R.C. BARNES

INK FOR THE BELOVED

The Tattoo Teller Series

This book was professionally typeset on Reedsy.
Find out more at reedsy.com

FOR:
RKB, DJAB, NESB

Contents

PROLOGUE - TROUBLE

"When did the trouble start, Elizabeth?"

The woman sitting across from me was wearing a neat brown suit that was cinched in all the right places. She was attractive with her hair pulled high into a messy bun. I got the impression she had quickly whipped it up, tied it back, and then slid the tortoiseshell glasses down her nose so she would appear as if she were ready for anything. Her lovely suit was not bought off the rack. It was the calculated outfit of a young woman, freshly out of law school, who has shed the sloppy sweatpants for clothes to get her noticed. She was ambitious. She wanted me to talk. I had the information required to wrap the case up.

"When did the trouble start, Elizabeth?"

"Bess," I said. "Call me, Bess." I looked her square in the eye to make my point.

"Okay, Bess," she smiled to defuse the tension. She thought she was making headway with me, gaining points by using the name I was comfortable with. I had no idea what I was going to say or where I should even begin, so I just smiled back. It was an awkward smile.

The woman displayed an immense amount of patience. I could see she had decided to wait me out. Well, I hadn't decided if I was going to talk to her. I might not grace her with any information at all. She was too put together, and the tailored outfit was starting to annoy me. I needed to feel a connection, and I wasn't getting it from her...I had already forgotten her name.

I picked up the business card that lay on the gunmetal table in front of me. "Tamara Blount, Assistant District Attorney" is what it said. Tamara. I bet she was Tammy to her friends. She just wasn't Tammy to me. She was brusque and business and refusing to look me directly in the eye. She focused on her notepad with the pen, hovering, waiting for me to talk so she could take notes and jot down my jewels of knowledge. I understood the severity of the situation, but this was going to be a long night, and I was already dog tired.

I looked over my shoulder at the policeman who had brought me in - Detective Kline. He had that rumpled look of comfort I connected with. He had held me in his arms, tight and secure, when he pulled me from the fire days ago. He smelled like cinnamon. I liked cinnamon. He had been kind to a sixteen-year-old black girl whose world had come crashing to a halt. Detective Kline knew the outer shell of the story, but he didn't know the details. They needed the details to prosecute.

I wondered if after I told them everything if the images and horrors would softly melt away. Or perhaps they would float out to sea the way the tide carries items from the sand. Would I be absolved of the guilt I felt? Would the doors to the past lock themselves shut, causing the pain to be snuffed out like a flame with no air? Will telling the police and the district attorney the story allow me to forget? Do I want to forget? Should I want to forget?

Detective Kline caught my eye when I turned around. "Are you thirsty, Bess? Did you need a soda or something?"

Something. I need something. "Could I get some coffee, please?" I asked. "Lots of cream and lots of sugar."

"Right away, sport," he said and hopped up and out the metal door, blocking me from the outside world. I wondered if Luther was waiting for me outside there. If not Luther, then I wanted Dusty. I hoped it was Dusty and Luther with Echo. I really wanted to hold Echo, tweak her nose, and see the shy smile emerge under her crazy red hair. I worried about my sister a lot.

I was thirsty and exhausted, and I had only been there an hour. My eyes felt heavy. The bright lighting in the room was not helping. In the back of my head, I could feel one hell of a headache threatening to make itself known. After weeks of being wound up tighter than a rattlesnake in the grass, this was my body's way of crashing. It was saying it's over now, Bess. It's over. You can rest now. You can close your eyes and not worry about the shadow images, the symbols, the threats, the sharp tang of ink, and her sparrows – especially the sparrows.

Assistant District Attorney, Tamara Blount was looking at me expectantly. She was so patient. I could see she was trying to be kind. I could see that. But what could I tell her? I didn't know where to begin. Wasn't it enough it was over? Dealing with family court and with the police in the past had soured me on everything legal. It was so easy to manipulate the system, get people to believe things that weren't the truth. Look at my mother. She was a master at deception.

"When did the troubles start?" she prompted. Again.

When did they start? I cocked my head as if I were in contemplation. That's a good question, Assistant District Attorney, Tamara Blount. How far back should I go? Trouble and my family go way back. We are as tight as thieves. Look up our thick file in family court. That's Wynters with a "y," not an "i."

The metal door groaned open as Officer Kline reentered with a cheap Styrofoam cup of coffee. In his grasp, he balanced a handful of creams and sugars. The creams were the good kind, not the crappy powder stuff. There was a red plastic stirrer for me to complete my drink. I looked at the assortment of items in front of me and started to add them to the cup. Officer Kline had poured in just the right amount of coffee so adding the three creams didn't create an overflow. Three creams and three packs of sugar. White and sweet.

I looked at the finished drink, and suddenly, hot tears splashed down on the table. I don't know where they came from. They just poured out of my eyes like a spigot. Detective Kline rested his hand on my shoulder. He glanced at Tamara Blount, Assistant District Attorney, and they exchanged a look.

"Bess, can you talk?" Detective Kline squeezed my shoulder. He leaned down and said the words softly in my ear. It felt too personal and intimate, but I didn't care. After all, the man had pulled me out of a burning building, and he smelled like cinnamon.

I nodded my head and tried to staunch the falling tears with swipes at my eyes. But I continued to stare at the coffee on the table. White and sweet. Just the way my mother liked it. This was my mother's coffee. Not mine.

Tamara Blount, Assistant District Attorney, had a concerned expression on her face. It was a patronizing look, and she was ruining the moment. I wanted to kick her under the table. Her arm was extended out as if she had thought about comforting me as the tears splashed down. Her palm was open and facing up. It was then I saw it. The ink was peeking out from under her wine-colored silk blouse sitting low on her wrist. It was hidden, but now I could see it.

"What is that?" I asked her. I sat straight up and gestured towards her arm.

She looked down and saw I was pointing where her shirt sleeve had pulled back, revealing the small design past her wrist bone. She subconsciously pulled on her cuff to cover it back up.

"Could I see it, please?" I asked. Tamara Blount, Assistant District Attorney, shot a puzzled glance at Officer Kline.

"Her mother ran a tattoo parlor," he explained.

"I ran the tattoo parlor," I muttered under my breath. I reached out towards Tamara Blount, Assistant District Attorney. "Can I see it, please?" I was dying to touch her arm. Suddenly, I knew how to make things feel right. To power me up and tell the story that needed telling.

She hesitated, looking about her as if there were eyes in the conference room and we were being observed. Perhaps we were. She made the decision and pulled the sleeve up from her wrist, revealing a small cavalcade of stars. It was a simple design showing multiple dark tiny stars, splattered as if a paintbrush had been flicked over that portion of her arm. Off to the side was a larger star with more detail and finesse to its creation. I had an idea as to what it meant, but I asked her anyway.

She stammered before telling me. I could see she was embarrassed by it. "I got it while I was in law school. I had it done right before I took the state bar. It's for courage. It means I'm a star." She said the last part with a whisper.

I thought it probably means you are a *super*star. "Can I touch it?" I asked. Tamara Blount, Assistant District Attorney, nodded her head in agreement. I reached over and touched the tiny stars on her wrist. I ran my fingers over the more significant star with the defined points and shooting flares as if it was speaking to me. I doubt Tamara Blount, Assistant District Attorney, was aware of this but the tattoo was – speaking to me.

They all do.

That's when I saw her. I saw Tammy. I saw the girl who studied diligently through law school. The girl who raised her hand in the large lecture halls and was ignored by the professors and other students. I saw the girl who knew she was better than how she was perceived. I saw the girl who bristled inside when she saw injustice and believed in staying true to those she represented. I saw the girl who the week before she took the bar exam, marched into a tattoo parlor on a whim, and sketched out this tattoo to the artist at the desk. She was a superstar amongst the stars. That was what this tattoo was about. Having it on her wrist allowed her to glance at it periodically to draw inner strength. This tattoo gave her the extra bounce when she began to falter. I decided I could talk to Tammy.

I pulled back, satisfied, and placed my hands in front of me on the table. I stared again at the coffee drink I had created and pushed it away. "I'm sorry," I said to Detective Kline. "I don't really want this. I'm ready to talk now, but can you do me a favor?"

"Sure, sport," he responded.

"I really really want some packets of hot sauce. That's what I want." As to be expected, whenever I made my request, I'd see raised eyebrows showing a combination of surprise and what the hell?

"I know how it sounds. I just want some hot sauce. Not a bottle or anything, but the packets they give out over the counter."

"There's a taco stand two or three blocks down. It's on the other side of the parking lot." Tamara Blount offered.

I bolted up in my chair. "That's perfect. Tell AJ to give you the extra hot ones. He knows me. Say it's for Bess."

Detective Kline shrugged and left the conference room again. Right when he went out, I could hear him murmuring to folks outside. There were many voices, and I couldn't pick out anyone in particular. But the voices didn't sound like there were only police officers or lawyers out there. Not that I would warrant that much attention, but I was just hoping there were people out there waiting for me.

Tammy, (yes, now she is Tammy in the sloppy sweatpants) was relaxed and smiling. She had removed her glasses as if she had decided since we shared a secret, she could let her hair down and be herself. We weren't besties or anything, but she sensed something positive had passed between us when I touched the constellation display on her wrist.

"Is it okay if I tape this?" she asked.

I nodded. "That's fine."

She reached down and brought out a recorder. It was one of those old-fashioned numbers with manual buttons that you pushed down. "I like to have it here on the table," she explained. "It's better than signaling to someone outside the room or using my phone. I also think it will help you if you see me listening rather than taking notes."

"Okay," I said. I felt myself warming up to her. I liked Tammy.

"However, I will jot things down from time to time. I will do that, so I remind myself to follow up with questions or to clarify something. I don't wish to interrupt you once you get started."

"Okay. Where's the microphone?"

"You don't have to worry about it. But it's right here." She pointed to an area that was facing me already. "Can we begin now? Or do we need to wait for Detective Kline to return?"

"We can start now," I said. Knowing hot sauce was coming was enough of a motivation to get me going.

"Okay. I'll begin." She pressed down the button on her tape machine and began talking. Her voice was precise and authoritative. "This is Assistant District Attorney, Tamara Blount, and I am speaking with Elizabeth Delilah Wynters, a minor, age sixteen. Elizabeth, also known as Bess, is here to make a statement regarding the fire in the Fruitvale district in Oakland, California and the events leading up to it." She looked at me, alerting me to the fact I now had the floor. "Bess, when did the trouble start?"

There was that question, again. When did it start? When had the warnings of trouble begun? Was it when Terry threw Luther out? Or was it when Annika began her solo work? Did the trouble go back to when Spiderwand disappeared? Or was it when Malcolm died? I realized I was going farther and farther back in time, looking for the thing that ignited it all. When had the trouble started was not a question I could answer because there had always been trouble.

But, in my mind, it all started with Todd. Todd was why we were here.

I looked at Tammy and started talking.

I

COSMIC HEARTS

ACTIVATED: ONE CHEETAH BRA

"**M**om is dating again."

The tiny voice spoke softly, but those four words sent a chill down my spine. I had been sitting at the small desk in my room, going over my analytic geometry assignment and despairing I was not arriving at the proper answer. I had skipped dinner, my eyes were tired, and my stomach was growling. The lines on the page were evolving into cartoonish squiggles, and my thought process was anything but analytical, so to say my mood was not receptive would be pretty damn accurate. I closed my eyes, took a deep breath, and counted to five before I turned and looked at my younger sister standing in the doorway.

"What do you mean?" I asked since clarification was in order.

Echo hung onto the doorway and leaned her body in to talk. She was trying to honor my rule of privacy and not enter my room uninvited. The toes of her shoes were planted outside the door frame. "I saw the dating bra."

"The dating bra? Mom has a dating bra?" I cracked a smile because my six-year-old sister was assigning labels to our mother's lingerie. Was there a cooking bra? A reading bra? A crossword puzzle bra?

"Yes. The dating bra is hanging in the bathroom." There was no mistaking the concern on Echo's face.

I laughed. "Do I have a dating bra?" I was curious because this

3

whole thing was more silly than ominous. Echo blinked. She looked at me like my question was the most ridiculous thing to be uttered in a conversation with a child about bras. Of course, I don't have a dating bra. I don't date.

"C' mere," she gestured for me to follow. I got up and went down the hallway with her. My bedroom is off the kitchen in the house. Originally it was designed to be the utility room or the walkthrough room. I like it because it is small and away from everyone else. Plus, I have easy access to the back porch if I need to escape. We walked past the front room, which was quiet and headed for our mother's bedroom.

It was the early evening. Dishes were still in the sink, probably waiting for me to do them. But the dining area was clear, which was a blessing. I guessed folks who had been here earlier had gone out, and mom was kicking back with her business partner, Dusty, having a beer at the studio. We had the place to ourselves - a rarity.

Our mother is the only one who has her own bathroom. It is connected to her bedroom and could only be accessed through her room. I followed my sister to the bathroom, where it was apparent mom had just washed all her lingerie and tiny see-through T-shirts. Many bras, panties, and delicate items were hanging to dry off the shower stall and towel racks. Echo pointed to the item in question, which was hanging on a hook on the back of the door.

The minute I saw the bra, I knew my sister was right. Mom was dating again. Shit.

The bra that caused all this anxiety was a padded number and gave my mother the illusion of cleavage. It was a bold cheetah print and so obviously designed to be seen and to be taken off. Our mother only wore this bra for one purpose. The fact she had recently washed it was evidence the dating had started. She wasn't just contemplating it; she'd already done some test runs.

I went into her room and opened the disc player next to her television. The tray slid out, and there sat the second confirmation our mother had found someone she wished to attract. In the disk tray was her cardio dance program. It was the program she used when she was interested in getting her body toned and firm. Damn it.

Echo stood next to me and looked at the dance disk as well.

"Any idea who it is?" I asked.

She solemnly shook her head, and her massive red hair flopped down over her face.

Another chill shimmied through my body. Our mother was dating, and she hadn't told us. I wondered why. Whatever the reason, I knew I wasn't going to like it. I took my sister's hand and led her back to my bedroom.

"Here. Stay here for a while." Echo smiled and made herself comfortable on a small patch of rug on the floor. I handed her some loose paper and the tin can where I stash my colored markers and crayons. Echo got to work, carefully selecting the colors she wanted to use and laying out her workspace. She began humming to herself, which was a sign of contentment.

Before I got back to my analytic geometry challenges, I pulled out a packet of hot sauce from my drawer and started sucking on the sharp, tangy liquid. The pop of the pepper in my mouth allowed my mind to focus. Sucking on hot sauce wakes me up and gives me an edge so I can think clearly. It also makes me a bit bitchy and mean, and I like that. I visualize myself as a rattlesnake, sucking on my own venom. It's liquid power.

I listened to the song Echo was humming and was surprised. I recognized it. It was a Negro spiritual known as "Wade In The Water." It looked funny hearing the majestic song come out of the mouth of a six-year-old white girl. A little girl with freckles splashed across her nose and a crazy hairdo, combining her red hair with plastic flowers and fairy doll hair clips hanging this way and that.

Echo started doing her own hair this school year, and her creative attempts were regularly photographed by my mother. Describing the hairstyles to other people didn't do them justice. They had to be seen to be adequately appreciated. Echo's newest obsession was these three-inch yellow and green fairy dolls. She liked to attach them as decorations into her curls. You could tell what kind of phase Echo was in by what she was sticking into her hair.

My mother had a social media page that highlighted Echo's hairstyle expressions.

My mother encouraged my sister's artistic appearance but washing Echo's hair and combing out the snarls and removing the things she had stuck into the curls was a pain in the butt. Which, of course, meant it was not a chore my mother ever found herself doing. I tried to keep Echo's hair in two braids down the side, and then she could stick whatever toys she wanted into the weave of the braids.

Echo had reached the refrain of the song, and I heard her quietly sing about all God's children being in the water. My sister humming this song could only mean she had been hanging around Luther, and she was forbidden to do so. There was a restraining order against Luther. If Echo saw Luther, that meant my mother wasn't the only person in this household keeping secrets.

I reached for another packet of hot sauce.

SPIDERWAND

Before I continue, there is something I should explain. *This information is not general knowledge. In fact, there are only a select number of people who know this about me.* One of those individuals is now in the hospital. At this point in my storytelling, I have not decided whether I am going to disclose this information to Tammy, the Assistant District Attorney, or to Detective Kline. I think I can relay the events without having to share this fact. Because to be honest, most people don't believe me when I tell them. I have already revealed myself to Tammy, but I don't think she picked up on what I was demonstrating.

It's very simple.

I know why a person gets a tattoo.

I know the story. The true story. Everybody gets a tattoo for a reason. The inked symbol always signifies something. It could be obvious like an oak tree representing strength or a clock representing punctuality and order. Or the ink on your skin can have hidden meanings, and they must be explained for the viewer to understand its importance. Perhaps the daisy on your ankle is a reminder of the perfect day you had with your first boyfriend. The guy has vanished, but his memory lives on in your heart and now on your skin.

People sometimes lie about the story of their tattoo. Perhaps they have become embarrassed over time and feel the need to make the image about something else. It doesn't matter. I know the truth. If I touch the tattoo and run my finger over the design, I see the truth. I know the cherubic faced angel on your shoulder is really the image of the little boy who died in the car accident you were responsible for. It's not a random guardian angel like you claim to others.

The fact is, I know the pain. I know the sorrow. I know the hunger. I know the desire. I know the why. I know the lies. I know it all.

One of the reasons why I decided to talk to Assistant District Attorney Blount is she told me the truth about her tattoo. She had it done for empowerment, which meant there were times in her life when she was not sure of herself despite the chocolate power suit and the wine-colored silk blouse. I imagined her sneaking glances at her special star before she rose from her chair to address the jury.

Some folks love to embellish the story behind the art on their bodies. They become enamored more with the story than the artwork. They tell the story so often; it becomes their truth. For example, they believe the lotus flower on their shoulder is symbolic of their struggles. The lotus flower is an amazing plant that pulls itself out of the mud and guck of the swamps and blooms into the most glorious flower the eye can see. The flower represents success extracted out of adversity. The person sees themselves as the lotus; they can triumph out of the thickness of the swamps. When in truth, they are not the beautiful blossom but the mud itself. They are the guck that mars and covers beauty. They are the obstacle keeping the beauty from expanding. My mother has a lotus flower on her back, and as you can see, the ink has many interpretations.

How did this ability grow? How did this gift reveal itself to me? It's hard to say. There were hints of the talent when I was little, but it flourished into being around the time I was twelve. It scared me at first because knowing the truth about people isn't always something you want to know. Luckily my strange psychic connection is limited to tattoos and the aura energy I can extract. But it doesn't help I am the daughter of a famous tattoo artist. Her name is Theresa Wynters. Perhaps you've heard of her.

If you haven't heard of my mother's name, then you definitely have seen her out and around Berkeley. She is the free-spirited woman running in the park with the kids and the dogs. She sprints with barefoot abandon, and her laugh hits this high squealing pitch. If there is a kite flying on the beach, she is the woman standing there glorifying the wondrous heights of the kite, complimenting the kite flyer, and giving words of encouragement and skilled advice. She is the woman at the flower stand, chatting brightly with the florist and remarking on how fragrant the roses are. At the coffee shop, she is the woman complimenting the barista on their selection of spiced cinnamon apple buns. My mother is Theresa Wynters.

Everybody knows her.

In addition to being the woman who happily greets and befriends all the people she meets, my mother has a body that stops traffic. Yes, I said it. And it's true. A flower garden is literally in bloom all over my mother's body, and it is magnificent. The tattoos are an artistic accomplishment, and my mother displays them by wearing clothes that show off the ink. Her usual attire is a thin-strapped dress in a solid color. This outfit makes it literally appear as if flowers are sprouting from the fabric and moving up across her body. I am used to the tattoos now. But it is amusing when someone gets their first glance at the eye-catching ink. Old men, toddlers in strollers, policemen, and Cal students in their university gear - they always stare. Always. You must.

In the same way, everyone knows my mother, hardly anybody knows I am her daughter. I look nothing like her. Where she is wiry, thin, and small, I tower over her with a solid athletic build. Where she has warm auburn hair that falls in ringlets around her shoulders, I have long, unruly, curly brown hair, which I usually must keep in line by braiding it into two braids on either side of my face. I use the same style on Echo. It's the only thing I know how to do with hair. It's what my friend, Joanie, calls the "Beyonce Formation" look. I'll do French braids in the front when I'm feeling fancy.

I have a bronze complexion, and I darken like a nut in the sun. I am of mixed race, and my father was black. My mother has a few pictures of him, and I've seen them, but the actual man is gone. The images I viewed show a happy person with a wide-open face, a bright smile, and deep dark brown eyes. The pictures are all taken at the same dinner party. His name was Charles, and he was only with my mother one weekend. I don't feel abandoned, however, because, in all honesty, I don't think he knows I exist. I don't believe my mother ever informed him she was pregnant, and once I came along, she had no desire to share me.

My mother has never been married. She is one of those women who doesn't believe in being tied down or allowing a piece of paper to declare the status of her heart. Those are literally her words – "the status of my heart." Ordinarily, this does not pose problems. But it has created complications from time to time when it comes to her children. My sister, Echo Haydn Wynters, is ten years younger than me. We don't share the same father. Poor Echo doesn't even have pictures of hers, but my sister looks like a miniature version of our mother, so no one questions her connection to the Wynters family.

And as I've said, my mother is known.

With all her floral body ink, she is a walking billboard for her tattoo studio. Cosmic Hearts Tattoo is located on a corner plot in the Southside of Berkeley on Telegraph. The studio is half a mile from our house, which makes it easy to get back and forth on foot or by bike. Being on a corner lot allows my mother to take full advantage of the side of the building and a splendid mural greets motorists and pedestrians who are traveling from the north.

A long time ago, an artist who called himself Spiderwand stayed at our house for several months. Initially, my mother thought he could work out of the studio as he had a keen eye for detail, and his outlining work was impressive. However, Spiderwand was never able to get a handle on skin work. Skin is a challenging canvas. He needed a place to crash until he could hook up with an artist friend in Minnesota, so my mother let him stay at the house with food privileges in exchange for the side mural she wanted him to paint. She had been having a tagging problem in the last year on the wall, and she believed getting a painting done would cut down or end the tagging. She was right.

The mural is a collection of multicultural eyes and hands. There are times where it looks like the hands are holding the eyes, and there are times where the eyes are floating in space. The cosmic universe is depicted with the Milky Way, the planets, and variations of the cycles of the moon. The painting shows vignettes, and some are humorous like a cow jumping over a moon and an astronaut floating around a space shuttle.

The mural has hands of all different shapes, skin tones, and genders. There are rough and stunted hands and manicured and elegant hands. Some are pairs, and some are singles. And whenever you think there isn't a balance to the piece, you step back and you realize you were wrong. Every little thing is connected. A constant balance moves with an ebb and flow.

My favorite hand on the mural is of a child with honey-colored skin and rainbow nail polish on their fingers. A beaded butterfly bracelet dangles from the wrist. The little hand points to one of the moons in the sky of the mural. A tiny mouse sits on top of this moon. He is nibbling on a piece of cheese as if he just pinched off a bite. The moon is smiling and slyly winking at the viewer. I was around six or seven when the mural was painted, and I liked to believe the hand with the butterfly bracelet was my hand. The little mouse was symbolic of me as this was my nickname for years. When I hit middle school, I told everyone to quit calling me "Mouse." It's embarrassing to be called "Mouse" when you're twelve.

It took Spiderwand four months to complete the mural. I remember I didn't like him at first, and I complained to my mother about him being around. Ollie had started cooking for us then. I liked Ollie, but I felt Spiderwand was taking advantage of us. I don't know where I got this idea, but it seemed like he was never going to complete the mural. There were days when he didn't go out and work on it at all. He would lay on the couch with a cloth over his eyes and claim he was thinking and visualizing. One of his thin-fingered hands would flit up and dance in the air as if he were painting in the sky. Ollie said Spiderwand got his name because of his long slender brown fingers.

Spiderwand would don these huge black rain boots and take walks up around Grizzly Peak and the fire trails. The boots looked ridiculous on him because he was this tall spindly guy, and when he walked, he stomped like an astronaut doing a spacewalk.

I told Ollie to over salt Spiderwand's food so he would go away. Ollie is a great cook, and people do hang around our house just to eat. Ollie released the low chuckle he has. It comes from his gut, and his whole body shakes and quivers like pudding. Ollie wagged his finger and told me I was too analytical, and I didn't understand the creative process. "Get your head out of them numbers," he would say to me. "You're always declaring stuff doesn't add up. You need to look at the art and beauty around you."

"Spiderwand is not beautiful," I declared, haughtily. "And he smells like garlic."

"His work is beautiful. Watch him. Watch him work. And if he ever complains about his food, I'm going to know who to blame."

So, I did. I watched Spiderwand work. I would return from school, get my snack from Ollie, and sit near the fire hydrant to watch

Spiderwand slowly move his brush across the wall. His long greasy hair would fall across his face, but his concentration was so intense he didn't seem to notice. An area, once a blob of color, would take form and become a woman's hand holding a single flower. Later, I realized the hand with the flower was my mother's hand. Spiderwand used a color on the painted fingernails, which matched a polish my mother favored. My mother keeps her hands well-manicured as she says nervous people will focus on her hands as she is working with the needles and having them clean and polished was reassuring. My mother always thinks of little details, and I could see Spiderwand was as meticulous and detail oriented as my mother. Even though he smelled like garlic.

I'll be honest and admit I was sorry when Spiderwand left. By the time he finished the butterfly bracelet on the little girl's wrist, I had become fascinated with his work and his strange process. I'm around artists constantly, and Spiderwand was the first person who would take substantial breaks and do something else while he was "working" and in the zone. He would even watch game shows on television as part of his process. He said game shows are the most organic way to see how people think.

Most artists I knew sketched out their ideas and images beforehand. Spiderwand didn't. I never saw a sketchbook in his possession. How he put together this enormous and beautifully detailed mural of the solar system and eyes and hands, I will never know. For a long time, when I approached the painted wall from the street, I would remember Ollie's words and marvel at the beauty. There was always something new to see.

Many people come and go in my life - especially artists and men, but Spiderwand left too soon. He never reached his friend in Minnesota. The friend contacted my mother about a month later, asking where he was. My mother called many numbers she had as references and friends for Spiderwand to try and locate him, but he had vanished. For months I would stare mournfully at the beautiful mural and wonder how someone could just disappear.

TEEN LIFE

I t was Friday, and I was leaving the high school campus with a giddy heart. I'm a teenager, so this is a rare thing. I was actually having a good day. My classes had gone smoothly, and I knew I'd aced the physics quiz. Earlier, my friend, Rueben, had handed me a big plastic bag of hot sauce packets from his aunt's taqueria. Rueben's aunt carried my favorite hot sauce, and whenever Rueben went to her restaurant in Sonoma, he would grab handfuls for me.

I was unlocking my bicycle and preparing for my escape when Rueben came running up. Rueben is a bit of an egghead. He is a little guy, and he keeps his hair cropped short and slicked back. Luckily, he doesn't wear glasses, but I do suspect he wears contact lenses because there are times when we are studying together when he squints his eyes while looking at the charts and images. It's how adults look when they need to read menus in a darkened restaurant.

Rueben is the friend who knows a little bit about everything, and sometimes he can be obnoxious about it. If you are meeting Rueben for the first time, he will slip in the fact he skipped a level of math in high school within the hour. Rueben has four older brothers, and they were all football players at Berkeley High when they came through. In fact, when Rueben started in high school, some teachers were shocked to find out he was the youngest brother of Javier, Carlos, Timothy, and David. Everyone knew the legendary Martinez brothers, and poor

Rueben is the runt of the family litter. But as the brawn went down with each son being born, the brains went up. Rueben is a national merit scholar and has plans of his own greatness. His current ambition outside of an Ivy League education is recognition on the game show Jeopardy. He says all the great trivia minds compete on that show, and he wants to make it clear he is the trivia master. We've been friends since eighth grade at Willard middle school.

"Hey!" Rueben called as he ran up. "You want to help me put together a study guide for economics?"

"Sure." I readjusted my backpack on my shoulders so it wouldn't slide too much as I mounted the bike.

"Why don't you handle fiscal policy in Macroeconomics and I'll do the charts on inflation. I think we should get the guide completed by this weekend because I suspect a pop quiz coming out of Meyer soon."

"Fine," I answered. "But please write up a regular study guide and don't use something from *Star Trek* or *Dune* as the widget example."

Rueben stared at me as if I had snatched a beagle puppy out of his hands. "What's wrong with *Star Trek* and *Dune?*"

"Nothing," I replied. "Just use something normal, okay. I get tired of reading about Tribbles and alien spices."

"Melange," Rueben said. "The spice in *Dune* is Melange. My Tribble chart showing their multiplication patterns was ingenious," Rueben argued. "I sent them to the writers on the *Star Trek* series. They thought they were fantastic, and they sent me signed autographs from everyone on the show."

By now, I was rolling my eyes because I cannot tell you how often I've heard the story about Tribble charts and the writers on *Star Trek*. Just note I do like this guy even though he can be incredibly annoying.

We were joined by Joanie, who is the third member of our friend group. Joanie is the most gorgeous girl in the school. Hands down, no questions asked. Joanie is tall with long elegant legs, and she shows them off with skinny jeans and ankle boots. She has impressive brown velvet hair that is the envy of all the high school girls. When Joanie walks, it bounces and moves behind her like it's starring in a shampoo commercial. Her skin is flawless. I don't think a bump would ever dare to mar her creamy brown complexion. It's hard to look at Joanie and not be envious; she took the blue ribbon in the genetic pool competition. I believe all the boys have secret crushes on Joanie. I know Rueben does.

Joanie is the opposite of me when it comes to her personal worldview. I'm the skeptic, always looking for the angle folks are taking and guessing what their selfish motives are. Joanie thinks well of everyone. I mean, everyone. She gets visibly upset when she observes nasty, manipulative behavior and cries at news stories on TV. She's not naïve; she understands what happens in the world. It just hurts her heart. I worry about Joanie, but then again, she worries about me.

Most people don't understand how we can be friends because Joanie is so lovely, and I am so mean. And I must admit there are times I can't understand it either. But we are.

"Are you guys getting together tonight?" Joanie asked. "Cause I want to come even if we're not working on the same thing. I can study my algebra, and you two will be there to help me."

Rueben and I have almost all our classes together. We both operate at an accelerated level and taking a course load of AP classes like Meyer's economics class. Joanie was on a more normal module of classes. I only saw her in between the bell periods when we were dashing to our next class and at the lunch break when we would hurry to the burrito stand located off-campus to get our bean and cheese burritos with extra onions, (and extra hot sauce for me).

"Isn't there a basketball game tonight?" Rueben asked.

Joanie is a cheerleader. She is a reluctant participant and rolls her eyes every time the subject comes up. The cheerleading squad at the high school insisted. In fact, the whole school kind of insisted. Administrators and students cajoled and sweet-talked Joanie into trying out, and then she was unanimously voted in.

The skeptic in me initially thought Joanie was being set up for a horrible *Carrie* style prank. But I was wrong. There must be a high school/cheerleader code. You can't have a girl who looks like Joanie walk around the high school campus and not be on the cheerleading squad. Plus, they were tired of people asking if that beautiful black girl was a cheerleader, so they placed her on the squad to shut people up. There is Joanie with her kicks and pom-poms, even if she is a bit of a klutz. She may be black and have the legs of a gazelle, but Joanie has no rhythm whatsoever. It is one of the things that keeps the rest of the girls at school from secretly hating her. Thank God for small favors.

"No game," Joanie answered. "We travel on Saturday to Vacaville. So, what's up?"

"Nothing," I responded. "We were just figuring our schedules out. But I'm working tonight, guys."

Rueben's eyes perked up. He loved hearing me talk about the tattoo studio. But since he and Joanie were minors, they weren't allowed to hang out there.

"Are you doing one of those ...ceremonies?" he asked.

I sighed. "Yes," and out of the corner of my eye, I could see Joanie turn away and look off into the distance as if something fascinating was coming around the corner. Unlike Rueben, she hated hearing about Cosmic Hearts Tattoo. Especially when I talked about the "Ink for the Beloved" ceremonies as she believed they were séances. Joanie is a Jehovah's Witness, and the religion frowns upon rituals and any type of contact with ghosts or spirits.

"Yes, it is a Beloved ceremony, and I have to get to the studio and prepare before 5:00."

Rueben was eager to hear about it, but I could see Joanie getting frustrated.

"Hey, listen, why don't you guys come over to study at my house around 7:00. The ceremony will be done, or at least my portion will be, and if you want to eat, I'll ask Ollie to add enough food to cover you." Joanie smiled and nodded her head. I knew I had her when I mentioned eating Ollie's cuisine. She loved hanging out with Ollie at the house, and his food was sublime. Joanie was an only child, and her mother had died in a car accident years ago. Her widower father brought home take-out regularly for the two of them, and Joanie's klutziness kept her away from the stove.

My mother is a lousy cook. Bowls of cereal in the morning was the biggest challenge she could handle. When Olliver DeMatteo offered his cooking services in exchange for the apartment studio on the second floor, it was an agreement that brought immense joy to everyone's gastrointestinal tracts.

Joanie dashed off happily, promising to see us later tonight. She managed to avoid plowing into the tree, blocking her path, but she tripped over the tree's roots, so it got her anyway.

"I want to hear the story for tonight," said Rueben. The boy was practically salivating. I guess I hadn't told him about studio stuff in a while. He was becoming very impatient like I was holding out. Then I remembered I had a large plastic bag of hot sauce packets from Aunt Rosine's Taqueria courtesy of Rueben. He deserved to hear a full story and not just the bullet points.

"Alright," I answered. "But I only have ten minutes, and then I have to get to the shop."

"Walk your bike," Rueben said. "And I'll go some of the ways with you."

"You'll have to take the bus back to your house," I pointed out.

"It will be worth it. Begin." He snapped his fingers. I began.

STEPHANIE GAIGE

The client at 5:00 tonight was Stephanie Amelia Gaige. Stephanie had requested the Ink for the Beloved ceremony, which is a unique service my mother performs. It is not a séance, as Joanie believes. There is no attempt to talk or communicate with the dead. My mother is a tattoo artist, not a medium or a fortune-teller. The ceremony honors the dead, we don't contact them. I seem to be the only family member with any type of supernatural ability. And even then, I don't like to call it that. I haven't determined if the tattoos are talking to me or if I'm super perceptive like Sherlock Holmes. I want to think I am super observant like Sherlock Holmes.

(And for obvious reasons, Joanie DOES NOT KNOW about the tattoo reading thing. Joanie is against tattoos entirely. Again, it is astounding the two of us are friends.)

The Ink for the Beloved service is one my mother executes when the tattoo an individual is requesting links to a loved one that has died. Not everyone who gets a design for a deceased person asks for the ceremony, but for many people who are using the tattoo as a part of their grieving cycle, the IFTB ceremony is a means to achieving closure.

Stephanie Gaige is a twenty-four-year-old woman who works as a marine biologist at the East Bay Aquatic Center. She is small in size but brazen with an adventurous spirit. She grew up in the landlocked state of Kansas with happy childhood memories of playing capture the flag using water guns and hoses on a fort her father had built for her and her twin brother, Aaron.

When Stephanie Gaige had her introductory meeting with my mother, she shared memories and photos from her childhood. This is in preparation for the ceremony. Stephanie told my mother a particular story that will be recited back to her during the ceremony. While my mother inks the design, she talks about the person who is being memorialized. Sometimes music is played, and other things like poetry are woven into the speech. It is a live performance but personalized for the client.

Stephanie told my mother about the day she lost her brother. And that was the story I shared with Rueben.

***

Aaron and Stephanie were inseparable. They loved water, and when they were old enough, they started taking swim lessons at the local community center. At the swim center, there were four levels of instruction. The beginning level was called the guppies, the next level was the tadpoles, the third level was the seahorses, and the fourth was the dolphins. Stephanie and Aaron couldn't wait until they reached the level of seahorses because it was at that level their mother said they could swing on the rope and jump into the man-made water hole at the rock quarry.

They were ten years old that summer. They started their lessons, and within two weeks, their mother said they were ready. It was a hot summer day in Kansas, and by 11:00, the quarry was filled with kids. Swimming was allowed in the morning until noontime, and then everyone was sent out of the sun until 3:00. There were tents erected and ice coolers with snacks and bottles of water for the kids that didn't want to go home for lunch. After three, when the sun was less intense, the kids were allowed back in. The whole area was well monitored by the adults. After all, most of their children from the ages of ten to sixteen were swimming at the quarry. At nightfall, the whole place was locked down for protection. There had never been a problem until Aaron Stanley Gaige took the rope swing.

The rules of usage on the rope swing were quite clear. Signs were posted all around the area where the quarry rope swing hung. And even if kids didn't read the signs (but they all did), the older youth always mentioned the rule when passing the rope to the next rider in line. Swing out. Swing back. Let go. Do not hold on to the rope. You must let go. Swing out. Swing back. Let go. (Actually, it was swing back halfway, so you dropped in the center of the water.) If you can't let go, you lose rope privileges FOREVER.

The older kids always said "forever", to make sure the meeker children understood the gravity of the situation. But really, the offender would lose rope privileges for the rest of the summer. The reason for emphasizing swing out, swing back (halfway), let go, is if a kid didn't drop into the water in the middle of the quarry, the rescue mission of getting them off the rope and pulling the line back to the raised shore took a full hour. Adults had to be called, and an inflatable yellow boat had to be paddled out into the water with life jackets. Lifeguard trained swimmers had to coax the reluctant child to drop into the water (this could take up to twenty minutes alone!), and then they were lifted into the floating rescue craft and returned to shore.

After swimmers were cleared from the quarry, the rope was hooked and pulled up to the high rocks. There were only two individuals in the area who were skilled enough to hook the line with a lasso toss within ten tries. And, if Maynard or Mark Cross weren't there at the quarry swimming themselves to retrieve the rope if needed, the swing would hang still until one of them showed up. Eighth graders, Stacey Upton and Craig Granger, timed the whole operation two summers ago when Kerry Rogers refused to let go of the rope. It had taken an hour and a half to reset. An hour and a half.

As the line inched up and they got closer to their first rope swing, Stephanie shared with her brother she was terrified she would be like Kerry Rogers and not let go. Not letting go of the rope swing was a public shame, tarnishing your reputation all the way through high school. People still weren't talking to Kerry Rogers. Stephanie was so worried; her body was trembling. Aaron reassured her. He rubbed her shoulders and reminded her they had gotten this far. They were mighty seahorses and had earned this privilege. He also told Stephanie their mom had packed a cooler for them at lunch, and it was filled with fried chicken, peaches, and oatmeal raisin cookies. Aaron loved food as much as he loved adventure.

When the time came for them to take the rope, Aaron told his sister to go ahead of him. He gave her a quick wink and squeezed her hand. Stephanie took the line, and the mantra ran through her head; swing out, swing back, let go. The rush of the swing swooping out was exhilarating. Stephanie had never felt anything like it. As the swing lifted her over the rocky ledge on the opposing side, she fearfully looked away and closed her eyes. The speed and the height over the water were scary, and fear took hold of her body. She instinctively tightened her grip on the rope. As the swing headed back to where the other kids were waiting for their turn, Stephanie opened her eyes, and her focus zeroed in on Aaron's face. Her brother looked happy. He looked proud. He was mouthing something to her. He was mouthing, "Let go!" And Stephanie did.

The fall into the water took less than two seconds. To her heightened senses, the quarry had rushed up to greet her, and the plunge roared in her ears. She sank deep into the water, allowed herself the opportunity to still herself in the coolness and the calm of the depths. She then kicked her feet to propel herself up and out.

The moment Stephanie walked, dripping, onto the shore, she turned up to look at Aaron, who now had the rope in his hands, eagerly waiting for his shot. The sun was shining in her eyes, and she could hardly see him, but she lifted her hand and raised her thumb in the "Okay" signal. She was smiling like she never had before. The adrenaline was rocketing through her. She watched her twin jump up and swing out on the rope. She was so happy to share this incredible rush of excitement with him.

Swing out. Swing back (halfway). Let go.

But Aaron must have been so fired up, his mind left his senses. He let go of the rope before it had reached its full height of the fulcrum swing. The momentum sent his skinny little body flying to the rocks on the opposite side of the shore. They said he died instantly.

The rope swing was shut down for the remainder of the summer. But even when it opened again the following year, Stephanie never got back on the rope swing. She never went to the quarry again, and on hot days she did her swimming at the community center pool.

Years later, after she had graduated from college, Stephanie's mother had a stroke and needed to be in hospice care. Stephanie was helping her father downsize their belongings when she found a box of childhood drawings in her mother's closet. Most of Stephanie's pictures had been simple illustrations of the stories and books she read, but Aaron had been the artist between the two of them. On top of the stacked artwork was a drawing of two seahorses. Their tails were curled under and wrapped together in solidarity. Around their necks were little capes. The capes were drawn as if the seahorses were flying instead of floating in the water. At the top of the page was written "To Stephanie from Aaron. We are mighty seahorses." Aaron had died before he could give this to her. Stephanie wept for days.

***

I finished talking and looked at Rueben. His eyes were glistening. I knew he would be crying on his walk home. We had reached the tattoo studio, so Rueben would have a long bus ride before coming back later tonight. "Do you want to just stay at the house and wait until I'm done?" I asked.

He shook his head. "Naw, I need to change and shower. I'll get Javier to drop me off later before he goes out for the night. So, is that what she is getting done? A tattoo of a seahorse? For her brother?"

"She's mirroring the drawing. She sent it to my mom a month ago, and my mother designed something from it. So, it will be two seahorses with capes, but it won't look like a kid's drawing. They will be done with a more realistic touch since she is a marine biologist." One of the added touches my mother incorporated was enlarging the eyes of the sea creatures to give them expression. Expressive faces in her designs are a strong suit of my mother's.

"Can I see it?" Rueben asked. He always wants to see the work after he hears the story.

"I'll show you the pictures when you come by later."

Rueben gave me a fake pout. But then he dashed up to the corner as he saw his AC Transit bus approaching in the distance.

I took a few breaths to clear my head. Telling the story of Stephanie Gaige and her brother, Aaron, had gotten to me a bit. It was sad. I was glad I would not be there during the ceremony and was just responsible for the prep and making sure everything was clean and ready.

SNAKE IN THE GRASS

I parked my bike and secured the lock. Right before going inside the studio, I zipped open my backpack and pulled out one of the hot sauce packs Rueben had gotten for me. Might as well treat me now. Besides, I needed to clear my head and focus. I shouldered the backpack as I tore open the packet. The sharp tang of the sauce felt good as it went down my throat. My nose picked up the smoky hint of chipotle just as my tongue captured the flavor. Damn, I loved hot sauce. I pushed open the door to Cosmic Hearts Tattoo and stepped inside.

"Ah, there she is," whispered a familiar voice. "Sucking on that hot sauce like a babe to the bottle. Replenishing your fangs, sweetheart?" The voice came from the back of the shop in the shadows.

"HA HA HA, Dusty," I replied as I walked towards the little desk in the back office. The place was empty and spotless. I could tell Dusty had just finished cleaning it up. There was jasmine in the air with a hint of cinnamon, and Dusty always used the spicy Jasmine essential oil when she was using aromatherapy.

"Did you have a walk-in this afternoon?" I asked and headed for the schedule log. I wanted to start on the following day's confirmations. I found it easily and pulled up the appointments for Saturday. It was easy enough. There were four, and the specifications and partial payments already recorded. Perfect.

26

Dusty was leaning back in one of the station chairs on the far end of the studio. Her feet were propped up on a wheeled stool, and she had tilted her black fedora over her eyes, siesta style so she could grab a couple of zzz's.

"Yeah, it was a teensy-weensy spider on a shoulder." She waved over in my direction. "It's all in the log."

Dusty Lorazo works alongside my mother at the tattoo studio. Dusty is a high draw herself in the inked artist world. Dusty's style is more on the realistic side, and she utilizes the black and grey technique. Her ink looks like photographs to me. Guys dig her stuff as Dusty is famous for her skulls, spiders, and vultures (I have no idea why vultures are popular, but they are). She is also beginning to do more bio-mechanical stuff. Her flash pieces are showing more of this. These are tattoos that make people look like they have metal gears underneath their skin. There is a huge bio-mechanical craze going on. I think those tattoos are incredibly creepy. But it brings in revenue, so I can't complain.

About six months ago, we had numerous messages inquiring about that type of work. Dusty experimented a bit and posted some good images on the website. Ever since we book at least four bio-mechanicals a week. These clients like large images, and its detailed work, so multiple sessions are required. And once she has done one, the satisfied client referral sends us dozens more as they proudly post their tats online. As I said, the money is good.

Dusty is quite a character in her own right. She is one of those people that just radiates "cool." She and my mom have worked together for years, and they are a great team with a ying/yang vibe. My mother is all frenetic energy and bright colors, while Dusty is low key shades of black and grey with a stillness that would fool the dead. My mother is girlish dresses and ballet flats while Dusty rocks western boots and wide-brimmed hats.

27

The one bit of silliness Dusty allows herself are her earrings. The most ridiculous pieces of jewelry can be seen hanging from her earlobes. She has items that are linked to her inkwork like skeletons holding roses and spiders with jewels in their eyes. But then you will also see her wearing flamingos raising up margarita glasses, pineapples with faces, and caterpillars smoking hookah like from *Alice in Wonderland*. A lot of the jewelry I see on Dusty's ears are things that make you wonder how anyone thought it would be jewelry, let alone something that someone would plunk down good money for and then wear.

Dusty has been around as long as I can remember. She is like a second mother. There are times where Dusty's logic prevails over the nutty ideas my mother sprouts. And all we can say is thank God for that.

"Where's my mom?" I asked.

"I have no idea."

"The client will be here at five. We have a Beloved ceremony tonight."

"Terry keeps her own hours, you know that."

I wanted to ask Dusty if she knew anything about my mother dating. But I couldn't think of a way to ease into the subject. Besides, I could tell Dusty was in a sulky mood and probably wouldn't be receptive to answering questions about my mother's social habits.

"It's really dark in here," I said.

"I'm trying to take a nap."

"I need light to set things up and sync the music."

"There's a flashlight under the cabinet by the scrub sink."

"Are you serious? You want me to use a flashlight?"

"I want you to go away. But I have no desire to place the orders, check supplies, and confirm the appointments for tomorrow, so I'm allowing you to be here. But please let me get a nap while the place is quiet." Dusty didn't remove the hat from her face the entire time she was talking. "If there is a walk-in now, I'm going to make you do the ink. I'm going to kick your ass, and then make you do the ink."

Got it. Dusty was grouchy. A migraine was threatening to broach the horizon. The Ink for the Beloved ceremonies required everyone to be on the top of their game. My mother might be the artist on record and doing the inking, but there was teamwork involved in the same way a surgeon has his team in the operating room. Everyone has a function to play and are integral to making the event go smoothly.

I groped for the flashlight under the counter, so I didn't have to turn on the bright overhead lights. I made my confirmation calls easy enough, keeping my voice low so I wouldn't disturb Dusty's nap. Two were messages left on voicemail, and the others had a few questions about the procedure. With one person, I knew I had gone over some of these questions before in emails, but I was pleasant and assured them after the work is finished, we will send them off with instructions on the care and cleaning of the tattoo.

I continued my work reviewing stock and making notes of what to order. Above my head was a framed magazine article about the unique services Cosmic Hearts supplied to its customers. The tattoo parlor was billed as a female studio, which was accurate at the time since my mother and Dusty were the primary artists. Since the article was done, there have been a handful of male artists that have blown through. There was this one guy who was great at doing the bio-mechanical stuff, and he helped Dusty really get the edge she needed to gain a following. If I remember correctly, this male artist was great at illustrations, but he had a hard time transitioning to skin as a canvas.

I took a moment to glance at the magazine article "The Women of Cosmic Hearts Tattoo." I knew the picture intimately. There was my mother wearing one of her trademark spaghetti strap dresses. This one is white and lacy, and her inked flower garden appears to be spilling out of the dress. It's like the dress is the vase holding the blooms up and out. Her thick red hair was pulled back into a proper ponytail, high and with a silky bounce. Her smile is wide and big. She is proudly pointing to the painted sign "Cosmic Hearts Tattoo" on the awning over the shop door.

In the photo, Dusty stands opposite my mother. Dusty is wearing black jeans tucked into weathered cowboy boots. A tight T-shirt shows off the ample time Dusty spends at the gym and then to top it off a grey fedora, cocked to the side, sits on her short blond hair. Big fluorescent pink elephants hang from Dusty's ears. Her arms are crossed over her chest, and her chin is lifted high, dishing out plenty of attitude.

However, the charm of the picture resides in the little brown toddler standing in between the two women. Her hair is a mass of dark curls; she would eventually have to tame by braiding. But now, a polka dot hairband is holding the curls in place. A big bright yellow and orange sun with Aztec symbols adorns the center of her shirt. Red shorts and bare feet. The toddler's face is joyful as she holds out a fistful of daisies in front of her as if she were handing the flowers to the person looking at the picture. It seems like I am bestowing the greatest gift with that bunch of flowers. I look so happy in the picture. Those were the days everyone called me "Mouse."

I just can't connect with that level of happiness anymore. Do I smile? Yes. Do I laugh? Yes. But would I ever feel that level of free abandonment where I could hand a stranger my most precious item of the day? Which when I was three years old, was a handful of white daisies? I don't think so.

But, obviously, once upon a time, I was able to do so. I stare at my younger self for a beat, wondering if the emptiness I feel is hormones, sorrow, or a reflection of something I lost. When did I become so angry and mean?

As if in answer to my thoughts, the back door to the studio opens, and the bells jingle. It's the private entrance which means my mother is entering the shop. I hear a bang as she smacks into something, and a few boxes fall over. There is the sound of hands fumbling along the wall, and I wonder what the hell is my mother doing. The light switch is not near where she is standing, and there is a lot of stumbling going on.

"Shit! Why is it so dark in here? Where are the goddamn lights?"

And then some more things fall over. It doesn't sound like anything breakable.

CRASH

I spoke too soon.

But then I heard something I didn't expect to hear. Giggling. Silly girlish giggles. And not just my mother was laughing. Her merriment was being joined by someone else. A man. A man was giggling with my mother, and they were clearly sharing an inside joke or something.

The overhead lights came on, flooding the entire shop. Dusty had awoken from her interrupted nap but remained seated in the chair. I just held my position, staring at the vivid picture in front of me.

There stood my mother. Her face radiant and flushed. Her abundant auburn hair was clipped high on the top of her head, exposing the nape of her neck. Small tendrils of hair had slipped out of the clip and fallen to her shoulders. My mom was looking at me and trying to stifle the giggles, erupting inside of her. She was giggling because a man was standing behind her with his arms wrapped around her waist. And he was softly kissing the nape of her neck. My expression must have been one of silent outrage as my mother started tapping on the man's arm, signaling him to stop. He didn't. Instead, it looked like he murmured something into her ear.

"Shhh. Shhh. Stop. Stop," my mother said, but she was still giggling. And finally, he did, and he looked over in my direction.

I was in shock. My mind was blank, and my mouth had probably fallen open. I've seen my mother with men in the past. But this was the first time I was seeing her sexually with someone who, by my understanding, she barely knew.

I didn't know what to do, so I kept staring at my mother. She was wearing eye makeup, something she never did in the middle of the day. Her eyes were focused on me with an expression of hesitancy and anticipation, but it was mixed with something else, and I couldn't put my finger on it.

A deep voice broke through the silence. "You must be Bess."

My gaze shifted to the male figure behind my mother. If it is possible to truly hate someone when you initially lay eyes on them, then that is what was occurring in my mind. First, I should mention this man was impossibly gorgeous. He looked like he had strolled off the pages of a gentleman's magazine. He had the rugged handsomeness that makes women think they have captured themselves a Han Solo scoundrel. Yes, there was a rogue quality with his strong chiseled jaw, sky blue eyes, and the kind of wavy brown hair that looks like the wind has tousled and teased it as his personal stylist. He was this walking sculpted body of hormones, and even my virgin nostrils could pick up the whiff of sex wafting off the two of them.

He had to be at least ten years younger than my mother.

My mother stopped giggling long enough to say, "Bess, this is Todd."

My expression hardened. Suddenly I knew what else was mixed in with my mother's facial features and body language. She was waiting to see my response to her new beau, but her decision had been made. Lust and desire were mixed into the equation, and she was exuding it.

I felt this rage whoosh up within me. It had been simmering at the beginning, but now it was coursing, overtaking my emotions, and it was bubbling out. I wanted to scream.

"What the hell are you doing?" I said steadily, but the malice was there.

Immediately the sparkling smile left her face, and her eyes tightened. She moved out of Todd's embrace and confronted me head-on. "Who do you think you are talking to?" she demanded.

I spoke without thinking. "A tart," I replied.

The hand came out and smacked me across the face. It stung, but I clenched my jaw and held my defiant gaze. My eyes flooded with tears. Dusty stepped in and forcibly pulled my mother back.

"Terry," she spoke in a calming manner and placed her arms around her shoulders. My mother was shaking with rage. She was speaking softly to Dusty, but I could hear what she was saying. Her voice was choked with emotion.

"Why does she have to be so mean?"

"You kind of sprung it on her." Dusty's tone was measured.

"We didn't know she would be here."

"It's Friday, Terry. And it's after four. She's always here at this time."

I focused on the two of them moving towards the station chairs. I refused to look at the interloper, Todd. He hadn't moved from the position in front of the back door, and I could tell he was staring at me. Stare on, asshole. And then get out.

"Maybe you should pay attention to what is going on in your store," I yelled. "Maybe you would see the work everyone else is doing."

Dusty looked up at me with an expression meant to silence. "Bess be quiet." She turned back to my mother and rubbed her shoulders. "A client is coming in half an hour," she murmured.

"I know." My mother was crying. "I wanted Todd to see what was involved. I wanted him to stay and watch."

"That is such a bad idea," I shouted.

Dusty released my mother's shoulders and marched up to me. Her face was hard, and her eyes black. She was mad as well, but I didn't know if she was angry with me or with my mother for bringing a guy so wantonly into our private and personal workspace. "I think you should go home."

"But I haven't finished with the supply list."

"It will wait. Go home, Bess. Go home NOW."

I held my ground for a moment, but then decided it wasn't worth it. It wasn't worth fighting with Dusty, and to be honest, I wasn't sure what I was throwing such a fit about. Perhaps after a five-month reprieve of no dating and an interlude where the household had finally begun to recuperate from the Luther phase, I had started to believe my mother was content with us, her kids. After all, she went through enough heartache to have us in her life.

Ordinarily, I would have left by the rear door, but he-man, Todd was still standing there. I didn't want to look at him and his freakishly handsome face. I walked past Dusty, and my mother, whose back was turned towards me and headed out the front door, keeping myself in check and not slamming the door like I really wanted to.

As I moved over to my bike, I was beginning to feel ashamed. I knew I had behaved badly, but in my mind, I kept justifying the fury I felt. I was tired of the boyfriends on the dating carousel. My mother's capricious nature didn't allow her to hold onto anyone for longer than three months. I hated the older guys because they would "move in" once they tasted Ollie's cooking and park themselves on the couch. I hated the younger guys cause they all thought my mother was a fun time. However, once they got an eyeful of the baggage she was carrying, they would scramble for the hills. I hated the women because, well, there was just one woman, and her name was Meredith. It was a phase my mother was going through, but nobody told Meredith it was a phase. The whole thing was frightful and dramatic with lots of screaming and name-calling and bitch this and bitch that.

Todd fell into the younger guy category. Aside from the fact he was abnormally good looking, he looked like a guy who could have any woman he wished. Lord knows what he wanted with my mother beyond a few laughs, a soulful dance, and good sex. Guys who looked like him were not keepers when you are talking about a single mother with two children, and one of them is a mouthy teenager.

I unlocked my bike and shouldered the lock. I then remembered I had left my book bag inside the studio. Well, I wasn't going back for it now. The study session with Rueben would have to be accomplished off his notes and my gift of recall.

As I threw my leg over the bike to pull out, I saw a green Prius navigate itself into parallel parking in front of Cosmic Hearts Tattoo. The driver did the maneuver tight and neat. Stephanie Gaige was half an hour early for her appointment. I hope the emotional cauldron inside the shop dissipated before she walked in.

I got home and entered from the back porch of the house, smelling the pungent aroma of garlic coming from the kitchen. On Friday nights, Ollie liked to build a marinara sauce, and he kept a variety of pasta going from baked penne to ravioli (which was Echo's favorite). Garlic bread was a staple. It was Rueben's favorite. (Ollie must have known I had invited him.) And then an enormous green salad filled with all the vegetables leftover from the week that Ollie would toss in.

I shuffled into my bedroom. I had cried all the way home, and I felt I needed to pull myself together before seeing my friends. The craziness of my life was bad enough, I didn't need them to see how it affected me. The other problem with leaving my backpack at the studio was in addition to not having my economics notes, I also didn't have the lovely bag of hot sauce packets Rueben had gotten me. I rifled through the top drawer of my dresser, tossing aside sports bras and socks. But I came up empty, no hot sauce containers to be found. I was out, and my defenses were low. Not a good place to be.

Ollie poked his head in the doorway of my room. "Miss Joanie is here," he announced in a sing-song voice. Ollie took one look at my face and gasped. He quickly stepped into the room and slid the door closed behind him. "What's wrong, sweetie?" Ollie was incredibly perceptive, but I'm sure my face was a wreck, and it was apparent I had been crying.

"I'm fine, really."

"No, I can see you've been crying. And you are not the boohoo type."

"Oh god, I don't want to make this into a thing."

"Make what into a thing?"

"Mom is dating, and I just met the guy."

Ollie sat his heavy frame down on the bed. "Oh, that."

I must admit, I wasn't expecting that reaction. "Am I the last one to know?" I asked. "Even Echo picked up the clues before I did."

Ollie looked puzzled. "Clues?"

"Yes, the dating bra."

"The cheetah print number?"

"Yes, that one."

A contemplative look crossed over Ollie's face. "I suppose she has been wearing it more frequently."

"Ollie, you're gay!?"

"Exactly. Which is why I notice these types of things."

I crossed my arms and leaned back against the bed frame. "Have you met him?"

"No, my dear. I have not had the pleasure."

"His name is Todd." I tried to say the name without wrinkling my nose in disgust. "He's really good looking."

"I've heard. I guess I will get the opportunity soon enough." Ollie heaved himself up on his feet and went for the door. "C'mon, my dear.

Your guest is waiting. There's a bottle of sriracha stashed in the frig. Give yourself a squirt. You'll feel better."

The worst thing about my mother dating was when she started to bring guys to the house and introduce them to Echo. She didn't understand this type of activity confused my sister. After a while, the suitors knew to stay away from me. I was the teenage rattlesnake with a nasty bite. But Echo was different. Echo wanted a dad. My sister didn't have any photographs to tell her what her father looked like. Any guy who walked through the door was a contender in her mind. She craved older male attention, and she got it because who could ignore an adorable little red-haired girl who sticks feathers and shells in her hair and wants to be a fairy princess Jedi knight.

Ollie was currently the steady male in the Wynters household. Ollie was a great guy, but he wasn't great with kids. Kids made him nervous, especially in the kitchen. When he first moved in ten years ago, Ollie made it clear to my mother he cooked, but he wasn't a babysitter. Ollie had a lot of hot pots going, and he was one of those cooks that used every bowl and utensil in the kitchen while he was cooking. Ollie left a huge mess, but it was okay. The kitchen was Ollie's domain, and he made sure you were aware of it.

I followed Ollie into the kitchen and saw Joanie perched on a stool in the breakfast nook. She was already digging happily into a plate of baked penne. Near her was a setting with an empty bowl that had once been filled with ravioli. Echo had been sitting there. I said "hey" to Joanie and went to look for my sister.

She was watching television in the front room, curled up on the couch with a blanket over her shoulders. I sat down next to her, and she leaned into me for a quick snuggle.

'What are you watching?" I asked.

"Cartoons." Like a typical kid, her eyes never wavered from the screen.

"Those cartoons are going to rot your brain."

"Too late," she answered and then squealed when I tickled her ribs.

"Echo, I need you to look at me for a moment." She turned her face my way. I swear she was the sweetest kid on the planet. "Remember when you came to my room the other night and told me about Mom?" She nodded her head.

"You were right, kiddo. I met the guy today. Mom brought him over to Cosmic Hearts."

"Is he nice?" my sister asked.

I wasn't sure how to respond to this. I don't know, Echo. I never gave the guy a shot. There was an instant dislike. Instant. Almost like a flashbulb went off in my head and he was transformed into a disfigured ghoul with fangs dripping with blood and hands grasping a machete, ready to swing in my direction. I just got angry and called mom a name. I don't know, maybe he is nice. But I really don't want him to stick around long enough to find out. This insanity with all the people in and out has to stop. In and out. In and out. Just because Cosmic Hearts has a walk-in policy, doesn't mean our personal lives have to as well.

"Yeah, sure," I lied. "He's nice." And pulled her closer to me for an extra moment.

I hated lying at that moment, but what was I supposed to say to my little sister. I could have said I had a bad feeling, but that sounds like something you hear from an old television show accompanied by lousy organ music.

LUTHER

"You called your mother, a Ho?"

"I didn't call her a Ho. I hate that word. Ho. And whore sounds harsh. I called her a tart."

"I'm sure she appreciated the distinction you were making for her." Luther pushed down the front hood of the Fiat he was working on, and he wiped his hands on the greasy rag hanging over his shoulders. His dark eyes bore into me like he was trying to comprehend the thoughts of someone as incredibly screwed up as I was. He must have given up because he sighed and went back to his work.

Luther is a big man with a muscular linebacker build. He played football at El Cerrito high school and a little bit later in college, but an injury kept him from going forward into the pros. He is a black man with a dark complexion and deep twinkling eyes that crinkle and sparkle when he laughs. And he laughs a lot.

Even though he never finished college, Luther is the smartest man I know. He reads all the time and is always quizzing me about the books assigned to me in school. Everything on the syllabus, Luther has already read. I'm in AP classes, so that is impressive.

He is reflective and honest, and he runs an auto shop, which is about twenty minutes on my bike near San Pablo. Every now and then, when I need the ear of an adult, I sneak away to see Luther.

Luther had his music playing, and he had turned it down when

I entered the shop. In the background, Nina Simone was singing about getting some sugar in her bowl. The song seemed to underscore the gist of our conversation. Luther played a lot of black female vocalists. His favorites being Nina, Aretha Franklin, Brenda Russell, and Teena Marie (who everyone in the black community considers black). Hanging out with Luther is like kicking back with an old friend where you can be yourself because that person already knows your damage. I love Luther immensely. When he was with my mom, I wished and wished and wished he could be my father. But it was not meant to be. No Terry screwed that up royally.

I was taking a small risk showing up at his motor shop on my bike. If anyone appeared here looking for me, I would have to run off and leave the bike behind. And then there would be physical evidence I had been there. I made a mental note not to compromise Luther in the future. I should lock up my bike a few blocks away or take the skateboard. I didn't want to make things even more difficult for him.

You see, there is a restraining order against Luther. He is not allowed to come within a 400-yard distance of the house or the tattoo studio. Technically, the restraining order lists my mother specifically and then the inhabitants of her "household." However, my mother's definition of a household is a loose one. I come to Luther on my own. I'm sixteen years old. I would become an emancipated minor if it were necessary to keep Luther in my life.

Luther and my mother dated for about three years. Echo was two years old, and I was twelve. Luther was the longest relationship my mother ever had with a guy. My mother met Luther because Dusty had gotten into a fender bender in front of the studio. It was her fault apparently, and since the big guy whose Audi she had hit was kind and not going off on her, she suggested they exchange car information inside. He agreed and met my mother, who was finishing up on a client who had gotten a design of the *Beetlejuice* character. The work was done, and the tattoo bandaged. My mother and the client were dancing with abandon around the studio. My mother had Harry Belafonte calypso music blaring through all the speakers, and Luther really dug the vibe of the music and the shop, and he dug my mother. They started dating immediately.

The time Luther was in our lives was magnificent. He showed a lot of interest in both Echo and me, taking Echo to the park and pushing her on the swings and going to teen girl movies with me.

I'll never forget him picking me up after a Robotics club tournament where my team had been soundly trounced in the competition. We had been soundly trounced because of me. I had screwed up something in the schematics, and there was an entire function our robot was not able to complete.

I was sobbing outside the auditorium when Luther pulled up in his car. He had been sent to get me because my mother was running late with other errands. Luther listened to my crying and all the guilt I was placing on my shoulders. He didn't try to say things like "it wasn't your fault" because it was or "you'll do better next time" because, of course, I would. I would never make a mistake like that again. He didn't state the obvious. He held me close and let the tears fall until I didn't have any left. Then he took me out for ice cream, and we watched a brilliant sunset from Indian Rock.

We didn't say another word about the Robotics competition. Instead, we discussed, in detail, the Lincoln assassination and the crazy manhunt involved with John Wilkes Booth. The sky was purple and orange as the sun drifted into the Pacific Ocean, and as we excitedly talked about the level of Booth's celebrity and how he escaped wearing drag, others jumped in with their opinions. It was such a Berkeley moment with university philosophy professors, artists, rocket scientists, carpenters, and auto mechanics engaging in a lively discussion about Lincoln's death, the layers of conspiracy, and the twelve day search for Booth. Luther held his own. He always does. I think it is my fondest memory of Luther Tucker.

Actually, I take that back. There is another fond memory. This one filled my heart with bliss. Being biracial and having a mother who is a redhead with translucent skin, I am always asked where my mother is. People don't automatically link the two of us together. As I have gotten older, there are certain features of my mother I have developed. I have her nose, and my mouth is shaped like hers. But no one looks at us separately and makes the connection. We must be standing next to each other for people to see it.

However, when I was out with Luther, it was different. There was one time when we were at a hardware store, and Luther was at the counter. We were purchasing knobs for my mother's bureau, and he looked at me, asking, "Are there four drawers on that unit, or three?"

"Four," I answered. But then I added, "I think."

Luther held up the blue knobs with pink roses on the ends (my mother was going to love them) and said, "Grab me two more of these. Just to make sure."

I ran down the aisle to retrieve the knobs, and as I was returning, I overheard the man at the register say, "You better watch out. You are going to need a shotgun when that girl gets older."

Luther laughed and answered, "Yes. Yes, I will." He didn't correct the man and say I wasn't his child. He claimed me at that moment, and when we walked out of the store, he put his arm around my shoulders. I knew I would love this man forever.

But then Echo got sick. It was terrible, and she had to be hospitalized. My mother was an emotional wreck and basically moved into the hospital, sleeping in a cot by her bed. She kept a constant vigil and read and sang to my sister whenever she was conscious. Dusty managed things at the tattoo studio, but she couldn't watch over me. Everyone knew not to approach Ollie, so I ended up staying with Luther for a few weeks.

Luther had a decent-sized apartment on Acton Street, and it wasn't far from the high school. We settled into a comfortable routine. I slept in his bedroom, and he took the couch. He made me breakfast in the morning, and I would walk to school or take my bike. After school, I would let myself back into the apartment, feed his cat, Chauncey, and do my homework. Around six o'clock, Luther would close the auto shop and pick me up and take me over to my mother's house. Ollie would have dinner for us, and we would visit with him. Maybe my mother would pop in at the time, but usually not. Sometimes after dinner, the three of us would watch television for a while, or Luther and I would leave Ollie alone to play his opera arias. We were all anxious about Echo and her recovery. The concern for her kept the evenings from being a family fun night, but the time was serene, and it flowed.

There had been a girl crashing at our house around this time. I can't remember her circumstances very well. She was a bit ditzy, had a large gap-toothed smile, and smelled like vanilla. She was like a groupie and lingered on every word that tumbled out of my mother's mouth. She had wanted to start an apprenticeship at Cosmic Hearts and had traveled all the way from Humboldt. Dusty had told my mother not to take her on because her work and sketches weren't strong. The girl needed to go to school or something. Anyway, my mother wisely didn't hire the girl for the studio, but she didn't have the heart to give the girl the boot from the house.

She hoped the girl would find something else and move on.

When Echo got sick, the girl didn't figure out it was time for her to vacate and go back to Humboldt. Ollie had to speak frankly to the girl, and finally, he packed her stuff up and left it on the steps outside the back porch. A week later, she came by with a bunch of druggie friends and retrieved her boxes. Ollie asked Luther to stand guard when they arrived to make sure no crazy shit happened. I remember Luther was pretty steamed about it. Not at Ollie, who had done the right thing, but the circumstance itself. This girl was taking advantage of a situation, and she hung with the wrong crowd comprised of addicts and thieves. I overheard Luther explaining to Ollie the girl had nothing to lose. You can't trust people like that.

Echo recovered, and you would have thought things would go back to the way they were. There was hope we would become the cohesive family; we were on track to becoming. I imagined Luther being the man who walked me down the aisle when I got married. But something curdled inside my mother while she was at the hospital watching her youngest child toss and turn in a feverish sleep. Her imagination went wild, and crazy waves of guilt crashed in her head. She kept thinking there were things she could have done to prevent Echo's illness.

My mother's brain does not operate rationally or logically. She focused on Luther as if he was the cause or the astronomical instrument behind Echo's illness. Suddenly, she viewed their relationship as wrong, and Luther was why she was being punished. She went on the attack.

She was suspicious of everything and challenged Luther constantly. Innocent gestures became over-analyzed, and proof he was trying to undermine her and make Echo and me love him more than we loved her. If Luther put syrup on Echo's oatmeal to sweeten it instead of brown sugar the way my mother did, it was an example of him trying to one-up her. If Luther picked me up from school instead of having me walk, he was coddling me, but then the next day, my mother would be in front of the school sitting in her Volvo wagon. My mother accused Luther of stealing her family. She would scream Echo and I were her children, not his. Things escalated, and her nasty charges became racial in nature.

I don't know how Luther put up with it. He loved her, that was true, and he probably believed Terry would back down eventually. She would see how irrational she was becoming and relax. But she was like a terrier that had gotten hold of the squeeze toy and was not letting go.

Terry started saying things like, "how can you walk down the street with Echo? Don't you think it looks weird? This big black man with this tiny freckled kid... Aren't you worried the police are going to stop you? Accuse you of kidnapping? You're endangering my daughter."

When that didn't make Luther flinch, she would add me to the picture. "Perhaps it's Elizabeth you want. You like it when people think she is your daughter. You get the glory, and you don't have to do any of the work! You don't have to raise her. You don't have to buy the pads when she has her period. Do you think she will ever share her troubles with you? Bess has a lot of issues. She's not your kid. Don't think that she is, just because she looks like you."

Echo and I would hide in my bedroom, and I would play Ollie's opera music to drown out Terry's ugly hysterics. It didn't help when Ollie spoke to my mother or when Dusty tried to apply reason. She was the terrier with the toy, and she wasn't letting go.

And through all of this, Luther just took it. My mother would work herself to exhaustion and collapse on her bed. Luther would tuck her in, smooth the hair back from her forehead drenched in perspiration, peek into the bedroom and say goodnight to us. He would lift Echo, who had fallen asleep, and carry her down the hall to her bedroom and tuck her in. Then Luther would leave for his home.

This went on for a few weeks until Luther decided he would no longer be my mother's verbal punching bag. Ollie had gone out of town to visit his sister in Idaho. He had a new nephew, and his sister needed some extra hands. Ollie was anxious about leaving. He had already rescheduled the visit twice. In addition to the blistering interactions between Terry and Luther, there was the overriding fear

Echo could have a relapse and need to go back to the hospital. His sister's pleadings finally convinced Ollie he had to go to her.

I don't know what caused Luther to snap. I don't know what new awful thing my mother threw in his face. I really can't come up with anything worse than what she had already hurled at him. But one night, Luther fought back. It must have shocked my mother to suddenly see the fury inside this man erupt. His baritone voice added to her shrill high pitch, and it was like a Great Dane suddenly barking back at the little terrier.

The voices escalated, and then there was the sound of things crashing and breaking. The time seemed endless, but in reality, it was a few minutes. But a few minutes is all you need to destroy something that once was real and worth saving. A loud bam and thud resonated through the walls of the house. Echo clung to me and buried her head under my armpit.

Red and blue lights flashed outside my bedroom window. The noise and shouting continued. I could hear movement outside, and I was positive someone was standing at the back steps of the house. They were silent, though, holding a position, and I didn't think I should call out.

There were sharp voices at the front door, commanding my mother to open it. She did, and I heard feet pounding the living room floors. After weeks of screaming and yelling, I'm surprised it took the neighbors this long to call the police. But it is probably because up until this night, the screaming had only come from a single voice, a female voice. Once Luther responded back, the whole thing must have sounded more terrifying.

A policewoman opened the bedroom door and saw Echo and I clutching each other on my bed. She motioned for us to follow her. She went through the kitchen to the back door and released the lock. Another policeman stepped in. Both officers had their weapons drawn.

"I don't think there is anyone else in the house," the female officer said. "The mother says it is just these two. But there are reports more adults live here."

"I'll check the other rooms," the other officer replied. They moved out of the kitchen and headed down the hallway towards the rest of the house. I could hear footsteps up above, so there must have been an officer in Ollie's living area, searching. The female officer led Echo and me into the living room.

"Don't bring those babies in here," a deep voice moaned. "Don't bring them in here. Take them out through the back."

The living room was destroyed. Furniture was knocked over. Lamps had fallen, and there were books and papers tossed on the floor. Vases and plates and picture frames had been smashed, and pieces of glassware were everywhere. Luther was on his knees, and a police officer was standing over him. Luther's hands were handcuffed behind his back. Sweat was dripping from his brow, and it began to mingle with the tears flowing from his eyes. "Don't bring those babies in here," he murmured over and over. I had to look away. When I did, I saw the hole in the wall, next to the clock that read nine-fifteen. The hole was the size of a fist.

Echo was clutching my legs and keeping her face buried into my pajamas. I had a blanket over my shoulders like a cape, and I used it to cover Echo and try to shield her from the horrific scene in front of us. I didn't see my mother, but I could hear her. Luther was crying and shaking his head. There were bleeding scratches on his face. He looked defeated like a bull before it is slain by the matador.

But having the police arrive had not calmed my mother's temper or her mouth. The terrier still had her toy.

She was on the front steps, with her hands handcuffed to the metal banister on the stoop, arguing with the officer standing over her. Her hair was electrified, and her face, a tight rush of red. Her dress was hitched up around her thighs, and her feet were barefoot and bleeding. She was in her words, "explaining the situation," but she was all righteous anger and furious she had been handcuffed. "This is my house! This is my fucking house!" She struggled against the restraints, telling the officer he had the whole thing wrong. Luther was stealing her children. She looked like the crazy lady who screams prophecies on the corner of Telegraph Avenue and Dwight Way.

Before the female officer took Echo and me out the front door, she squatted down so she could look us both in the eye. She pointed to our mother, flaming with spitfire, on the steps, and asked: "Who is that woman there?"

"Our mother," I answered. I was scared and trying to keep myself from shaking. The woman looked like our mother, but now, she had been transformed into one of the hellish harpies I read about in Greek mythology that tortured Odysseus in his seafaring travels.

The female officer pointed to Luther in the living room, and asked: "Is that your father?" She directed the question more to me since I had answered her first question, and clearly, Luther looked like he was my father. But Echo nodded her head yes. I don't know if the officer noticed this, but our mother did. She had finally seen we had been brought out of the house and were standing outside.

She started screaming with increased fervor. "He is NOT their father. He's stealing my kids! He's stealing my kids! Ask anyone. You have to stop him!"

I looked at the officer and answered, "He's my mother's boyfriend." It hurt my heart to say it like that. I immediately began to cry. The female officer looked at me again. "Did he come here tonight to take you away?"

"No," I answered. I wanted to add, *but I wish he would.* I wanted to add that, but I didn't.

SHE'S THE WORST

The female officer placed Echo and me in the back of a squad car. I grasped she was planning on taking us away from the house and begged for proper shoes since both of us were wearing slippers. She came back out with socks and sneakers. She clearly wasn't going to let us go back inside. My sister and I were both wearing pajama pants and sweatshirt tops. Our strange attire with the sneakers just seemed to add to the surreal nature of the night.

I realized this is what being in shock is like. You don't think; you just watch. Perhaps later, you get the opportunity to piece things together. But while it's happening, you're there as a witness, not a participant. The other officer who had gone through the rest of the house came out and holstered his gun. He spoke with the female officer briefly, and she gestured to the police car where Echo and I were sitting.

"Is she taking us away?" Echo whispered to me.

"I think so."

"Where?"

"I don't know." I suspected both Luther and our mother were going to be questioned for a while. I didn't know how these types of things worked. Seeing them, both handcuffed had scared me, but later I learned it was standard procedure with domestic violence calls. The police took one look at the devastation in the living room and restrained them both. They didn't know if there was a gun in the

49

house, and they couldn't risk my mother bashing them on the head with the vase. The vases and picture frames were her handiwork. The hole in the wall was Luther.

"Don't leave me, Bess," Echo whispered.

"I won't. They can't make me."

Surprisingly enough, the police did try to separate Echo and me when we were taken to the station. They wanted to talk to me alone since I was fifteen, and they were worried about Echo hearing what I had to say. They had a child crisis room to hold Echo. It contained sad looking cots, faded linens, and grubby toys. I laughed rudely and pointed out they had just marched us through a living room that looked like a cyclone hit it, Echo was already aware of the violence being displayed in our household. My sister stays with me.

I answered all the questions about our mother and about Luther. I asserted my mother's rants were all wrong. Luther had been a part of our family for years now. The only change had occurred when Echo had been sick, and I had stayed with Luther at his apartment while my mother was tending to my ill sister. They asked me about Ollie and who he was. They asked questions about people who had come through the house but were no longer residing there. They apparently had gotten information from the neighbors because they asked about a few people who had not been around for years. There were people even I had forgotten about, and I found out the gap-toothed girl's name was Amy Honeywell.

Since Ollie was out of town, there was no one to retrieve us from the station. Echo and I went home with the female officer who had us sleep on the floor of her living room with two sleeping bags – one orange and one blue. She gave us hot chocolate from a mix. The marshmallows were stale, but I ate them anyway.

The following morning, Dusty arrived, and there was a big to-do about her taking us since she wasn't family, and our care and wellbeing was the issue at stake here. But eventually, the police relinquished us to Dusty when she showed them proof; she was legally my mother's business partner.

My mother was held in jail overnight since she had apparently tried to accost the officer when they went back to get Echo and me from the rear of the house. That was the other reason for the handcuffs and why they placed her outside. But it was just one night, and then they let her go.

But the horrible thing is this – she insisted on pressing charges against Luther. Her claim was insane, but she was the terrier with the toy, and she must have realized this was her dynamite. This was how she could blow Luther out of the water. She insisted Luther was a threat, and she filed a restraining order. And she made race an issue. Terry played up his size and his dark skin and the fact he worked in auto repair.

She made it sound like all types of nefarious characters came through his shop. "Officer, I have no idea what kinds of dealings go on there. I mean, it could be anything...things my children shouldn't see... there's so much CASH." This was her offensive attack because she needed to characterize the tattoo studio as a haven for artists, and free love and mutual respect. It was truly awful what she did.

Luther had no legal leg to stand on. My mother was not only ending the relationship, she was also detonating it. The phrase "burning bridges" was coined with her in mind. My mother torched her bridges with a flame thrower. She made sure nothing could ever grow again. But Luther was slightly different than the others because Echo and I had become involved. My mother wasn't just burning the relationship; she was shooting rocket launchers at Luther. She wanted him out of her life and away from us. It didn't matter what we wanted. SHE decided it, and then got the law to back her up.

She lied in the paperwork and made Luther sound like he was one-inch shy of being a gangster and someone who became too attached to other people's children. The fact they had been dating for several years didn't matter. Luther and Terry had not married, so we were not legally his children. We weren't biologically his children. We couldn't ask to live with him. He had no claim, and neither did we. My mother reduced him to "some guy".

It was over. Done. Finished. Kaput. Because Theresa Ann Wynters declared it so.

Later a judge tossed out my mother's claims Luther had tried to steal us from her. Many folks submitted depositions indicating the truth of Luther's character and the nature of their relationship. I believe my robotics coach sent in a witness statement and one of Echo's kindergarten teachers at Malcolm X Elementary. No one from the household or tattoo studio sent in any type of report or deposition, despite the requests from the family court. People like Ollie and Dusty remained silent. I was so angry at them, but then I learned Luther warned them to stay out of it, or they would be subject to my mother's wrath.

The judge dismissed anything that could lend itself to a misdemeanor or character harming, but the restraining order remained in place. The police had been called, and a woman was claiming she felt threatened. Luther was not to come in contact with my mother and her household. The only man who had ever shown interest in being a father in my life had been sent away because of my mother's insecurities. To call the situation unfair, does not begin to address the magnitude of the injustice.

That was when I started on the hot sauce packets. I wanted to burn the hurt inside. I was angry, but I wanted to feel more than that. I just wanted to become mean. I wanted to inflict pain. I had to protect myself and lash back.

***

Luther had started humming along with the music playing over his sound system. It was still Nina Simone singing, but now she was crooning about the rock in the hiding place. I was reminded of Echo humming the spiritual the other day and thought I would test my theory.

"Luther? "I asked.

"Yes, Baby doll," he answered. He was over by his workbench, cleaning off tools and sorting out bolts. His back was to me. And I could see the words "Good Job Motor Care" stenciled across the top of his work shirt.

"When was the last time you saw Echo?"

Luther stopped his work entirely and cocked his head to one side. He slowly turned around to face me, and his expression was one of high suspicion.

"Why you asking me that?"

I thought I would play my response from pure ignorance.

"Well...because... I'm here. But I can sneak away and see you. But I don't tell Echo about my visits, because...well...it would seem unfair...cause then, she would want to see you, and that is harder to arrange with my mother picking her up from school, and I just wondered if you snuck peaks at Echo ever. Like...you know...watch her at the schoolyard..."

He didn't go for it. Luther crossed his arms across his chest, held his suspicious gaze, and waited for me to continue.

"I wanted to know if you have been able to see Echo at all. I know she would like to see you."

"I suspect you already have the answer to the question. And why are you phrasing it in a creepy way like I'm some type of stalker? Why are you asking?"

"Okay, I know Echo has seen you. I just don't know how. I know she has either been in your car or she has come to the shop."

"And how do you know that, Ms. Nancy Drew?"

I released a proud smile as I was rather pleased with how I had figured this all out. I pay attention to details. "Echo has been humming "Wade in the Water" which you have on your Mavis Staples CD. You only play your CDs in the shop or on the stereo system in your apartment. So..."

Luther gave me a mock look of exasperation. He placed his hands on his hips and shook his head. Luther appeared to not be able to decide if he should scold me or hug me. I then watched his stern expression melt away, and he broke into a wide grin, embracing me with a teddy bear hug. It felt good to have his large arms around me. It had been too long since I had received a Luther Tucker special deluxe. "Damn, nothing gets by you!" he said.

Luther released me and leaned back, holding me at arm's length. "This has been incredibly hard on me." He acknowledged. "But it's been really hurting the girl."

I knew what he was referring to. Echo peppered me constantly with questions about Luther. I didn't let her know I was sneaking visits, but I tried to answer the questions the best I could. Many times, it wasn't so much the questions, but her statements of longing and wishful thoughts. We'd be in the kitchen eating ice cream, and Echo would reminisce about some quiet evening where we were watching a television show with superheroes, and Luther was there, and we were eating ice cream. They were memories that hardly registered with me, but she would bring them up. "Member when we watched Iron Man with Luther, and we were eating peppermint ice cream... I hope Luther is still getting his peppermint ice cream..."

Luther explained Echo had been doing this with Ollie, and it was driving the older man nuts. Ollie adores Echo. He really does. But his adoration needs to come in small dose exposures. Ollie likes to blare opera music during the day and insert himself mentally into the world of the aria. He doesn't want people hanging out in his kitchen. He likes his space in my mother's house. The only exception he makes is in the evening when the meal is on its way to completion, and then someone can perch on the kitchen stool in the breakfast nook and talk about their day. That person is usually me. And sometimes, Joanie. But Echo is another story. Echo rambles. Echo asks those kid questions that make you appreciate the existence of the Internet and Google. If Echo is in the kitchen, Ollie cannot employ his means of handling stress and escape by listening to opera music and pretending he is the lead tenor at the San Francisco Opera House. Because if Echo is in the kitchen, he must remove the chef hat and put on the responsible adult hat. And nobody in my mother's household likes wearing the responsible adult hat. That's why it gets tossed to me all the time.

It seems to be the secret society they all share – an honest to God, Peter Pan Society.
    "Hi, I'm Bob."
    "I'm Carol."
    "Are you a member of the Peter Pan Society?"
    "Why, yes, I am." Wink wink
    "There is this incredible house in South Berkeley. It is owned by Terry Wynters. Perhaps you've heard of her."
    "I think so. Isn't she the beautiful redhead with the blooming garden on her body?"
    "Yes, that's her."
    "I see her all over the place. I think she was at the Ohlone park on Tuesday, running around, catching kids on slides, and making silly faces."
    "That's definitely her. She has a communal spirit. Well, you know, Berkeley and all."
    The person nods with utmost familiarity.

"Terry Wynters runs a house where if you act like a kid, you get to stay."
"Really?"
"Yes, you are free to unleash your creative spirit."
'Wow, that sounds fantastic. What's the catch?"
"Haven't found one."
Hahahahhahaha

Luther was the one person who viewed membership in the Peter Pan Society as a revolving door. It was suitable for a night or two but not every night. He was on board with the ridiculous because, in its place, it could be fun. He did the mamba with my mother and wore crazy hats and feather costumes. When we did musical theatre night, he would lend his deep voice to the role of Caiaphas in Jesus Christ Superstar and sing along to the soundtrack. Whenever we watched movies, he would bring out the popcorn and yell, "Oh no, he didn't!" at the television screen.

But Luther was also the one who made sure Echo completed her homework and would patiently work with her on her penmanship. Luther was always telling me to put on a sweater and asking where I was going because he cared. Luther was the guy you would call if you needed a ride, needed advice, needed a hug.

Without Luther around and with no means of allowable communication, Echo was driving Ollie nuts with endless questions about Luther's wellbeing. She was entering Ollie's kitchen sanctuary, sitting at the breakfast nook and pummeling Ollie with questions about Luther. Since Luther isn't eating at the house, where is he eating? What is he eating? Is he having his favorite peach cobbler? Where is Luther sleeping? What does he do all day? Is he watching television? Is he playing games? Is he dancing the mamba? Echo was having a hard time visualizing Luther outside of the Peter Pan house he had been tossed out of.

Ollie had figured out the same loophole I had. If Luther can't come to us, we can go to him. So last Tuesday, he had walked Echo to the AC Transit bus stop, and the two of them boarded the bus to Luther's apartment. Ollie chose a day when my mother had an evening appointment at Cosmic Hearts, and I would be at the downtown library with Rueben preparing for a debate club competition. They took the bus so his truck parked out front wouldn't give him away.

They spent an hour at Luther's place, and Echo got to see where Luther lived. She got to see his kitchen. She got to see the bookcases filled with the works of Richard Baldwin, Langston Hughes, and Maya Angelou. She got to hear the soft spiritual music in the background with Mavis Staples singing, and she got to meet Luther's cat, Chauncey. Luther's place is peaceful and inviting with its warm colors and smells of earth and spice. I'm sure Echo wanted to stay.

It was a clandestine meeting, but it had its desired effect. Echo could now visualize the life Luther was living. The unfortunate thing was we were not a part of it anymore.

Well, not legally.

After telling me about Ollie's secret visit, Luther warned me not to try the stunt myself. "Don't you be bringing that child over here. Your mother can still shut the whole thing down. And I don't want to see you in more trouble than you are already in."

Obviously, the man doesn't know me very well.

CEASEFIRE

"Who was the father of Paris?"

"King Priam," I answered.

"Paris?" Dusty wondered. "How do they determine the father of a city? How does that even happen?"

"Paris is a character," I explained. I was going through the supply cabinets in the shop, taking inventory notes. Dusty was cleaning the sterilization chamber. It was a typical Saturday morning, and we were preparing for the appointments of the day and whatever else walked through the door.

While we worked, my mother did her crossword puzzle. She did them daily. Usually, she liked the one published in the newspaper, but she kept a paperback book of crosswords in the rear office in case she needed to engage herself mentally during a quiet interlude. My mother loved crosswords. I, on the other hand, liked visual puzzles. I was the Queen of Tetris and loading the dishwasher.

"What did you say, Bess?"

"King Priam. The answer is King Priam."

My mother was silent for a moment as she did the configuration. "It doesn't work."

I held my ground. "The father of Paris, the man who is responsible for the Trojan War, is Priam. I'm pretty positive that is the answer."

My mother and I were operating within a truce. After two weeks of her giving me the silent treatment and my delivering the same with equal venom, we had reconnected in a late-night ice cream raid. We had both snuck into the kitchen at the same time targeting the last spoonfuls of Chunky Monkey in the freezer. We realized we had a shared goal, dropped our weapons of hostility, and consumed the ice cream together.

She was still seeing Todd and was sharing more and more about him.

I was trying to be open-minded. Luther had counseled me to do so – to not be closed off and dislike Todd because ..well because he wasn't Luther. My mother was happy. Let her be happy.

I was finding this thinking hard to maintain. It was like a nasty pit in my stomach; a nasty pit with thorns and toxic goo. There was nothing I heard about Todd that I liked. He didn't seem genuine to me. Every glowing thing my mother told me about him felt like something I could spin to show he was a fake and a liar. I couldn't put my finger on it, but I felt like Todd was just an act. From his impossibly good looks and freaky crocodile smile, he seemed like a guy who got up in the morning and put on this Todd suit before he presented himself to the world. He was a wolf in sheep's clothing. And we were the stupid sheep letting him waltz through the door.

This evening my mother was planning on having Todd come over to the house, and Echo was going to meet him. I argued it was a bad idea, and it was too soon. But my mother put her foot down. It had been almost half a year since she and Luther had broken up, and she had a right to date and secure her happiness.

There are times I wished she could listen to herself. I'd love to playback her words so she could hear how often she says "me, me, me" and "mine, mine, mine." I conceded to her dinner party. My one request was that Dusty be there. I didn't want the evening to feel too much like family. In fact, Dusty had started dating a woman named

Carrie, and I suggested Dusty could bring Carrie as well. I wanted to fill the house with people, so I mentioned Rueben and Joanie should come over too. That way, Todd wouldn't be special. I didn't want him to think he was special in the slightest.

In my mind, Todd was not a keeper. He was the rebound guy, and that's it.

My mother was erasing what she wrote down into the puzzle. "It's not working, I tell you. That's not the answer."

"Let me see." I moved behind her and peered at the puzzle over her shoulder. She had a good portion of it completed. I could see where she had written down the answer to Paris' parentage, and she was right; it was not linking with what she had written down for the response to where Paris had met with the goddesses. Mount Ida was the correct answer there. This was a crossword with a Greek mythology theme.

I saw the problem immediately. "You spelled Priam wrong." I pointed out. "It's with an "I" not a "Y.""

"That's how you pronounced it." My mother was annoyed at the correction.

I shrugged. "That's how it's pronounced, but it is spelled the way I just showed you." I should also point out my mother is great with crossword puzzles, but she does employ creative spelling. Usually, if she can't decipher something accurately, it is because she misspelled one of her answers. The answer is right, but the spelling is uniquely hers.

"Okay, maybe you know this one as well. I was trying to see if the answer would slowly reveal itself, but you might know it off the top." She pointed to the question asking the name of the God of Wind.

I closed my eyes and let my mind drift a bit. I had a book on the Greek gods at home and at one point, had memorized them pretty thoroughly. But the real trick I had accomplished was I had mentally photographed the pages in my head. I let my mind drift, and I visually turned the pages of that book until I hit upon it. "It's Aeolus," I said, a bit triumphantly. I knew my mother would not be able to spell it, so I did it for her. She clapped her hands, gleefully like a child. She then leaned over and gave me a quick peck on the forehead.

"Thank you, honey. You are so clever. My little problem solver."

"Stop giving her problems to solve," said a husky voice across the room. The statement was intended to be as loaded as it sounded.

My mother flipped the bird at Dusty. (See what I mean, she is the founding member of the Peter Pan Society.)

The door opened. There was the jingle of bells, and our first customer of the day walked in. He was clearly someone looking for Dusty as his loose-fitting utility shorts revealed bio-mechanical tattoo work on his calves. Dusty greeted him. She knew his name, but he was not scheduled in the books. It looked like an impromptu consultation.

"I was thinking..." my mother started. I looked over at her. From her expression, I could tell she had been looking at me for a while. I know parents do that. They stare at their kids, and strange thoughts run through their heads.

Since she had delivered the layup, I had to take the shot. "Thinking is dangerous for you."

She smiled at my unoriginal response. "I've been thinking we should plan a weekend getaway soon. We haven't been up north in awhile. I'd like to take some family time up in Guerneville. Wouldn't that be fun?"

"Stay at Dusty's place?" I asked.

"Yes, just us."

Dusty has a tiny one-bedroom cabin up in Guerneville, a small town that sits near the Russian River. It is a little artist's glen with craft fairs and festivals and it's a popular destination for lesbian couples - the same way Palm Springs has become a popular place for gay guys.

I have no idea what the mass appeal for Guerneville is outside of its proximity to wineries and its rustic ambiance. But that's why Dusty has a place there.

"Just us *and Todd*?" I had a suspicion.

My mother looked away, and her agenda was revealed in that one maneuver.

"It's too soon," I said. "Stop foisting him on us."

"I haven't," my mother countered.

"But you want to," I pointed out. "You want Todd to be included. You want him in our family unit. What little of one we have."

"And what is that supposed to mean?"

We were speaking in hushed tones, but the volume of our discussion increased as our emotions were rising. Dusty looked up at us from her station and frowned. The client was engaged in his description of what he was looking for. He was pointing to his forearms and then gesturing at a piece of paper on the drawing table.

For me to broach, our precarious nature of family was walking into dangerous waters with my mother. I hesitated, not wishing to touch this live wire – the third rail of our family. How do you mention something my mother feels is her business and no one else's; the fact I am literally the result of a one night stand and she didn't marry Echo's father and had no intention of doing so. She has a fly-by-night life and hides behind her creative genius, and everyone is supposed to accept and deal with it. No judging. This is what I hear all the time from her. No judging. Don't you dare judge me.

But stating a fact is not judging. It's stating a fact. And she has placed my sister and me in unstable and precarious situations because neither one of us has a male name listed on the line which says "Father" on our birth certificates. My mother believes this gives us freedom. And has this absurd notion she is rebelling against patriarchal views and moral judgment. But of course, she is not the one that has only one birth parent listed on her certificate. She has two birth parents. She has the luxury of rebellion.

I was rescued from delivering the sentiment racing through my mind and would have surely plunged my mother and me into another war when Dusty called me over to "get the paperwork started on her client."

Dusty's bio-mechanical guy had a name. It was Glenn. Glenn must have a secret desire to become a virtual cyborg as he already had full tattoos covering his calves depicting metal and wiring beneath his skin. The concept behind the ink was of somebody slicing through the core of Glenn's humanity and discovering hardware; that secretly, he was an android or something. Dusty had once explained all this to me, but anybody with a brain could see it.

It was evident from the sketches Glenn was hoping to continue with his desire of art, transforming him into a metal creation. Drawings at the station were to be tattoo sleeves for his arms, and it looked like Glenn may even have something more substantial in mind as I saw a piece that could only be turned into work for his back or chest. This was a huge commission if Dusty was going for it.

Dusty introduced me to Glenn and explained I was kind of like the office manager of the place, and he would work with me to book the sessions. Glenn toured with a traveling theatre company as their road manager and had some dates where he would be out of town. With all that established, Dusty pulled me away to the shelves and sterilization unit to discuss ink and needle orders.

That's what she told Glenn, but in truth, what Dusty wanted me to do was a little more clandestine. Let me explain - there are times when somebody enters Cosmic Hearts, and they are studio shopping. They are planning on doing a large tattoo – something that will require multiple sessions, and they want to make sure they have a good rapport with the artist, and they trust the artist's skill and overall vision for the piece. They will go to a few places they have either gotten through recommendation or seen an appealing tattoo on the Internet. They book an appointment for a small piece of work. Usually, the design is something done under two hours. They scope the place out. They see how the artist responds to their idea, and if the experience is a good one, they come back for the more significant piece.

When someone comes in who has had extensive work done someplace else (and Dusty wants them as a client), Dusty usually asks me to check out the person and "get the paperwork started." Dusty thinks I get my information by asking questions, the right questions, and people just guilelessly cough up the information. I'm like a perceptive fortune teller. She has no idea why I am so accurate.

Glenn was hoping to commission an artist to do a sleeve on his upper right arm and a sleeve on the lower left. Eventually, when he saves up enough money, he wants to do something on his back. Glenn wants the same person to do all the work. When Dusty asked him why he hadn't gone back to the artist who did the ink on his calves, he said the person had left the area and was no longer in California. Dusty suspected an artist she knew personally, Curtis, had done the work, and as far as she knew, Curtis was still in town. She wanted to know why Glenn was shielding the truth.

I talked with Glenn and asked him basic scheduling questions, making sure everything seemed smooth and fluid on the financial end. There are times with big pieces where we don't take the entire amount upfront. If the artwork is going to take four sessions, I will break the payments up into three installments. The idea is that the whole piece is paid for before our artist finishes the work. Tattoos don't work on a layaway plan. I can't tell you how often we hear people say, "I'm good for it," and they're not.

My mission was to discover what problem Glenn had with Curtis –

easy enough. I asked him if he minded sitting on the stool and laying his leg across the table so I could photograph it and allow Dusty to use as a comparison as she created new sketches. This is all part of a standard consultation anyway. He did. And then came the weird part because I had to touch the tattoo, and calves can be a sensitive area of the body. I pretended there was something on the leg and blew on the ink designs as if I were a perfectionist, and I couldn't possibly have any lint in the way. After blowing, I looked at Glenn and asked permission to touch his leg.

"Do you mind?" I asked. I want it to be a clear picture." I've done this before, and nobody ever sees the imaginary lint I am trying to dispose of, and everybody says it is fine to brush this imaginary lint away.

Mission Accomplished. With a sweep of my hand, I acted as if I had finally gotten rid of that pesky lint, touched the tattoo in the process, and then snapped my picture with the digital camera we keep in the shop.

When I touched Glenn's tattoo, incredibly strong emotions pounded through my body like a jackhammer. I felt fury and anguish all at once. It was an intense feeling, and I had to hide the shudder that raced through my bones because I didn't want Glenn to think that touching him had repelled me. I backed away under the pretense something had gotten into my eye – maybe the pesky imaginary piece of lint. After a beat, I squared my shoulders and looked at Dusty with a smile. The smile was to let her know I had what she needed. I knew why Glenn had not returned to Curtis at Vulture Tattoo for any follow-up work. And he never would.

Later, I gave Dusty the rundown...

Curtis is the lead artist at Vulture Tattoo and has a steady clientele of men who are into displaying their machismo with ink. Military guys, motorcycle guys, wanna be motorcycle guys, and guys with gang affiliations all take up residence at Vulture. From what I learned by touching Glenn's tattoo was that Glenn had two problems. One, despite his extreme interest in becoming a science fiction muscle guy, Glenn did not look like a muscle guy. He was kind of soft and nerdy. Glenn was the type of guy that should wear glasses because then there would be a point of interest on his face. The clientele at Vulture Tattoo terrified him, and he inwardly hated that they terrified him, and part of his metal transformation was to combat these feelings of male inequality and literally have inner titanium strength "implanted" within him. He was finding it impossible to build on his tough-guy persona when he was surrounded by real tough guys who could squash him like a stinkbug.

The second problem Glenn had, and it was something Dusty could use as a bonding tool, was that Glenn had developed a massive crush on Curtis' wife, Erika. She was this buxom number with short blond curls and a full open face who ran Vulture Tattoo. When Glenn first started going there, Erika was still just a girlfriend, and Glenn thought he actually had a shot. There were probably many men who believed they had a shot with Erika. She was known for her flirtatious behavior and the way she would rest her size DD breasts on the display counter when going through a flash design tattoo binder.

However, a month ago, Erika and Curtis ran off to Reno and tied the knot. She now was Curtis' wife, and Glenn felt bad ogling another man's wife. He thought he needed to take his business elsewhere. I wondered if that move on Curtis' part was going to cost him other business. Not that many men have a problem checking out the rack a married woman displays, but some men don't like it and try not to place themselves in situations where temptation is beckoning. Glenn was one of those men, and I made a mental note to remind Dusty perhaps this is a potential avenue to pursue – Honorable men who want tattoos but can't go to Vulture anymore.

There was another interesting piece of information I gleaned from Glenn. Glenn wanted to create a club of sorts. A secret club kind of like fight club. His idea was that these people, he thought both guys and gals, would be like "future people." They would be identified by their bio-mechanic artwork. I couldn't tell if this was something Glenn was attaching to a post-apocalyptic zombie attack or if he thought merging humans and androids was the wave of the future, or what. But it was a secret desire that had been emotionally attached to his tattoo work, and it was either odd strange or odd cool.

When I shared the bio club aspiration with Dusty, she got this quizzical look on her face, but I could tell there was some deep thought processing going on. "Hmmm, that's interesting," she said while nodding her head.

"Weird, huh."

"A little. But harmless and perhaps a money maker for me." She planted a kiss on my forehead. "Thanks, kid. Now, I'm sure you have homework to do. Get out of here."

"I need a seven-letter word for ardent. Hopefully, it will begin with the letter "Z"," cried a voice sitting on the other side of the store.

"It's zealous," I answered.

"Are you sure?"

"Yes."

"Z E A?"

"Yes."

"It fits! Yay!"

IS EVERYBODY HAPPY

The dinner party was going well – all things considered. Everyone was trying to make sure there were no fireworks. My mother and I had drawn up further lines of distinction in our truce, and the two of us were doing an excellent job of keeping ourselves in check. Terry tried not to fondle Todd with every opportunity she had – however, I did see them sneak an embrace in the hallway with Todd grabbing two large handfuls of my mother's behind in his paws.

For my part, I worked at not sending out nasty verbal zingers even when the temptation was laid bare. I sucked down a lot of hot sauce packets. We both were hiding our frustration with over the top smiles. What do they say? – "Fake it until you make it" or some mess like that.

It seemed the guests understood they were human buffers to keep the drama from flaring up. I had both Rueben and Joanie with me. They always help me from mouthing off in front of my mother – Rueben dissolves the tension with his humor. His jokes are usually stupid, but that's what makes them work.

And Joanie, well... let's just say I never want Joanie to see me misbehaving. It's not that Joanie is a saint. She is a complete goofball, but Joanie does not have a mean bone in her body. I do, and I don't want her to see it. I don't want Joanie to disapprove or be ashamed of me, and possibly rethink our friendship. It's weird, but with all the concern about folks not judging each other, I care about how Joanie sees me.

My mother had Dusty and Dusty's new squeeze there as her buffers. It turned out Dusty's new gal pal was Carla, not Carrie. And I created a firestorm by calling her Carrie and Dusty had to convince Carla there wasn't a Carrie. Carla was a tiny birdlike looking woman with short, cropped black hair. She looked fearful of the crowd, and a bit overwhelmed. She was cute, but I could already tell she was not going to keep Dusty's interest for long. Her quick accusations of infidelity based on me tripping over her name was indicative of someone who was incredibly needy and insecure.

Later Dusty asked me to perform my parlor trick on Carla. She wanted me to touch the tattoo on Carla's wrist and talk with Carla and then give Dusty the extra information I would glean. As I've said, Dusty thought I was overly sensitive and intuitive. She leaned towards the Sherlock Holmes route of acute perception.

Carla had the inscription "words fly away" on her wrist, and even I could see without touching the tattoo, there were tiny slits of scars on her wrist. These had come from cutting herself. I feigned interest in her ink and asked to look at it. She was hesitant because the tattoo was there to cover the scarring of her self-destruction. However, she didn't want to look like she was a baby in front of Dusty, so she laid out her arm for my perusal. For me to "read" anything of significance, I must directly touch the tattoo. Carla looked like she was about to flinch and move her arm away, so I gently placed my other hand under her arm to steady her. I rubbed the tattoo with my finger as if the words were in Braille, and I was reading them in that fashion.

"Words Fly Away," I repeated. "I like that. I also like the wings you have sprouting on either side like bookends. It's really cool."

She gave me a weak smile. She feared me. And after touching the tattoo, I understood why. This woman had been viciously bullied. She had been taunted and ridiculed and screamed at. Through the tattoo, I was able to see the central tormentor in her life. The person who had been instrumental in her misery and was the reason she had tried to take her life when she was in college. The woman in my vision spewed hateful things from her lips. "You idiot. What are you doing? You're stupid. You weak, pathetic thing. Of course, you like girls. What guy in their right mind would want you? You're not a woman, you're a waste of breath." The barrage was endless. The sad thing was I believed the tormentor was a family member, perhaps a sister. As the features on the face were like Carla's, except the hair was longer.

"Thank you for showing it to me," I whispered. I was embarrassed for her and felt sorry because, despite the fact she had survived her suicide attempt, and she intended to not allow hurtful words to road map her life, Carla was still vulnerable.

About half an hour later, I shared my thoughts with Dusty. Just like when I read a client for her (i.e., Glenn), I structured my findings as if I was a detective reading hidden clues or a soothsayer.

"So, what do you think?" Dusty asked.

"I think Carrie has been abused."

"Carla," Dusty corrected.

"Huh?"

"Her name is Carla. Oh god, I hope you didn't call her Carrie again."

"No. No. I'm sorry. But she seems like a Carrie. Anyway, I think she was abused..."

"Sexually?"

"No. Definitely not sexually. But seriously verbally abused. She had a bully in her life. A female bully. It was constant. Someone who called her names and told her she was stupid."

"Her sister, I bet!" interjected Dusty.

I nodded my head as I was pretty sure that was the identity of the tormentor.

"Do you know she attempted suicide?" I asked.

Dusty looked down at her boots and shifted her weight from one foot to the next. "Yeah, I knew. I guessed when I saw the tattoo was covering something up on her wrist."

"She seems nice," I shared with Dusty. "Good Luck." I wondered how Dusty would handle things now that she knew Carrie/Carla had been bullied. Carrie/Carla was the type of gal you would have to walk on eggshells around, and Dusty liked to stomp around in those cowboy boots of hers.

On the other side of the room, I heard Joanie's familiar squeal of laughter. She and Rueben were hanging out with Ollie and a guy named Duane. Duane had come with Todd.

Todd had brought human buffers as well. My mother had already met his crew as she greeted them both with her trademark scream of a welcome and warm embrace. They laughed about some previous jokes and talked about going to some concert in Sonoma County. Both of Todd's friends called him "Mackey" which is Todd's last name. (insert eye roll) Watching this exchange from afar, I wondered just how long my mother and Todd had been seeing each other. These guys knew her.

Todd's friend, Duane, was the oversized doofus of the group. He's the one they keep around for a laugh, probably gets drunk quickly, and then does some outrageous stunt. He was large and round and delivered a boisterous chuckle, causing his torso to heave under his flimsy t-shirts. Duane went outside the house a lot during the night. I smelled cigarettes on him, so I assumed this was the reason for his disappearances. I hoped there weren't a bunch of cigarette butts outside my bedroom window for me to find in the morning.

The other friend of Todd's was tall and angular. He had a sharp nose and small dark eyes. When he first looked at me, it felt like his gaze was a knife sliding through me. I felt exposed. I shivered. I glanced over to the couch where Echo was sitting quietly with her collection of tiny stuffed animals. I quelled my instinct to go over there and touch Echo as if I were warding off a dark spell. This man had that effect. Later I learned his name was Nick. Nick Ryder. Nick Ryder gave me the creeps.

The house was filled with music and joyful noise. Ollie had created a taco bar, and my mom had the tub in her bathroom filled with Mexican beer and ice. It was a regular house party.

The evening came to a delightful climax when Dusty brought out her guitar and began strumming. Everyone sang along to the seventies folk tunes Dusty loved to play. Joanie has a strong, well-defined voice and sang "If I Had a Hammer" on her own as nobody wanted to drown out the clarity of her sound. Afterward, everyone begged for her to do something else, and she sang "Bridge Over Troubled Water," and I could see both Ollie and Carrie/Carla wiping away tears from their eyes.

Joanie had driven to the dinner party and she gave Rueben a ride home. I had Echo come sleep in my room as I never trusted her being on her own the nights my mother had strangers in the house. Some people might think I was overly cautious, but Echo's room was next to the bathroom. Bad things can happen, and I didn't want someone accidentally stumbling into my sister's room at night. My bedroom door has a lock on it. And I locked it that night.

As I suspected, Todd spent the night. When I came into the kitchen the following morning, he was there going through the dishwasher and pulling out two coffee mugs. He was wearing nothing but his boxer shorts. I walked out of my bedroom, saw him, saw his attire or lack of it, and turned around and walked back into my bedroom. I slammed the door to register my disapproval.

"Put some clothes on," I shouted through the door.

"Sorry," Todd answered with the voice of a car salesman. "I didn't think you were there."

"It's my house. Of course, I am going to be here." I shouted back. I whispered, "Dumbass," under my breath. I glanced over on my bed and saw Echo lying there with her eyes open, looking right at me. I gestured for her to pull the covers over her head. She did.

I could hear my mother entering the kitchen. "What's all the shouting?" she asked. "Bess, open the door!"

"No. Go tell him to put clothes on."

My mother knocked on the door like she meant business. I opened it a crack and saw she was standing there in a bra and panties, and Todd was still over by the dishwasher.

"For crying out loud, mom! You go put some clothes on too. Why are you guys running around in your underwear?" I cried.

My mother's hands flew to her forehead. "Stop with all this racket," she scolded. "Great, now I have a headache."

I groaned and closed the door. "Just go away," I shouted through the door.

"Come out, Bess!"

"No. Not until the two of you are decent." A thought then crossed my mind, and I opened the door a crack. "Tell Todd he shouldn't prance around like that. He might give Ollie ideas." I slammed the door and locked it. She smacked her hand on the door and tried to open it.

"I hate that lock," she mumbled.

I heard Ollie cry out from upstairs, "I heard that comment, Missy. Don't think I didn't," as my mother stomped off.

Despite the disastrous way the day began, after I emerged from my room later, my mother was in high spirits. Ollie had come down and had made scrambled eggs and had mixed in the leftover taco fillings and shells to create a delicious brunch. We were so lucky we had Ollie.

My mother said he was better than Mr. French. (I have no idea who that is, but I think he was on a TV show) As I consumed my food, I could hear my mother scurrying around in the living room. Todd must have left the house as I didn't hear his voice at all, and no sounds were coming from the bathroom.

I was tired of fighting with my mother. Bolstered by the delicious food and carrying a soothing cup of chai tea in my hand, I decided to approach her in the living room. Her face broke into a wide smile when I came in. She was on the couch and patted the area next to her for me to sit down. She then fixed me with a look like she was about to bust with anticipation.

"I had the most fantastic idea last night."

"Yes?" I was wondering what it could possibly be. Her excitement was palpable, and I wanted to match it, but it was making me uneasy.

"We've wanted to add a fixed musical component to the Beloved ceremonies. We have clients bring in playlists, and that is effective. But a live performance is both compelling and emotional. What if we had a soloist who could sing certain selections for the client. Songs like "Amazing Grace" or love songs associated with the person connected to the tattoo. Wedding songs or the song from their first dance. Stuff like that. It would be an added service. And a paid position for the singer."

It was brilliant, actually. It was a smart idea. Many people would want this added touch of intimacy to the service. The businessperson inside of me did a mini happy dance as I thought about all the revenue it would bring in. Then suddenly, I realized where my mother was going with this, and my heart dropped like a stone.

"I thought your friend, Joanie, would be perfect for this. It would allow her to make a little extra money. She has such a lovely voice. I am sure there are many songs she already has in her repertoire. We can do a two-tiered invoice structure, where if a song is something we consider a standard, and we will list them, then we will charge one cost, but if the song is something that is a special request, we can charge a bit more because Joanie will have to learn it. What do you think?"

Inwardly I groaned inside. I knew Joanie would never go for it. And now another fight was going to unfold with my mother, who failed to comprehend other folks may not approve of her lifestyle and her unstructured outlook of life.

"We can launch this pretty soon," my mother continued, not noticing the look of dismay which must have been splashed across my face. "We have a woman coming in next week...either it's next week or the week after that. You can check the books. But she is doing a Beloved ceremony, and the tattoo memorializes her mother. Check the books. Her name is Liza, I believe, and the piece is a dragonfly – apparently, her mother loved them as a little girl. She wanted music, and I was pulling together soundtrack themes and orchestras and violins, but if we could get a solo work from Joanie, that would be marvelous. Oh my god, I am getting goosebumps just thinking about it. Look at my arm!"

My mother threw her arm out for me to inspect. She looked at my face for confirmation, and that is when she must have seen my expression. She slowly lowered her arm, and her face shifted from wonderment to suspicion. "What is it? Don't you like the idea?"

"It's a great idea, mom. No, really, it is a great idea." I gave her a smile, but I knew it was weak.

"So, what's the problem?" My mother's eyes were penetrating.

"Joanie would never do it."

"Why not? You just said it was a great idea."

"Joanie thinks tattoos are a sin. She wouldn't want to be a part of it and..., and her father would never let her."

"WHAT?!!!" My mother leaped from the couch like an army of fire ants had taken over the cushions.

"Witness' believe marking your body is a sin against Jehovah."

"That girl has been to my house and had dinner with my family and friends, and she thinks I am a sinner?!"

According to the Bible, my mother is a sinner. The tattoos were a minor infringement compared to the big fornicator part. I wished I had never opened my mouth, but what was I going to do? Lie to her? And then have her approach Joanie and then Joanie telling me I had to come up with some reason for her to decline. All that drama was a pathway to awkwardness and messy deception.

Tattoos and sexual freedom are my mother's path. They are her choices, and there are consequences to those choices. One of which is Joan Whittier will not be a soloist at her spiritual ceremonies housed in a tattoo parlor.

My mother was screeching now.

"Mom, wait. Wait. Calm down." I said.

"I am not going to calm down. You just told me your little friend thinks I am a sinner. Who the hell does she think she is?"

"Mom, a lot of people think you are a sinner. If you go by the ten commandments you are." I always go right to the ten commandments because everybody has heard of those even if they don't attend bible study. I don't have to list the commandments or the ones she has broken. We both know what's on her list.

My mother was glaring at me. Her arms crossed over her chest in pure defiance. "I can't believe she has come over to my home and has the nerve to eat my food."

"Mom, the house is different. The house is not Cosmic Hearts. She can be here. Her father allows her to come here. She just wouldn't feel comfortable in the shop. Joanie is a Witness, and she abides by certain truths. That is how she refers to it. She lives in the truth. But you don't live in the truth. She is not expecting you to live in her truth."

These words seemed to soften my mother a bit.

"It goes both ways. Joanie respects you and is respectful of you in your home. She doesn't have to approve of the flowers all over your body. Mom, there are tons of people who dislike tattoos. You know that. You just have to respect the fact she is uncomfortable with the notion of marking your body."

"Why do they not like it? What's wrong with it?"

I shrugged, not really sure, but then the answer came to me. "I'm sure it has something to do with idol worship. Many pagan believers marked their bodies with runes and symbols, and they worshipped many gods. You know... a god for this and a god for that... Greeks, Romans, Native Americans, Druids...all pagans. Christianity is about worshiping the one true God."

"Does she know about you?"

"Does she know about me, what?"

"Does she know...has she seen your foot? I mean, goodness Bess, you spend a lot of time with that girl."

"Yeah, but I'm never barefoot."

"Are you ashamed of it?"

I didn't know how to answer, so I kept my mouth shut and let the silence speak for me. The inked symbol on my foot was a tether to my mother, and one Joanie would completely understand despite her probable disapproval. I just wished to avoid the hard conversation it would provoke, so I have never allowed Joanie to see me without tennis shoes on. It really wasn't hard with the skateboarding and bike riding; I'm not a barefoot kind of gal.

I think Joanie is terrific, and I feel lucky she is my friend. She knows I am the daughter of a mega sinner, and she is okay with that. I just don't want Joanie to think some of my mother's queasy morality has tainted me. Even though all logic dictates it has and will. How could I escape the sin if I was living in her house?

Seeing I was also enveloped in this judgment on our household, and it wasn't just about her, my mother dropped her angry stance and allowed her arms to fall by her side. She twisted her body this way and that in a sulky childish swing.

"Shoot. It was such a good idea."

"It IS a good idea. Find somebody else."

She plopped back down on the couch next to me and picked up my cup of chai tea and helped herself. She wrinkled her nose in disapproval and did a mini gag.

"Don't you sweeten this at all?" she asked.

"It's my tea. I make it the way I like it."

"We have honey in the cupboard. Why don't you put honey in it?"

"I don't want honey. I like it the way it is."

She pouted like a two-year-old. "You don't sweeten your drinks just to keep me from taking them."

Wow, she figured it out.

But I said nothing. I was waiting to see if another ball was going to drop. But it appeared her angry emotional wave had crashed on the rocks, and the water was rescinding into the sands, vanishing from sight.

My mother was back to smiling, and she reached over to the coffee table and picked up her current crossword puzzle.

"Stay here," she said. "I may need help with this one."

I leaned back into the cushions of the couch and released the breath I had been holding. I had dodged a bullet with that one. The argument about sin could have blown into epic proportions. My mother could have decided to ban Joanie from the house just from the idea that someone else could possibly have a different viewpoint than hers.

It is astonishing to me a woman who has had multiple lovers and some of them married (yes, she has wrecked some homes) and two children out of wedlock, would still get riled up by the notion other

78

people may view her lifestyle as sinful or even unsavory. I hated feeling like I had to defend my mother. It's hard because I don't agree with her half the time.

My mother has had a challenging life. If you understood her, you would see her pain is inked on her body for all to see.

"I need a three-letter word for a stress reliever."

"Hug"

THE SPARROWS OF SORROW

There are five sparrows tattooed on my mother's left forearm. They are sweet little dark birds with beautiful detail in their wings, and each has a tiny red heart sheltered underneath the span of their outstretched wings or carried within the clutch of their beak. The birds circle around my mother's arm like an extended charm bracelet. The five little birds represent the five miscarriages my mother had in her life. Each one of these babies was a dagger to my mother's soul, like a judgment held against her ability to become a mother. They were not early pregnancies, but second term. These were the ones she felt move within her. The ones that kicked and made her gasp as she envisioned a life and a future for them.

When my mother feels lost or sorrowful, she wraps her left arm across her chest, so the sparrow angels are near her heart. I don't think she is even aware she does it.

Before I was born, there were two lost pregnancies. She named them. She names them all. I just don't know the names of those two. However, I know their stories. I know the stories my mother shares. Because of the level of grief associated with these babies, I refuse to touch the sparrows. I am not a masochist, and I don't need to experience that level of pain with my mother. It is enough I know they are there and what they are about.

The first one was when my mother was barely in her twenties. She was in love, or she thought she was. She had left the confines of my grandparent's house and run off with this boy who blew into town. There were dreams of living on the whim and living off the land. They covered over 3,000 miles of amber waves of grain and purple mountains majesty. In Tennessee, she discovered she was pregnant. In Texas, they ran out of money and started heading back west. In Arizona, she lost the baby, a girl. She was six months along.

Thus, the first sparrow was commemorated on my mother's wrist. It was personal. The boy had long gone. Not able to hang with this young woman who was grieving so heavily.

The second pregnancy came out of a loose relationship with a fellow tattoo artist she was living with as she was apprenticing with Kaya Marklund at Brown Sugar Tattoo. This relationship was comfortable and low key. Two people who were more like friends than lovers. Things ratcheted up into intense levels once my mother discovered she was pregnant. She kept it to herself for months, fearing she would miscarry. Finally, after four months went by, the guy noticed he wasn't seeing my mother drink alcohol anymore, and she had stopped asking him to use condoms when they were having sex. He asked her flat out. She wanted to deny it, but she couldn't - she was already beginning to show. The guy flipped out, yelling about trust issues and the lack thereof. He left. Six weeks later, she miscarried. The baby was a boy, and a second sparrow was inked on her wrist.

Then at the age of twenty-six, my mother had a wild weekend with a man she met at a friend's Friday night dinner party. He was handsome, hot, and had a great smile she felt she could melt into. He was my father. He kissed her goodbye on Monday morning after two days of constant bliss. There was no promise of calling or hooking up later. He said his goodbye and then was gone for the sweet unknown. His name was Charles. Two months later, my mother realized she was pregnant. She told one person. A woman she had met while apprenticing at

Brown Sugar, a fantastic artist who had a unique style all her own. She could work with male clients without flirting with them (A challenge my mother was never able to overcome). They talked about opening their own shop together in a few years. That was Dusty Lorazo.

My mother had moved back in with her parents. My grandparents were thrilled to have their spirited daughter in their home and asked no questions about the circumstances of her pregnancy. They must have seen the fear and caution in her face as they took care of all her health concerns while she was pregnant. When I was born, they said nothing about the brown nut tint to my skin or the massive dark curly hair. With the success of my birth, my mother was convinced money was the key factor. She had carried successfully to term because she had been diligent on the health care, had eaten properly, and taken all the megavitamins. Unfortunately, that assessment was false.

When I was two, my grandparents were both killed in a car accident. It happened fast, and they were gone.

My mother went into an emotional shock. Dusty says she didn't smile or laugh for weeks and stopped dancing – even if Earth Wind and Fire were playing, she wouldn't twitch a hip. She stayed engaged in life as she had a toddler and a new business to operate. My grandparents left her the house and enough money to open her own storefront, and with Dusty at her side, the business, Cosmic Hearts, took off. She was busy paying attention to her work and being the best mom she could be.

Besides, she was focused on me. I was the light of her life. I was her cosmic heart. She loved me so much, she wanted another one. She kept trying. Many times she lost the pregnancies in the early weeks. And the spiral of grief and despair started again. She realized her challenge in carrying babies to term wasn't money and access to health care. She now had plenty of that. No, it was her. The problem must be her.

Then what happened was the "hot mess" phase as Dusty refers to it. My mother was like this glorious siren, radiating with unworldly beauty. She would lure men into these frenzied relationships, desperate to show she was both desirable and matrimonial. She would dress for the park in these super cute outfits and then have me attired like a little curly-haired doll. I was the bait. I was on display in the playground, at the supermarket, in coffee shops. She was working this image of the sexy mama and her adorable little girl. What man could resist that package? Sadly, they didn't.

Many men fell into the web my mother spun. She was looking for a guy who could get her pregnant and then would stick around and be the family man. I was encouraged to call these men "Daddy" after a certain period. Then my mother would get pregnant, and there was euphoria in the home for a few weeks with the anticipation of joy and becoming a family unit.

Then came the inevitable smackdown nature can employ. The gut punch. The miscarriage would occur. Her uterus' rejection of motherhood.

Sparrow number four is for Simon. My mother had snared a guy named Peter, who was a grad student at UC Berkeley. He was an international exchange student from Denmark, and when my mother got pregnant, he began searching for grant funding, allowing him to continue his work in the United States. Peter was tall and thin like a stork. He would work on his English pronunciation while reading picture books to me. He was best at the ones that rhymed like 'The Owl and the Pussycat". However, when my mother lost the baby, Peter was not prepared for the emotional tsunami, surging from her body. Her enormous despair scared him back across the Atlantic.

Sparrow number five is for the sister I'll never know. Her name was supposed to be Candace. With the addition of Candace, the sparrows have completed the bracelet of grief and have started another level, winding up her arm. I don't remember very much about the man who fathered Candace. I was eight and had discovered the sanctuary of books. I was able to hide in my bedroom and read stacks of stories and transport myself far far away.

My mother gave me a baby doll she had commissioned to look like how she believed her new daughter would physically appear. Candace's father was a redhead like my mother, so they both thought the baby would have red hair as well. Because of Candace, my mother gave me the only white baby doll I ever owned. The doll had bright shiny green eyes and a splash of freckles on the nose and cheeks. There was an abundance of copper hair on her head for me to brush.

Two weeks before the due date, Candace stopped moving. At the doctor's office, they told my mother and Candace's father Candace had died. There was no longer a heartbeat. My mother had to go to the hospital and have labor induced. Candace had been strangled by the umbilical cord. Her hair was brown.

At this point in my life, I began to hate the fact I was a survivor. I had emerged from the womb and taken a breath, but my existence wasn't good enough for her. My mother kept putting herself up on the auction block for more maternal despair.

You may think I miscounted earlier, and I am off by a sparrow. Sparrow number three is on my foot. My mother had Dusty do it when I was a toddler. I don't remember how I felt when it happened, but Dusty says I was very brave and sucked on an orange lollipop with tears streaming down my pudgy face. Why the foot and not a more fleshy place, like my hip or thigh? My mother (and this is her logic, her mind) didn't want to interfere with my own desire to have my own tattoos designed for my body.

Plus, a tat is easy to hide when it's on the foot.

Also, because I was a child, my mother didn't want people condemning her for putting a tattoo on her kid. She made Dusty do it. This is where my mother's twisted logic comes entirely into play. She doesn't care about the morality of inviting all kinds of people into her home, but she is worried people will care that she, a tattoo artist mind you, commissioned to have a tiny tattoo of a bird done on the arch of her child's foot.

Some people would see the tattoo as child abuse, but laws surrounding this can be murky because they focus on parental consent. Someone would have to file a complaint, and who was there to do that?

Sparrow number six is on Echo, who miraculously came into this world shortly after I turned ten years old. To this day, I believe she was a birthday present. Somehow the higher being that totally confuses me daily decided I had endured enough crazy grief from my mother, and this little incredibly pale baby girl would live and take a breath in our world. It's also uncanny how much the doll that was supposed to represent Candace ended up being Echo.

For the first few months of Echo's life, my mother kept waiting for her to die. In my mother's own words, she did everything wrong. Echo's conception came out of a casual dalliance, and my mother hardly bothered to attend her doctor appointments. She didn't monitor her diet and instead ate whatever she wanted. My mother had lost her desire to invest in more heartbreak.

But Echo was determined to be born. She came prematurely and had to be with the other tiny babies for two months. And even after she came home, my mother was convinced she would succumb to crib death or some other illness that snatches an infant in the blink of an eye. Echo remained. And like me, she received her sparrow, which had become a warped sense of branding on my mother's part when she was three. By then, my mother believed Echo was sticking around.

I never learned who performed the sparrow ink for the dead babies on my mother. I asked Dusty one time if she knew, and she shrugged her shoulders, shaking her head no.

Whoever the artist is, there would be one more request of their services as there are seven sparrows on my mother's soul. Two are her surviving children and five on her arm for the pregnancies. These are the seven sparrows representing the fragile heart of Theresa Wynters. The seventh sparrow was the child of Luther's. His name was Malcolm, and my mother carried him for six months. He came prematurely like Echo. But unlike Echo, Malcolm did not survive, and his time in the incubator was brief. My mother was deeply crushed as she believed this one had the odds going for him as he mimicked elements of her other two surviving babies. Luther was a strong black man, just as Charles had been, surely his seed would prevail. Scrawny little Echo had survived being premature; surely, Malcolm could do the same.

Luther consoled my mother and brought her all kinds of symbolic gifts to diminish her grief. He was grieving as well but buying the special cinnamon buns my mother loved and bringing her white daisies helped him tremendously. He assured my mother he didn't need a child of his own; Echo and I were enough. She began to believe him. There was comfort in the notion the family was whole. We didn't need anybody else. Unfortunately, Luther's consoling words would be used against him later.

Luther would have Echo and me curl up on the couch with him and be his "baby blanket" while we watched television. He would sit on the couch propped up with the cushions and say in a baby bear type voice, "Where's my kiddie blanket? I can't find it." Echo would come running into the room, giggling, and I would walk in rolling my eyes, pretending I was too old for this type of thing. Luther would put his bear arms around us, and we would snuggle in, our arms and limbs being the blanket he had requested.

One night we were watching some silly family comedy on the television. There was a baby on the show. It was bopping up and down the way toddlers do when they are trying to dance. I felt something warm splash down on my arm. I glanced up, and I saw Luther was silently crying. Large tears were rolling down his cheeks. He saw me looking at him with a worried expression. I had never seen a man weep. He gave me a little smile and pulled me into a squeeze so tight I lost my breath.

The days with Luther were the best in my life.

ANNIKA KANE

Much to my horror, Todd became a regular presence in the household. My snake venom was losing its bite as the smiling Ken doll came over to the house every single day. I behaved myself and watched my tongue. But. It. Was. Not. Easy.

I practically gagged on the number of times I swallowed my tongue and the venom that went with it. I swear there were times we would be in the same vicinity (a situation I tried to avoid as much as possible), and I felt Todd was baiting me. There was something about the guy that made me feel like he was trying to get me to unleash and lose my cool. And how screwed up is it when you have a grownup trying to egg on a 16-year-old girl? Because wouldn't a grown man have better things to do?

Whenever I mentioned these thoughts to somebody else – people who were in my safe zone, I would get these comments, these looks of exasperation – all of which came down to "Get Over it, Bess." I knew how it sounded. "He smiles too much. He's too nice. He's fake, I tell you. He's fake." It looks like I am the one with the problem.

Time and time again, I was told to deal with it. Handle it. Don't let his presence get the best of you. This was the logical stance, the rational viewpoint, but as I said, there was something about him that rubbed me the wrong way.

Any time I tried to point out the weirdness to my mother, she would shut me out. My mother would side with Todd, tell me to back down, and state I imagined things. It was enough to make a girl want to scream.

One of the reasons Todd felt he had a secure position is that he helped tremendously with the revenue at Cosmic Hearts. Todd exuded a certain amount of entitlement outside of being my mother's boyfriend because he delivered Annika to Cosmic Hearts, and Annika was a big hit.

Not long after the dinner party at the house, I walked into the shop and saw this girl hanging around Todd and my mother and she was not a customer. "Who's that?" I asked Dusty, pointing over at the tall thin girl. The girl was wearing skinny black jeans, clunky boots, and a long peasant blouse. Her hair was sheet straight with a blue/black dye job. My mother was going over items on the shelves in the back, and I could see the tattoo flash books were out on the display counter with Todd flipping through the pages. His expression was a mixture of boredom and feigned interest.

"Annie," Todd called out. "I think this is something you could work off of." He was pointing to a design on the page. Judging from where he was in the binder and he was flipping through binder number 3, I knew Todd was pointing to something falling into the dark faerie realm.

Annie came over and peeked. "That's perfect," she cried and gave Todd a quick peck. It was a friendly peck, not a lover peck, and just when I was starting to sort out what was happening here, my mother saw me. An enormous smile radiated from her face.

"Bess," she beamed happily. "Meet Annika."

Annika/Annie hopped over and put out her hand for a formal shake. Her face was long, and she wore makeup in the blue and purple category. Her sleek hair fell across her face in a practiced fashion. She smiled and took my hand.

"I've heard so much about you," Annika beamed. "I can't wait for us to become friends."

I'm sure my mouth dropped open at that last remark. Thank God, no flies were buzzing around to zip in. With an incredulous expression, I looked up and caught an unspoken exchange between my mother and Todd. My mother had her eyebrows raised, and Todd was flashing the "thumbs up" move. But when Todd looked back at me, I'm sure his expression was more like checkmate. I got the vibe he had one-upped me in some competition only he knew about. What was going on?

I'm just going to point out something here...just because everyone thinks you are paranoid; doesn't mean you shouldn't be.

I was introduced to Annika. Annika Kane. Annika was going to begin her apprenticeship in the shop. Apparently, Annika was a big fan of my mother's. Years ago, when she was just old enough to get a tattoo without parental consent, Annika had raced to Cosmic Hearts and had my mother do a sleeve on her arm of the colorful characters from *Alice in Wonderland*. The girl had a mosaic of the Cheshire Cat, the Mad Hatter, and the Caterpillar, and all of them were surrounded by red roses, dripping with paint. The dripping paint was Annika's idea, which works if you know the story. The soldiers, who were made up of playing cards, were painting the white roses red because they were afraid of what would happen if the Red Queen discovered the wrong colored flowers had been planted. My mother pointed out it would look like dripping blood to most people no matter what she did to tweak the design. The dripping red from the flowers combined with the unsettling grin of the Cheshire cat made the whole design look diabolical. Regardless, Annika was happy with her Terry Wynters original ink work.

So happy that she had spent the last two years in art school and her ambition was to follow in my mother's footsteps. Blah. Blah. Blah. Rah Rah. Rah. (Here is where I *shake the red and yellow pom poms*)

What a way to feed my mother's ego. I could see Annika was a royal ass kisser.

It also turns out Miss Annika is the lead singer in an emo/electronic band known as Sugar City. (*This just keeps getting better and better*) Sugar City is a popular local band. (*But I can't say since I am not allowed into clubs*). Annika is a big draw with her smoky hipster voice and slick blue/black hair. Todd thought she would be just what the doctor ordered as an asset to the shop and the Beloved ceremonies.

There's that Todd again.

"Think about it," my mother explained. "It's a perfect *marriage.*" My eyes widened at her usage of the word "Marriage." "She's got a direct pulse into another generation of clientele. People see her onstage. They think she's hip, she's cool. They see the *awesome* work on her arm." My mother laughed, and Annika giggled, waving her arm around with the *Alice in Wonderland* artwork.

I thought I was going to gag. My mother used the word "awesome."

"Plus, people KNOW HER. It will be great to be able to use her name value as leverage. Wouldn't you like Annika Kane of Sugar City to serenade your mother's favorite song as part of the Beloved ceremony? Oooh, I'm getting goosebumps." My mother giggled AGAIN and then shivered to sell her earlier comment.

This whole thing was beginning to smell like a sales job. Why were the three of them (thankfully, Dusty was off minding her own business) surrounding me as if I had to sign off on this new addition to the tattoo shop?

"I didn't know we were looking for another apprentice," I offered, and, I admit, the comment sounded lame. "I thought you said you wanted to keep it just you and Dusty for a while." My mother hadn't said that directly. She had hinted she wanted some downtime, and she didn't feel up to training a new artist. Frankly, she said it was exhausting.

However, this is an interesting note - the last apprentice in the shop had worked with Dusty, not my mother, and his name was Rafael. The exhausting element for my mother was the fact Rafael developed an enormous crush on her, making things complicated and really, really awkward. This was shortly after she had kicked Luther out and filed the restraining order, so Rafael took it upon himself to be the protector of Cosmic Hearts. Because goodness knows, we couldn't have the big bad Luther show up and huff and puff and blow the place down.

Rafael would continuously check with me as to what the security aspects of the place were as if he were in charge. He wanted to know when doors were locked, how and when supplies were delivered, and the information about the security company we employed. I complained to Dusty about this. I pointed out Rafael shouldn't be asking me all this information. It was information beyond what an apprentice should know. Besides, he shouldn't be bugging the teenage girl. I hate it when people look at me as a soft touch because of my age. Dusty had to go to Rafael and tell him to reel it in. He was crossing the line. However, Rafael firmly held on to the idea he was my mother's savior. She winked at him and touched his arm, and the ignorant fool didn't notice she did this with everyone – man or woman.

Extracting Rafael from Cosmic Hearts had been exhausting. It took days and weeks of teary exclamations, and my mother dodging him on the phone and at the house. Now that I look back on it, new apprentices at Cosmic Hearts are tiresome for everyone involved, and it flashed in my mind the addition of Annika may be intended to distract me. Her comment about being friends played in my head. I don't need any new friends.

Todd had a pleased as punch grin on his face, so it was apparent he had orchestrated this and was pounding his chest like the dominant gorilla.

"This will keep our bookings at a two-month waiting period," my mother continued with the exuberance she was feeling. "This will take the Ink for the Beloved ceremonies to a whole new level."

"It's great for advertising," Todd interjected.

My jaw dropped at that. And inwardly, I was shaking my head. Part of the appeal of the Ink for the Beloved ceremonies was they were an underground thing. Word of mouth and direct recommendations is what made it special. You had to know about it and then know where to go. Like a secret handshake or password to enter an exclusive club. If we advertised, then any Tom, Dick, or Harriet would come waltzing in. It would become tacky and gimmicky. I shuddered at the thought.

"I have an idea." I threw out with as much sarcasm as I could muster. "Why don't we hang constellations from the ceiling like Jupiter and Venus with beaded strings of stars and hearts. You know Cosmic Hearts – get it. And then Annika could sing songs like "Lucy in the Sky with Diamonds."

"I know that song!" Annika said excitedly. "I can sing that." My mother giggled AGAIN. This was nauseating.

I glared at the trio in front of me. "I was kidding," I said. "But oh my God, you people are serious. I can't handle this. I'm outta here."

I went in search of a hot sauce packet. I kept a stash in the cupboard over the sterilization unit. As I found my way to inner balance with the soothing pepper kick in my throat, it dawned on me that perhaps Todd's intention wasn't to distract me with Annika, but maybe keep me out of the shop. He knew a personality like Annika would drive me bananas. She may look cool, but the need to please part of her character was annoying as shit.

I opened a second packet of sauce and watched them talk about suggestions for enhancing this new element of the Ink ceremonies. It was a good idea, I knew that. On the one hand, I was glad my mother had found a replacement singer for Joanie. However, it bothered me Todd had been the one to find the replacement. I admitted it bothered me because now he looked like a hero. I watched and listened as Dusty joined the conversation. The laughter increased as Dusty suggested songs like "Weird Science" or even Bjork's "Mutual Core" for people who were doing biomech ink. Annika screamed about how much she loved Bjork, and my mother did too, at the same time. Then they giggled and hugged. Todd gleefully pumped his fist in the air.

At that moment, I realized I was standing outside the inner circle.

MUG WARS

Todd's continual presence at Cosmic Hearts kept me away. I would go in, do the task that needed to be done, and get out quickly. But I was also beginning to feel under siege in my own home. The man was an intruder, and he kept doing things to remind me he was an intruder. My mother would try to cloak the misfires like we all were adjusting to him being around, and the awkwardness was natural. I was not having it.

Their morning routine was plain ridiculous. For weeks after my mother and Todd began seeing each other, my mother maintained this pretense that Todd was not spending the night. The whole charade bordered on the absurd. If it had only been Echo in the house, then maybe, and I emphasize maybe, they could have pulled this off. But there was a teenage girl in the house for goodness sake! (*I really try not to say God or use Jesus Christ in my exclamations since Joanie told me it bothered her. I still catch myself at times. Well, frankly, I catch myself a lot.*)

This was the charade my mother and Todd would pull after Todd had spent the night. This was their answer to the awkwardness after Todd had displayed himself in his underwear. My mother has her own bathroom attached to her bedroom, so morning constitutions were not a problem. There wasn't the danger of having a child or teenager waltz in while Todd was in the bathroom. The problem was having one of us see him emerging from her bedroom and heading down to the kitchen. That scenario screamed of over-familiarity and sex.

In the morning around seven o'clock on school days and eight am on weekends, Todd would get dressed in his clothes and climb out the window of my mother's bedroom. That's right. He would scramble out the window like a forbidden lover who is running from a shotgun. Then, and this part is absurd, he would walk around the side of the house and ring the front doorbell, and my mother or I would let him in as if he was just arriving. My mother made a big show of it, wrapping herself in her robe, hurrying down the hallway, and opening the door with a big 'Hi sweetheart! Good morning'. If it was me who answered the door, I just opened it, mumbled at his disheveled look, and then rolled my eyes for good measure. Todd would flash his Tom Cruise grin like he was happy to see me. Oh, happy day.

One time Todd didn't have his balance in check, and he tumbled out the window, landing hard on his back. From my room, I could hear the fall and the snap of the bush branches. I stifled a laugh because I could tell that one hurt. After his tumble, they placed an old plastic stool of Echo's under the window for Todd to lower himself onto. Whenever I was in a vindictive mood, I would move the stool. I loved hearing Todd fall out the window on his ass.

We had our little warfare going on. Our silly games of oneupmanship. Each one of us was seeking ways to get underneath the other's skin and tapping emotional buttons like they were slow controls on a frustrating elevator.

One of Todd's favorite ways to get my goat was to use my mug in the morning for his coffee. I had a favorite mug, which is common in most families. It wasn't anything special - just a bright red mug with no designs or words on it. I liked the shade of red and had purchased it when the mug caught my eye in a shop on College Avenue. Due to the communal nature of the household, there was a large stack of multi-colored cups in the cabinet over the counter space where the coffee maker sat. There was also a mountain of tea boxes and tea tins for folks who liked a smaller dose of caffeine in the morning. That would be me. I disliked coffee but loved tea. I had designated which mug was mine so the coffee drinkers would not taint my mug with the essence of coffee. You think this is weird, but it's not. Ask any devout tea drinker how they feel about coffee grounds.

There was a vast variety of coffee mugs – something for everyone. Anybody who came into the Wynters' kitchen in the morning when the pot was brewing had their choice of mugs with birds, mugs with presidents, mugs with dinosaurs, mugs with cute messages, and mugs from some out of the way destination nobody remembered. Some mugs hadn't been purchased by anyone in the household but had magically appeared in our kitchen anyway. For instance, there was a tall yellow mug with a chicken on it that said 'Rochelle," and nobody had any idea who Rochelle was. Then you had the mug I had purchased personally and claimed as mine. Everybody knew the bright red mug was Bess' mug. Todd knew it, and that's why he would use it if he got into the kitchen before me.

The first time I saw him sitting nonchalantly at the breakfast nook reading the newspaper with my red mug clutched firmly in his grasp, I felt a slow heat rise through my chest.

"That's my mug," I said, trying not to sound like a bratty three-year-old.

Todd raised the red mug, like a toast, and smiled at me. "I didn't think you would mind."

"I do," I replied. "Everyone has their own mug. Even Echo has one for her hot chocolate. I don't see you using the dinosaur one."

Todd looked at my mug like he was examining a finely chiseled diamond of rare origins. "I like red," he replied and then delivered his dopey pearl white grin.

"What's going on?" my mother asked as she entered the kitchen. She headed over to the cupboard to extract her favorite mug, which was black with an explosion of white daisies.

I said, "Nothing," but at the same time, Todd said, "Bess is unhappy with my mug choice." And, of course, my mother went with what Todd was saying as an assessment of the situation.

"Good God, Bess, just take another one." My mother reached back up into the cabinet and grabbed Echo's dinosaur mug and handed it to me.

I looked at the mug with the growling Tyrannosaurus Rex flashing his impressive incisors as if they were mocking me. And they were. "Are you serious? I asked. "This is Echo's."

My mother waved her hand as if she were saying "potato patatoe," which is probably what she was thinking. "I knew somebody used it. It's a mug, Bess. What's the big deal?"

The slow burn I had felt earlier erupted into a firestorm. I knew it looked childish to complain. And making me look childish was Todd's endgame. I held up the dinosaur mug like I was displaying it on the Home Shopping Network. "Mom, this is clearly Echo's. There is a dinosaur on it. Look at all those sharp teeth. Roar. All I am saying is everyone has their mug. Everyone has their OWN mug. You have the daisies. Ollie likes the one from Yellowstone. I have the red one I got from Sweet Dreams on College Avenue. Todd can choose his own OR buy one and add it to the collection. Hey, that's a thought. Todd could BUY something."

Todd and my mother just looked at me like I had grown alien antennae and was making beeping and farting noises in the middle of the kitchen. Todd threw on his customized Tom Cruise smile and said once again. "I like red." My mother leaned over and kissed him on the cheek. She then nuzzled his neck and added: "And he makes a damn fine pot of coffee."

Oh. Gross.

It was then that Echo shuffled into the kitchen, yawning and using her fists to rub away the sleep in her eyes. Dinosaur figures that had come from a birthday cake were popping out of her braids. Her feet were in dinosaur slippers, and she was wearing dinosaur pajamas. Of course, Echo looked at me immediately and said: "What are you doing with my mug?"

I. HATE. TODD.

PITY FOR A BROWNIE

My last class of the day was the easiest. I was taking beginning guitar, and it was an excellent class to end the day with. When Terry had seen it on my registration sheet for junior year, she had praised me for my desire to study music. She has wanted me to pick up an instrument for the longest time, but I shied away from it. Band and orchestra aren't my thing. I needed art credits to fill out my college preps for applications. There was no way on God's green earth, I was going to take anything that smelled like a tool from Terry's toolkit. No art, ceramics, design, or painting.

I knew Terry liked the idea of me playing the guitar because she had visions of me sitting in the living room and strumming songs like "Michael Row Your Boat Ashore" or something from *Godspell*, with everyone singing along like we were at a campfire. There was a music camp near the Russian River Terry talked about. They had family sessions, and she had memories of going there as a kid with her parents. My mother reminisced about listening to the music under the giant redwoods and the concerts with steel drums and other ethnic instruments. Whenever she told me these stories, I was reminded my grandparents were a bit on the hippie side. They didn't attend Woodstock or anything, but they were on the cutting edge for their time. My mother's artistic rebellion and her biracial child weren't as big a deal as she likes to believe.

It's okay for my mother to have this dream I'll join the creative members of the group in this way. But I doubt it will happen. I just see myself managing talent rather than being a part of them. Or maybe I'll become a lawyer.

But seriously, I'm taking guitar for the credit.

I locked up the instrument assigned to me for class and headed outdoors with the throngs of students exiting the structures heading out towards downtown Berkeley and the buses home. I usually met up with Rueben and Joanie near the bike racks near the C building, where I locked my bike. We'd talk and then head off in the various directions the rest of our day dictated.

Joanie was already there waiting. I could see her wearing the leggings and long T-shirt she wore for cheerleading practice. Her book bag was on the ground, and she was staring at the screen on her phone, reading something, and then she would look up at the sky as if she were trying to think or remember. Her movements are so transparent.

I called out to her as I approached. "Is that a new phone?"

"It's a new cover," she answered. She held out the phone, so I could see it. "Look, I got one with red and gold all over it. You know like the yellow jackets. *(FYI the yellow jackets are our school mascot and red and gold are the school colors)*

"You're taking this cheerleading thing too far."

"I'm trying to show school spirit. You should try it."

I made motions of gagging myself with a finger. Joanie ignored my immature actions and kept talking.

"I downloaded an app that gives me a new SAT word every day. See." She showed me the display on her phone where the word "atrocity," and its definition was clearly presented. "Plus, I'm starting an SAT study workshop next Tuesday. I can't do the one scheduled on Saturdays."

The reason Joanie can't do anything Saturday mornings is she is going door to door as a Jehovah's Witness.

I pointed out. "You know you're going to have to miss pioneer work to actually take the SAT's."

"Yeah, I know. But that's one day as opposed to many." Joanie was worried about her father not letting her go away to college. She had been building a strategy to satisfy his concerns about her being away and still allow her to pursue a level of independence.

"Are you taking any SAT workshops?" she asked.

"Nope."

"Why not?"

I shrugged my shoulders. "I don't think I need it."

Rueben came up behind us. His last class was in the science building, so he had a farther walk across the campus. He had also stopped at his locker since there was a lunch bag in this hand. Rueben usually brings two lunches.

Joanie looked over at him and asked the question. "Are you taking any SAT workshops?"

Rueben pulled a sandwich out of his lunch bag. "Don't need to."

"Just listen to us talk more, Joanie," I said. "We use SAT words all the time."

Rueben nodded in agreement. "We'll pontificate for you."

"I think you mean discourse," I said.

"Verbalize?" he asked.

"Converse," I fired back.

"Jabber" was his response.

"Oh," I laughed and clapped my hands. "One of my favorites."

By now, Joanie was glaring at the two of us.

"Oh no," Rueben said with a bogus voice of sincerity. "We're haranguing her."

I turned to Joanie. "Seriously, they changed the SAT vocabulary test, so they don't have as many obscure words."

Joanie scrunched up her face. "But you see, I had to think a minute before I remembered what "obscure" means." She sighed and shook her head.

Rueben took a bite of his sandwich. "Read the Bible more. It's filled with obscure words," he said while chewing.

"I hate you guys."

"Whoa." Rueben stepped back, throwing his hands in the air with mock horror. "Can you even say that?"

Joanie's face flooded with anger. "Don't make fun of my religious beliefs," she snapped.

I gestured for Rueben to back down. Joanie was not the fiery type. In fact, she usually ignored our ribbing.

"Hey, what is it?" I asked.

Tears flooded the rims of Joanie's eyes, and she quickly turned her back away from us to wipe them away with the back of her hand. She glanced around to check if anyone was watching us, but as usual, we were being ignored by the rest of the Berkeley High student population.

"You guys can joke and laugh all you want. But you know you are going to college when you leave here." She pointed at Rueben. "You are pretty much guaranteed admission at an Ivy League school, which means you are going to be on the other side of the country." She then pointed at me. "And you, once you figure out what the hell you want to do, will be accepted anywhere. Anywhere."

I stood there saying nothing because I was pretty shocked Joanie said the word "hell." Rueben was shocked too. He had stopped eating. Joanie continued to berate me. (Berate is an SAT word. I know, I know, I'm an asshole)

"We all know you're not going to stay and go to Berkeley," she continued. "So that means you will be leaving here as well. You're both going to leave ME."

"I might go to Berkeley," I sputtered out.

Joanie waved her hand to dismiss the thought. "I doubt it. I sincerely doubt it. You can't wait to put miles between yourself and your mom."

"What do you mean?"

Joanie faced me, square on. "Do I have to spell it out? Bess, you complain about your mother and stuff at home all the time. You'd gladly trade in Ollie's cooking for dorm food if it meant you could be rid of the craziness your mother makes you put up with. And with the grades you get, you're going to get a full scholarship somewhere." She looked over at Rueben to make sure he was listening. Rueben was standing there wisely keeping his mouth shut.

Did I really complain that much? I tried not to. I really didn't want to complain about things around Joanie because I wanted her to feel it was okay for her to come to my house. I didn't want to endlessly talk about the weird artists who came by and the smell of stale beer, marijuana, and patchouli. If Joanie heard about those things, or if her father heard about those things, it would be a big NO to go to the Wynter's house. But perhaps in not complaining about the weirdos that frequented my home, I was focusing my complaints about my mother. Doesn't everyone complain about their mother? Then I remembered Joanie didn't have hers.

"You're forgetting something," I said.

"What?" she demanded.

"Echo. I can't leave because of Echo. Especially now this creep Todd is in the picture. Do you think I can trust Echo to be safe with all the people flying in and out of the house?"

Joanie sighed and closed her eyes. "I'm sorry. I did forget." Tears pooled back into her eyes as the anger drained from her body. We were still standing in the central courtyard of the high school, but I steered her over to a section of benches that were clear of the student traffic exiting the school. Rueben silently followed us. He had finished off his sandwich and was working on a bag of cookies.

Joanie took a seat on the bench and pulled a tissue from the front pocket of her back bag. She dabbed at her eyes and then blew her nose. "I'm being so silly," she said.

I knew that wasn't true because she had said "hell" earlier and had not copped to it yet. Joanie may not have any tattoos for me to read, but I do understand her.

"What's going on?" I asked.

"I'm doing terrible in my history class, and we've got this paper coming up, and I have to do well if I'm going to be able to go to college."

That wasn't it, but I didn't say anything. Luckily, Rueben was following my lead and keeping quiet, except for the sounds he was making while chomping on his cookies. I waited for Joanie to continue.

"You guys are going to leave. I know you are." She looked in my eyes. "Even if you stick around for Echo, you're not going to have time for me. You'll be off doing whatever it is you decide to do, and I'll be stuck here with no friends and no opportunity to make new ones if I don't get out of here."

This sounded like the crux of it. Joanie's father kept a short leash on her, and it wasn't just because of the Jehovah's Witness stuff. It was mainly because he had tragically lost his wife, and he wanted to keep his daughter close by. Mr. Whittier was scared. We all could see that. Rueben and I were Joanie's escape. We were the only friends she had not connected to the Kingdom Hall.

The cheerleading had been an opportunity for Joanie to build a stronger connection with the school and the community. She had used this argument to win her father over. Mr. Whittier had consented because the uniform covered her properly, and there weren't any conflicts with the football or basketball games and the pioneering work she does as a Witness. But she didn't really like it, and she wasn't that great. Joanie looked cute, messing up on the field because her expressions were priceless. But the shtick was getting old, and I knew she wouldn't be continuing with it her senior year. Joanie hadn't made friends with any of the other girls who were cheerleaders. But they hadn't wanted her friendship to begin with. They had wanted the cheerleading squad to look like a complete set of pretty chocolate girls.

There was one other girl who was a Witness at Berkeley High. Joanie had pointed her out to me. I remembered her name was Candace since that was the name of the little sister I was supposed to have before Echo. Candace was a short girl with pale skin and crazy bushy hair. She wore cardigans a lot. She seemed to have one in every color. Joanie said Candace was clingy and talked too much. In fact, Joanie had sought me out as a friend early on in ninth grade to escape from Candace. Joanie said I had a reputation for being strange. *(I laughed when she said that and didn't question it further – perhaps I should have)* Joanie knew Candace would stay away if she saw Joanie hanging with me.

It worked.

There was a learning curve to being Joanie's friend and understanding she was a Jehovah's Witness. I thought for sure Joanie had chosen Rueben and me to be her personal project, and she would try to convert us. Initially, I challenged her and said crazy things about the Bible to try to provoke her. She never took the bait. She'd reply, "if you are really curious, I can look up the answer for you. I'd be happy to".

Joanie didn't care we weren't Witnesses, and she rarely brought her religious beliefs up. Joanie is goofy and kind and has a loud laugh pinpointing her location if she is on the other side of the room. When Joanie hooked up with Rueben and me, she wanted to talk about music and television shows and the things going on in the world; the regular stuff. It is easy to make fun of Jehovah's Witnesses and the door to door thing. I think every comedy show I've seen has taken a crack at them. Now that I know Joanie, I cringe when I hear those jokes.

Listening to her concerns, I think Joanie was deathly afraid we would leave Berkeley, and she would be stuck with Candace and her rainbow cardigan collection.

"Why would you think I wouldn't have time for you?" I asked. "We're friends. I'll always have time for you."

Joanie sniffed and dabbed her eyes again. Rueben silently stood there, slowly munching on his cookies, listening.

"You're smarter than me, and I'm just the dumb person you keep around to make you look good."

"Joanie, how could you say that? How could you think that? I have the most screwed up family life."

"No, you don't," Rueben interrupted.

"What?" I looked at Rueben, confused. "Of course, I do."

"I think I might beat you with that one," Rueben countered "How so?"

"I'm the runt in a family that only values muscles. I can't even do a proper push-up. I'm ridiculed all the time by my brothers. They don't think the schoolwork I do is important, and they accuse me of trying to be better than them. And the fact is I AM trying to be better than them. I have no desire to bag produce in my uncle's grocery store or be a waiter in my aunt's restaurant. My cousins and brothers are flocking to those jobs. Timothy is becoming a plumber like our dad, but I can't, I refuse to work with my hands. I'm the only one in my family that even desires to go to a university. I want to go to Carnegie Mellon, and no one in my family can even spell it. They don't even know where it is."

Both Joanie and I were staring at Rueben, who rarely delivered tirades on this level.

"You're right," I said. "That sucks. But I don't know if it beats a crazy tattoo lady."

"Or a father that watches over you like a hawk and constantly sends text messages asking you where you are..."

"At least you have a father..."

"At least you have a mother..."

"Ladies, ladies, are we fighting over the last brownie? Is this a pity party? We all have crappy home lives, okay?"

"You have both of your parents," I pointed out.

Rueben snorted. "And I would gladly trade both of them for Ollie's lasagna."

That made me laugh. He was sincere. The emotion had dissolved, and Joanie was giggling as well.

Rueben crumbled up his now empty lunch sack and tossed it into the nearby trash bag. "I gotta hit the library," he said. He looked over at me. "You coming?"

"Yeah, for about an hour," I responded.

"I'll see you there. 5th floor." Rueben moved on as I collected my bike to meet him at the Central library branch.

Joanie retrieved her book bag from the ground and leaned in to whisper. "Where is Carnegie Mellon?" she asked.

"I have no idea," I responded. "Someplace where it snows."

"Can you spell it?"

"Hell no," I said. But I was lying. Of course, I know where Carnegie Mellon is, and of course, I can spell it.

SUGAR CITY

Annika became a thing. She actually became a big thing. The idea to have a soloist for certain Ink ceremonies blew the lid off the enterprise. It got to the point where people in high school were approaching me about it and asking questions like "Is Annika Kane really performing at your house?" The questions were dumb and never on target, and I had to continually explain we weren't giving free Sugar City concerts at my home, and no, you can't come over.

The tone of the Beloved Ceremonies changed from being an intimate private presentation to a full out church level memorial. There were now multiple tiers of pricing for the Ink of the Beloved Ceremonies. There was the basic level which involved the price of the tattoo and the storytelling. But now we had all these add-ons.

There was a performance cost of Annika. There was an additional cost if Annika had to learn a song that was not on the approved song list. There was the cost of adding another musician if they wanted to perform along with Annika. We got to charge a lot for that because of the rehearsal time needed. Sometimes there were catering costs, and we got Ollie in on the action. Then some people wanted the ceremony to be more public with witnesses, so I had to start asking how many guests would be attending the event. I was becoming an event coordinator for Cosmic Hearts. It was insane.

But my mother loved it. She loved being the mother figure for all these young people coming through the door and seeking her out. She had always enjoyed being a mentor for ink artists, but now she was getting creative recognition from musicians, poets, actors, and film directors.

Dusty's bio-mech client, Glenn brought in somebody who wanted to film the ceremonies for a documentary. Glenn's friend also had a bunch of biomech ink on his body, so I guess Glenn really was putting together this strange little club. Glenn's buddy filming my mother meant there was something else I had to add to my booking questions. "Are you interested in having your event filmed as part of a documentary? If so, we have a release form we will need you to fill out."

In the past, I rarely sat in on Ink for the Beloved ceremonies because of the intimacy involved when it was just Terry, the client, and an audio player. There were times I would sit off in a corner with my head buried in a book, trying not to observe. It seemed as if the privacy of sorrow should be respected. But sometimes the stories were so emotional you couldn't help but be swept up by the life being honored and the power of the words my mother was saying.

But now things were completely different. It was a production, and everyone was required to pitch in to get ideas into action. Terry Wynters was the star even though the focus of the ceremony was somebody else. The client shared a co-starring role. They expressed their wishes, and then the team was off, making the magic happen. Dusty was like the props and costumes master, and I was the house manager. Annika oversaw sound and music. Her singing was not always requested, but she ran the audio decks and alerted me if an outside musician needed to be brought in.

But Todd. Todd was everywhere. He was the director and the producer all rolled into one. If I wasn't so busy with this and schoolwork, I might have complained about it more. It felt like when I left a room to get away from him, he'd appear in the next place before I arrived. It was like he had been cloned. I heard his voice everywhere, greeting people when they came in, shaking hands, and throwing out his movie-star grin.

We were preparing for a big Beloved ceremony. This one was going to have Annika in costume. Glenn's documentary friend had been filming my mother earlier in the week, noting the preparations she went through. For my mother, it wasn't just about the design. She became an oral storyteller and compiled a script from the memories the client shared. The Beloved ceremonies were like a memorial gathering, but with only one person speaking about the dead. My mother shared the words as if they merged with the ink she was sinking into the person's body. The stories became the design and the essence of the tattoo.

The idea for the Beloved ceremony was birthed around the time my mother realized what I could do with tattoos. However, there are important distinctions. Tattoos are a window for me, and I glimpse a piece of someone's soul, but my mother uses the story behind the artwork to make a statement. I shy away from touching tattoos because of the unapproved familiarity my ability offers, but since Terry receives consent, she revels in it. She makes the Beloved tattoos performance art.

I had stopped by directly after school to help Dusty unpack the programs that had arrived. This client had wanted printed books for her guests attending the ceremony honoring her mother. The small books contained photos of the deceased woman throughout her life, along with excerpts of her favorite feminist poems. The woman being memorialized with a tattoo also loved the singer Cher, and Annika was dressing up as the star when she sang, "If I Could Turn Back Time" as a ballad. Dusty hired a woman who would create a gown that looked like a Bob Mackie original with feathers and sequins. She was picking up the dress in an hour which is why I was helping with the programs.

After unpacking the boxes, we needed to visually scan all the pages and make sure the printing had been done correctly and there weren't any ink splots.

While we were working, Todd came up behind me, holding my backpack. "What's this?" he asked.

"What does it look like?" I responded.

"You can't leave this in the back room, lying around. People could trip over it."

This meant Todd just tripped over it.

"Where am I supposed to put my backpack?" I asked.

"How about you don't bring it here at all? Leave it at the house."

Thankfully, Dusty jumped in before I shot back with a blistering response.

"I asked her to come straight from school. We've got a lot to do here. So, if you don't mind..."

Todd looked at the stacks of programs we were reviewing. He nodded his head like a dictator approving the work of the masses. "Good, good. Those look good." He handed me my bag. "Keep it in the back on the top shelf. We don't need a lawsuit if someone trips on it and smacks their head." He moved away from us.

"WE?" I said. "WE...when did you...?"I started after him, but Dusty held me back.

"Don't, she said. There's a lot to do, and I don't need you going off at the slightest thing."

"How come he is giving orders around here?" I asked. "He's telling me where I can keep my stuff!" I was fuming and reached into my backpack to pull out a hot sauce packet and suck it down.

"Who the hell does Todd think he is?" I demanded. "Luther never did that."

"No, he didn't," Dusty agreed. That was the first time I heard Dusty make a comment in Luther's favor. Most of the time, she was noncommittal.

Dusty was getting ready to leave and pick up Annika's costume. We needed to have it tonight, so Annika could try it on after closing. The Beloved ceremony was in two days. My mother had already gone home to look after Echo and work on her script.

"Can you finish these?" Dusty asked, pointing at the programs. "I want to pick up the Cher dress and be back for my five o'clock appointment."

"Sure," I replied.

But fifteen minutes after Dusty left, a messenger showed up with the dress. Apparently, the information had gotten confused, and the dressmaker had the gown delivered. I called Dusty to let her know the dress had arrived, and she could turn back.

"UGH!" she said over the phone. "I didn't want her to do that because I wanted to check the costume over before taking it away."

I finished proofing the programs around the time Dusty returned. She stomped in on her cowboy boots and went straight to the gown. Dusty aggressively removed the plastic covering and shouted, "Where's the headpiece?" She held up the hangar and flipped the dress back and forth. "Do you see a headpiece?" she asked.

I shook my head.

"I don't have time for this!" Dusty shrieked. "Bess, I need you to go get the headpiece. I can't leave now; I have a client coming at 5:00, and Annika will be here at 6:30. I'm calling you a ride to take you there and bring you back."

"I'll take my bike," I offered.

Dusty shook her head. "The piece is too big. You can't shove it in a backpack."

Dusty ordered the ride and told me to go outside to wait. "Make sure there are green stones in the tiara," she said. "Not white, green." I picked up my backpack and went out the front. "I'm taking my backpack, so you don't have to worry about falling on your stupid face," I yelled to the back where I knew Todd was hiding.

"Good," he hollered back.

I. HATE. TODD.

DUANE RODRIGUEZ - MAN OF ACTION

Night lights from the boulevard illuminated the quiet interior of the tattoo studio. Duane Rodriguez entered through the rear door from the back alley and flicked on his flashlight. He used the code he had been given to deactivate the alarm. He kept the beam low so he wouldn't attract attention from the outside.

Rodriguez was nervous, and he felt a line of sweat drip down his back. This was the first time he was entering the shop alone. He knew Mackey had to keep his hands as clean as possible with minimum exposure to the product. Besides, Mackey's main job in all of this was distraction. Duane was told the stash could be found in a dark bag in the storage area. A bag like a book bag or a backpack. The product was in there and should be kept in there to remain portable.

The shelves in the back were filled with boxes, jars, and tubes. Rodriguez ran his flashlight over the area, hoping he wouldn't have to go through these boxes. He was already worried about time and getting back to the party before people noticed.

It was Mackey's idea to have Duane leave the dinners and announce he was having a cigarette. "They'll get used to you being gone," he said. "But make sure you smoke a cigarette, so you smell when you return." Duane hated when Todd Mackey talked to him like he was an idiot.

Mackey's cue for him to leave was the story about his German

Shepherd. Rodriguez loathed hearing this story, so he was glad Mackey had used it as the informal signal for him to leave the premises and move the product. Wolfie, the dog's name, was the code word. Mackey said it was always easy to find a way to bring the story into a conversation. There were many elements to the Wolfie story: old girlfriends, pets, loss, and everyone liked how Mackey showed how he honored the dog with a photo-like tattoo on his left shoulder blade. 'Close to his heart,' he would say.

Wolfie had initially belonged to Mackey's old girlfriend, Lucy. She and Mackey had dated for a year or so, and Mackey had moved into her place in Hayward. Wolfie was Lucy's dog, but all the activities the couple did together involved taking the animal out. There were hikes up in the Oakland Hills and excursions into San Francisco. They were a trio, and Lucy lavished a lot of love on the dog. Which is why Mackey was confused when Lucy walked out on him but left Wolfie behind. Mackey was positive; there had been a mistake. Lucy would never leave Wolfie. But she didn't come back. The way Mackey tells it, he couldn't afford to keep the apartment on just his salary, so he had to find a smaller place for him and the dog.

And this was the part Rodriguez hated. One day Mackey came home and found Wolfie dead on the front landing inside the apartment. Somehow the poor animal had strangled himself on the doorknob of the front door with his collar. He had gotten caught, and in his struggles, his body weight tightened the collar around his throat. Todd was heartbroken and had the tattoo done of Wolfie's image. He had used a happy photograph of the animal from one of their hikes on Mount Tamalpias. It hurt Rodriguez, thinking about that poor dog dying because his collar had hooked itself onto a doorknob. He shuddered. What a horrible way to die.

Rodriguez pulled several items down from the shelves. They were heaped around on the floor. None of them looked right. But then

Rodriguez' flashlight picked up a dark book bag on the top shelf. There it was. He stretched up to pull it down and then went back out the side door leading to the alleyway.

He hurried down the street and went to his truck to toss the book bag in the cab. He wanted to have people see him coming from his vehicle when he returned, so he could use an errand as the excuse for his absence; aspirin, gum, something like that. Gum felt right, there had been a lot of garlic in the fat man's spaghetti sauce.

Rodriguez forgot to reset the alarm. He remembered that after he was already back in the house and laughing with the chubby chef about getting the gum to clean his garlic breath. He also took the wrong bag, and he would realize that later.

BOOKBAGS AND BREAKINS

I t was early in the morning on Saturday, and I was tossing the shelves in the back room at Cosmic Hearts. I was pretty sure I had left my backpack at the shop when I came back to assist with the Cher focused Beloved ceremony. I didn't have much to do at the event except check the guest list and hand out programs. But I did want to see Annika in the green sequined dress and feathered headpiece I had made a special trip to retrieve. When Annika finished her first song, I snuck away to make a pit stop at Luther's auto place. I know I left my backpack on the high shelf, where Todd told me.

I hadn't taken my bag when I went to see Luther because I could accidentally leave it there. I made that mistake once already and really needed my books for a test. I had to contact Luther secretly and arrange for Ollie to pretend he had an errand and retrieve it down the street. My mother would have asked too many questions if I had taken my bike at night.

I noticed Todd fed her questions to ask me. I swear the guy was trying to trip me up. For instance, I'd say, "I'm going out for a bit." My mom would respond, "Okay," but then Todd would be like, "Ask her where she's going?" And then I would get indignant and say, "why do you need to know where I'm going?"

He would look at me with an innocent expression and say, "well, if you're going to the drugstore, I could use some deodorant. And I could give you the money to pick some up for me." The idea of getting Todd's deodorant was repulsive.

But then my mother would pipe in and go, "Oh, yeah, where ARE you going?" And then I would have to come up with an answer when I never had to before.

"Uhh, I'm going to the store."

"The grocery store?"

"Yeah." Thinking that was it, I would head for the back-porch exit.

"Oh, can you get some ice cream?" And then my mother would run up waving a ten-dollar bill and giggling "Todd's buying. Get peppermint for Echo."

Todd this. Todd that. The man was a home invasion.

I knew one of the reasons fueling my frustration surrounding my missing bag was I had placed it where Todd told me to. Maybe if I had left it on the bottom shelf where nobody could bend down to reach, my bag would still be here. I can't imagine anyone would walk off with a kid's backpack. Dusty was also at the shop. She was early as she wanted to finish cleaning up from last night's ceremony. After the Beloved service was done, and the client and guests left, people came back to the house for a celebratory dinner. Ollie made spaghetti, and there was a lot of wine flowing with toasts to the success of the event.

Dusty was seeing a new client this morning, another recommenda-tion from Glenn, and she didn't want any feathers on the floor. The Future People Alliance (the name I bestowed on them) was starting to use Cosmic Hearts as their place to get their tattoos, so working with Glenn had been a good investment.

I was standing there staring at the shelves, willing my backpack to come forward when Duane came in with Todd through the back door. I hated the fact Todd and his buddies used the back door as an entrance. The back door was for employees and family members, and this action implied they felt they were in that category.

Duane had a book bag on his shoulders using the one strap method, and for a second, I thought it was mine.

"Hey, I've been looking for that!" I said, a little too sharply. But the moment the words came out of my mouth, I realized it couldn't be my bag.

Duane quickly stepped back, and Todd threw up a hand to block me. "What are you talking about?" Duane said. He held onto the strap of the bag protectively. Odd.

I felt stupid, but clearly, I had to explain. "I'm looking for my backpack. I can't find it. I thought you had it for a second."

"Why would he have your backpack?" Todd asked. He was smiling, but there was something weird about his smile. It was like he was overly interested in my answer. Todd was excessively interested in a lot of what I did. I was used to having a parent who was barely invested in my comings and goings. But now with Todd I had someone who continued to quiz me as if he had authority over me, and when it was pointed out to him he didn't, he would go to my mother and comment on the fact (as if it were an innocent observation) that as a teenage girl I had too much freedom.

"I don't know," I answered. I was getting flustered, and I could feel the heat of embarrassment on my face. "I just can't find it, and I have a paper due on Monday, and if I don't find it soon, I'm going to have to start all over." I stomped away from Todd and Duane because I really wanted to place some distance between us.

"Maybe you left it at the house?" offered Dusty.

"I DIDN'T!" I screamed. *And yes, I know it was said with too much volume. Way too much volume.*

"Don't yell at me, Missy. I didn't take your backpack." Dusty was giving me a warning look, and I didn't want to have a conniption fit at the shop, so I left quickly.

Well, I tried to leave quickly and headed for the front door to avoid Todd and Duane, but I forgot it was early morning, and the front door was still locked. Dusty's early morning client was going to knock for her to let him in. So, after trying to open a locked door, I had to maintain my composure and head for the back door out to the alley. I shouldered my way past Duane and Todd, stomping the entire time, so people understood I was angry. (And, no, I am not too old to have a tantrum.)

I finally took a breath when I was on my bike, and I had cleared the alleyway. I don't know why I was so upset. Later, and I mean really later, the question flitted through my head as to why were Todd and Duane even at the studio that early? My mother is a late sleeper, and she would never schedule anything before 11 am. Dusty will take a 10 am, and she was making an exception for the new client by seeing him at 9 for a consultation. So why were Todd and Duane there?

My backpack was not at the house, and I knew it wasn't. I swung by Luther's shop, but he wasn't there yet, and the place was locked up. I sent text messages to both Joanie and Rueben on the outside chance they had picked it up. No Luck. To say I was pissed does not begin to describe the situation.

At two o'clock, I headed back to Cosmic Hearts. I wanted to look one last time before I threw in the towel and recreated my notes from memory and banged out a new draft. I'd be able to get some assistance from Rueben, but I hated starting from scratch like this – especially given all the work I had already done.

When I came through the door, both my mother and Dusty were talking to a woman with short hair and silver highlights. She was Latina, and her round figure did not mesh well in the policeman's uniform she was wearing. She was the type of woman who should be sporting bright colored blouses and floral skirts and sandals.

The officer was taking notes while my mother stood with her hands on her hips, and Dusty answered the questions. Dusty's hands were gesturing all over the store as she spoke.

I had been standing there for a while before Dusty noticed me. "Wait. Here is Bess. She can give you more precise details. She was in the backroom for a while."

"What's going on?" I asked.

My mother had her lips pressed firmly together. Her eyes were tight and hard. In fact, her whole demeanor was tight and hard. 'It looks like we've been robbed," she spit out.

"What? How much?"

"Not the cash. There wasn't much there anyway. I made a deposit on Friday night. The supplies in the back. They seem to have been tossed about, and I'm sure stuff is gone." Dusty pointed behind me at the stock room. She then gestured under the sink near the station she now shared with Annika. "And I think stuff is missing from here, but I can't be sure until Annika shows up."

I moved over to the office phone, but Dusty waved me off. "I've already called her. She wasn't home, but I left a message on her machine."

"She will be in at 3:00 anyway." My mother was talking. "We have a Beloved ceremony at 4:00." She leveled her eyes on me. "The Kaufman sisters."

I remembered that one. I booked it last month. Two sisters who were getting matching tattoos to honor a younger sister who had died in a boating accident. She had been a Lord of the Rings fan, and the surviving sisters were getting elfin symbols of eternity on their arms. During the ceremony, the soundtracks to the movie trilogy were set to play while they were getting the ink work done. Annika was set to perform the song done by Annie Lennox in the movie at the end of *Return of the King*. Annika was very proud of the accomplishment as she claimed it was a tough song to learn. Since it had been a personal request, she was getting a high commission on it. But compared to last night's ceremony, this was an easy one. The sisters were keeping the event private.

"Bess," my mother was talking. "This is Officer Lopez. Can you take her through what you noticed from this morning? Dusty said you came in after her and saw the state of the supply room."

"Yes, my backpack was missing. That was the first thing I noticed. While I was searching, I noticed many items on the shelves had been knocked over and moved around."

The Officer found this interesting. "What kind of backpack was it"

I shrugged. "Just a Northface. Dark blue. All my school notebooks were in there."

"Any textbooks?"

"Yes, but who would want to steal a physics book?"

"There's actually a market for textbooks. You'd be surprised." The Officer smiled and winked with her right eye. "eBay. Amazon. But I don't think that's why your backpack is missing."

"Do you think it was stolen?"

"At the moment, I'm just listing everything being reported as missing from this shop."

I looked at both my mom and Dusty. "What's going on?"

"There have been some break-ins in the area. Increased activity. More robberies. Smartphones being snatched. Needles found in the alleyways." My mother's tone implied this was an everyday occurrence.

"And there have been some complaints," Dusty added.

"About what?" I asked.

"About us," Dusty answered.

"Us?"

Having the tattoo shop be a focal point for problems, was a sore spot with my mother. "It's the usual bullshit where if there is anything bad going on, folks look at the tattoo place as the scourge of the neighborhood," she threw in. "You should be talking to the restaurant that supposedly opened its doors two months ago," she said to the policewoman. "I never see it open for business, and I never see people going in there. What's up with that? Huh?"

The policewoman swiveled her gaze around the interior of the shop. Her eyes took in the sparkly moon lanterns and the silly skull lights hanging over Dusty's station. "I don't think it is because you are a tattoo shop," she explained. "Not so much that. There are complaints of increased activity at night." She looked directly at my mother and smiled. "I have a tattoo."

My mother was surprised. "You do?"

Officer Lopez opened the buttons at her wrist and pulled back her shirtsleeve to reveal a bio-mechanical inked design with gears and blood vessels on her forearm. "I also have something like this on my hip."

"You know I am running a special on bio-mech work." Dusty's eyes were saucers, and she was practically salivating.

"Really?" Officer Lopez pulled her uniform sleeve back down. "I might have to find out more about that. I'm thinking about adding on to what I have."

She then flipped the pages on her spiral notepad and consulted an item she had written down. "Have you ladies changed your hours recently?"

"No," Dusty answered.

"Have there been any clients coming in and requesting appointments off the clock?"

"A few. But that's normal."

I wondered why Dusty and my mother didn't mention the Ink for the Beloved ceremonies. I mean we just had a big one last night.

Officer Lopez moved her eyes down to another item on her notebook.

"Many of your neighbors have commented about more people coming in and out of the shop. More people than usual. More people hanging out on the streets. They are claiming your shop seems to be the center of activity. Are you having a surge in business? Any Groupons happening? Offering any specials? Lopez smiled at Dusty. "Any specials outside of the biomechanical artwork?"

My mother ticked off items and counted them out with her fingers. "No Groupon stuff. We can't offer because our work is too specialized. No advertised specials." She gestured at Dusty. "The work she has been doing with the biomechanical has been through word of mouth and a specific recommendation."

"Glenn Porter?" Lopez asked.

"YES!" Dusty exclaimed.

I guess I was right about the Future People Alliance, and Lopez was a member.

My mother was staying on track focusing on the matter at hand. "Our business is our business. We are usually booked one to two months in advance, not counting consultations. Dusty and I are the main artists. We sometimes have an apprentice. Sometimes two. But currently, we have one. Her name is Annika. She started with us about a month ago. She also sings and performs at night with a band..." My mother snapped her fingers, she was spacing on the name of the band.

"Sugar City," I volunteered. "They play at the Albatross on Fridays and do art spaces like Cloud 9."

"Sometimes we have private parties at the studio," my mother offered. We had one last night.

So, that's how she was going to describe the Beloved ceremonies.

The officer was back to writing in her notepad. The pen was scratching across the paper.

"You seem pretty young to be here." The question was directed at me, but she didn't look in my direction.

"I work here," I answered.

"Really? And what do you do?" Officer Lopez looked over at my mother and Dusty for confirmation. But Terry Wynters had moved away from the conversation and placed herself at the display counter. No longer engaged, she had picked up her current crossword puzzle. Dusty just cocked an eyebrow.

"I am responsible for the financing and planning for the professional enterprise known as Cosmic Hearts," I answered. "I manage and plan the budget. I engage the contract work, and I respond to the needs and requests of the staff in their various services. I oversee quarterly reporting and annual accounts. Usually, I am tracking three years simultaneously, the previous, current, and forthcoming..."

"That's amazing," the officer laughed. "Do you always talk like this?"

"Only when she is showing off," Dusty responded, and then she mumbled in my direction, "Show off."

I smiled. "I saw it printed on somebody's resume once, and I decided to memorize it as a joke. It's a long-winded way of saying I manage the office."

"Do you work part-time here while you are in school?"

"You could say that."

The officer was back to writing in her notepad. "Berkeley?"

"High School," I responded.

The officer lifted her head with a puzzled look.

"Berkeley High School," I clarified. "I'm in high school. I'm her daughter." I said, pointing at my mother, who still had her head deep into the intricacies of her puzzle.

"Oh, sorry. I missed that."

A lot of people do, I thought to myself.

The moment felt weird suddenly, and I sensed Officer Lopez was scrutinizing me now that she knew I was personally connected to the shop. I was afraid she would mosey over to child services and dig up the Wynters file, which in my mind was enormous, held together with rubber bands, and with red flag post-it notes slapped all over it.

I thought it would be best to go back to the reason why the Officer was in the studio. "I was only here for a short time this morning. I couldn't find my school backpack. I frantically looked around and then left to continue the search in other spots."

"Was the alarm engaged?"

"It was off. She (I indicated Dusty) was already here."

"I was?" asked Dusty. "I thought you beat me here."

"I didn't turn off the alarm," I stated.

"Neither did I," said Dusty.

Officer Lopez looked at the two of us. "So, it's possible the alarm was never engaged."

I nodded in agreement, but it was hard to believe. We were all diligent when it came to the alarm.

"And which entrance did you use?" Officer Lopez asked me.

"I came in through the back and exited through the back," I answered. I left out the part about my hissy fit. I realized then in my anxious state to locate my backpack, I had failed to notice the supply area had been rifled through. There were things moved out of place, and stuff on the floor, but it also could have been tied to last night's event.

"Have you found your backpack?"

"No." And then I remembered a crucial factor. "But you should talk to Todd. He came in while I was here in the morning. He had Duane with him."

Officer Lopez looked up from her notes. "Who is Todd?" she asked.

"Good question," I replied and pointed to my mother. "You should ask her. Because the rest of us do not have a clue."

"Oh God, Bess, don't start," said Dusty.

I didn't reply. I just looked at Dusty with an expression challenging her to take it farther.

"Who is Todd?" Officer Lopez repeated the question.

Dusty jumped in before I could give my definition. "He is her boyfriend." She gestured to my mother sitting over by the display counter, acting as if she couldn't be bothered with the rest of us.

"Does he work here as well?" asked Lopez

"NO!" I responded a little too loudly.

Officer Lopez jumped at the level of my voice and frowned.

"I need help here," my mother called out. She waved her arm to draw the attention her way. "Eye candy male horse," she said. "It is a six-letter word."

"Stallion," offered Dusty.

"Nope. Tried it. Too long."

"Eye candy male horse? What the hell could that be?" murmured Dusty. "Stud. Stud-ly?"

"Nope," Terry replied. "The third letter is A."

Officer Lopez looked at me like she was stumped. But it had nothing to do with the possible answer to the puzzle. It had to do with the fact both my mother and Dusty were now ignoring her.

"She does this all the time," I explained. "She's deflecting."

"Bess," my mother called. "I could use your help with this."

"Ma'am," Officer Lopez moved to the display counter. "I have a few more questions for you, and then I'll be on my way."

My mother looked up at the policewoman with an annoyed expression. "Yes. Yes. What?"

"Your daughter brought up that a gentleman by the name of Todd was in the shop before opening hours. Could you tell me who he is?"

There was a long pause. "He's my boyfriend," my mother replied. I realized Dusty must have called the police because my mother was throwing icy chill all over the person in the blue uniform. It dawned on me the perfect way to get back at my mother would be to marry a cop.

I stood over to the side, watching the exchange.

"Foal," Dusty shouted out. "No, wait, you said six letters."

"Does your boyfriend work at the shop alongside your daughter?"

"No. As if Bess would let that happen." My mother's response was snippy. I was confused. Why was she purposefully not assisting the Officer with her answers?

Officer Lopez sighed. She was sensing the contentious vibe my mother was flinging at her. "Can you tell me why he was at the tattoo studio in the morning before opening hours?"

"And Duane...," I added, but it was kind of a whisper.

Officer Lopez looked at me over her shoulder and then turned back to my mother. "And he had someone else with him. Why were they here?"

"Spayed?" Dusty asked. She had taken a seat at her station and was drumming her fingers on the counter. Dusty was nervous. Even she was picking up the hostile energy in the room.

My mother looked around Officer Lopez to address Dusty. "Male horse," she said, emphasizing the word "male."

Terry decided to answer the officer. "He was here to pick up my glasses." She reached under the counter and retrieved her eyewear, placing them in front of her. "I wanted to read the paper this morning, but I had left the glasses at the shop. He came to get them." She looked in my direction and held my gaze. "Duane must have given him a ride."

The minute the words were out of her mouth, I knew she was lying. She was covering for Todd. She had no idea why he had been here. This was why she was angry. She hated being questioned, and she hated the police and anyone who represented law and order. The last time she had interacted with an officer was when she had been carted off to jail the night, she and Luther had THE FIGHT. The fight that blew up our happiness and was the primary reason why Todd was even in our lives, to begin with.

Emotion was flooding my body, but I couldn't tell if it was anger or shame. All I knew was I was dying for a hot sauce hit. I turned away from my mother's gaze and went in search of my backpack. And then I remembered it was missing. I was moving, so I almost missed what Officer Lopez said to my mother.

"Ma'am, did I do anything to offend you?"

My mother's response was clipped. "I just don't like cops."

"I'm sorry to hear that." Officer Lopez bowed her head. She flipped her notepad closed and slipped it into her ill-fitting pants pocket. "I'm done here. I'll have the report mailed out to you. You should receive it in a day or two." Lopez headed for the front door, but she stopped and turned back to Terry. "I think the answer you are looking for is "teaser." Teaser ponies are used to arouse mares." She smiled at my mother. "My uncle is a horse breeder in Mexico."

Teaser. That was the answer. If I hadn't been so freaked out about my missing backpack, I would have seen it was the answer to a lot of things.

SANITY CHECKIN

"**S**o now police are coming around, and you think there is some kind of mystery for you to solve. Give it a rest, Nancy Drew."

I was sitting with Luther having lunch at a walk-up burger place down the street from his "Good Job" auto shop. He had ordered a double bacon burger and an enormous platter of french fries, completely ignoring my comments about his lunch being a rocket jet pack heart attack special. "At least cut back on the bacon," I added.

"I'll cut back on bacon when you cut back on those hot sauce packets," he replied. He said it while I was currently emptying one out and scraping the packet with my teeth. I narrowed my eyes at his blasphemous comment and let the pepper tang hit the back of my throat with a satisfying explosion.

"Never."

"Alrighty then. You leave my bacon alone." Luther got up when his order was called and brought the wonderful smelling meal back over to the booth, where I had made myself comfortable. I figured I would take the view of the street, and then I could see if anybody passed by who could possibly report the fact I was sitting with Luther to my mother. If anyone she knew told her they saw me sitting with a big black guy, she would be able to put two and two together.

I helped myself to some of Luther's french fries. "This guy Todd is all up in my business," I complained.

"What do you mean? And what kind of business do you have?"

"Well, he's always asking me about where I'm going and who I am seeing." I reached over and grabbed the ketchup and squirted a big blob on the side of the french fry basket. I then added about five to seven drops of Tabasco into the mix. Perfection.

"What's wrong with that? You need some looking after. Maybe I should be up in your business," Luther said.

"It isn't his place!" I protested. "He's not my father." I gave Luther a silencing stare, so he didn't throw out the obvious that he isn't either. "The guy is at least ten years younger than her, you know. He's not old enough to place any type of parental authority over me."

Luther nodded his head as if he agreed with me. I grabbed some more fries and dabbed them into the spiced ketchup. I then remembered something and brought out a tiny spiral notebook from my pocket.

"What's that?" Luther asked.

"Joanie is making me keep track of how many hot sauce packets I use a day. She says I'm having too many and will screw up my gut."

Luther nodded his head. "I like that Joanie," he said. He began to get down to the business of eating and got the burger secured in his hands to take a bite. A tomato slid out of the sandwich and fell to the plate.

In the notebook, I made a notation of the day's date and made a marker on the page. I was up to three packs so far today. I included the tobasco I had added to the ketchup as one. My daily average was five. Joanie said that was high.

The smell of Luther's burger and the food coming from the kitchen was making me hungry. I should have gotten a plate of my own.

"Who the hell does Todd think he is?" I continued with my rant. "He's this big blond Ken doll with moussed hair, safari jackets, and perfect teeth, and everything about him is fake, fake, fake. It's so obvious he is creating this pretty boy image. What does my mother see in him?"

"I love you, Bess. You know that. But some things go on in the adult world I just don't feel comfortable sharing with you." Luther took a big bite of his incredibly layered burger.

"What are you talking about?" I responded. "Lust? I know about lust."

Luther continued chewing. He couldn't talk without choking, but his eyes opened wide in mock horror.

"I'm sixteen. Of course, I know about lust. I haven't experienced lust if that is what you are wondering at this moment, but I do know what it is. Obviously. Obviously, lust is an element here. But isn't my mother beyond that? She has two children from lust. You would think she would grasp the consequences here. Does she really want another lust child? Ewww. Ewww. The thought of a Todd baby..." I did an enormous shudder of horror.

Luther tried not to choke on the food he was eating. He grabbed the water in front of him and got the bite down safely.

"Am I really the person you want to be discussing this with?" he asked. "The things you come up with. I take back what I said about loving you. I don't even like you. You are not worthy of..." He reached over and snatched the French fry I was holding from my hand. "And leave my fries alone. Don't be putting your nasty pepper sauce on my potatoes."

Luther took a deep breath and slowly let it out. He looked off in the distance as he spoke. "Bess, I love Terry. I still love Terry, but there isn't anything I can do about her current situation. I have been told, no, ORDERED, to stay away. Another night in county jail is not on my bucket list."

"Don't you think the whole thing is odd?" I continued.

"It's not my business."

I was not going to let this drop. "I know I'm just a kid, and I don't know much about the complications of adult relationships. I should just stick to family sitcoms on TV as everything else is over my head. Romeo and Juliet, there's a relationship up my alley. Oh, but they died. Spoiler Alert."

Luther raised his hand with his palm in my direction, signaling enough already with the sarcasm. I dropped that tactic and moved on to another thread that bothered me. "Here's something. What does the man do all day?"

Luther ate a french fry. He dipped it into his own unadulterated pepper free ketchup before responding. "Why don't you ask him?"

"I HAVE!" I thrust my arms in the air for emphasis. "All I get is the 'I am an entrepreneur' line. Or I'm a businessman."

"That's what rappers say," Luther responded. "What kind of business?"

I punched my index finger in the air as if I were hitting a big red button. "That's the question, isn't it? And that's when he gets vague. He gives me this "little darling" speech as if he were suddenly from the South and throws out statements about meeting with investors and raising capital and manufacturing products as if this is giving me answers."

"But he's not telling you squat." Luther finished the thought.

"Precisely." I leaned back in the booth and looked directly at Luther. I held my gaze for a long time. Luther kept eating, and then after my silence and stares went on a little too long, he looked up.

"What's the product?" he asked.

"He won't say," I responded. "He just throws out a stream of little darling this and little darling that, like I was three years old and too young to understand these types of things. But he's full of shit, and my mother goes along with it as if he were really saying something of substance. It's all unbelievable!" I threw up my hands like I was tossing in the towel.

"You think I can do something?"

I nodded my head. Yes. Yes, he could. He could be Luther and save me and Echo from this mess. I reached over and snared a few more fries.

"Baby girl, what am I going to do? There's a restraining order on my ass."

"Make some calls. You know people..." I cried.

Luther snorted.

"You DO!" I insisted. "Can't you have someone look into him? At least find out what the guy really does."

Luther sat in front of me, undaunted. He looked into my eyes as if I was telepathically sending him answers. He was thinking. I could see I was getting to him. I delivered the coup de grace.

"He brings all kinds of friends over. People from clubs. Not just musicians and artists, but wannabes. Folks like that."

Luther continued staring at me.

"Strange guys. Weird guys."

Luther kept looking at me, not breaking the visual connection. I could see he was processing what I was saying. Luther could see where I was heading, and he was bracing himself for what he thought I might say. What he hoped I wouldn't say.

"I have a lock on my bedroom door."

Luther remained stoic, but I could see the silent anger working into the muscles of his shoulders. He already knew I had a lock on my door. I then delivered the stinging blow.

"Echo does not."

Luther sighed and hung his head. The fight was out of him, all at once, just like that. He remained still for a while, resigning himself to the situation and his continual role in the tortured drama of our lives.

"I'll see what I can find out," he said softly.

It's all I ask. I thought to myself.

He then lifted his head and gave me a wicked grin. "Change of topic. How come you are not dating anyone?"

"Are you serious?" I cried in outrage. I fixated my patented look of mock fury and anger on him. I could hold that expression for a long time, and sure enough, I won the contest. After two minutes of trying to keep his teasing expression, Luther broke into a grin and shook his head, laughing.

"I knew that would shut you up so I could finish eating," he said.

Luther looked down at the platter, and his eyes widened. "Damn, girl, you ate all my french fries!"

COOPER HAWKS

Rodriguez drove his beat-up pickup truck down the quiet residential neighborhood. Neat and attractive. Modest homes, but ownership was apparent, not renters. University students didn't live down here.

He slowed his truck at an intersection where flyers were posted on telephone poles asking the residents not to use rat poison. Interested in reading the fine print, Rodriguez got out of the truck, leaving the engine running. The notice was about the Cooper's Hawks in the area. They were nesting in the trees in the neighborhood. The hawks ate the rats, and if the residents used rat poison, then the birds would ingest the poison and die. Rodriguez gazed up at the lush, full trees lining the blocks in the area. Hawks were cool. He was down with the concern of the local residents.

He got back in his truck and searched for the address. The address was the home of the teenage daughter's friend, and Nick had said to leave the backpack somewhere on the property. The girl's bag had to show up to keep her from searching and asking too many questions.

Rodriguez wanted to return the backpack to the tattoo shop. He didn't like the fact the school bag was still in his possession. It was evidence and the wrong kind of evidence as well. Not only was it a direct example of a big mistake on his part, but it was also a link to the tattoo shop, and the police were already sniffing around.

Nick had stopped him from going back to the shop because everyone had searched the area. "You can't suddenly have the girl's bag appear in the place where people have been looking for it. You've already compromised the operation." Nick mocked Rodriguez, "What kind of idiot are you?"

A few days later, Nick handed him a slip of paper with an address written on it. "Toss it here, stupid" he hissed as he slammed the paper into Rodriguez's palm.

Rodriguez found the tiny, green, house near Gilman. There were steps headed up to the house, with an entryway with boots and clutter in the front. It looked like an area where outdoor things were deposited and judging by how far back the driveway went to the house, the occupants used their back door more often than the front. He could put the backpack here and have the girl believe she had left it. Or she could just wonder what happened. He was okay with an element of mystery. People question their actions all the time.

Rodriguez hopped out of the truck and ran up the porch. He threw the backpack so it would land behind a pair of gardening boots, but he overshot, and it tumbled into the rose bushes. Good enough. Rodriguez hurried back to his vehicle. Getting that condemning bag out of his possession gave him an immense feeling of relief. Rodriguez had left the engine running again on his truck. Sometimes restarting the vehicle could be a challenge, and he didn't want to draw any more attention to himself. In a neighborhood that posted flyers about taking care of the Cooper's Hawk, they would notice and remember a beat-up truck, creating a lot of noise as it overturned its engine.

HOT WATER

"**W**hat is this, Missy?"

Ollie was standing outside my bedroom with my bookbag hanging from his outstretched finger.

"It's my bag. Where did you find it?"

"I tripped over it as I was heading out the front door just now to go food shopping. Do I really have to comment about leaving your things...?"

I interrupted him. "Ollie, you KNOW I didn't leave it there. I've been looking for the bag for days. Besides, I don't even come in through the front door." The moment I finished the statement, my cell phone buzzed. I looked down and read the message from Joanie saying she had left my book bag on at the doorstep, and why did I throw it in her mother's roses?

My face must have been screwed up every which way as Ollie's tone shifted to concern. "Who was that?' he asked.

"Joanie," I replied. "Her dad found the bag in their yard, and they just drove it over here."

"Okay, mystery solved." Ollie handed me the backpack like it was a dead animal. "You're going to need to wash this it smells like smoke. And your mother will have a fit if she smells this. When did you start smoking?" He threw up his hands to stop me before I could protest, causing his kimono sleeves to flutter out like butterfly wings. "Don't tell me. I don't want to know. The less I know, the better in this household."

Ollie exited out the front with his recyclable bags and turned left. He didn't take his truck, so I guess he was headed for the Berkeley Bowl. I was left with my stinky backpack and tons of questions. I stared at the bag, which, in its absence, had become unfamiliar. The awful smoky odor wasn't helping the situation. I opened the backpack and confirmed my possessions were inside. A now overdue library book sat nestled in a side pocket. My hot sauce packets were tucked in a little zip-up area. It appeared nothing was missing, but wherever my bag had been, it was the home of a smoker. It definitely hadn't been sitting with Mrs. Whittier's rose bushes. I sent a message to Joanie asking why my bag smelled like smoke.

I went inside to dump the contents on my bed and give the backpack a ride in the washing machine - maybe two cycles. When all the items were laid out on the covers, the smell of tobacco hovered in the air. The smoke had permeated the interior of my bag. Joanie sent me back a text stating she was going to ask me the same thing, and she added an angry face emoji.

The smell was overpowering in my small room. Ollie was right, my mother would freak over this. I hoped everything would air out over time. I couldn't very well wash a library book and my folders. I sprayed my room with air freshener and cracked a few windows open to catch a breeze.

The minute I did so, the smell of marijuana filled the air. *Shit, this was all too much.*

I opened the back door that led out to the porch and saw Nick Ryder standing below on the sidewalk, enjoying a doobie. He was just standing there, smoking a joint outside my bedroom. I hated the fact he was hanging out on the street waiting for Todd. My body rumbled with anger.

"Do you mind?" I said. "The smell is coming into my room."

"I'm almost done," he responded. *Not sorry, mind you.*

"Can you take a few steps away from the house, so it doesn't come through the window?"

"Shut up," Nick said. "I said I'm almost done."

I think it was "shut up" that tipped me over the edge.

I closed the door, walked into the kitchen, took out a plastic pitcher, filled it with water, reopened the door, stepped to the edge of the porch, and threw the water onto Nick, hopefully dousing his smoke.

"You're done now," I yelled, and then I slammed the back door and locked it with the double bolt. I then rushed to the front of the house and double bolted the front door. Outside I could hear Nick screaming obscenities and calling me a bitch. He came up the front steps and begin pounding on the door, demanding I let him in.

Was he out of his mind? There was no way I was opening that door.

Echo came running out of her bedroom. Her eyes were wide and fearful. "What's going on?" she asked. "Who is that?"

"It's Nick," I told her. I was watching the door and hoping it would hold and not splinter. Nick had picked up something and was smacking the door with it, screaming at the top of his lungs.

"Don't let him in," Echo whispered. "He sounds like the Big Bad Wolf." My sister moved over to my side and took my hand. In her other hand, she held a plastic fairy doll. There was a ton of blue glitter in her hair. "Is he going to break the door?" she added.

SHIT. I had really done it. We were alone in the house, and a crazy man was screaming for my blood outside. I looked down at my sister. She was visibly shaking. My mind raced as I tried to think about what I could do to make the situation go away. I didn't want Nick to move to the back door as it was not as fortified as the front one. If he went around to the back, he would get inside. I had to act fast. I pulled out my cell phone and called 911.

The dispatcher, on the other end, took the information quickly. Once she heard the address, she told me a call had already been placed about the disturbance, and a unit was on its way. She told me to stay inside. I responded she didn't have to worry about that. And then I asked for Officer Lopez. I don't know why her name popped into my head, but I had liked her when she had come into Cosmic Hearts. And I don't usually like cops. The dispatcher said she would notify Lopez, but Lopez handles robbery, and this was a domestic dispute. I bit my tongue, not wanting to correct the lady. Nick Ryder screaming outside my home, was not a domestic dispute.

I could hear the unit pull up outside the house while Nick was still banging in his fury. There was a tussle as they must have secured him, but the level of his rage was frightening. He kept screaming I was a bitch over and over.

"He doesn't like you," my sister said. Six-year-olds always state the obvious.

The 911 dispatcher signed off after she learned the police were there, and she had left a message for Lopez. Within minutes there was a knock on the door, and the police were identifying themselves. I told them I was coming, and when I pulled back the curtain to peer out the front window, I could see two officers standing outside the door with their weapons drawn, waiting. I motioned for Echo to move back, and then I said again I was opening the door before doing so.

The officers showed me their identification and quickly entered the house. Outside I could see Nick sitting in the backseat of a police car, agitated and his mouth moving. He probably was still calling me a bitch.

I sat on the couch with Echo next to me. My sister was clinging to my torso and hiding her face. All the officers could see of her head was a mass of red hair with two fairy dolls tangled in the glitter splattered curls.

The officers asked me for my name and my sister's and then asked if there were adults in the house. I mentioned my mother and Ollie and told them Ollie had just gone to the store. They asked if I knew who Nick was, and I said yes. When they asked if he lived in the house, I said no. They asked if he had a connection to the house, and I said no. One of the officers got up and went outside. I didn't move from my seat. I only rubbed my sister's back as she pulled on my clothing, keeping her face away from the police. When they asked her questions, she would shake her head, showering glitter all over the couch cushions.

"Is she okay?" The officer who asked was young and black, clearly uncomfortable with the interrogation we were receiving. He stood across from us, waiting for his partner to return from outside.

I wanted to respond with, "Of course she's not okay, you moron." But I counted to five (ten has always been impossible for me to reach) and looked at the officer and replied: "She'll be fine."

"She looks scared."

Another count to five. "She is," I replied. *Dumbass. A scary man was pounding on the door outside our house. Looking down at Echo's hair, I kept wondering who was going to be in more trouble; me for throwing water on Nick and causing the police to come or Echo for spraying glitter in the living room.*

The other officer returned from outside. He was older, clearly the veteran of the pair, with silver hair and a bit of a paunch over the belt. He sat back down in the comfortable chair across from us, but on the edge, so he wouldn't have trouble getting back up.

"Nicholas Ryder, the guy we have outside, says he is friends with the man who lives at this house, and he was waiting for him to return."

"He's not Ollie's type," I responded.

The officer looked at me, confused. "Olliver DeMatteo is the only male at this house," I said. I was thinking "legally," but I didn't add the word. I knew I was treading water in a sea of sharks. My status as a minor was the only reason they were tossing me softballs.

"There's no Todd Mackey who lives at this residence?" The silver-haired officer was looking at his notebook, reading off the name.

"No," I answered. There. I crossed the line.

"Nicholas Ryder claims you intentionally threw a bucket of water on him."

"It was a pitcher of water, and yes, I did."

"And why did you do that?"

"I wanted him to go away."

At that point, there were some voices at the doorway, and Officer Lopez entered the room. She was not in uniform, and I had been right, she was better suited for bright tops and colorful skirts. She had on a yellow floral outfit with a denim jacket, and she looked pretty cute.

The silver-haired veteran stood up and spoke quietly with Officer Lopez. I could hear her say she had been requested, which was why she was there. I also heard her mention something about a bag being found. The veteran cop's interest piqued, and he motioned for his young partner to go outside with him.

Officer Lopez sat down in the seat the silver-haired veteran had vacated. She looked at me, and there was a slight smile hinting around her mouth.

"That your sister?" she asked.

"Yes, this is Echo. She's a bit freaked out. What's going on?"

"I think I should be asking you," Officer Lopez replied.

"Why'd they go running out like that?" I asked.

"A substantial amount of opioids and meth were found outside in the bushes. A couple of bags were a bit...waterlogged."

My eyes went wide, and I think my mouth dropped open.

The young cop came back in, holding Nick's black leather jacket. He held it up for me to look at. "Can you tell us who this jacket belongs to?" he asked.

"It's Nick's," I answered. I had just figured out where the drugs were found. Nick wasn't wearing the jacket when I doused him with water. The jacket was probably lying nearby and received a healthy splash. The drugs were hidden in the pockets. I'm sure when the cops asked him, he denied owning it, so they came in to ask me.

The young cop went back out with the jacket, and after a few beats, I heard one of the police cars drive away. I nudged Echo to get her to sit up. After a while, she did, but she just stared at Officer Lopez. I knew she wasn't going to talk. Echo won't speak to the police.

"We weren't able to reach your mother," Officer Lopez said. "No one is picking up at the tattoo shop. Is that where she is?"

"I'm not sure," I responded. "My mother has a big appointment tonight, so she may be taking a break. She likes to go to the park. When she is in her creative zone, she doesn't answer the phone unless it's me calling or the school."

Officer Lopez nodded her head. "Is there anyone else expected to be here? I'm going to wait here until an adult arrives."

"Ollie should be here soon," I answered. "He walked to the store, so he'll be back to make dinner."

The three of us sat in silence. The squawk of a police radio outside reminded me of something. "Is there a police car out front?" I asked.

"Yes," Officer Lopez replied.

"I better ring Ollie from my phone," I said. "He may not come up to the house if he sees a police car sitting out front." I took out my phone and hit the numbers to contact Ollie.

I heard Officer Lopez mumble under her breath, "What is it with you people and the police?"

I shrugged and answered, "We don't like cops."

She looked at me, quizzically.

"No offense," I added.

"None taken."

The phone rang a few times, and then Ollie picked up. "Shit! What's happening?" were the first words out of his mouth.

Dear Jehovah, I had eight packs today. I'm stressed. You saw what happened.

A LOST CONNECTION

"My friend is in jail."

"That's not my fault."

"You threw water on him."

"I had a theory he would melt like the wicked witch of the west. I was wrong."

Todd threw up his hands and turned to my mother. She was standing next to him with her arms crossed. We were in the kitchen, and I was sitting on the stools. They had me cornered in the breakfast nook. Todd's face was red, and my mother's face had this pinched look as she was pressing her lips together.

"Elizabeth...," she started. *Oh shit, she was leading with Elizabeth. This was the clue I was in trouble. But the fact is, I really didn't care.*

"Your actions put Nick in jail," my mother said. "This is serious."

"I didn't put Nick in jail," I responded. "The big bag of pills and the other stuff in his jacket put him in jail." *And, I thought to myself, his previous drug charges are going to keep him there for a while.*

"The police wouldn't have found the bag if you hadn't called them."

"The police came because the neighbors called. He was screaming at the house with Echo and me inside."

"He was screaming at the house because you threw a bucket of water on him." Todd jumped in.

I shifted my gaze to look squarely at Todd. "He gets wet, and he goes ballistic? He needs anger management."

I could see Todd's fury intensify. In fact, his hands were forming into fists. My mother saw this as well, and she lightly touched his arm. The hands relaxed, but his fury stayed engaged. He was shooting laser bolts with his eyes in my direction.

"Elizabeth, why did you throw water on Nick?' My mother asked.

"You ruined the pills in the bag. Water slopped in his jacket." Todd interjected.

I looked at Todd with an expression I hoped read as "so what." "The police took the drugs. So now they have ruined drugs and melted pills. Who cares?"

Once again, my mother touched Todd's arm to keep him from balling his fists.

"You're going to have to pay for that," Todd said.

I looked at him with an expression I hoped read as "You are crazy if you think that," and then said, "I don't think so."

My mother stepped in between us. "Let me talk to her," she said. "Darling, go on down to the bedroom. I'll be there soon." My stomach knotted at the term of endearment.

Todd stormed out of the kitchen, and we could hear him stomping to the bedroom. The door slammed. Perhaps he was the one needing anger management.

My mother sat down across from me at the table. She reached for my hand, but I refused to give it to her. I kept my arms crossed over my chest.

"Elizabeth, this really is serious."

"Don't you see Todd cares more about the drugs than he does that his friend tried to break down the house?"

She tilted her head and peered intently at my face. She looked like she was attempting to telepathically extract something from my brain. "What's going on with you?" she asked.

"Nothing is going on with me," I tossed back. "What's going on with you?"

She pulled down the neckline of her sweater, revealing the petals of a flower and a vine crossing over her shoulder. "What are you talking about? I'm an open book to you."

I reared back. I wasn't going for it. I knew my mother's despair was inked all over her body. I wasn't touching a single tattoo to learn anything about her. The beautiful designs on her body were expressions of grief. There was no joy embedded in the color.

"Don't do that," I said. "You know I won't touch them."

"Then what do you want to know?" she cried out. "What do you want to say to me?"

"TODD!" I exploded. "He's a creep. An enormous creep. He's awful. He lies to you, and you're just blind to it all."

"What has he lied to me about?"

"He lies to you about what he's doing. He misleads you all the time," I said.

"Like what? Give me an example."

"What does he tell you he does for a living?"

"He's in-between jobs right now, but Todd brings people together and gets a commission for it. Like an agent."

"Does he do this for someone?"

"Not now. Like I said, he's in-between work, but he's like a connector person."

Seriously, mom. Do you hear yourself?

"Does he have any money?" I asked.

"Not a lot," my mother responded. "But he pays for things. And I've started giving him money from Cosmic Hearts because of all the work he does with the Beloved ceremonies."

"How much money?
" I challenged.

"Not much." She shrugged. "Like a commission."

I was pretty sure the funds were coming out of the 5% increase I had seen in the rates.

"How about when we had the break-in at Cosmic Hearts, and he was at the shop in the morning," I brought up. "You said he was there to get your glasses."

"He was."

"You're lying."

"Elizabeth, I won't have that. He was getting my glasses; I had forgotten I asked him to do it."

And there it was again, another lie. My mother was covering for him, and she didn't even realize she was covering. Because I knew her glasses weren't at the shop that morning. I had seen them in the kitchen when I had gone out the back door. Todd must have picked them up after I left and then offered to retrieve them from the shop after convincing my mother she must have left them there.

It was a ruse to be at the shop. He was doing something there.

"Bess," my mother was attempting to get my attention. 'What is going on with you?"

"Nothing."

"You're so hostile."

I took a deep breath and blew the air out of my nose. Her body leaned forward on the table. She had her arm out and her palm up, waiting for me to place my hand in hers. In moments like these, she laid out the clean arm - the one without the sparrows. Given my ability, it was a conscious choice. It was an indication our bond was separate from her sorrows. I was her daughter, not just a survivor. I looked at her gesture of peace and shook my head. No, I wasn't taking her hand tonight.

"I want him to go away," I said. Water rushed into my eyes.

My mother bowed her head and withdrew her hand. She placed it on her lap. "That's not going to happen," she said.

"Why?" I asked. Tears had started to run down my face.

"I love him," she said.

The words penetrated my heart, and I gasped out loud. The catch in my breathing created a hiccup through my tears. My brain felt numb, and the hiccuping and the tears were keeping me from getting oxygen into my system. My mother just sat across from me. Her head turned as if she was blocking out my heartache and refusing to watch me fall apart on the other side of the table.

Finally, I got a hold of myself, so I could speak. "That's impossible," I blubbered out. "You can't love him."

"I do," my mother replied. But she sounded like the decision had just been made. As if something in her mind had just clicked firmly into place. "He makes me happy."

She got up from the table and exited the kitchen, leaving me with my arms folded across my chest, protecting my heart, and crying like a fool. She wasn't going to do anything. It was up to me to fix it.

Dear Jehovah, I lost count. I think I had twenty. Does that sound right? Weren't you watching?

SANITY CHECKIN NUMBER TWO

The text message was vague, but I knew who it was from. Because of the restraining order, I had scrubbed Luther's contact info from my phone. I couldn't risk Terry picking up the device and seeing messages from Luther. I knew his number when it popped up and then quickly deleted any message.

"I have info," was all the text said.

I hopped on my bike and rode out to his shop. The business was already closed for the day. However, there was a note taped to the door. No name was written on it, but I assumed it was for me. I was right. The paper simply said, "Shattuck theater 5:20".

The Shattuck theater had many movies playing, but only one was scheduled for 5:20. It was a historical drama. I groaned. I'm not a fan of dramas, but Luther loves them. Clever, Luther, clever. You trick me into seeing some movie about the first black person to do whatever because you know I want to hear what you have to say. Plus, movie theaters are dark, and no one can see us inside.

I went up to the ticket booth. The lady behind the glass stared at me. She was wearing an obvious wig of a hairstyle that was twenty years too young for her, and serious dewlaps were swinging from her neck. (Dewlaps is a bonus SAT word, by the way) "Are you Elizabeth?" she asked.

I nodded, "yes." I was mesmerized by the way the extra folds of skin bobbed as she spoke. It was like seeing an enormous dog with floppy jowls talking to you. There is a special breed that has them. I was trying to come up with what those dogs were called, and the woman spoke to me again. "Here," she said and pushed a ticket under the glass window. "Your dad already bought your ticket."

I took the ticket, watching the skin flap as she spoke and turned her head. It was very distracting.

Mastiff! An English mastiff! The name of the dog came to me as I handed the guy in uniform my ticket. I must have said the name out loud because his nose wrinkled up in distaste, the way you do when someone is acting a little strange. Maybe he knew I was talking about his fellow employee, but he simply responded, "You're in theater number 6. It's in the back."

The theater lobby was decorated with holiday lights. A big plastic tree with red plastic snowflakes sat off to my right. I passed the concession stand, and my stomach started rumbling as the smell of popcorn always triggers that response. I think they do it on purpose. They make the popcorn right when you are entering the theater, so you must buy it, or your brain is too distracted to watch the movie. I didn't have any money, so I would have to hit Luther up for some.

As I neared the area where the back movie screens were located, I saw a horror film I did want to see was playing next door. Maybe I'll run in, see Luther, talk to him, and then leave and catch the movie I really want to watch. I like horror films, but Joanie refuses, and Rueben doesn't like movies unless there is a hobbit in it.

But leave it to Luther to have every angle covered. I entered the theater. It wasn't that big, and I spotted Luther immediately. He's hard to miss - even in the dark. I took the seat next to him, and his eyes sidled over in my direction.

"Took you long enough," he muttered.

"Hey, can I have money for popcorn? I'll get a large and share."

"I don't know. I'm trying to watch my weight." He patted his stomach.

"I'll get a small then."

"Naw, get a large." He leaned forward so he could remove a wallet from his back pocket. He pulled out a twenty. My eyes went wide. "I want my change," he said with emphasis. "And hurry back, the previews are about to end."

"I want to know what you were going to tell me. That's why I came."

"You know I'm not saying anything until after the movie is over. I'm keeping your butt in this seat. You need to learn stuff about important people in our history. So, no going next door to see Slasher Dan or whoever kill dumb teenagers in the woods."

God, this man had me pegged. He literally read my mind. I was actually happy with the notion of sitting and watching a movie with Luther, no matter how educational, but I didn't want him to think he had won, so I scowled at him before I left. At the concession stand, I had the girl put extra butter on the popcorn.

The movie was actually pretty good, but it was one of those where the lead character was too earnest for his own good. I get the importance of legacy, but these people in movies who accomplish great things are never exciting characters. They walk through the film with giant halos over their heads.

As I pondered this, I literally thought about my mother for half a second. Now she's exciting, and many people want to be in her presence. Many people love her. I was sitting next to a man who loved her. He still loved her. I loved her. But I realized that I don't really like her. She's complicated and tough to live with. I once read somewhere that Benjamin Franklin was a lousy dad. A founding father was a terrible father. I think about that sometimes when I think about my mother.

Luther is one of those people who sit through the entire credits. He calls it giving respect to the people who make the movie happen. I call it making me wait another fifteen minutes and getting back at me for the extra butter on the popcorn.

Finally, the credits were done, and the last remnants of people exited the theater. Luther turned to me and asked, "You remember when Echo was sick and in the hospital?"

Of course, I remembered. It was the best of times and the worst. That was the trigger that sent my mother into raging loony town.

Luther continued, "There was this girl. She was staying at your house. She was this odd girl with yellow hair..."

"She smelled like cookies," I piped in. "I remember her."

"She died about a year ago. Drug overdose."

My jaw dropped open as I stared at Luther. I don't know why I was shocked except to say that this was the first time that someone I knew had died. I didn't know this girl well, but I remembered her. I remembered how she smelled, and I remembered the way she giggled. "Amy Honeywell was her name," I said.

"Yes, that's it," Luther confirmed. "I saw something in Berkeley-side, and they had her picture, which caught my attention. I don't know if your mother saw it. She doesn't look at a newspaper unless they have a crossword puzzle."

Luther was hunched over and speaking in a conspiratorial manner, even though we were the only ones left in the theater. The cleaning crew had come in with their plastic bags and brooms.

"So, this is what I want to tell you...Ollie and I had to make that girl leave the house. Echo was sick, and your mother was away, worrying in the hospital. This girl, Amy, was sleeping on the couch and eating up the food. Then Ollie started noticing things were missing. They were little things, but stuff that could be sold. Your mother doesn't have a lot of jewelry, but a watch of Ollie's' went missing, and there was a leather designer purse that had belonged to your grandmother that disappeared from the hall closet."

Hearing something belonging to my grandmother had been stolen made me angry. Not that I would have ever used the purse, but it was the principle of the thing. She was the only grandmother I had.

"One night, we sat down, and the two of us told this girl, Amy, that she had to leave. We didn't accuse her of the thefts but just pointed out that it wasn't proper for her to continue to stay at the house. Believe it or not, this girl argued with us, saying that Terry had said she could be her guest and that Terry said it would be fine, and Terry said, Terry said, Terry said. Ollie looked like he wanted to throttle the girl, I don't blame him. Ollie explains Terry isn't in her right mind now; her daughter is dying, and you need to leave. Amy was still all huffy. I get it, she had no place to go. But she was stealing, and your mother wasn't around to do anything about it."

For a few seconds, I didn't hear what Luther was saying because I was focusing on the words "her daughter is dying." Had Echo really been that close to death? I shuddered, thinking about how different things would be if that little loving mess of a child were no longer in my life.

"And then Ollie tells her that we're going to throw her out. Which was news to me. But he looks in my direction, and Amy takes it that I'm the muscle and will physically remove her. Ollie was furious about the watch."

"Why didn't you have the police get rid of her?"

Luther looked at me like I had a purple horn coming out of my head.

"Never mind," I said. "That was stupid. Keep going."

Luther continued. "The day comes when Amy is picking up her stuff that Ollie had left on the porch outside of what would become your room. I guess she was worried about me because she had all these guys with her. She said it was to help carry stuff, but there were only three boxes, and she had five fellas with her. I just stood there and watched them remove her belongings from the porch. Ollie hid inside the house. He was done with the whole thing."

I nodded. This was like what I had overheard Luther tell Ollie back when it happened.

"While everyone else was taking the stuff down the steps, there were these two fools who stood in front of me like they were going to take me or something. One of them even says you can't make Amy leave; you don't live here. I said something about the tenant of the house wanting her gone. Meaning Ollie. And then this guy sneers and says something about Ollie not being a tenant that he just crashed there like Amy was doing. I didn't respond to this guy because the girl's stuff was already off the porch, and Ollie had changed the locks to the house."

A chill went through my body. "What did he look like? This guy?"

"That's the thing, baby girl. That's what I wanted to tell you. This guy was tall and blond. His hair was in a long ponytail. But you once mentioned this Todd smiles with a big shit-eating grin, and that's what this guy was doing. He threatens you, and he smiles while he's doing it."

My head was continuing to bob up and down. "That's what Todd does. It's like a crocodile."

"And then I did something foolish," Luther said. "One night last week, when your mom was having one of those tattoo ceremonies, I took a window seat at the pizza place across the street. And I looked to see if this fellow was the one that I saw several years ago. It's been a long time, and he's cut his hair, but that Todd guy looks like the friend of Amy Honeywell's who challenged me. It was the big toothy smile that you talked about that got me thinking."

My mind raced with this information. Amy Honeywell was a druggie, and perhaps Todd had been one of her druggie friends. Years ago, Todd had been at the house and even questioned the tenancy arrangements.

I looked up at Luther. "Doesn't Ollie have a lease arrangement with my mother?"

Luther answered. "He does now. But at that moment, back then, Ollie didn't. It was a verbal arrangement, but I told him he needed to get Terry to put it in writing. He did after Echo was better and things were fine. But having that lease saved him when Terry and I had that fight, and... you know..." He sighed.

Yeah, I knew well enough.

Amy Honeywell was dead. Had Todd been her supplier back then? Fear was creeping inside me like chilly fingers of fog that blanket us from the Bay.

"Luther," I said. "I think he's a dealer."

Luther cocked his head and looked at me. His expression was dark. "A dealer or a doer?" Luther asked.

That's when I told him about Nick and the drugs in his jacket and the arrest. I added my suspicions were aroused when my backpack went missing for several days. The cleaning crew for the theater politely came over and asked us to go into the lobby. The next showing was about to start, and they had to let those patrons in. Luther and I exited the theater. It was then I noticed he had a bag with him.

"What have you told your mother?" asked Luther. "Anything?"

"I've told her all of it," I replied. "She doesn't believe me. She thinks I'm making stuff up to make Todd look bad."

"Well, what about this Nick, and the drugs he had. Your mother used to have a strict policy about stuff like that in the past."

I nodded my head. "No drugs in the house and no drugs if you are an artist under her employ. But Nick wasn't an artist, and my mom believed all the drugs were his. She thought Nick was the problem. And now he's gone, and she believes it is over and done with."

"So why don't you?" Luther asked. His eyes narrowed, scrutinizing me. "You know what I believe? I believe you need to stay away from this guy. Stay away from Todd. You can do that, can't you?"

I hesitated, not sure why I felt it wasn't over and why I thought it was Todd and not Nick, who was pulling strings in the operation. Nick had always given me the creeps, that's for sure. But I wasn't convinced he had been the one in charge. I had the sense Todd was the alpha in the pack. Nick had been holding the drugs because Nick was there to meet Todd at the house. He told the cops that. Would the alpha cough up somebody else so quickly?

Todd was crafty. I knew that well enough by the way he played me with the coffee mug dance. I thought Todd was too smart to allow the drugs to be on his person. Nick already had drug priors, so maybe Nick was expendable in Todd's mind.

The whole thing made me wonder how much I know, how much was I guessing at, and how much was wishful thinking.

I looked over at Luther. We had taken seats on the benches in the lobby. Luther was finishing up the popcorn, picking at the edible kernels, and popping them in his mouth. He scowled at me and rubbed buttery oiled hands over his jeans. "I believe there was a lot of butter on that popcorn, baby girl," he said.

I didn't comment.

Luther got up and pointed to a package under the bench. "My hands are all greasy now, so you have to pick up that bag there and carry it out."

"What is it?"

"Christmas gift for Echo. You can figure out how to give it to her."

I looked inside and only saw one present wrapped up in silver paper. "Where's mine?" I asked.

Luther leaned over and gave me a soft kiss on the forehead. "There you go," he said. "Merry Christmas."

At the moment, that was all I needed.

Dear Jehovah, I had four packs of hot sauce. Not bad, huh. Seeing Luther helps.

CHRISTMAS FUBAR

C hristmas happened.

Todd spent the night.

He tried to do Santa in the morning.

It was awful.

That's all I'm going to say about it.

SHEEP

The pig was enormous. I mean, this sucker was huge. He was huge and ugly. Echo stuck her hand through the wooden slats to pet the animal. I reached out to stop her and pull her arm back, but she had already touched the pig's dripping snout. Oh, Echo. Ewww.

"He's nice," my sister claimed. "Look, Bess, he's letting me pet him."

That's because you're cleaning the snot from his nose, I thought. Thank God I had brought wet wipes with me. I had one ready as Echo withdrew her hand from the pig's pen.

I've never been a fan of farm animals. I lean more towards the exotic creatures at the zoo. But Echo wanted a day at Tilden Park, so I got Ollie to drop us off at the Little Farm so Echo and I could have a picnic lunch, hike around Jewel Lake, feed the ducks and then visit the donkeys, cows, sheep, goats, and pigs, residing at the farm. Seeing Echo touch and stroke every animal she could reach; I was glad we had already eaten our sandwiches.

There was a bus route that had a stop near the Little Farm. Instead of contacting Ollie, I thought it would be nice if we took the bus down the hill and then got ice cream somewhere downtown. I proposed the idea to Echo, and she was happy to say goodbye to the pig to have a frozen treat.

The bus came within fifteen minutes, and soon my sister and I were seated, enjoying the ride, which was scenic in some spots. We were coming down from the Berkeley hills, and you could see the Golden Gate Bridge across the bay. Looking at the Golden Gate Bridge never gets old.

"I've got a riddle," Echo started. I groaned loudly, and she pinched me on the arm. "Stop it. This is a good one."

"Go ahead," I said.

"I live on a farm, and I give milk."

"You're a cow," I said before she finished. She frowned.

"Here's another one. I have feathers, and people like to eat me, and that doesn't make me happy." I said, "chicken" right after the word "feathers" left her lips. I laughed. However, Echo was not amused.

"Bess, stop it. You have to let me finish. You're not being nice."

"Okay, okay."

She tried again. "People like to count me when they try to go to sleep."

To play along, I answered, "you're a goat."

"No," she responded, delighted I hadn't said the right answer. "I'll give you a hint because this is a hard one," she said. "I'm white and fluffy."

"Ugh, you're right. This is hard," I responded. I scrunched up my face like I was giving serious thought to the answer, and then I opened my eyes wide as if an animated lightbulb had flashed over my head. "Is it a rabbit?"

"No," she squealed. "Do you want another hint?"

"No, no, that's okay. I'll get it."

"Okay, here's a hint," Echo said. "Todd has some."

That stopped me. Because in all honesty, the answer had to be sheep, and there was no way city boy Brad Pitt had sheep.

"Todd has sheep?" I asked.

"Yes," she answered. Her eyes glistened, excitedly. "I heard him on the phone. He said he had new ones. A whole bunch." My sister had started playing with the beads of the bracelet she was wearing. It was an old one of mine with sparkly butterflies and colored wooden beads.

"When was this?" I asked. I tried really hard to keep my voice interested but not too interested.

"When he picked me up from school yesterday. He was talking on the phone about his new sheep."

I waited a bit before talking further with my sister. I wanted to know about this sheep thing, but she had just given me a piece of information that made my blood surge like volcanic lava into my brain. I reached into my backpack, which I had used to carry our lunches and the wipes for Echo and pulled out two hot sauce packets. I opened the first one quickly and sucked down the sauce like people throw back a shot of tequila. The next one I savored more as I continued to talk to Echo.

Todd had picked Echo up at school. How the hell did that happen?

I knew how this worked. I remembered the paperwork my mother had filed with the school to give Luther permission to function as an intermediary parent when Echo was in the hospital. Schools don't let just anybody pick students up, especially when the student was in elementary school. At the beginning of the year, the schools require parents to fill out these emergency cards, and you are supposed to list the names and contact info of three or four people who can take your kid. This is very important in California, especially if there is a fire or an earthquake keeping the parents physically from being able to get to the school. In fact, California makes you list a person who lives out of the immediate area, just in case the emergency is an earthquake, and a distant family member from Nebraska must come get you. You see, our state taxes are well spent. Some bureaucrat actually thought of that. They don't want kids waiting in a holding area, because their home and family has fallen into the Pacific Ocean. Of course, in the lousy earthquake scenario, Echo and I are out of luck. There is no distant family member in Nebraska to come get us.

Echo was in first grade, so she got picked up directly from the classroom when school was out. There were three people on the emergency card for Echo; me, my mother, and Dusty. We were all familiar faces to Echo's teacher. If Todd had picked Echo up, it meant my mother had added him to the emergency card.

Terry had never done anything like this before. No boyfriend had ever been added to the emergency card. There was that one time, the crisis situation when Echo was in the hospital, and she had placed Luther on my card. I was already in middle school, though, and not being physically picked up in a car.

This was some sick tangled shit.

Todd had burned himself recently, and it was all bandaged up. He looked like he was wearing a giant mitten on his right hand. He told my mom it would scar, but he didn't have to have skin grafts or anything. How he injured himself was something stupid like putting his hand down on a hot skillet and not knowing it was hot. If I hurt myself like that, I would come up with a better story.

When I had told Ollie about my conversation with Luther and that Todd had been friends with Amy Honeywell, Ollie's first response was Luther was over-reaching. Ollie insisted he would have known if he had seen Todd before. Then I reminded Ollie he hadn't seen the guys that came with Amy when she cleared out her things. Ollie marinated for a while and then answered, "I have to think about this more." But I noticed he stayed out of Todd's way and watched Todd from a distance (usually the kitchen) with dark and hateful eyes.

I decided to tuck away Todd's possible connection to Amy Honeywell for later, and instead focus on the improbability Todd had farm animals in his possession.

"Tell me what he said on the phone," I said to Echo. "Todd doesn't live on a farm, so where are his sheep?"

"How do you know he doesn't live on a farm?" My sister threw back.

My mother and Todd were continuing the "out the bedroom window and knock on the front door" farce, so Echo still didn't know Todd was shacking up with mom.

I didn't want to get caught up in a discussion of Todd's sleeping arrangements or even mention the fact Todd had been using his cell phone while driving with my sister in the car, so I came at it a different way.

"You said he was talking about new sheep," I prompted.

"Yes, he was on the phone and said to the guy he had new sheep he was bringing in and that things were going well, and he could carry more."

"Carry more...what?" I asked.

"I don't know." My sister shrugged. "More sheep. Do you think he will let us see them so I can pet them?"

"Of course," I replied. Happy with that answer, my sister settled into the bus ride, playing with her butterfly bracelet and announcing every five minutes what flavor ice cream she was going to try. My mind wandered as I looked out the window, and she chattered about chocolate chip, fudge ripple, or raspberry sherbet. It didn't matter, she was just going to get vanilla with rainbow sprinkles.

Dear Jehovah, I had eight packs of hot sauce today. I know that's on the high side, but I have a lot to think about. I must get rid of Todd, and I'd appreciate some help here.

INVITING THE VAMPIRE IN

I'll admit at the start of this that my timing wasn't perfect. I needed to talk to my mother about letting Todd pick Echo up at school, but I needed to speak to her alone. Todd was around all the time at the house. I guess he wanted to make sure I didn't send another acquaintance of his to jail. The only place I could catch my mother without pretty boy hanging around was at Cosmic Hearts during the day. More importantly, it had to be a time in the shop when Dusty didn't have an appointment, and she would excuse herself when she realized a family throw-down was about to begin. Now Todd only came into the tattoo studio at night when there was a Beloved ceremony going on.

I had to bide my time. My stunt with Nick did not keep the traffic down as I hoped it would. In fact, it got worse. Todd and his crew were behaving more and more like the house was their space. New faces would pop up, and I would be introduced as "the teenager of the house." When I left in the morning, I would see Todd sipping his coffee in the breakfast area, reading a magazine, or checking messages on his phone. The mug wars had ceased because I was keeping my red mug underneath the bed in my room. But I felt I was being tracked and he was stationing himself outside my bedroom door like a jailer.

When I came home from school or after stopping at Cosmic Hearts, I would find Duane or Todd lounging around the front room, drinking beers, and acting like this place was a clubhouse. Sometimes Annika was there with her annoying giggle, but usually, if there was a girl, she was someone the guys had just met, and I didn't bother learning her name because she wouldn't be around for long. They were all space cadets.

Whenever I challenged the presence of Todd or his cronies, I always got some excuse or reason for them to be using our home as their drop-in spot. "I'm running an errand for your mother" or "I'm waiting for Annika to show up or Todd or whoever it was (it didn't matter)." I felt like Todd told them what to say, and they were just challenging me to throw water on them. I stopped asking.

I would just go to the back where my bedroom was and keep my door locked. I would only come out for dinner and then slink back into my room. Ollie made the meals, but instead of calling us to eat together, he would leave stuff out so folks could help themselves, and then he would retire to his space upstairs. The muffled sound of opera arias wafted down. The dramatic music underscoring everyone's mood.

According to Luther, the information I had on Todd didn't amount to squat. I couldn't call the police and say, "I think my mother's boyfriend is a drug dealer." Without evidence the police could use to arrest him, I was just a pissed off teenager who didn't like her mother's latest fling. The best evidence was the drugs themselves, but I never saw Todd holding the backpack.

Then there was the added problem of bringing the police into the mix when I didn't have concrete evidence. Given my family's relationship with law and order, if I tossed drugs into the recipe, I could count on Echo and me spending weeks in foster care while family court sorted everything out. No, the key for this to work with minimal bleeding was to have everything point to Todd and have my mother be blameless. I had no idea how I could do that.

Joanie and Rueben had stopped coming by, and I couldn't blame them. I would see them at school and pretend everything was okay. They knew I was unhappy, but they didn't ask questions. What was there to ask? "Is the creep still staying at your house?" My regular consumption of hot sauce was testimony enough.

Am I painting a depressing picture? Good. It was fucking depressing.

Todd was winning.

A week passed, and I was finally able to grab some alone time with Terry. I entered the shop after school, and purposely came in through the back. Since the missing backpack fiasco, I had continued to leave my backpack in the same spot on the highest shelves. I was thinking about trying to get a look inside the other pack to confirm its contents if I ever saw it. A green ribbon was tied on the top of my bag. I had done this intentionally in front of Duane so he would see the identifying ribbon and know it marked my bag. Then later, I would tie my ribbon onto Duane's backpack and then sneak off with it so I could look inside. I saw this done in a movie with a briefcase. However, the excitement of laying a trap fizzled out when I realized I would only be ensnaring Duane, and there was no fun in that. I wanted Todd, and he never touched the backpack.

While I was doing inventory in the studio, a call came in, rescheduling their appointment with Terry. They needed to push it back a week. I saw this was work that had already been paid for so I could accommodate the request. I made the notation but didn't tell my mother about the change because I realized it would give me a window of time to talk to her. Dusty was out for another hour, and my mother would be finished with the detailed oak tree tattoo she was inking on the thigh of a young woman in about thirty minutes.

When it was completed, and my mother was cleaning up. The young woman with a tree on her thigh came over to the counter to get the follow-up kit we hand out to our clients. I complimented the young woman on the work, telling her that she is going to be really happy when the tattoo heals.

"It's so beautiful," the woman gushed. "Even with the red skin all around it."

I gave my spiel, cautioning her about peeling back the plastic bandage too soon. Then I handed over the oils we ask our clients to use and checked to make sure the account was paid in full.

Once the woman left, I turned to my mother, who was wiping down her chair in preparation for the next customer who wasn't going to appear.

"Can we talk for a moment?" I asked.

"Not a good time, Bess. I've got someone coming in ten minutes."

"They rescheduled," I replied.

My mother slowed her movements down. She was thinking. She looked over at Dusty's empty station and then back at me, realizing she was stuck with me for some time, and she couldn't escape. She then sighed and moved over to the display counter, taking her customary seat and pulling out her crossword puzzle.

"Okay, what do you want to talk about?"

"I'd like your full attention."

"You have it," she said as she scratched an answer within the squares.

"You're letting Todd pick up Echo from school," I stated.

"So?"

"You don't have Ollie on the emergency cards, and he's been with the family for ten years."

"Ollie has made it clear he doesn't want any type of childcare responsibilities."

I held my tongue not wanting to disclose the fact Ollie drove Echo to Luther's place from time to time. In an emergency, Ollie will definitely step up.

"You've only been dating Todd for five months. Isn't it a little soon?"

My mother shrugged and scratched in another answer to her puzzle.

"Todd offered, and I accepted. Why do you have a problem with it?" She looked up at me.

"It's too soon for him to have that..." I didn't know what word to use. "Privilege" is what sprang to mind.

"Bess, I don't know why you have a problem with this. Work at Cosmic Hearts has doubled - thanks to Todd, by the way. And I need help with stuff involving Echo."

"Ask me," I pleaded.

"You're already doing too much. I need that analytical brain of yours here at the shop. Todd may have helped in boosting business, but you're the reason it is translating into money." *Thanks for the compliment. I think.*

My mother went back to working her crossword. "It's just picking Echo up and bringing her home. Sometimes he grabs her an ice cream. You know how much your sister loves ice cream. It allows Todd to have some bonding time with her."

My heart sank, thinking of the bonding times with ice cream Echo had done with Luther, and now those memories would get swept away by new ones imprinted with this pretty boy impostor.

"Why do you give him so much access?"

"What do you mean?"

"You're just letting the vampire in. You're opening the door wide open for him. You involve him with Cosmic Hearts, and you involve him with US."

"Bess, I told you. I want him in my life. I love him."

"But we don't. I don't. Don't my feelings matter?"

"That's because you are refusing to get to know him. You keep holding on to the idea that Luther is your father."

That was a low blow, even for her.

"I know Luther is not my father."

"That's right. HE ISN'T." She used the pencil in her hand to punctuate the point.

"Todd will never be a father to me. Don't even think that."

"I'm not. Don't worry. But he could be a father for Echo."

The burning shock I felt was like she had just thrown boiling water at my face. I drew in my breath and then screamed, "No. No. NO."

My mother looked up from her crossword at my outburst. Her eyes widened, and her mouth dropped open. My fiery response had caught her by surprise.

"Are you out of your mind?" she asked.

"No, but you are. How can you not see...?" I threw my hands up and paced around the space of the shop. I needed air. I was suffocating. "You can't do this! How can you not see what he is?"

"My god, Bess. Cut back on the theatrics. You're calling Todd a vampire, and you expect me to listen?"

I stopped the pacing. My chest was heaving up and down as I tried to keep my emotions under control. I looked squarely at my mother. My absolute oblivious mother. "How can you trust him?" I asked.

Her response stabbed me in the heart. "I trust Todd with my life."

***

I need an eight-letter word that means treachery. There's a y second letter in.

"Betrayal"

"Thanks. That's it."

"No problem."

Jehovah, I consumed nine packs of hot sauce that night and fell asleep with the tenth one in my hand.

MAYOR OF COSMIC HEARTS

N ow that things were out in the open, I knew trusting my mother was not an option. It was going to be my word against Todd's. In my mother's mind, my complaints and my whining (I don't whine, but she says I do) were examples of my "displaced anger." I wanted Luther back, and Todd was in the way. Once I accepted the fact Luther was out of the picture, I would be able to accept Todd. Todd made her happy, why can't I accept it.

But Luther made me happy. Why couldn't she accept that? Without sounding crude, why do her sexual needs come before my emotional needs to have a complete family?

We were at a standstill. Terry wanted me to welcome Todd. I wanted to get rid of Todd. Todd was at the center of this.

After contemplating the situation for a while, I realized my mother was right about one thing regarding Todd. I would have to get to know him better. I had to know him to find a way to get rid of him.

Around the time she first started dating him, my mother had asked me to touch Todd's tattoos. She casually requested I do my little parlor trick (her words) on him so she could use the information if needed. It was the equivalent of asking someone to run a credit check. It was one thing to read people's stories as a means of drumming up business. I had justified the intrusion as a revenue tool.

However, I am not a touchy-feely person, and I'm not keen on knowing people's dark secrets. I was feeling weird about doing the parlor trick, and I especially didn't want to have to touch Todd at all. It was easy for me to shoot down the request, so I did. Touching Todd on any level creeped me out, and knowing a special thing about him, would creep me out even more. But we were at war, and it was the only advantage I had.

Todd was reinventing himself as the Mayor of Cosmic Hearts. He was good at schmoozing people, and he was great at shaking hands and squeezing shoulders. He made folks feel welcome. It was easier for me to justify going after his personal information as a business move, then a vengeful one. It's like getting your references, Todd. It's business, not personal.

Once I knew something he was lying about, I could use it to his disadvantage and catch Todd in a lie. I'd have to create a scenario so it would happen in front of my mother, and she would see he was fake. He was a wolf in sheep's clothing.

The sheep comment he had dropped in front of Echo was starting to make sense. I bet Todd saw us as sheep, and he was pulling the wool over our eyes. When he talked about getting more sheep, he was talking about getting more people to fool, and more clients. When you add that to Luther's information that Todd was connected to Amy Honeywell in the past and had known drug associates like Nick, a larger picture was materializing.

I thought about something my mother said the other night when she claimed work at Cosmic Hearts had doubled. That wasn't exactly true. HER work at Cosmic Hearts had doubled. Dusty was doing the same amount of business and handling a teensy bit of overflow, but the main attraction was Terry Wynters and the Ink for the Beloved ceremonies with soloist Annika Kane. I saw how the numbers were growing.

We went from being open in the evening maybe four times a month to accommodate an Ink ceremony to ten in a month, and we could quickly flip that number up to twenty. Terry Wynters was in beast mode. It was both fascinating and scary to watch.

Beloved Ceremonies were being videotaped and shown on social media. I was getting calls from people who wanted to watch a ceremony even if they didn't know the individual being inked and spoken for. Once I got permission from the person receiving the tattoo, I created a payment scale - twenty bucks if you knew the person. Thirty-five dollars, if you didn't. The seats were full. I gave a percentage to Annika if she was performing and a portion to the individual getting the tattoo (it felt fair), and then the money that would go to my mother went to me. I kept trying to give it to her, but she waved her hand and told me to go buy something nice for myself. I realized then, it was blood money.

The Beloved ceremonies at the tattoo studio were the only time Todd, my mother, and I shared space without Echo being around. On those nights, I knew Echo was safe with Ollie in the house, who had now reached the point where he was allowing Echo to be in his apartment upstairs. Ten years, he's been with our family, and Ollie has never let me up there with his "No kids" rule. But it showed how protective he was becoming of Echo and working with me to diminish the amount of time she spent with Todd. I knew I was interfering with my mother's wishes, but something in my gut told me it was the smart thing to do.

Echo had a friend named Maisie Kelly who didn't live far from the elementary school. I called Maisie's parents and asked if they could take Echo home three days a week for an hour until I could get her. The other two days, I could pick up my sister myself.

I wrote out a note to Echo's teacher from my mother saying the Kelly family would be bringing Echo home for a play date and had my mother sign it. After my mother signed it, I added the days the Kelly family would be responsible for Echo, so it was clear it was an ongoing thing, and not just one play date. Since Maisie Kelly was in Echo's class, I didn't have to deal with the emergency card stuff at the front office. Then, to ensure everything ran smoothly, I took $60 out of the money I was getting for booking seats at the Beloved ceremonies and put it in an envelope. Each week I would give the envelope to the Kellys thanking them for picking up Echo and saying the money was from my mother and could be used for snacks or some fun activity for the girls to do.

Worked like a charm.

With Echo taken care of, I felt I could focus on trying to figure out what Todd was up to. I couldn't believe a guy as handsome as Todd and as connected (his words) would settle for a woman who was fifteen years older than him and with two kids. My mother had a thriving business and owned property, but there were so many other women in Berkeley and the East Bay who had much better portfolios. I've seen these women standing in line for pizza at the Cheeseboard or shopping at Star Grocery, so I know they exist.

Plus, Todd knew I actively hated him. So why put up with me when there are easier women (and wealthier) women to be had who would fall for his Tom Cruise grin.

There was something else going on, and I knew it centered around the backpack. Drugs were the obvious conclusion, but I didn't have proof, and I had already burned multiple bridges with my mother.

My mother said there were three tattoos on Todd. I had seen the image of his German Shepherd, Wolfie, on his shoulder and the tribal bands that wrapped around his arms as if he were some type of Maori warrior. (HA) Those were the tattoos I could see. The third one was probably someplace I would never venture. I figured the Maori warrior bands were some type of machismo declaration. In the past, when I've touched tattoos belonging to men that had a masculine or frightening image, the symbols were significant to boost the guy's ego. *No judging here. I'm just speaking the truth, I see.*

I hoped the warrior bands were either gang related (*I can dream, can't I?*) or would give me a story showing Todd trying to prop himself up as a macho guy. I had heard the tale surrounding Wolfie and knew the ink was a memorial, so I decided to focus on the bands. They were easier to access anyway. The moment Todd walked around with arms bare, I would be able to take my shot. Even when he wore short sleeves, enough of the warrior bands were visible for me to touch.

Thankfully, the weather was getting warm enough for short sleeves. Todd was into lifting weights at the YMCA (he had joined up on my mother's account), and he was the type of guy who would wear a smaller shirt size, so his muscles came off well-defined under his t-shirts. Saying Todd is vain is an obvious statement. It was why he liked walking around our place wearing nothing but his undies.

Once I had decided to touch Todd on one of his tattoos, the opportunity presented itself almost immediately. It was another busy night at Cosmic Hearts. It was an evening where the Ink for the Beloved ceremony was public, and I had sold fifteen extra seats in addition to the twenty chairs of friends and family. I was going to make close to $300 even after paying out Annika and the client.

The client getting the tattoo was thrilled by all the attention. Her name was Wendy, and she was getting a tattoo to commemorate a boyfriend who had died from an illness four months ago. She had spent the last year of his life taking care of him, and she was throwing out a "Aren't I fabulous" vibe along with her martyr credentials. Her story was now she was moving on with her life and the tattoo of Greg (I think his name was Greg) was a symbol he would forever be in her heart.

To be honest, there was something ghoulish about this woman, and I got the idea she had been using the dying boyfriend story to get noticed, and now her friends were over it and over her. Having an Ink for The Beloved Ceremony was a last-ditch attempt for sympathy and attention. Wendy had paid for a full package. Not only was the ceremony being recorded, but she had requested three songs from Annika. Food was being brought in from the pizzeria down the street. Basically, Wendy was throwing a party.

The place was at capacity, and Todd was moving around the area, getting chairs set up, and being very gracious to everyone involved. This was Todd at his absolute best. He was charming and flirtatious. Ladies loved him because he smiled and touched their arms as he guided them to their chairs. I saw Duane hovering in the background with his backpack slung over one shoulder, and I made a mental note to see if he placed it on the shelves so I could make the switch. This was going to be a busy night.

Because the space was packed with people, the AC kicked in (which is rare in Berkeley). Todd had already stripped off his jacket and was moving around in his T-shirt, showing Bruce Lee at a record turnstile like a DJ. A T-shirt I completely don't understand, and clearly, it's me, because Todd gets tons of compliments on the shirt.

My mother was also down to her bare minimal outfit. She looked great wearing one of her spaghetti strap dresses. It was green, and her floral garden of ink erupted over her body like a wild tangled mass of color. Her hair was down, but once she started working, she would clip it up and out of the way. She was surveying the room with pride. I could see she was watching Todd with appreciation (UGH), but she was also pleased with the thought of working in front of an eager audience.

"Big crowd, isn't it?" I said as I moved up alongside her.

"Annika really brings them in," she observed.

"They are here for you," I emphasized. "It's the storytelling with the ink, that's the draw." She smirked at my pun, and I smiled. "The music sets the mood, but people like being a witness to the personal event. It's like a memorial with flair."

My mother leaned over and kissed the side of my head. "I love you so much," she said. "You can really be fantastic when you want to be. I miss my little Mouse."

Since I now cleared her in height by about two inches, I rolled my eyes. But I let this moment of honest connection set in and linger.

"She's a bit of a weirdo, don't you think?" I asked.

"Who?

"Wendy. The client."

We both watched Wendy as she smiled and waved to her friends and the strangers at the event. She behaved like a bride, greeting her guests at the reception.

"What's weird about her?" my mother asked.

"She just gives me the creeps for some reason."

"How did she come in?"

I hesitated for a bit, thinking back. "No direct referral. Wendy left a message after hours about booking an appointment, talking about her dying boyfriend. He wasn't dead yet. It took four months to fit her in."

"Should I be concerned? Have you touched her other tattoos?"

"No," I replied. Sometimes my mother makes it sound like I run around touching people because I love to do it. Believe me, it's not something I enjoy doing. Depending on the tattoo, it can be painful.

"Well, see if you get an opportunity. She's spending a lot of money here tonight, and this video is going to be used for publicity. I need to know if there's an issue. Do that thang that you do."

I gave her a mock scowl. She had hit "thang" way too hard. I hated it when she used slang. She always embarrassed herself. My mom smiled at me and moved back to the workstation and chair, checking and prepping equipment that had already been checked and prepped a million times. Every now and then, she would halt and close her eyes and sway her hips a bit. I knew she was working Wendy's story over in her head.

I watched Todd embrace Wendy, call out to a guy across the room, and then give one of Wendy's female friends a hearty handshake. The woman wore a flowing silk jacket with red poppies. Off to the side, Duane was standing with the bag hanging loosely off his back. His hands were in his pockets, but there had been a quick movement, and I could have sworn he slipped a bag into Todd's left hand while Todd embraced the woman with the poppy jacket. The generous material on the jacket hid the next movement, which was Todd sliding the bag into her pants pocket. I looked away so Todd wouldn't catch me watching. So that was it.

Duane stepped away from Todd and slunk towards the back behind the cameras, apart from the crowd. I would need to see an exchange again to make sure. But the activity seemed clear. Todd was moving drugs at the tattoo studio and had a system that kept him from ever having the drugs on his person. He was the frontman, and everything else was in the shadows.

This guy had calculated a way to move more people through the studio in a manner that would not be obvious to anyone - especially my mother.

With all the lax rules and regulations my mother followed, you may have thought she was loosey-goosey when it came to drugs as well. But brain enhancements outside of alcohol (or even marijuana which is everywhere in Berkeley) were a big no to her. She was an artist that didn't believe talent was unleashed through artificial stimulants. In fact, she felt it was the opposite - that drugs hindered the creative work.

That was why the gap-toothed, Amy Honeywell, had been bounced so quickly from our home. Luther saw the girl was doing smack and out she went. She was stealing to support the habit. If my mother hadn't been so distracted by Echo's illness, she would have noticed the signs with Amy herself.

This made me think. Was there anybody in Todd's entourage that did drugs in a manner my mother would see? Outside of Nick and his marijuana, there wasn't that I could recall. This was why drugs didn't spring to mind when I first pondered the situation regarding Todd. The guy came across as clean cut. He didn't use the product he was pushing.

What was I going to do? I had to convince my mother, and that was not going to be an easy task. She questioned and challenged everything I said when it came to Todd.

The Beloved ceremony began with a slow drum beat and then a soulful song delivered by Annika. Before the final note of the song ended, my mother spoke, saying the name of Wendy's belated boyfriend, Gregory Steven Fox. Wendy stood beside my mother, beaming with excitement. My mother introduced herself and said she was here to tell the story of Gregory. To share his life and ink his tale onto Wendy, his beloved caregiver. Wendy then took her position in the chair, facing out so she could watch her audience. (By the way, most people don't like to watch their friends. Instead, they chose to face away, and the audience is looking at their profile). But this was Wendy's party, and she wanted to see the faces and expressions of everyone as she got the tattoo honoring Greg.

As my mother's clear voice carried across the room, she began the outlining ink. She talked about the earlier bits of Greg's life as a child growing up on a farm in South Dakota. Greg dreamed of working in biotechnology and finding cures for the suffering or a means of alleviating their struggles. But Greg's work focused on animals, and he began building prosthetic limbs for animals suffering a loss either through illness or amputation. He loved his work.

Listening to this, I started to think more highly of Greg and, by extension, Wendy. Greg clearly was a good guy with his heart in the right place. When I first heard Wendy was getting one of my mother's rockabilly creations and using a fox. I snorted at the unoriginal connection of having a fox and that Greg's last name was "Fox." But as I heard about Greg's work, I could see there was a deeper connection. Dusty had mounted pictures of the animals Greg had helped, and she displayed them to the audience. There was a series of photos showing a red fox that had gotten its paw snapped off in a hunter's trap. He was now running around an animal sanctuary with an orange prosthetic leg thanks to Greg Fox, the animal lover.

There were more pictures and more animals, and as Annika sang another song, folks began to cry. I was ready with boxes of kleenex I had purchased earlier. I moved up to Todd, who had positioned himself in the back. I tapped him on the arm right where his Maori warrior band was and handed him the kleenex boxes. He smiled at me appreciatively (UGH, my stomach clenched) and moved around the chairs, offering the teary-eyed ladies something to dab their eyes. He relished his role as the Mayor of Cosmic Hearts.

By the time Annika was finished, and the displays of Greg's human-itarian work concluded, the outline work of the tattoo for Greg was done. My mother paced things out so when the ceremony (party) ended, most of the tattoo would be completed. This was mainly because it was being filmed. Many times, the full tattoo was not done because of the hours involved, but she was trying to give the audience more of a sense of completion.

My mother began to talk about Greg having leukemia and meeting Wendy at a support group holding sessions in a church basement. Wendy's smile grew as the story expanded to encompass her. I was just beginning to wonder what Wendy was doing at a support group if she didn't have cancer when I saw the delivery guy from the pizza place hovering near the entrance. I went out to meet him and directed him to the back entrance so he would not walk in front of a bunch of people with boxes of pizzas. As I was orchestrating the situation with the pizza, I reflected on what Todd's warrior tattoos had told me about the guy.

Unfortunately, it wasn't much. As I had suspected, Todd had gotten his warrior bands with a bunch of friends on a drunken night of bonding. They all had chosen the bands to show solidarity and strength. The choice of Maori bands wasn't even significant. The guys had no idea the bands represented something. They just thought they were cool. So, it was a bust. I would have to glean something about Todd another way.

People were starting to shift in their seats as the aroma of garlic, and hot melted cheese filled the air. My mother was nearing the point where she was going to take a break and let the guests eat. She would continue with the inking work but get back to the story of Greg Fox after people had eaten.

I was working to move the food along and make sure that plates got tossed in the trash can and not left unattended on a counter somewhere. The atmosphere was filled with expectancy and enjoyment. This was going well, and based on the strong reception, I suspected we would get future bookings at this profitable scale with food and multiple performances by Annika.

(Hmmm, with this much money, maybe it was time to hit my mother up for a new bike. That would be cool. The minute the thought crossed my mind, I felt guilty. I loved my old banged-up bike.)

While the guests were eating, I went up to my mother and Wendy. They were continuing with the inking work. I asked Wendy what type of pizza she would like me to set aside for her. I already knew my mother would want the mushroom and green pepper. Wendy gave me the order and then babbled on about what a great time she was having and wasn't this party fantastic. (See, I was right, she viewed the event like a party.)

While I was talking to Wendy, I noticed she had a bright red apple tattooed on the wrist of her right hand. A little worm was wriggling out of the fruit. I looked over at my mother, who was watching me, and she saw I had caught sight of the tattoo. My mother nodded her head, indicating for me to continue. She wanted me to touch the apple.

I did. I didn't ask for permission either. I made the touch look like an impulse, and I couldn't help myself.

"That's so pretty," I said as my finger glossed over the image.

"Thanks," Wendy beamed. She took a sip from her wine glass and then waved at a friend across the room. She didn't see the horrified look I gave my mother.

"So, what do you like?" I asked. "Apples or worms?"

"Pardon?"

"The tattoo," I continued, forcing myself to be pleasant and interested. I was keeping a level tone in my voice because inside, I was vomiting. It was like mass hysteria in my gut. Imagine all the hot sauce packets I consumed over the weeks and months revolting and exploding within me.

"The apple is New York, you know, the big apple," Wendy answered. "I lived there for a while. Once a New Yorker, always a New Yorker." She laughed.

"Why did you add the worm?" I continued. At this point, I knew I was going to throw up. I needed this witch of a woman to answer my question immediately because I was heading outside to vomit in the alley.

"The worm was cute. I saw this on a design in the studio and just added it. I thought it was sweet the way it was wiggling out of the apple. I guess it was like me trying to escape, New York." She laughed harder, throwing back her head. "I couldn't wait to get out."

My mother was looking at me quizzically, and then she looked back at Wendy. She was worried. I think she could see I was sick to my stomach. Maybe my face was green. It felt like it was.

I bolted out the back door of the studio and ran a distance so I could vomit, and no one would hear. Tears were running down my face, and I needed to wipe my nose. I had nothing but my shirtsleeves, so that would have to do. I made a mental note to throw my shirt in the laundry before Echo greeted me at home. She always buried her face in the folds of my clothes. If I had dried vomit on my shirt, that would be gross.

Almost as gross as what I had just witnessed. People might wonder why I don't touch tattoos that often, why I hold back. It's simple. It's an intrusion. I learn something about a person's inner thinking that is private and not for public scrutiny. It might seem it is like reading someone's diary, but it's more profound than that. People can edit their thoughts while writing a diary. They don't always write the truth or the whole truth. They might not even be aware of what the truth is.

When I touch a tattoo, I learn the truth, and it's not the truth that is loved and crafted within the heart. Sometimes the truth matches what the person says, but many times the truth is unblemished, and it is not given the touch-up memory allows. It's like the photo service high school portraits offer. They will remove the acne and discoloring from your skin, so the pictures your parents' purchase make it look like you don't have a pizza face. As the years unfold, it is the picture of the smooth skin that stands the test of time. Everyone else begins to forget the ugliness that used to be there. When I see the truth of the tattoo, I see the picture before the touch-up. I see the sprouting zits.

Wendy was a horrible woman that was pretending to be a saint. What I saw was a woman who intentionally befriended guys who were ill or had suffered from an accident. As a nurse, she had easy access and was able to find men with soft hearts. She pushed the relationship, and these men were so happy to have a companion showing interest in them and their situation. They just didn't know she was pretending. And what did Wendy get out of these uneven relationships? She got glory and admiration. People were in awe of her and her remarkable patience and ability to be optimistic in the face of tragedy. It was a drug to her; it was better than Ecstasy.

She had thrown bereavement parties in the past. Greg was the third boyfriend of Wendy's that had died. The worm in the apple was boyfriend number two. Which meant there was a number one somewhere.

The thing that had made me ill from touching the apple tattoo was the knowledge she had nudged things along. She had grown impatient because the guy wasn't dying fast enough, and she wanted to leave New York. She didn't directly kill him by putting a pillow over his face or something. But she had intentionally moved this guy's medicine out of his reach and then left the apartment for hours so she could return to a still body on the floor. Wendy was a murderer.

I would have been happy to live my life without knowing this about Wendy. It wasn't going to change anything. She was going to continue to have her inked memorial for Greg and her bereavement bash at the studio. I wasn't going to call the police in New York and tell them a death they ruled as an accident ten years ago was murder. Where was my proof? Her tattoo told me, officer. Yeah, right.

I wasn't even sure if I was going to tell my mother. I leaned my back against the concrete wall that ran down the alley defining the boundaries. A few deep breaths of crisp air, and my mind began to settle, allowing me to think clearly. I could hear the soft sounds of the Beloved ceremony continuing in Cosmic Hearts. My mother's voice carried through the night air as she shared the virtues of Wendy, now becoming Greg's saint and finding ways to continue the excellent work he was doing with injured animals. The party would end with a closing song by Annika.

A few more breaths and clarity revealed itself. My mother liked to hear what I learned from clients' tattoos, but this was a situation where the knowledge was not going to benefit her. It wasn't like Glenn and his discomfort with returning to Vulture Tattoo. This was not going to be something that brought in business or hindered the business. Even if Wendy and her despicable actions were revealed, our association with her wouldn't be tarnished. I mean, how were we supposed to know she was a fiend.

I wouldn't tell my mother. I would say I was sick from the hot sauce, and that's why I bolted for the alley. She'll cluck her tongue, wag her finger, and tell me to stop that nasty habit. I'll shrug my shoulders, and that will be it.

There. I was decided. I'd make up something that matched what Wendy said. The worm was her wiggling out of New York to freedom.

Because I had to know, I stayed up on the computer that night, downing coffee to keep the screen from blurring. It took a while, but I eventually found it in the New York obituaries. His name was Jason Grubb.

FIRST FIGHT

We were seven months in on the Todd Mackey relationship. Seven months and finally, they had a fight.

It was Tuesday, and I had started the kettle to brew my morning tea. My red mug was ready with a chai tea bag in place. WHAM. A door slammed open, and my mother stomped barefoot down the hallway, not caring that she wasn't covered up for public view. She wasn't wearing a bra, so her breasts jiggled, and I got a full view of her floral ink job. Her short silk robe flew behind her like a cape as she entered the kitchen. She quickly snatched up a cup and stood behind me as the coffee maker slowly did its business of making coffee.

"What's taking so long?" She was testy.

"It's brewing."

"How long ago did you start it?"

"It's on a timer, Mom. It starts at 7:15, like it always does."

She impatiently waved her hands in the "hurry up" gesture as if the coffee maker could see and respond in kind.

"Can't I pull the pot out and pour a cup now."

"That only works for coffee makers that have the stopping mechanism."

Hot breath blew out of her mouth and floated stray hair tendrils hanging over her forehead.

"I thought we could do that. I remember doing that before."

I looked at her out of the corner of my eye. "That coffee maker broke nine months ago." I wanted to add you threw it across the room, but I didn't. "This is the backup coffee maker," is what I said instead. "I don't like your tone. Don't talk to me like a child." We stood there for a full minute staring at the coffee maker chugging away. Finally, I was saved by three chimes, which signaled the task was done, and we could remove the glass pot.

Terry pulled out the pot and poured her cup. She then added the milk and sugar to her drink. I reached up and removed another coffee mug from the cupboard. I thought Todd could have the camel humpday mug, even though it wasn't Wednesday, but my mother was already heading back to her bedroom.

"Hey," I called. "Aren't you going to bring him a cup as well?"

She stopped and turned around. "I'm not getting that asshole anything." She snarled with the viciousness of a harpy who has been denied her food. She then whirled back around and flew down the hallway on her harpy wings.

Inside, I felt like a beacon of light had just exploded inside, and I swear I could hear angels harmonizing in my ears. I placed the camel coffee mug back up in the cupboard. I wanted to do the type of dance football players do when they score. A smile crept across my face as I poured the hot water into my red mug, but that movement felt too contained for how I was feeling. I wanted to dance. I wanted to sing. I wanted to scream. I must have started humming as a voice behind me interrupted the happy thoughts in my head.

"What's that noise? Are you singing?" A harsh honking laugh then followed the words, and I turned around to look at the person who had already caused emotional havoc this morning.

"I was humming," I responded defensively, and moved to head towards my bedroom.

"Oh, don't leave on my account." He was over by the cupboard retrieving a mug and pouring himself some coffee. I noted he did not take the camel one, but instead chose a cup which read "100lb gorilla". The mug wars were still on even though I had been stashing my mug in my room. Todd poured his coffee. He looked up at me, watching him and smiled. He glanced down at the tea I was holding in my red mug. The smile was confirmation he knew. He knew what was going through my mind. Even though I was hiding my mug in my room, the coffee mug war was still on.

He took his coffee and moseyed over to the kitchen nook and pulled out a stool. He looked like he was about to say something to me when Echo hopped in all bushy-eyed and ready for breakfast. In the heat of her anger, Terry had not set out the cereal for Echo and placed it on the table, so I did it while she pulled out the stool across from Todd and climbed up.

We hovered at a stalemate while Echo was at the table.

"Can I have juice please?" The tiny voice cut through the tension vibrating in the air.

"Sure." I poured out orange juice and placed it in front of my sister. She was still in her pajamas and was wearing a mismatched pair. This was intentional as Echo liked to play around with different patterns. Her pajama bottoms were an autumn print of fall leaves, pinecones, and acorns while on top she was wearing a design with puppy dogs and bones and balls. I think the uniting color was yellow, but that was about it.

"Oh, there's orange juice. Could I have some?" Todd was smiling when I looked over in his direction. His smile was more like a smirk. He gestured in my direction. "While you're up."

I poured him the juice and placed it down in front of him, glaring the entire time.

"THANK YOU," he responded, but he delivered it as if he were singing in a community theater production of *Oklahoma* with an aw-shucks smile.

I reminded myself to pull back and not engage, even though he was egging me on.

Down the hall, I could hear my mother banging doors and slamming drawers as she got herself together to walk Echo to school. Walking her children to school was one of life's pleasures my mother insisted upon. It didn't matter if she was in a bad mood or slightly hungover, walking to the neighborhood school was my mother's method of connecting with the community and her past.

Since we were living in the house she grew up in, both Echo and I attended the school my mother had gone to when she was a girl. It was one of the things my mother liked to expound upon. She enjoyed pointing at the different trees along the path and talk about the days she would climb them as a girl. The house with the blue shutters had once been a house with green shutters. The triplex with the noisy grad students was once a duplex where a family from New Zealand kept an ostrich in the backyard.

On the days my mom was chatty, the walks to Malcolm X Elementary were enjoyable. Well, I'm guessing they were. I don't remember those as well as the days when she was a female troll in pajamas and fluffy slippers. When my mother was in a mood, she wouldn't bother putting on street clothes and would escort me to school in her pajamas and slippers and a large traveling mug of coffee. I hated walking to school when she was like that. Not because of the lazy attire, but because it meant she was in a nasty mood, and I had to suffer for it. She snarled and barked and made the whole thing unpleasant.

Instead of pointing out the charming changes in the neighborhood, my mother would complain about the people who let their properties fall into disrepair and the folks who were renting or selling to the wrong kinds of people. Just so we are clear, my mother's definition of the "wrong kind of people" are people who don't appreciate the eclectic nature of the city and instead want to make Berkeley another Palo Alto.

Good mood or bad mood, Echo didn't mind the walks with mom at all. She never asked me to walk her instead. I think it was because it was the one portion of the day, that you knew you had Terry's undivided attention - even if it was only for fifteen minutes.

"ECHO!" my mother hollered from down the hall. "I'll be ready to take you in five minutes."

"She's finishing her breakfast," I hollered back. I looked over at Todd. "You taking off soon?" I said it like a question, but we both knew it was a statement.

It was at that point Terry entered the kitchen to load her traveler mug with coffee. She stopped when she saw Todd sitting at the table with her six-year-old.

"What are you doing here?" she snapped.

"Thought I'd savor my orange juice and enjoy the morning rays of the rising sun."

"I told you to leave."

"Oh, you meant that?"

"Get out of here, Todd. I don't think we should see each other for a while."

Before replying to Terry, Todd looked over at Echo, who was staring out the window, uninterested, and then myself, who was staring at him very interested. I folded my arms across my chest like I was the muscle of the operation and posing for a badass militia photograph.

"You were angry this morning. You still are." His face contorted into concern. "Why don't we take some time...the entire day, maybe, and rethink the words we said to each other."

"I don't need to take an entire day to rethink anything. You're an asshole, and I don't need you around my kids. Don't make me throw something at you."

Yes, my mother swears around us and yells at other people about their evil influences. However, I did clear my throat, and Terry glanced over and noted Echo sitting there.

"Echo, go get your bookbag." She then glanced at me. "Can you give us some space?"

I threw up my hands. "Happily." Inwardly, I was back to feeling like I was doing an end-zone dance, and angels were singing my favorite funkadelic song. But I put up a good show of being annoyed and inconvenienced and slipped back into my bedroom. I wasn't ready to go just yet.

I rooted around for the flannel shirt I was going to throw over my T-shirt. I could hear them bickering in the kitchen. I was able to understand quickly the argument had something to do with a woman.

"Why is she calling you?"

"You know how exes are. She was lonely."

"My lonely exes don't call me at two in the morning."

"Terry, I told her not to call me. What do you want me to say?"

"You told her not to call you at two in the morning. Seems to me you're saying she can call you at other times."

Todd raised his voice. "This is ridiculous. I'm not going to argue about it."

"Then don't. I won't tolerate cheating. I don't need my girls to see that kind of treatment."

"I'm leaving." I could hear the kitchen stool being pushed back. He stomped over to the back door near my bedroom and opened the screen. "I'll call you later. Give you some time to calm down."

"Don't bother," my mother yelled, but by then, the screen door had slammed closed, and Todd's feet were pounding the sidewalk down the street.

I waited for my mother to leave out the front door with Echo before emerging from my room. Seven months before the explosion. Seven months, but it had finally happened.

If there was one thing my mother wouldn't tolerate in her relationships, it was infidelity. Terry Wynters had to be the top chicken in any man's hen house. Todd was a good-looking guy who most assuredly caught the eye of many a girl. It didn't surprise me he would communicate with other women.

This breakup had been easy with little bloodshed. I didn't have to bring in my suspicions about the drugs or continue with my snooping. A cloud lifted. I could visualize a new and happy life ahead of me. My good mood carried me through school. I even smiled at that idiot, Felicia Norris, in US History when she waved at me. Twice, Joanie asked me what was up. I just laughed.

I hope you noticed Jehovah, but I only had three hot sauce packs today.

WOLFIE

My jubilation did not last long. Jehovah didn't even give me a full twenty-four hours of happiness. Unaware of what lay ahead, I biked home, imagining the pleasure of seeing Todd's belongings tossed out into the street. This glorious image made me salivate. Hell, I'd even place my red mug on top of his stuff, if it meant that he was truly gone.

However, when I reached the house, there was no sign of my mother's fury or even that she was home from getting Echo from school. No opera music or smells from the kitchen. The place was quiet. A rare occurrence. I had the house to myself.

I made myself a cup of tea and moved into the living room. With no one else in the house, I didn't have to hide in my bedroom. I stretched out on the couch, sipped my tea, and relaxed with images of Todd's clothes lumped out on the sidewalk (my mother never bothered with boxes) and dogs walking by and peeing on the piles.

A hard thud brought me out of my relaxed state. Another one caused me to place my tea down and sit straight up. I looked around me, trying to discern the direction of the noise. BAM. Then a silence followed by smaller thuds. The commotion was coming from my mother's bedroom.

I quietly got up and moved down the hallway towards the room. In addition to the pounding noises, I was hearing grunts and the sounds of someone straining themselves. I knew my mother wasn't home, so I wasn't too worried about walking in any sexual activity. The door was slightly open, and I pushed it wider so I could peer inside.

There were long-stemmed red roses tossed around the floor of the room, and the grunting noise I was hearing was Todd stuck in the window. He appeared to be in the process of climbing in. I walked into the bedroom and stood there looking down at him as he strained and tugged. His head was low, so he didn't see me. One arm was inside, but the other was caught as his shoulders were too broad. He was a fat Pooh bear stuck in Rabbit's house. I continued to watch him. He must have sensed my presence because he stopped his movement and lifted his head.

"You're home," he commented.

"Yes, I live here," was my reply.

"I didn't think anyone was here."

He paused for a second as if he was thinking something through. "Hey, can you give me a hand?"

I started to move forward, but he stopped me with a quick shaking motion of the hand that was inside. "Wait. Wait. Don't step on the flowers. I was bringing those in when the stool fell out from under me outside."

"Would you like me to put them on the bed?" I asked.

"That would be great. That would be great." His voice was tight. He was breathing hard.

I gathered up the roses and placed them out of the way on the bed. By my estimate, Todd had purchased about fifty stems.

"Do you want me to push you or pull you?"

"What?"

"Pull you in or go outside and push you in. Or I could push you out."

"I'm stuck," he said

"I can see that."

"No, my sweater is caught on the bush. Could you take care of it? I don't want to lose this sweater."

I sighed and went out the front door of the house and around the side. From this viewpoint, Todd's situation looked even more ridiculous. The stool had fallen over, and I righted it so he could rest his feet and stop swinging them around. I saw the problematic branch had snagged the edge of his sweater and unhooked the garment. There were a few snags, but they could be pulled out to the point where they would be unnoticeable. However, I saw there was a much bigger problem, and I came back into the house.

"Did you fix the sweater?" he asked when I re-entered the bedroom.

"Yes," I said. "But you are going to have to take it off. I can't pull or push you through without it getting messed up on the windowsill. If we work it off you, I can keep it from tearing. Then I'll pull you through."

You may wonder why I was so helpful. Well, I saw the scenario, and this guy was trying to surprise my mother by leaving flowers in her room. The evidence was there, and I couldn't keep him from making this romantic gesture. Anything negative I did at this point would only boomerang on me. Besides, my mother would be home soon with Echo, and being helpful could work to my advantage. Or so I thought.

There was a step ladder on the back porch off my bedroom. I went to retrieve it and carried it outside. The ladder gave me enough height to work Todd's sweater up to his shoulders and then gently work the material over his head and through the small gaps between his body and the window frame. I had gotten most of it safely through when I saw I would have to do the rest from the inside.

"Hold on," I said. And ran around the house and back into the bedroom. Boy did this guy owe me big. I was assisting him far and beyond what he deserved. I began to wonder if this was something I could barter with. But what? I could see the current wave of events were not going my way. The gesture with flowers would get my mother's attention. It was soon enough after the morning fight for her to bestow forgiveness. If a week had gone by or even a few days before Todd made a move, she would have blocked him. But his timing was perfect. Shit. She would take him back. I felt the four walls of frustration, failure, disappointment, and despair shifting into place to form a box to contain me.

The last section of Todd's sweater that needed to be worked through was the area on his arm inside the house. By holding up the window frame with my shoulder, I was able to use two hands on the task. I got the material past his head and was working the part that was on his shoulder. And that's when it happened. I touched the tattoo. I touched the tattoo of his dog.

I fell back like I had been zapped by lightning. A small scream lodged in my throat. Todd looked over at me. His eyes showed concern as if he was worried about me, but that was impossible given what I just saw.

"Wolfie," I said softly. There was a moan in my voice, and I tried to keep my emotion from betraying me. "Oh, no. Oh, no."

Todd's eyes held mine. He was trying to figure out why I was suddenly mournful. "You've seen this tattoo," he said. "I lost him years ago."

Our eyes remained locked. Comprehension was seeping through me as I began to understand what I saw.

"Can you pull me in now?" he asked.

The mood in the air shifted. My sorrow was turning into anger and then fear. But Todd... His eyes stayed on mine because he knew. He knew something had happened, but he wasn't sure what. I had quickly gone from Miss Helpful to Miss I'm Not Touching You. To emphasize that point, I jumped up and fled the room.

"Bess," he screamed after me. "Bess, C'mon. I need your help."

I ran.

I ran out of the front door and almost collided with my mother, who had Echo behind her. Echo was carrying a bag of art supplies, which explained their delay in getting back to the house.

"Bess, where are you going?" She was bewildered.

"I forgot something at school," Saying anything to keep her from stopping me. I cried over my shoulder. "Todd's inside."

"What? What? Where are you going?"

But those last words were caught in the wind. I was running.

It seemed like my feet couldn't move fast enough. I wanted my bike, but there was no way I was going back. At first I thought I was running just to get away, to put distance between myself and the loathsome man stuck in my mother's bedroom window.

But I wasn't running away I was running towards something; to someone. Twenty minutes later, I was at Luther's apartment building. I collapsed on the steps outside and pulled myself up into a ball. Rocking back and forth with my head buried in my knees - that's how Luther found me when he got home.

With no words, he took me inside.

I slept.

When I awoke, I was lying on the couch in the living room. A cedar colored knitted afghan was covering me. It was one Luther's grandmother had made for him years ago. My nose picked up the smell of a sandwich in front of me - ham and cheese with mustard on wheat. Sitting in the chair across from me was Luther. He uncrossed his legs and put down the little glass of whiskey he was sipping.

"Good, you're awake," he said.

He went into the kitchen, and I could hear him puttering with the kettle. Seconds later, he came back in and set a cup of chai tea in front of me.

"Eat," he said. "I'm out of hot sauce. You cleaned me out the last time you were here."

"What time is it?"

"It's late. Past nine o'clock."

"Oh, my God." I sat up and threw back the blanket.

"Holdup. You're not going anywhere. You're spending the night here."

"I can't," I protested.

Luther moved back to his chair and picked up his whiskey.

"I took the liberty of using your phone and calling that friend of yours, Rueben," he said. "Told him to contact your mom and say you were studying and going to spend the night at his place."

I nodded. Terry would buy that. Especially since she would go in the house and see the roses and Todd in her window and think I was upset about him being there. After the fuss with the flowers and the requests for forgiveness, she would forget all about me.

"Is that my shirt you're wearing?"

I looked down at the flannel shirt I was wearing over my Tshirt and shorts.

"Yes," I responded.

"I wondered where that one went to. How many of my shirts do you have?"

"Three."

"Did you know you cry when you are sleeping? Not out loud, but tears. They fall down your cheeks, but you don't utter a sound." Luther pointed at the sandwich. "Eat," he said again. "And then you are going to tell me what's going on."

"I can't."

Luther motioned to the sandwich. "Eat." Then after I started taking a few bites. He added, "You have to."

Luther watched me finish the sandwich. He waited as I sipped the spiced tea. He took a few sips of whiskey and then put the glass down on the table next to him.

"Bess, you have to tell me."

"She won't believe me."

He nodded his head as if that could be true. "Try me. Tell me."

"It's awful."

"I know, baby girl."

And I talked.

***

Lucy had raised Wolfie since he was a puppy. When Lucy and Todd decided they would move in together, Lucy brought her beloved dog with her. In those days, Todd worked as a bartender in Hayward. He gravitated towards jobs that gave him daily access to people. "Service jobs," he would say. "I love to be of service." Most of the story Todd shared about what happened with him, and Lucy was the truth. Except he left out a crucial part.

When Lucy broke up with Todd, she left a note. She was away on a trip, and in the letter, she said she would be moving out when she returned. She would be picking up her things and her dog. For three days, Todd stared at that dog. He was stunned Lucy was leaving him, and all she wanted was her dog back. Hatred built up inside of him as he reread the note again and again. Then, the night before Lucy was due to return, and the animal was sleeping with his head in Todd's lap, Todd reached down and snapped Wolfie's neck.

***

"He killed the dog," I said to Luther. "With his bare hands, he killed the dog."

"Why would he tell you this?" Luther asked.

I had to fudge here, because Luther didn't know what I could do,

202

and that Todd hadn't told me directly. "He wants me to know what he's capable of," I said in a whisper.

Luther shot out of the chair like a rocket. His hands were clenched into solid rocks. "That motherfucker," he roared. "He threatened you?"

I started to cry. I couldn't let Luther interfere. If he did, he would be in violation of the restraining order and thrown in jail. Luther was the only way Echo and I could escape from this mess. He had to remain an option. He could be a safe haven.

"I'll be okay," I said to Luther. However, now, I didn't know how that was possible.

"What are you talking about, Bess? That man has threatened you. And your little sister is in the house. This is crazy! What is your mother thinking?"

"She doesn't know," I responded. And if I tell her, she won't believe me. She'll think I'm lying. She says she loves him." I was sobbing now.

Those words deflated Luther. I could see sorrow wash over him, and the fury he had been displaying earlier melted inside. He still loved my mother and hearing that she loved another man was heartbreaking. Luther stood still for a second and then approached me, taking me slowly into one of his giant bear hugs. "What can I do? What do you need me to do?" he asked.

I took some deep breaths, engulfing myself in the security of his scent and the aftershave he wore. I answered him as honestly as I could. "I need you to stay out of jail. I need you to be our strength and our secret."

NANCY DREW & HER CREW

I n the next few days, I was fueled by an anger I didn't realize resided within me. I raged, and every moment awake, and every breath I took was centered around bringing Todd down. I sucked back hot sauce to maintain my focus and fire.

Joanie gave up asking me how many I was consuming a day, and just handed me a bottle of Tabasco sauce to carry in my backpack. "Here," she said. "This is cheaper."

It was while I was fired up that Operation Green Ribbon was fully launched. I brought Joanie and Rueben into the activity. I knew I would need them as alibis and witnesses and legwork. Luther having Rueben cover for me the night before, planted the idea. If I am going to keep Luther out of things, I will need my friends.

I told Rueben and Joanie I was building a case against Todd so my mother would dump him. This was something they could readily get behind. Neither one of them liked Todd, and they knew my home life had been miserable since he came on the scene. They both believed the evidence we were accumulating was connected to Todd cheating on my mother and not drug related. I let them think that. If they thought we were building a case against Todd because of drugs, they would have insisted the police get involved.

Neither Joanie nor Rueben understand how the legal system works the way I do. Neither one of them is in it. They didn't have a fat file sitting in family court with multi-colored post-its sticking out of it. After the situation went down with Luther, and I saw how my mother could bend the story against the man she used to love, I realized certain elements were always going to be in play. If it's going to be your word against someone, you had to have leverage, and the leverage doesn't have to be facts. A white person has leverage over a person of color. A man has leverage over a woman. An adult has leverage over a child, but a child can gain leverage with specific keywords. I couldn't pit Luther against Todd because Todd had the advantage.

So, yes, I am a terrible friend because I misled my buddies, but on the other hand, because of me, they have great stories to share and can write interesting personal statements for college. Win-win.

Earlier observations revealed Duane was the flunkie when it came to carrying the drugs. He was the flunkie because, due to his low position on the totem pole, the drugs were on his person most of the time. This allowed Todd deniability. You would think Duane would change his drug bag once he realized how close it resembled mine, but he didn't. He must have thought it was an asset. By marking my bag with a bright green ribbon, I had helped the situation. Both Duane (and Todd) believed I was ensuring we would always be able to tell the difference between the bags. A de facto system was in place where I would leave my bag marked with a green ribbon on the top shelf, and Duane left his bag on the bottom. It was practically a routine.

But the critical element was in my demeanor. I stopped fighting Todd. I didn't suddenly become nice (that would have sent out rocket flares), but I stopped resisting him. I would step away from situations and not counter with an opposing opinion. If Todd suggested pizza for dinner, I didn't fire back with the response of "I hate pizza," which I used to do, even though I liked pizza. I didn't pretend I was gagging when he gave an opinion or roll my eyes when he spoke. With this defanged teenager lurking around, Todd believed he had won. Not that he had won me over, but just that he had won. I put up with his smugness because I knew this was a chess match.

I realized something else quickly with my attitude change. I was being ignored. My earlier hostility to Todd had painted me red, but now I could leave when I wanted, and there wasn't a sudden request for me to announce where I was going. I had become invisible. YES!

I was meeting with Joanie and Rueben on the 5th floor of Central library. There was less foot traffic up there, and we could spread out our schoolwork on the rectangle tables. At the moment, though, we were huddled together. My mother was so happy about the flowers and the reconciliation with Todd, she was having a dinner party this weekend. I was sharing with them my (false) suspicions that Todd was cheating on my mother, and Rueben was confused.

"What is in the book bag, and why are we following it?" Rueben asked.

I sighed. I had to make this sound credible and worth the effort. "I am pretty sure Todd is communicating with his other girlfriend via messages in the backpack Duane is carrying."

"Whaaat?" said Joanie. "Why doesn't he just text her?"

"Yeah?" Rueben added.

"Because my mother looks at his phone all the time," I answered.

I didn't know if that was true, but it sounded good. Joanie must have agreed because she nodded her head in affirmation. "Sounds like your Mom," she said.

I continued. "At the dinner parties is when we can catch them because Duane always leaves for some reason."

"That's right! He does." Joanie was starting to see I may have a point.

"Yeah, he got me skittles one time," Rueben said.

"And then he comes back without the backpack," I said, making it sound mysterious.

"This seems really complicated," Joanie protested.

"So, what does he do with the backpack?" Rueben asked. I knew I could count on Rueben to see what the real purpose of the exercise was.

"That's where you guys can help me out."

"How?" asked Joanie. She really wasn't getting it.

"We could follow him," Rueben interjected. "Next time he leaves the dinner; we'll have a reason to leave as well. Bess will stay at dinner, and it won't look suspicious."

Bingo. That's exactly what I wanted Rueben to say. Now it wasn't my idea. It was Reuben's idea. My friends will act when it looks like I don't have it all figured out. It's the curse of being perceived as bossy.

"That could work," I said, nodding my head to encourage Rueben to keep going.

"I'm still confused," Joanie said. "What does Duane leaving with a backpack have to do with Todd having an affair?"

"Joanie, listen. We need to follow the backpack." Rueben was running with it. "When Duane leaves the party, we make some excuse to go. I'll say I'm not feeling well or something, and you're driving so you'll take me home. But really, what we do is follow Duane."

"Is this safe?" Joanie asked.

"Of course, unless he goes someplace sketchy or something," Rueben answered. "But he's not going far because he is back within half an hour most of the time. We just watch and see where he leaves the backpack and report back to Bess."

"And then what is Bess going to do?" Joanie asked.

Both Joanie and Rueben turned their heads to look at me.

"I'll see who picks it up and what she looks like." I fidgeted with a piece of paper and looked down. "And I'll take pictures," I added.

"I'm still not getting this," Joanie sighed.

"Don't worry," said Rueben. "It will be fun."

With Rueben on board with the subterfuge, it was a piece of cake. Rueben can make any challenge a game. And if it wasn't dangerous, Joanie was on board.

Two nights later, Joanie and Rueben were at the house in preparation for their portion of Operation Green Ribbon. Rueben had brought this kit with him containing items that would make it look like he was allergic to something. This would be their pretense for Joanie to rush him home when Duane left. Rueben planned to go to the bathroom and come back with a face of irritated skin and red eyes using a harsh exfoliating skin scrub he had taken from his mother and a few strips of chili pepper he planned to touch with his fingers and then place the oils near his eyelid. I cringed when I heard that part.

"Rueben, dial it back," I said. "You are not going to have the time to do all this. But you get an "A" for effort."

"That's what I was telling him," Joanie huffed. She was standing there with her hands on her hips, looking exasperated. I could tell mentally; it had been a long car drive from Rueben's house to mine.

"Rueben, when Duane leaves, you are going to have to immediately say you are not feeling well and bolt. There will be no time for you to craft a Ferris Bueller excuse." I smiled and looked over at Joanie. She was chewing on her lower lip. Second thoughts or just Rueben fatigue?

"I'm impressed you were willing to put hot pepper oil near your eye," I said, clapping Rueben on the shoulder. "That's commitment."

Rueben looked disappointed, but he understood delays would hinder the operation. I took his "allergy" kit and tossed it on the bed in my room. Out in the kitchen, Ollie was working up a meal that smelled like fried chicken and macaroni and cheese. With a fantastic aroma in the air and my friends by my side, I was starting to get excited. I motioned for Rueben and Joanie to enter the room so I could close the door. "Besides," I whispered. "What would Ollie do if you pretended you got sick because of his food."

"But isn't that what I'm doing?" asked Rueben.

"No, just say you don't feel well, like its a fever or a headache. You don't need to link it to the food."

Rueben approved. "Good thinking."

Outside my bedroom, I heard Todd's voice greeting Ollie. Todd and Ollie maintained a civil relationship. Todd knew the rules about staying out of the kitchen when Ollie was at work, so their paths didn't cross very often. I poked my head out, and Todd saw me. He smiled at me like we were best buddies.

In the past, that dopey smile would have gotten me to grab a hot sauce pack. But this was a fired up and focused Bess, and I was not going to let this monster get my goat. I brushed past Todd and entered the living room. Rueben and Joanie were behind me like devoted followers.

Duane had already arrived, and it looked like he had brought Annika along with him. Clutched in Duane's hands was the backpack - the focus of the enterprise. I was pretty sure Duane was going right to Cosmic Hearts tattoo parlor. And Todd had given him the access code on the alarm, and he was leaving it there. Then either Todd or someone else was filling the bag with the stuff. The bag was not seen in Todd's possession. That's what I believed this whole thing was about. Todd could not be seen holding the bag.

Nick had blown it back when I threw the water on him. Not that they were thinking I would do that, but it opened their eyes to the problem of using the house as an operation post. I was an obstacle to move around. I had ruined that batch, and Todd had probably had to pay for it in some way. I wondered if the bandaged burned hand Todd had been sporting shortly after the Nick episode had been a form of punishment and not an accident. Maybe his boss had pointed out it was stupid to have the drugs on the premises where minors lived. There was a lot of increased traffic coming in and out of Cosmic Hearts. The tattoo parlor was now the perfect place to operate out of and the ideal place to hide the stuff.

I watched Annika for a bit and the way she interacted with everyone. She giggled and squeaked and thoroughly washed away any ideas you might have about the types of people who dress up in Goth fashion. She may wear black clothing and heavy kohl around her eyes, but Annika was an insipid bubbly sunshine girl. The dark ripped attire and the pounds of makeup were like a costume she wore. But it didn't matter, Goth or sunshine; she still annoyed the hell out of me.

Joanie came up beside me and handed me a water bottle. It was one of the personal ones folks fill up, so they are not littering the planet with wasteful plastic bottles and worrying about BPA toxins in their bodies. "What's this?" I asked.

"Your personal hydration system. Water with squirts of Tabasco. I even added a little lemon and honey."

I smiled with appreciation. "Nice," I replied.

"I got your back," Joanie said.

Oh my God, I was beginning to feel all warm inside. Like hope was bubbling up inside me. I had to admit this was becoming fun, but I refrained from doing something dorky like high-fiving Joanie or giving her a thumbs up.

"Let's eat," Ollie called out, and the game was afoot.

***

Dinner was concluded, and Joanie and Rueben and I cleared the table of dishes. People were kicking back with beer and wine, and Ollie had picked up ginger beers for the younger folks.

Echo didn't like hers and after taking a sip, announced very loudly, "Blah." She reared her head back to deliver a spit take for comic effect (she's been watching WAY too many cartoons), but Terry sharply cried "No!" and snapped her finger to get Echo's attention. Terry then pointed to the bathroom down the hall. "Spit it out there in the sink." Echo scowled and reluctantly left the room. She was clearly angry; her perfectly timed comic bit had been foiled by her own mother. Everyone laughed, and Terry shook her head and exclaimed, "You see what I have to deal with!"

Annika piped in. "She's adorable. I love her spirit."

Terry responded, "Her spirit is delightful, but try combing her hair!" That got an even bigger laugh. They all roared, which is good because I was sitting there with my mouth wide open. I couldn't believe she said that. One-she never does Echo's hair. I'm the one that runs a comb through those copper snarls and pulls out the leaves and flowers and toys. Two-she always complained about MY spirit, but I guess it looks cute when it is housed inside Echo.

It's a good thing Joanie and Rueben were there, or I might have said something flippant, gotten my mother angry, and jumped into a shouting match, and then Operation Green Ribbon would have been toast. Instead, I took a giant swig from my water bottle and immediately began choking. I had forgotten Joanie had doused the drink with Tabasco sauce. My mouth sputtered, and I ended up doing the spit take Echo had attempted five minutes ago. Tears were in my eyes as I tried to regain my breath. Everyone was looking at me with concerned expressions.

Ollie came over to deliver the Heimlich, but my mother stopped him by saying, "If she can cough, then she can breathe." Ollie shimmied back to his wine glass, and exited into the kitchen, announcing he was warming up the cobbler.

Joanie leaned in from my right. Her arm was on my shoulder. "Are you okay?" she asked.

I nodded in the affirmative and waved my hand, indicating everyone else should carry on. They quickly did, and the topic moved to some of the challenging design work my mother and Dusty had done in the last week. I whispered to Joanie, "Soon." She nodded and looked across the table at Rueben and mouthed, "Soon," slightly bobbing her head in the direction of Duane. Rueben's eyes widened, but I couldn't tell if he understood the message. He started to fidget with his napkin.

Sure enough, once ink designs were mentioned (and they always are with this group), Todd found a way to discuss his tattoos and talk about Wolfie. Now that I had uncovered the truth about Todd, I realized Wolfie or talking about the dog must be a secret communication between Todd and Duane. Todd spoke about the dog a lot, and everyone had heard the sad story. The first number of times I heard Todd talk about Wolfie, I thought he was a dog lover, but his behavior around dogs at the park and on the street didn't bear that out.

Then I felt the Wolfie story was a way of showing off and revealing a tender side for the gullible women who would fall for that type of thing. Rueben was right. After the dinner, Duane would find an errand to do. I was piecing the situation together, and I suspected "Wolfie" was the trigger word between Todd and his flunkie.

Todd was saying how much he missed having a dog around, and my mother reached over and patted his arm. "Perhaps we'll get one for the girls," she cooed. Todd smiled at her. I wanted to barf and inject Echo wanted a kitten, not a puppy. She wanted two kittens, but we were told Todd was allergic.

Suddenly Duane was up saying he needed to get a prescription filled before the pharmacy closed.

"How come you don't use a 24-hour place?" I asked. I peeked over at Rueben to see if he was ready. Rueben was sitting red-faced and staring at his hands. The napkin he had been fidgeting with was tied up in enough knots to make Popeye the sailor proud.

"I use the spot around the corner from my place," Duane stammered. "They close at seven."

"Are you coming back?" asked my mother. "We've got dessert. I think it's a berry cobbler."

"Yeah, yeah," Duane responded, and he was gone.

"That was fast," my mother remarked. She turned and looked at Todd. "Do you think we'll need ice cream? I should have told him to get ice cream." She yelled into the kitchen, "Ollie, do we need ice cream?"

Ollie shouted back, "Naw, we're good."

Precious seconds were passing. Joanie and I both turned our heads to look at Rueben. He was just sitting there.

"Psst," Joanie hissed.

Rueben didn't move.

"PSST," Joanie hissed again. She was practically spitting.

Rueben stood up quickly, almost knocking the chair back. "I..." He sputtered out. "I...I...think..." He now had everyone's attention. "I...think..." He was stuttering, staring at the numerous faces looking at him. His face was the color of strawberries. I could see he was losing his nerve, and he just wanted to sit down. *What the hell?*

It was Joanie to the rescue. "I think you're sick," she said. "I'll take you home." She swooped down on Rueben, snatched his jacket off the couch, and whisked him out the back door. Seconds later, we could hear the car engine of Joanie's dad's station wagon turning over and Joanie pulling out.

All the adults turned to me as if I had an explanation for the odd behavior of my friends. I didn't have one, but I tried. "He had a rough day at school. Some kids threw him in a locker." The adults all nodded their heads and murmured in universal understanding. It was kind of weird.

Minutes later, I received a message from Rueben. "I'm sorry. (sad emoji face) We are following him now. Save me some cobbler. (happy emoji face)"

BIG DADDIES AND ORANGE KITTIES

I heard back from Joanie the next morning. She sent a flurry of brief text messages. "Can't talk. Dad. Went 2 Tobacco Joe. Telegraph. Left inside." It was Saturday morning, so I knew she would be going door to door doing pioneer work for the next few hours. After that, her group went to lunch and then Joanie usually spent the rest of the day spending time with her father. The earliest I would get to talk to her was Saturday night.

Rueben was also unreachable on Saturdays. He worked his Aunt's tamale booth at the farmer's market until two o'clock. I could go down there, but I didn't want to infuriate his Aunt Rosita, who was my primary connection when it came to brand name hot sauce packets.

I was feeling antsy. I needed something to do. I needed to engage my brain. I needed to have friends who didn't have family obligations on a Saturday morning. I opened my phone and looked up Tobacco Joe. It was a smoke shop located on Telegraph near the university campus. I scrolled through a few pictures. It didn't seem like there was much there. It wasn't the type of place that would jump out at you. You'd miss it if you weren't looking for it. It looked like the size of a closet.

I knew better than to go there. If anyone who knew me, like Todd or Duane (or possibly Annika, as I still didn't know how connected she was) saw me in the area, then the gig would be up. I decided it wouldn't hurt to ride my bike past the place. I threw on an oversized denim shirt of Luther's I had been wearing lately, grabbed my bike helmet, and headed out of my room.

However, when I went out to the kitchen, I saw my sister at the table. The expression on her face was heartbreaking. On the table were pieces of torn paper, and Echo was trying to tape them back together. Tears were flowing from her eyes as her fingers tried to maneuver the paper correctly so she could apply the tape. She kept wiping the water from her face, and unfortunately, damp fingers make using tape more difficult.

I slowly approached the table to see what picture she was trying to tape back together. But I knew. I already knew.

"What happened?" I asked softly.

Echo's crying intensified, and now sobs were heaving from her chest. I looked at the crayoned images on the paper, and my gut feelings were confirmed. Echo had drawn a family picture that included Mom, me, and Echo. We were standing in a garden of flowers and green grass and, suspiciously, there was a white kitten at Echo's feet. (Echo was dropping hints) Echo's drawings of me always showed me with wild curly dark hair down around my shoulders, even though I didn't wear it that way. My abundant dark hair matched her red hair, and I believe it was her way of showing we were sisters.

Her drawings of our mother always had the high ponytail that she wore while doing her inking work. And instead of covering our mother's body with floral tattoos, Echo would suggest the ink by placing one or two on the body and then having our mother stand in a bed of flowers. I always thought it was an effective creative decision.

My brain was whirling as I pieced the images together. Why had Echo's family picture been torn up? But as I said earlier, I knew. Deep down, I knew. Within seconds I saw the confirmation. One of the images Echo was trying to tape back onto the picture was of Ollie.

She had drawn Ollie with his blue and white kimono and the butterfly sleeves. But it was the other image I was sure had created the fury. It was Luther. Echo had drawn him big and smiling, holding an orange kitten in his arms. Luther and Ollie were ripped out of the picture. This action also caused my right arm to be torn off as well.

I bent down to assist Echo with repairing the picture. Echo's crying was so loud, I didn't hear my mother enter the kitchen. Suddenly, she was upon me.

"Give me your phone," she demanded.

"What? What's going on? Who ruined Echo's picture?" I asked.

"Just give me your phone, Elizabeth. NOW."

I went to my room and retrieved the device. As I walked back, I thanked Jehovah for giving me the wisdom to delete the earlier text messages from Joanie and Rueben and not storing Luther's number in my phone. The minute Terry snatched the cell out of my hand and scrolled through the recent calls and messages, I knew she was looking for evidence of Luther.

Echo's sobs dwindled down to baby whimpers as my mother searched for confirmation we were betraying her. Her fingers swiped up and up as she scrolled through the phone numbers and text messages. Every now and then, she'd pause and read something through, but thankfully, thankfully, I knew there was nothing there to incriminate me. Terry stopped at a number. Her eyes narrowed.

"Whose number is this?" she asked, holding up the screen so I could see.

It was the phone number for Officer Lopez.

"The policewoman who came to investigate the break-in a few months ago," I answered.

"Why do you have her number in your phone?"

I shrugged. "She gave it to me. I thought it would be good to have it on the phone instead of searching for a card, in case there was another break-in."

My mother scrutinized my face for signs of falsehood. "You should delete it." She said and handed the phone back to me. She looked back over at Echo, who had patched the picture back together. I noticed the drawing of Luther had not been added back in, and it was gone from the table. Where had Echo hidden the picture?

My mother turned and looked at me again. She was pretending she had calmed down, but I could feel the sparks flying off her body. "Would you like to tell me why she is drawing pictures of Luther?"

Instead of answering that question, I asked, "What happened?"

"She showed me this picture she did at school of the family."

"What was in it?" I asked.

My mother's face was turned away. She was looking at Echo, watching her. "She had the three of us." I noticed my mother didn't mention the kitten. "I said someone was missing. I asked her if she could add him to the picture, and then I would display it on the kitchen cabinet."

She paused before continuing, but I already knew what was coming next. Echo's tears and the torn picture told me what had happened. "And when she came back, she had added Ollie in that ridiculous costume he wears."

I waited, knowing there was more.

My mother continued. "I laughed, trying to play it off and said she was still missing someone. She smiled at me and said, "of course, mommy," and off she went." My mother turned and looked at me. Her face was stone. "So, you tell me why she came back with Luther in the picture. Tell me, Bess! WHY?"

Her fury was barely in check.

"She loves him," I answered. My voice was a whisper. I said it as if it was obvious. It was obvious.

And the fury escaped. "When are you girls going to drop this?

LUTHER. IS. OUT. I blame you, Bess. I blame you. I know she is seeing him somehow. I know it!"

I peeked a glance over at Echo. Her face had reddened when Terry mentioned seeing Luther. Echo must have cracked under pressure, but she hadn't mentioned Ollie. Thank God.

"It is embarrassing to have my daughters sneaking around to visit a man I kicked to the curb," my mother shouted. I don't know what's wrong with everybody here. Todd volunteered to go to the auto shop to speak to Luther, but I told him it was not necessary."

My body stiffened when she said that. If there been an altercation with Todd and Luther, that avenue of escape would have been compromised. Luther needed to remain on the sidelines.

"There is still too much Luther around this house!" my mother went on. She pointed her finger at me. "You read his books and listen to his music. Don't tell me that you don't. I can tell. I CAN TELL. I swear, sometimes I think I can still smell the man!" she exploded. "No more Luther. No more Aretha Franklin. No more pictures of him. I got rid of him. He is a menace. Or have you forgotten what happened? Have you forgotten, Bess? He threatened me. He punched a hole in my wall."

I couldn't let that statement go without a challenge. "He punched the wall so he wouldn't hit you. You started the fight. You attacked him. You scratched his face. You trashed the room."

My mother went silent. Her chest rose as her breath vigorously went in and out of her body.

"Is that what he told you?"

I didn't answer because Luther hadn't said anything about that night. I knew because I overheard the cops talking while Echo and I were sitting in the back seat of the squad car.

"Don't put Echo through what I went through," I said.

"And what, pray tell, was that?"

"An endless train of potential daddies."

I expected her to slap me, but instead she glared with flames in her eyes. "That's coming to an end. You understand? That's coming to an end. The current one...he's... he's a keeper. He's good to me. That's who you should have drawn in your little picture, baby girl." she snarled in Echo's direction. Echo whimpered and kept her head down.

"Not if I have anything to do with it," blared through my head. I kept that thought to myself.

"I'm going to the studio," my mother announced. "Clean yourself up!" she barked at Echo. She looked at me and added, "Do something with her hair! It looks like a rat's nest."

After the front door slammed, I took my sister and her ruined picture into her bedroom. I smoothed the image out on her polka dot bedspread and gazed at the happy figures my sister had drawn. By taping Ollie back into the picture, my right arm had been restored. Echo's artwork was always bright and cheerful, and the fact this picture had been attacked for what it depicted, saddened me greatly.

"Can I have this?" I asked.

Echo nodded. She then pulled out a folded-up piece of paper from the elastic waist of her leggings. "But this is mine," she said. It was the drawing of Luther and the orange kitten. She had hidden it away. Echo kissed the paper and then reached under her bed and pulled out a shoebox. The shoe box was one I had seen before. She made it in kindergarten, and it was covered with a collage of pictures cut from magazines. Rainbows, cookies, and kittens were represented all over the box. They were things my sister loved. She placed the drawing inside the box. Before she closed the lid and slid the box back under the bed, I saw there were other drawings of Luther in there.

Echo climbed into my lap, and for a while, I just held her. I rocked a bit from side to side, more to soothe my troubled thoughts than to

220

comfort my sister. I looked at the picture on the bed. Our sunny and lively family unit.

Echo spoke softly. "Mommy didn't understand. The teacher said we were to draw what made us happy. And that's what I did. I drew what made me happy, Bess."

I smoothed her hair and pulled her in tighter. "I know, baby. I know." We stayed that way for a long time.

SALLY'S STORY

Terry heard the tinkle of the star chimes when the door opened from the street, but she didn't look up to watch the person who had entered the studio. It had been a quiet morning with little traffic coming in. Dusty was due to arrive any minute, and Terry was glad her business partner hadn't seen her throwing up in the bathroom when she had gotten to the shop after her argument with Bess. Nerves, that's what it was. Nerves and emotions had made her nauseous. Now she was enjoying her cup of coffee and the crossword puzzle on her lap. If the person had questions, they would ask.

At the moment, the crossword puzzle was taxing her into a mental frenzy. These were answers she should know. The subject matter was centered on mermaids, and she was quite familiar with the breed as she had inked enough of them to last her lifetime and the lifetime of her daughters, and probably their daughters as well. Still, she found herself taking too long to answer questions like "Hans" for the four-letter spot asking, "Danish author of Little Mermaid" or "Manatee" as the seven-letter response for "sea cow."

So often, she could see the answer dangling in front of her, taunting and teasing, but not coming into focus enough for her to grasp the answer. Her brain was foggy. She wasn't sleeping enough. Terry took a sip of her coffee and reflected on the fact that even with the current lack of sleep, her life was good. She was happy. Yes, she was damned happy. Business was booming, as they say, she had a man in her life, and her children were healthy - thriving even.

The next question, eight down, was not making sense. "Location of little mermaid statue." The answer was Copenhagen. Terry had been there, she had seen the statue herself, touched it. But the space would only allow seven squares. *Christ, this wasn't making sense.*

Bess would know this, but Bess wasn't really speaking to her. Especially considering the blow-up, they just had.

Terry sighed, exasperated at the estrangement that was growing like thorns between herself and her oldest daughter. *If only Bess could move past Luther and put him in the rearview mirror where he belonged.*

She listened to the footsteps as the patron roamed over by the counter, showcasing Dusty's ability to create ghastly spiders and lightning bolts that appeared to sizzle off the skin. Listening to the person's movements, Terry realized the individual was wearing high heels, but there was no click on the floor. This person's soft steps were measured and mature. Terry stole a glance at the customer's footwear and confirmed a very stylish pair of Jimmy Choos were adorning the end of a sculptured leg. *That was surprising.* Jimmy Choos didn't usually step into Cosmic Hearts.

The polished older woman was still examining Dusty's work but had moved over to the biomech display. Terry was now brimming with questions, but she waited to see if the woman chose to engage. Was this someone shopping for a tattoo for her daughter? Her son? Husband? Or had she entered Cosmic Hearts to escape the panhandlers on the street, and now she was viewing the tattoo shop as a fascinating art museum with presentations of the tawdry, the obscene, the enchanted, and the childish?

The woman had now made her way past Dusty's section of the shop and was moving up on Terry's right. Terry kept her face down as if she was disinterested, but every pulse of her blood was dying to look at this woman who had entered her studio. But now she had committed to not-speaking until spoken to first, it would be hard at this point to look up and just watch. Terry decided the two of them were engaging in a secret battle of wills.

Out of the corner of her eye, Terry could see a tailored cream suit. It floated with the body's movement, and she caught a whiff of perfume. It was a crisp floral scent and expensive.

The movement had stopped, and Terry could feel the heat of the woman's gaze on the back of her neck. *C'mon lady, talk.*

She kept her focus on the crossword on her lap. Where the hell was the little mermaid statue, if not Copenhagen?

"Are you the artist?"

Finally, the woman had spoken. Terry released a silent breath of relief and looked up with alert eyes and her best "May I help you" expression.

"My work is over here to my left. If you're looking for something less sinister and dramatic, I'd suggest heading over there."

The woman didn't move. Her manicured hands rested on the counter.

"That's a striking display on your body," she said. "You clearly didn't do it yourself. Your partner, then?"

"No, I go see someone who is up in Guerneville." Terry leaned back in her chair so she could get a proper look at her unusual customer. "I did, anyway." Terry amended.

"Did they die?" the woman asked.

Terry gnawed on her lip when she answered and looked back down at her puzzle. "They moved on."

There was a silence, and the woman looked past Terry's head as if she was studying another piece of inked artwork, but Terry knew there was nothing behind her except for the calendar and the framed photo of her and Dusty and Bess outside the entrance of Cosmic Hearts the day it officially opened. Bess had been a huggable doll baby at that age, not the willful She-dragon hatchling that lived in the house right now. Terry missed her little "Mouse." When had she stopped calling Bess by that nickname? Hey, diddle diddle.

"Are you the person that does the tattoo ceremonies?" The voice startled Terry out of the lovely memory she was having. And the question caught her by surprise. Jimmy Choo lady didn't look like a woman who would ever seek out her premium service.

"Yes, I am. Is that what you are interested in?"

The woman paused before she spoke as if a decision was being made within the moment. A decision she couldn't take back.

"My name is Ellen Somerville."

And then, everything fell into place.

"I know who you are," Terry replied, and she gazed at Ellen's face with compassion. It was an elegant face with few signs of aging, just some crow's feet crinkled at the eyes. "I'm very sorry for your loss," she added.

The woman nodded, accepting the words she must have heard multiple times in the last year and would hear murmured gently for the rest of her life.

What happened to the Somerville family reverberated throughout the town. Their sad story was now a cautionary tale.

There were four daughters in the Somerville family. They were tall statuesque beauties with long hair and the bodies of slender giraffes. When they had walked together as children, they resembled steps moving in unison. When the girls reached adolescence, they all hit five feet ten and looked like a volleyball team missing two players. Three of the girls were smart, delightful, and engaging; wonderful to be around. But then there was Sarah, known as Sally.

Sally Somerville hit adolescence like a ton of bricks. She hated being the third girl in the family and decided to break out and rebel in every fashion she could. Sally chopped off her hair and dyed what was left of it black. She regularly wore makeup and bright colored lips in direct contrast to the freshly scrubbed look her sisters had. Sally started smoking pot, and when that didn't get enough of a rise out of her parents, she switched to cigarettes. She'd proudly come home and strut through the door, smelling like an ashtray. It was so bad Ellen asked the housekeeper to separate out Sally's clothing when the laundry was being done so the smell wouldn't permeate the attire of the rest of the household.

Ellen and Byron Somerville convinced themselves Sally was only going through a phase and if they made a big deal about her appearance and behavior, she would escalate matters. Ellen noted Sally's grades were still good in school, and her friends weren't too objectionable. If black hair and smoking was the worst thing Sally was going to throw at them, so be it. They were getting off lucky.

What the Somervilles didn't count on was inexperienced teenage driving. Berkeley is a city where almost a third of the population lives in the hills. The Berkeley hills contain homes, trails, and parks. If a person wishes to buy milk, or do anything involving a commercial transaction, they must come down from the hill.

It was Friday night, and Sheri Connors was the designated driver with her family's Pontiac. The Connors lived in the hills off Euclid. Four girls, ranging in age from sixteen to eighteen, were in the vehicle; Sally, Randee Hanson, Leah Higson, and Sheri behind the wheel. The car was low on gas because Sheri's brother had been driving earlier and had not filled up the tank. Sheri bitched about this because when the girls pooled their cash, they only had twenty bucks between them. Later in a statement, Leah Higson indicated it was Sally's idea to put the car in neutral to save gas and coast down the hill. The car had power steering and power brakes, and once it started rolling, the doomed girls were trapped. With no way to slow or steer the vehicle, they smashed into a tree before they reached the bottom of the hill. The car was crushed like a can. It was a miracle Leah survived.

Sheri may have been behind the wheel, but with Leah's statement and the radical visual rebellion the city had witnessed with Sally, it was only a short period before bad teenage driving became synonymous with Sally Somerville. Families would talk in hushed voices to their teenagers and use the phrase "Remember Sally Somerville" to get their kid's attention. Terry herself knew she had uttered those words to Bess when the private driving lessons started. Bess had scowled at her and sucked on one of those horrendous hot sauce packets.

Now here was the grieving mother standing in front of her wanting to know about the Beloved ceremonies. A thought pinged inside Terry, and she immediately swept it away for the guilt it brought on. Ellen Somerville was the perfect client. Doing an Ink for the Beloved ceremony for a Somerville would take the business to a level that, at this moment, she couldn't even fathom.

Terry explained the ceremony in detail to Ellen and drew up a contract for her to sign. They discussed design ideas and the size of the tattoo and its placement. Ellen was wary about the notion of getting something so permanent, but then Terry said, "She was your wild child. It is only fitting you memorialize her by doing something wild yourself". Ellen knew immediately what was in her heart to do.

By then, Dusty had entered the shop, and Terry was able to move Ellen to the back where they could have more privacy. Terry fixed two cups of tea as Ellen talked at length about her daughter. The bright girl who liked rabbits and sunflowers and chewy brownies, with no walnuts. Terry took notes and sketched a bit, but already she could see how the tragic teenager would be immortalized in spirit and ink.

Terry mentioned music could be added, and they had a lovely soloist, Annika, who could learn anything. Ellen asked for two songs written by Janis Ian "At Seventeen" and "Society's Child." Terry felt a surge of emotion. Tears almost escaped from her eyes as she wrote the entries into the contract.

"I love those songs," she whispered to Ellen. "But be careful, Annika will pierce your heart when she sings them." Ellen smiled. Their friendship was solidifying.

So much so that Terry shared the secret of the tiny sparrows inked on her left arm. "I understand loss," Terry said. "These birds are for my angels."

"There are five," Ellen observed.

"Yes. Five. I have two that survived, the others..." Terry's voice faded off as she brushed away the tears forming in her eyes. She brought her arm up and laid it across her heart the way she always did when she thought about her lost babies.

"Love them," Ellen said. "Hold them."

"One is now a teenager..." Terry was going to say more, but Ellen touched Terry's arm and lightly tapped the sparrows.

"Cherish that one," Ellen said softly.

Ellen's touch was similar to the way Bess stroked tattoos, but Bess refused to touch the ink on Terry's body. Terry understood why, but it hurt because they could only hug when Terry was wearing long sleeves.

A hug was needed now, and the two mothers embraced and breathed in their shared grief and pain.

As Ellen was preparing to depart, Terry stopped her and asked, "What do you know about mermaids?" and showed the woman the puzzle she was solving. "I've seen it in Copenhagen," Terry insisted. "Am I missing something here?"

"The answer is Solvang," said Ellen.

"How's that?"

"There is a replica of the little mermaid statue down in Solvang because of their large Danish population."

"Really?"

"Yes."

Terry laughed and filled in the answer. "I'll be damned."

Ellen smiled and left.

TOBACCO JOE

I ended up taking Echo to a movie and getting her ice cream. She was sullen for most of the afternoon, but by the time evening rolled around, she was laughing at cartoons on television, and you never would have known the sorrow she experienced when she started her day. They say kids bounce back, but what we really do is learn to survive. I wondered if Echo had learned never to show her heart's desire to our mother again.

Rueben wanted to hang out on Sunday, and I had a specific plan in mind. I kind of tricked him into accompanying me to the spot where the tobacco store was located by telling him I would buy him lunch. We had our choice between BBQ and a Thai noodle place. We chose Thai noodles. As we ate, I told Rueben about my plan and pointed out the tobacco store across the street.

"I should go in there with you," he said.

"You can't. Don't be offended, but you look like you are twelve."

"Okay, I'm offended."

"If something happens. I need someone to know I'm in there. If we both go in there, there's no back-up."

"It's just a woman in a tobacco shop. What are you thinking? FATAL ATTRACTION or something?"

I had forgotten about the "Todd is having an affair" excuse I had used on my friends.

"It could be a front," I countered.

"A front for what?"

"Drugs," I answered. It feels weird when you tell the truth, but it's part of a lie.

"And you say I have an over the top imagination," Rueben mumbled.

"Your stories always involve aliens and wizards," I replied

"I'd rather have a wizard than a drug dealer."

Me too, buddy. Me too. (I didn't say that out loud)

Rueben looked over at me and stared for a long time. I began to worry that he knew I was lying about the importance of the tobacco shop.

"Here." He gave me his CAL baseball hat. "Take out the braids and cover up your hair. You don't want her to be able to recognize you. If you are not out in ten minutes, I'm coming in."

***

The man behind Joe's tobacco counter had a pockmarked face and a permanent scowl. A plate with the remains of his lunch sat in front of him. It looked like he had gone to the BBQ place. Judging the congealed meat and the soggy fries, I was glad we had made the lunch decision to go with the Thai noodles.

"You're too young to be in here," he said. "I'm going to need some ID."

"I just have a few questions," I responded and moved up to the counter, hesitating to see if he was going to throw me out.

He picked up the small knife he had been using to cut his pork ribs and began picking his teeth. *Subtle. Real subtle.*

"What questions?" he snarled after removing the knife from his lip area.

"Have you seen this guy who is tall and blond around here?"

"A lot of guys are tall and blond." He shrugged like he was already bored with me.

"This one looks like Brad Pitt." I hated saying that but describing Todd as handsome didn't work. But comparing him to a movie star somehow made the connection for people.

"You talkin about Mackey?" *Bingo.* Mackey. Todd Mackey.

I was, but I didn't want to show my hand too soon. "I think so," I answered.

"Why? You looking to score?"

I hoped my eyes didn't grow into the size of saucers at that remark, but I felt my hands begin to sweat as my suspicions had suddenly been validated.

"Yes," I answered. *God, I was scared.* "But I'm not looking for weed."

"Pretty boy Mackey don't do weed," the ugly man answered. "Anybody can buy that now." The man's scowl deepened, and he gave me a hard once over. "You don't look like someone who gets high," he said. *Shit.*

I forced my face into my best sarcastic expression. "And what's that supposed to look like?" I replied. I threw my hands up as if to say *I'm done.* "I'm just looking for something to help me study - to cram for finals. Someone told me Brad Pitt could help me out, and I could find him here."

The ugly man held up one finger, telling me to hold. He then made a fist and struck himself hard in the chest. This brought out a nasty burp, and a beat later, I could smell the BBQ sauce. Disgusted, I turned around to leave. Outside, Rueben clocked me, moving towards the door, and I could see him heading to intercept me.

"Hold on, girly. Hold on." The ugly man called out, and when I turned back around, he waved me over. I gestured behind me, signaling Rueben to move back and out of sight.

"Sorry about that. You know I don't work on commission for that guy." *Which meant he did.* "But I can probably help you out. What is it you want?"

"I don't know. Pills."

"What kind of pills?"

"You're right. I don't usually do this, but I need something to keep me up."

"Speed?"

"Is that pills? Cause that's what I want."

"Yeah, yeah. Mackey's got pharmaceuticals with his hospital connections. Those are what you want. Minimum purchase is a hundred."

"A hundred pills?"

"No, a hundred bucks."

"How many pills is that?"

"Sixty."

"SIXTY?!"

"You want them or not? You're cute, but I don't have all day."

"I don't need sixty pills."

"Whatever you don't use, you can sell." *Holy Crap! Is this how people become dealers?*

"Do I buy them from you?" I asked. "I thought I was buying from Brad Pitt."

"Let's say I put in an order for you."

I paused the negotiations because there was no way I was going to buy the drugs. Technically, I had gotten the information I wanted. But this gross human being seemed to be a fountain of knowledge, and he was willing to share since he had burped in my face. Even humanity at the bottom of the barrel has a semblance of manners.

"What else does Brad Pitt have," I asked.

"I thought you wanted to study for your UC exams." Right. I had forgotten about the baseball cap claiming I was a college student.

I shrugged. "I might want to be more experimental later, After the exams. To celebrate."

The ugly man shook his head. "Nah. Stick to the pills, girly. You don't look like you can go crystal."

With the statement I'd be back once I went to the ATM, I walked out of the tobacco shop. I moved slowly because I felt if I didn't, I would run and betray my fear.

I rattled off a poor excuse for my spooked demeanor to Rueben. I told him the woman recognized me and threatened to tell Todd I had been in the store. It was a stupid lie, but my brain was more focused on the information I had received.

Back when my backpack had gone missing, Duane had taken it by accident and delivered it to this shop. This was where the drugs were placed inside their bag. The backpack was then retrieved, and the drugs were distributed. The guy at Tobacco Joe's worked with Todd, but he wasn't the boss. It was the comment about a commission that confirmed their arrangement. Todd was a dealer, and he moved many types of drugs. He was using our tattoo studio to handle transactions inconspicuously.

This was confirmation, but was it enough to take to the police? Was it enough to take to my mother?

I still had Officer Lopez's number in my phone. Could I call her? I realized the next step I took could blow my poorly bandaged and fragile world wide open.

MR. WHITTIER

I t doesn't often rain in California, but when it does, it pours. We can't just have a regular rainfall like everyone else. No. We must have a freakin storm.

When it comes down that hard, I don't bother with the bike. The side streets are flooded, motorists can't see for shit, and it's easier to dodge out of the way if you are a pedestrian. I had an umbrella, but what I really needed were boots - any kind of boots. I didn't want to soak my tennis shoes.

I thought I had seen an old pair that looked about my size about a year ago in the front closet. The front closet is the depository of all things communal. It's the Lost and Found bin of the house. Once a week, Ollie does a thorough clean of the house, and if he comes across something he doesn't recognize as belonging to one of the Wynters women, he chucks it into the front closet. There are lots of jackets, sunglasses, sweaters, and umbrellas in that closet. There are even some questionable items like skirts and bras. However, I don't think Ollie has ever come across a pair of panties. If he did, I'm sure we would hear about it. I think the whole neighborhood would hear about it.

In the past, the closet has been a goldmine at Halloween time. Echo and I would rummage through it and have the base items needed to create cool and colorful costumes.

Today, I wanted boots, and I was pretty sure I saw a pair in the far backspace. After blindly reaching around with my hands, I landed on something that felt like what I was seeking. I pulled out the items and found myself staring at a familiar pair of black hiking boots. These boots had belonged to Spiderwand, the creator of the mural on the side of the tattoo studio.

Memories of Spiderwand and his odd habits flooded back, and I sniffed the boots to see if they smelled like garlic. They didn't. I lined the shoe alongside my foot and saw they could be a fit. However, before I plunged my foot inside, I held them upside down and shook the boots hard. I once heard someone put their foot in a shoe that had been in a closet for a long time, and they were bitten by a spider that had taken up residence in the big toe. The story came out of Australia, but you should never take chances.

No spider came fluttering out, which would have been funny now that I think about it - a spider in Spiderwand's boots. I put the shoes on, and they were loose, but two pairs of socks made them workable, so I could go out in the rain.

It was a Saturday, and I was planning on sneaking a visit with Luther at the Auto Shop. My mother and Dusty were at Cosmic Hearts and Ollie had left to drop Echo off at a friend's house. I was feeling antsy and I needed to talk to somebody. Luther would be furious when he heard about the sleuthing I had done. But the information I had was proof Todd was using the tattoo parlour to house his drug business. Things were clearly pointing in that direction. I wanted to know if I could go to the police. I could contact that police officer, Lopez. Even though she was robbery and not narcotics, she would listen to what I had to say and then tell me who to speak to in the right department.

I wondered if I would get to wear a wire and trick Todd into talking. I smiled. That would be kind of fun. I could see myself getting Todd to admit what he was doing and maybe I could even get him to admit what he did to Wolfie. That would really freak out my mother. She'd back off then and perhaps even throw a frying pan at him.

My thoughts were about drugs and criminals and the court system, so imagine my surprise when my phone rang, and I saw the name flashing on the screen. Back in freshman year when Joanie made the twosome of Bess and Rueben into a trio, she had insisted we give her father our cell phone numbers. She said it was for her dad's peace of mind. Rueben and I weren't in the Kingdom Hall and her father needed a means to contact us. She made it sound like her father wouldn't let her hang out with us unless he had our numbers. It didn't seem like a big deal at the time, and we wanted Joanie to join our friend group, so phone numbers were exchanged. Over the years, I had never received a call or message from Mr. Whittier. Nothing. Until now.

I hesitated, but then hit the button to accept the call. "Hello?" I said into the phone.

"Is this Elizabeth Wynters? This is Keenan Whittier. I believe you are friends with my daughter, Joan."

"Yes," I replied. This was weird.

"Ms. Wynters, an opening in my schedule has presented itself this morning. I should be in your area in about an hour. I would consider it a kindness, if you would meet me for coffee."

"Okay..." I said.

"There is something I would like to discuss with you, and you should know Joan will not be present."

Mr. Whittier gave me the name and address of a coffee shop located on College Avenue. I was already familiar with the place. I ended the call feeling off kilter as if I was shifting between mindsets. I had to admit as weird as this was, I was insanely curious. I couldn't remember ever spending more than two seconds with Mr. Whittier. He'd wave at Rueben and me if we were in the house, but that was about it. I worried I wouldn't recognize him when I arrived.

When I entered the dark and musky cafe, he was the only black man wearing a suit on a rainy day. He was seated expectantly at a small table in the front. He nodded his head when I came in and formally stood to help me into the little wooden chair. He asked me what I would like, and I asked for a chai tea. It was all very strange like we were meeting on a blind date. My heart was beating like a rabbit. I was worried Joanie was in trouble. I was worried Mr. Whittier would tell me to stay away from his daughter. I was worried he thought I was a bad influence on Joanie, and since there was no way I would become a Witness, it was time to cut the purse strings.

However, asking me for coffee didn't make sense in that scenario. Mr. Whittier could have just called me or sent me a letter if this was his intent. Do you sit down and have coffee with someone if you are going to tell them to go away?

Mr. Whittier returned to the table with a chai tea for me and a single espresso for himself. We shared basic pleasantries for a minute. He asked about my family and my schoolwork. We even talked about the Golden State Warriors as Mr. Whittier mentioned he had playoff tickets, but Joanie had declined to go with him. Is this why he wants to talk to me because Joanie didn't want to see the Warriors play? Now that I think about it, that's odd. Joanie likes basketball.

"I imagine you are curious about why I asked to see you" *Yes. Yes, I am.*

He took the lemon peel and rubbed the rim of his espresso cup. "Recently, there have been many spirited discussions in my home, and most of the time, you are the center of the debate."

Oh shit, here it comes. The only thing in recent memory I had asked Joanie to do was follow Duane Rodriguez to the Tobacco Joe smoke shop. But her father couldn't possibly know about that. Could he?

Mr. Whittier continued. "I understand you are an excellent student."

I shrugged. I mean, what are you supposed to say? Hell yeah, I'm an excellent student.

"Your other friend, the boy. Joanie says he is going to be attending a school back east."

"Probably," I responded. "But Mr. Whittier, I'm not sure what this is about. This is our junior year. Rueben and I haven't made any decisions. We haven't even applied yet."

"Allow me to get to the point," Mr. Whittier said. He took a sip of his coffee. I decided this would be a good time to take a sip of my tea. It was still too hot.

"You know I lost my wife, Joan's mother, when Joan was ten years old. Since that time, I have struggled to raise my child as a single parent. The last few years have been very difficult because Joan is looking more and more like her mother and behaving like her. I must fight within myself to not be overly protective. Allowing Joanie to drive when my wife perished in an automobile accident took an enormous amount of prayer and faith. But I don't want to lose my daughter by clipping her wings or shielding her from the outside. Many Witness families watch their children flee from the domestic cages they construct - never to return. Denying college or higher education can be a cage. I understand allowing my daughter to leave and not keeping her from leaving will ensure that she returns. That is more important to me than whether or not she remains a Witness."

I remained silent. I wasn't sure what to say. I felt if Mr. Whittier had a tattoo on his body, this would be the story I would see. I was hearing what the tattoo would show me. It felt odd to have someone directly share their pain. Most of the time I inadvertently stumble across it by touching their ink. As Mr. Whittier spoke, I envisioned a tattoo I see on many bodies, showing a cage with the door open allowing the bird to escape.

There is a single portrait of Joanie's mother in the house, and hearing Mr. Whittier talk, I began to understand why there was only one picture. His grief was too much to withstand multiple images throughout the home. He saw his wife daily through Joanie. Every day he heard his wife's laugh. Every day he saw her pull her hair back from her face. That must be painful but also strangely comforting.

"You are a good friend to my daughter," Mr. Whittier added. "I am aware your home is ...." He paused for the word. *Uh oh, here it comes.* With Ollie's homosexuality and my mother's promiscuity and my illegitimacy, our home was a living embodiment of Christian values *"Don't do this."*

"Challenging" was the word Mr. Whittier settled on. "But all homes are challenging. Joan says yours is filled with spirit and freedom and love. Those are her words."

I almost choked on my tea. Joanie thought all that?

"Elizabeth, I want you to know I support my daughter's friendship with you. I trust her and I trust her judgment when it comes to you and your family."

While Mr. Whittier continued talking, I felt like sinking into my chair. All I could think about was the lies I had told Joanie and how I was deceiving her regarding the situation with Todd.

I had never had an adult talk to me about trust and felt so shitty about it.

"I will finish our meeting by saying Joanie has my blessing when it comes to attending college. I know this is important to her and you, and Rueben - you said his name was - are setting good academic examples and increasing her desire for learning without compromising her values."

I wanted to blurt out, "You're saying if she can be friends with me and my challenging family values and still be a good Witness, then she can withstand anything Satan throws her way." But I didn't say that. I'm not stupid.

Instead I said. "Thank you, Mr. Whittier."

"It's because of my daughter's association with you, that I believe she can handle going to college or pursue opportunities beyond my home."

I nodded in acceptance to what I viewed as a back-handed compliment.

"Joanie's friendship means a lot to me," I said. "I value her a lot." But deep down, I wondered. Do I value her if I'm lying to her? I was only telling her what I believed she could handle as if she were a four-year-old. I realized I was treating Joanie like a child while her father was sitting here, saying he was ready to allow his baby bird to leave the nest. I didn't want to lose Joanie as a friend. I had to stop deceiving her.

Mr. Whittier sipped his coffee and smiled at me. I smiled back and sipped my tea. It was cold.

VIENNA WAITS 4 U

Saturday
It was Dusty who provided the initial concept of the Ink for the Beloved service for clients. It came out of an inspired moment after she had gone through a cathartic inking herself.

Dusty has an Italian background. Her blond hair comes from a bottle. She grew up in a Catholic household in New York City with two older brothers. One was a priest, and the other was a cop. The three siblings were close in age, and the brothers allowed their kid sister to hang around them. They were probably aware her tomboy inclinations went far deeper than just a desire to avoid dresses and the nice boys their mother kept picking out for Dusty to meet.

The siblings all planned to take a trip to Vienna after Dusty reached the age of 21. But Anthony, the brother who became a cop, didn't make the date. He was killed in the line of duty two weeks before they were scheduled to leave for Austria. Dusty and her surviving brother, Francisco, took the bittersweet trip without Tony. They both felt he would have wanted them to go and not cancel the excursion. When they returned, both Dusty and Francisco had a few lyrics of Billy Joel's song tattooed on their shoulders. In beautiful calligraphy, the words "Vienna Waits For You" and the coordinates of the city are inked to honor the loss of their brother.

Years later, Dusty shared this with my mother during a late night of red wine and female bonding. Terry jumped on the fact the emotional meaning of the tattoo and song had profound significance for Dusty and Francisco, and there was something to be built out of that. The story of the tattoo was compelling and could be communicated. Plus, by then, my mother was aware of the psychic ability I was displaying around tattoos. The idea behind "Ink for the Beloved" was born. The Ink for the Beloved ceremonies were always money makers. But they were time-consuming as well, and when Echo and I were younger, my mother didn't like doing more than two a month. But with all the added support and the enhancements Annika (supplied by Todd, cough, cough) brought, the ceremonies have turned into sold-out money-making extravaganzas. Okay, I'm exaggerating, but whenever we sold tickets, a lot of money was generated by looky-*loos*. *Some of these people, I now believe, were Todd's customers.*

When Todd discovered Ellen Somerville was opting for a private ceremony and not selling tickets, he blew a gasket. At the time, my mother could not figure out why Todd was going berserk. Their argument was filled with thunderous roars and vicious spite. I was in my bedroom, pretending to study, but I was listening to every single vowel being spat out between the two of them.

"What is wrong with you," my mother was screaming. They had already reached high pitch levels, so it was easy for me to follow what was being said. Echo was at a sleepover - *thank you, Maisie Kelly and the Kelly family!* And Ollie was out who knows where. He was probably clubbing in San Francisco. He had left his truck if I wanted to use it. I was going to call Rueben and see if he wanted to have pizza, but then the fight had started, and I remained quiet so they would forget I was there.

"Look at the books, Terry. We have to sell tickets to the ceremony."

"It doesn't matter if we need to or not. Ellen has requested it be private."

"She's paying for Annika."

"Yes, and she still wants it private."

"Nobody else? No family members?"

"Private means private, asshole."

I could hear some stomping across the floor. It sounded like Todd was pacing back and forth.

"What is the problem here?" my mother continued. "I'm offering a service, and this client has made her specifications. If she wanted a manicure done with pink polish, I wouldn't then paint her nails blue."

"I just know you can make more money off of this appointment," Todd responded.

"It doesn't matter if I can make more money. I'm not going to force people on her if she doesn't wish it. The woman is mourning the death of her daughter. The death was already public, and so was the funeral. I'm happy to give her the privacy and peace she is seeking."

"It's because the funeral was public, that you can sell seats to the tattoo."

"The funeral was public because THREE TEENAGE GIRLS died. The entire high school attended and half of the city. What is wrong with you? My God, this thinking is ghoulish."

"Just talk to her again," Todd spoke as if this was a demand.

"I will not. The fact Ellen is even getting a tattoo is private. She doesn't want it broadcast all over town. She's one of those old money "town and gown" people."

"Then why did you say doing the work for Somerville will bring in more business if it is not publicized?"

"Because women talk, you idiot! They talk among themselves. Why do I have to explain this to you? If I respect her wishes, she will share that with other women and other families. But if I'm crass and rude and using her grief to make money, then she is not going to refer me to anyone. I know my business, Todd. Don't interfere."

"Fine. Fine. But I am going to remind you with all the time you have taken off..."

"You know why I took that time off." My mother spit those words out with venom. It was said with such hostility I found myself leaning in and listening harder (if such a thing is possible). When had my mother taken time off? As far as I knew, she was at the studio regularly. I was the one who wasn't at the studio as much. One, I was keeping my distance from Todd and two, I had been focusing my after-school time on Echo so Todd wouldn't be the one my mother sent to the school.

"Good. We don't need to discuss that again." Todd's response was forceful but not combative. It sounded like he was crossing the floor. I hoped he didn't bring the argument into the kitchen, because then they might see I was home. The door to my room was slightly open, and I feared if I got up to shut it, they would hear the creaking of the wooden floor. I heard some items being moved around before Todd spoke again.

"I need you to hear me out," Todd said. My mother must have scoffed and moved away because then Todd raised his voice, and it bellowed through the house.

"HEAR ME OUT DAMMIT!"

"WHAT?" I could almost see my mother standing there with her hands on her hips, staring him down with the flaming gaze of a pissed off dragon. "What is it, Todd? Are you going to tell me how to run my business? Is that it? I've been doing this for over twelve years. What do you think you can tell me?

"I've helped you out a lot. You were just breaking even a few months back. You told me you were worried about your property taxes and the expense of Bess going to college."

My eyes widened, and I leaned in even harder. This was the first time I have ever heard my mother mention there could be problems with me going to college.

"There were also the hospital bills from Echo being sick. I saved your ass. I brought in Annika."

"That was my idea," my mother replied.

"Perhaps, but I found the girl. You owe me."

"I owe you what?"

"That Beloved ceremony for Ellen Somerville has to be open to the public. You owe me that."

"WHY?" my mother screamed. "WHY?"

Todd's response was quiet, but it sounded like he said he had sold tickets or something because then my mother screeched even louder.

"Are you stupid?! Why would you do that?! You can't sell tickets to an event that is not happening. That's fraud, you idiot! Jesus Christ!"

"I know," Todd thundered back. "That's why you have to convince her to allow outside people to attend."

"I'll do no such thing."

"I'm going to spell this out so you can understand it." Todd's voice was low, and the edge was so sharp it sliced through the air. "I have sold four tickets to the Somerville ceremony, and they will be honored, and I have five more tickets that I plan to sell. Maybe six. And all those people will be allowed into the studio. ALL of them."

"Let. Go. Of. My. Arm." My mother's voice was hostile, but there was pain behind it. And I could detect a little fear.

"I just want to make sure you get the pretty picture I'm painting for you."

I was leaning in so far; I knew any second I would topple over. Gravity was pulling me down. I was saved by the physical sounds of two people wrestling with each other. I think my mother was pulling herself out of Todd's grasp, and something got knocked over. That sound cloaked the squeaking noise the bedsprings made when I readjusted my weight by pulling back on the comforter.

I sat very still and waited.

And listened. I wondered if I had to make my presence known. How far was the physical action going to advance?

Right when I wondered if I should do something, the tussle stopped. I could hear them both in the living room. Their breathing was hard. I imagined my mother was staring angrily at Todd, fury zinging out of her body like lightening.

"You are such an asshole," my mother said.

"That should come as no surprise," was his measured response.

I waited to see what my mother would say. I waited for the sharp retort to his power play, but instead, she went out the door with a slam. A few beats later, and Todd left as well. I was now alone in the house with my thoughts, and they were very disturbing thoughts.

First, there was the stunning realization, my mother had given in. She was going to let Todd sell tickets to the Somerville ceremony despite the wishes of the client. She was not going to fight him. In fact, it had sounded like Todd had physically grabbed her, maybe even had hurt her. In all the years and all the men my mother was involved with, no one had ever hurt her. I believed at that moment; she was in shock.

The second piece of information that had stunned me was the mention that my mother had not been at the studio for a few days. She had taken time off, <u>willingly</u> taken time off. My mother is devoted to her work and her art. The only time she didn't engage with clients was when Echo had been sick and when she had spent a night in jail back when she and Luther had the fight. But even then, she had only missed a day and had scheduled her mandatory community service around client appointments. This sounded like planned time off, and I hadn't been aware of it. It couldn't have been more than one day maybe two days, otherwise I would have known. What did she do?

Third, were we having money problems? If so, this was news to me. Echo's hospital bills would only be disastrous if we didn't have insurance, but I knew we did. Unless it had lapsed. Also, why was my mother worried about college tuition, and why would she even discuss that with Todd? All of this told me my mother divulged a lot more than I thought to Mr. Mackey. My body trembled with the knowledge of exposure and raw vulnerability. This guy was dealing drugs out of Cosmic Hearts, and we were so fucked.

I sucked down four packs of hot sauce in a row, and for the first time, my stomach revolted, and I vomited the fiery substance back up.

DANGER, WILL ROBINSON

There was a period in my life when I used to play "The Charles Game." I was about five when I created the game. It was around the time when you are at school, and the teacher is asking you to list family members, and I would put down my mother and sometimes Dusty, and my mother would get upset because she didn't want people to think she was in a lesbian relationship with Dusty. I was confused when she would tell me to just list her. That was the family – her and me. I would do this for some time, but then I would get puzzled by all her attempts to enlarge the family with the boyfriends and the babies.

Clearly, it was not just the two of us in her mind. She was dating men and after a few months, wanting me to call them Daddy. I didn't want to draw pictures and include Simon or Thomas or whoever my mother was giggling with in the other room, so I started drawing pictures of Charles. My father.

I knew what he looked like. I had seen the pictures from the dinner party – the night I was conceived. I didn't know anything else about him because either my mother didn't know, or she just didn't want ME to know. So, Charles became a prince. Or a fireman. Or a scientist. I would draw tons of pictures of Charles and give him multiple occupations. They were detailed pictures complete with backgrounds. Prince Charles was sitting on a throne with beautiful tapestries behind him. The scientist Charles was holding up a beaker with bubbles and smoke coming out of it, standing *in front of a blackboard with scribbles of numbers and equations. The pirate Charles had a ship and a colorful crew, and of course, a parrot on his shoulder. The fireman Charles was saving a child from a house where flames were coming out of the bedroom window.*

My mother thought these drawings were brilliant. (Her words). She loved the fact I was showing a man of color in all these different occupations and workplaces, both fanciful and real. She would just ask me what it was a picture of, and I would answer it's a pirate, it's a pastry chef, it's a race car driver. I never told her they were pictures of my father. The man I didn't know. Even at the ages of five and six, I knew that to indicate my desire to place flesh on the ghost would be upsetting to her. And as a child, I never wanted to upset her.

Tuesday

Right now, my mother was very upset. It had been a few days since the blistering argument with Todd, but the two of them were behaving as if the fight had not occurred. In the presence of Echo and me, they remained pleasant and greeted each other around the house. Terry wasn't stomping her feet or slamming drawers or staring angrily in Todd's direction. Except I could see a switch had been flipped within my mother. Her body hummed with intensity. Her attention was focused, and her gaze fixated. She wasn't relaxed, and she didn't smile. Ollie picked up on the shift in my mother as well and did what Ollie usually does - gave her a wide berth.

The Somerville ceremony was scheduled later this week on a school night, a Thursday. Todd continually talked about how he was rehearsing with Annika (as if he was a music producer and not a drug dealer) and the timeline for the decorations being mounted in the studio after the business officially closed. Somehow Todd had gotten my mother to agree to have the area where Annika would be singing adorned with celestial items as if Annika was in heaven. There would be the suggestion of clouds, and soft lighting, and Annika would have props like a lyre and a pair of angel wings. Thankfully, my mother had stopped Todd from ordering a golden gown and a halo, because that's just...No.

All of this came about because in the preliminary meeting, when Mrs. Somerville met Annika in all her dark Gothic glory, she had gasped. The shock was not because of Annika's questionable fashion choices, but because Annika bore a resemblance to Sally, the daughter being commemorated in ink.

Never one to miss a marketing opportunity, Todd convinced Mrs. Somerville Annika's performance in song would be as if Sally was singing to her mother. This was a natural emotional string to pull since the songs Mrs. Somerville had chosen for the ceremony were songs she associated with her daughter. Then, (and I must give this to Todd - this was clever) Todd told Mrs. Somerville the performance of Annika singing should be filmed so Mrs. Somerville could go back and experience the event again when she wishes. He added this would be a professionally edited video, and she would be able to share it with her other family members when she was ready to let them know about the tattoo. Only one person was needed to work the camera, so the rest of the film crew Todd planned on bringing in were the supposed ticket buyers to the event (the ones he had mentioned to my mother). And since they were clients of Todd's anyway, they would hold a makeup brush or a microphone for five minutes if Todd told them to. All this to sell the idea of a film crew to Ellen Somerville in her private tattoo ceremony.

At dinner on Tuesday, I listened to Todd go on and on about his scheduled plans for the ceremony. Todd was excited, but as I listened, I pieced together in my head how all this activity covered up his distribution of drugs. He was animated and boasting and totally oblivious to what he had done to my mother's enterprise. Or maybe he wasn't oblivious, and he just didn't care. Across the table, my mother silently ate her food, but you could tell she didn't taste it. Her eyes were down on the plate, and occasionally she would nod her head and murmur "uh-huh". I could see the strain as she fought to keep herself from erupting and unleashing the anger burning inside of her.

Echo perked up when she heard Todd mention the angel wings, and she stopped trying to hide her broccoli under the mashed potatoes. "I want angel wings," she declared.

"Oh, you can have them after Annika finishes using them," Todd said magnanimously. His chest was puffed out as if he gave away angel wings daily. Of course, I knew Echo with angel wings meant feathers all over the house for somebody to clean up and that somebody was me.

Echo turned to our mother with pleading eyes. "Please, can I have them? Please."

"These wings are bigger than you are, baby girl," my mother responded. "They're not for kids. They were designed for an adult." She glanced over at Todd. "Perhaps I'll wear them. They're beautifully made. I tried them on when they arrived at the store today."

"And you looked great in them." Todd tossed in. "A very sexy angel." He raised his eyebrows suggestively. *Oh barf, Todd, not at the table.*

"I'm a bit concerned with all these props that this film crew idea may be too over the top," my mother said. Todd began to protest, but my mother held up her hand to indicate he should let her finish. "I know Ellen has agreed to it, but I'm worried about so many people around and so much stuff, she might get uncomfortable and cancel the whole thing."

"If she wants fewer people in the room during the ceremony, I'll just shoo people out," Todd answered.

"I thought they purchased tickets to watch." My mother made

her statement and then immediately took a sip of wine. She was cloaking something. Taking a drink, after baiting a person was how she steadied herself. She had just tossed a grenade.

Todd was silent on the other end of the table. His eyes were pinpricks of darkness, and his jaw was rigid.

"Do you want me to be there?" I asked. I didn't want to be there, but I thought I should offer. Besides, the mood in the room had suddenly gone hot, and a deflection was needed.

My mother's eyes zeroed in on me. I saw her thinking, contemplating. It was like she was seeing me, seriously seeing me for the first time in ages. After a beat, she said, "No. Stay here. Stay with Echo Thursday night."

It was the way she said it. An odd tone in her voice made me sit up and take notice. I looked at my mother, and she gazed back. Her eyes flared. There was no smile, but she was communicating something to me. And then she winked.

What was she up to?

TERRY

ednesday

W It was very early when Terry entered the Cosmic Hearts studio. She would have plenty of time before Dusty arrived. She came through the front, turned off the alarm, and took a moment to appreciate the space. Her space. It was eerily quiet. The morning sun illuminated the tranquil studio. She was rarely at her shop at this hour. But something was hiding here. There was a cancer growing; a cancer that threatened to destroy this artist's haven.

She began her search. First, she checked the areas where personal items were deposited. Annika and Dusty both used the space under the sink. Terry usually tossed her purse on the shelving below the display counter. Those areas were clear. She headed back to the storage area and opened recently delivered boxes. While she was back there, Terry remembered the day Bess claimed her backpack was missing. Initially, they had thought it was taken in the break-in. But there wasn't a break-in, was there.

Terry quickly spotted the backpack, resembling her daughter's on the bottom shelf. She pulled it out and zipped it open. Inside were bags and bags of neatly prepared white powder. Terry was not knowledgeable enough about drugs to be able to identify what she was looking at, but it didn't matter. Todd's manipulation of her, Todd's strategic influence in her life, was due to these little packets of powder.

Terry looked at the evidence before her and took a picture of the bag's contents. She placed it back on the shelf. She then emailed the picture to herself and deleted the image from her phone.

She wasn't sure what she was going to do. The ramifications of what was happening, of what she had allowed to happen, threatened to cripple her thinking. She needed a focused mind. She forcibly pushed back the thoughts, creating havoc in her brain. She had to come up with a plan, and she had very little time to do it.

The Somerville ceremony was the following evening. The items necessary for the event were already in the studio. She was practiced and prepped. Inwardly, Terry said a prayer of thanks that she had already done the prep work for the engagement because now she had something far more critical to tend to. Saying a prayer brought Luther to mind. Of all the men she had dated, Luther was the only churchgoer. Embarrassment flooded through her as Terry thought about that bear of a man. Her wretched ego had decimated her relationship with Luther, and that man had truly loved her. And Luther loved her daughters. But her inability to bear him a child coupled with the natural way he had become a father to her girls had struck a chord she was ashamed of. Perhaps there was still a way to fix things. Maybe she could do that.

What had she seen in Todd, besides the handsome features? He had been funny, sweet, and aggressive in his attentions. Was she that shallow where she could be swayed by the charms of a younger man who found her desirable? The sex had been good. It had been great. But she was old enough to know sex wasn't everything. It didn't hold a relationship together. Not even babies can hold a relationship together, but she had tried, hadn't she...?

Terry wanted to be a good mother. She believed she was a good mother. But that wasn't enough. You must be a good mother. Just be. Put your children first.

Terry wondered if her maternal insecurities had driven her into the arms of Todd. He was someone who clearly could not best her in the parenting department. And it turns out he is a drug dealer. She had opened the door and invited the vampire in. It was precisely what Bess said.

The drugs were here in the studio. Logically, Todd was planning to move them during the Beloved ceremony. Terry pulled out the folder containing the booking information for the Somerville event. Ten names were listed as "invited guests," even though the service was supposed to be private. Todd had constructed the whole film crew scenario to fool Ellen Somerville. Terry bit down on her lip as the rage from that deception fired up within her. She couldn't allow her emotions to get the better of her. She had to out-think this guy.

It had been his insistence on being present for Ellen Somerville's personalized inking ceremony that had triggered Terry's suspicions. A musician getting an octopus on their shoulder, yes. A local baker having an inked sleeve of donuts, sure. But not a grieving mother dealing with the public death of her daughter. Todd's demands to be present at the ceremony had made no sense.

Terry scanned the list of names of the invited guests who were posing as a film crew. She sucked in her breath as she realized these names were all fake. The giveaway was seeing Rick Grimes on the page. Terry knew the name belonged to a popular character on a show about zombies. These weren't real people; they were code names.

Over the last few months, she hadn't bothered reviewing the lists or checking the names. She had allowed Bess and then eventually Todd to collect the money and organize the guests. He seemed to love to do it as it gave him something to do at the studio. Bess snarked, calling him "the Mayor of Cosmic Hearts." Terry rummaged through the drawer and pulled out the files for Beloved ceremonies dating back to when Bess was managing the paperwork. Scanning the names and organized receipts of the paying attendees, Terry saw another name pop up that she suspected to be false. Bess had placed a red "x" next to the name. Was that because the person didn't show or had Bess known that it was a fictitious name. Todd had been sloppy using the name Rick Grimes, Bess would have seen that immediately because she liked to watch gory stuff, but then, Todd knew that Bess wouldn't see this list. Terry wouldn't have the opportunity to ask her daughter these questions, but she understood Bess' observation skills could be an asset now.

Bess. Bess was the key. Todd had been avoiding Bess as much as he could. She had thought it was a smart move over the last few weeks, thinking Todd was doing it to create peace in the household. But now Terry thought Todd stayed clear of Bess because he didn't want Bess to watch him too closely. Her daughter was very observant.

Thinking about Bess, Terry knew she had an ace up her sleeve. With everything that Terry had divulged to Todd, she had never talked to him about Bess' ability. Todd didn't know Bess was extraordinarily empathic. He complained about the things Bess did and how she interacted with people, but Terry had never gone into detail about Bess' gift. Terry didn't know how to describe what Bess could do, but she knew she could use it to her advantage.

She thought about her daughter and the things she knew and the things she had tried to bring to her mother's attention, and Terry realized Bess already knew a lot. Bess probably knew about the drugs. Warm tears flooded her eyes, and she released the breath she had been holding in. The pain Terry had brought to her little girls and to her household was immeasurable. How could she be so stupid? With all her rules about drugs, how could she end up falling for a drug dealer? She felt naive and used, and the anger that hit her body caused her to smack her hand down on the countertop.

There was a tingle on the skin of her forearm. It was a reminder. She was wearing long sleeves, and she pulled up the clothing to peer at her arm. The inked wound was ready to receive air to continue healing. She had skin oil in a basket to her left, and she applied a little now. Tears escaped and rolled down her cheeks as Terry comprehended; this was healing that would never reach the depths of her soul. She would never be able to find the forgiveness to accept this action. Terry had known then. Deep down, she had known there was something not right with this man. If he could force her...her, of all people...to do that action and be an accomplice to... The waterworks flowed, and she had to take a moment to handle the sobs vibrating through her.

She wiped the tears with the back of her hand and stared at the list of false names. This list in of itself was not evidence of anything, but it was giving her an idea. She pulled out her client notebook and flipped through the pages. The pages contained names and sketches of the work she had inked over the last few years. Every now and then, Terry stopped and mentally recorded a name and an image. A plan was slowly taking shape. It was a strategy targeting her little ace, her mouse. Todd was no dummy, so Terry had to leave information without him seeing it. The idea was risky and audacious, but it could work. It had to work.

Her eyes shifted across the room, where the backpack sat on the bottom shelf in the storage area. Tomorrow night, after the ceremony, the drugs would be gone, and the bag would have money in it. Friday morning, he would come in and move the backpack. Terry mentally reached back to the various times Todd had been at the studio in the early morning hours. He only touches the bag when it has money, she realized. She would have to strike before then.

Understanding what she had to do and willing herself to do it, Terry went back to her client notebook. Terry knew Todd's fury would be taken out on her. She knew she was placing herself directly in harm's way, and she was ready for that. But most importantly, if Terry did this right, her girls would be protected. She would be a good mother. Terry needed more time, but there wasn't anymore. With her studio appointment book in front of her, Terry dialed the musician client, hoping the man was in town.

She had to leave a story map. A map for her daughter who lives in pictures. And she had one day.

Hey, diddle diddle.

COSMIC HEART

Friday
"Elisabeth Wynters to the main office. Elisabeth Wynters, please report to the main office."

I was sitting in physics with my head down, concentrating on a formula I knew was not correct. My brain was fading in and out. Numbers and symbols floated about, making things disconnected and foggy. My mother had not come home last night. Sucking on hot sauce packets barely helped the situation.

My physics teacher came up to my desk and tapped with his hand to get my attention. The office runner was standing there, waiting to accompany me out of the classroom. I gathered up my things. Everyone stared at me as I walked out.

This can't be good.

I was right. Dusty was waiting at the front office. Her face was pale, and her eyes were red.

"Who's at the studio?" I asked. It was about eleven-thirty in the morning.

"We're closed right now," Dusty answered. "C'mon, I'm taking you to the hospital."

***

The nurse led me into the room where the woman who was my mother lay covered in bandages and tubes. Mercifully, she was unconscious. Both eyes were swollen shut. The right side of her face was raw and red. Someone had repeatedly struck her there again and again. The assailant was left-handed. Todd is left-handed.

I was told other areas of her body were ruptured and cracked. She had been beaten and kicked within an inch of her life.

Sobs escaped from my chest as I stood over the hospital bed. I couldn't embrace my mother or even take her hand. Every part of her was covered. There was nothing I could touch to create a connection. She looked so broken, and looking at her, I realized this could be it. The hushed tones, the beeping machines, and the sorrowful faces of the nurses told me that.

My mother was dying, and Echo and I would be alone. I didn't think she had made custody arrangements for us. I wracked my brain, running through the possibilities of our future. Ollie couldn't take us. He was an old man who smoked pot and had no clear source of income. Dusty was good for the little moments of advice or phone calls in the night, but she could never handle the school drives in the morning or cupcakes for the PTA meetings like Terry could. Luther could do it. Luther wanted the job. My mother just had to remove her ego and give him a legal right to claim us, or at least Echo.

Otherwise, we were looking at the foster system while the state tried to figure out who our biological fathers were. With a little detective work and asking the right people, it could be deduced. Blood tests would finalize the deal. The thought of becoming a financial burden to someone who had never signed up for the gig was demoralizing.

Our fathers weren't men who had ditched a pregnant woman and run off to escape the demands and responsibilities. Our fathers were men who never knew they were fathers. My mother had cheated them of the knowledge, but if they learned the truth now, Echo and I could be separated. Two men would learn they had abandoned children they didn't know existed. And just like that, their rights, their legal custody rights, would take precedence. There were no grandparents to fight for us and challenge the custody. My mother would be vilified.

I sat down in the visitor's chair, pulling it up alongside the bed so I could lay my head on the blankets covering her legs. "I love you," I whispered to the battered creature lying on the bed. I don't think I have ever felt so scared and alone.

An hour passed, maybe two, and Dusty poked her head into the room. "The police are outside," she said.

I stepped into the corridor and saw Officer Lopez was there along with another policeman. He was a tall guy with rugged features. Officer Lopez was in uniform, but the other cop wore clothes that looked like he slept in them. He was all disheveled in khaki pants and a battered bomber jacket, but he held an erect posture like a steel rod was going right through him. His badge was clipped to his jacket. A toothpick moved back and forth in his mouth.

Officer Lopez spoke first. "Elizabeth, Bess, I'm so sorry. I'm so sorry this has happened. Still, my colleague and I have several questions, and Ms. Lorazo, here believes you have most of the answers."

"Todd did this," I hissed. "Todd Mackey."

"We believe that, as well. Ms. Lorazo is the one who found your mother on the floor of the studio this morning. Your mother was still conscious, and she named Mr. Mackey as the attacker. We'd like to get a time-line from you if possible."

"And there is another problem," Dusty interjected.

"What?" I turned to Dusty, who looked as awful as I felt. Her face was still white, and the only hint of color was her bloodshot eyes.

Officer Lopez eyeballed Dusty as if she was speaking out of turn. Suddenly, the other policeman spoke up. "We believe Mr. Mackey has your sister."

"WHAT?!" I screamed.

Dusty ignored Officer Lopez's stern look and filled me in quickly. Her usual slow country drawl was gone, and now she spoke like the Italian girl from Brooklyn that she genuinely was. "I went to the high school to collect you as soon as the ambulance delivered her to the hospital. I thought it best to leave Echo at school, given your mother's condition." I nodded as that was sound thinking. "I was going to contact the family that watches Echo every now and then and see if they could take her. Then the school called to check on your mother's condition."

"How did they know?" I asked.

"Exactly" was Dusty's response. "Apparently, Todd went down there at noon and removed Echo from the classroom. He told the women at the front your mother had fallen ill, and he was taking Echo to the hospital."

"So, where is he?" I demanded.

"We have multiple units on the lookout for him and your sister," Officer Lopez responded. "We don't believe he is going to harm her. However, we need to focus our efforts. I have to ask you why Mr. Mackey would have taken your sister, to begin with."

The shock of the situation and fear for my sister's safety clogged my brain. My mouth opened, but nothing came out. I looked at Officer Lopez for relief. She guided me to a row of chairs in the hospital corridor. The act of sitting helped to bring the level of panic from a high to a moderate level. "My mother didn't come home last night," I said to the officers.

Dusty reacted in surprise. "What do you mean?" she stammered. "I saw her leave with Todd around eleven o'clock."

Officer Lopez gently placed a hand on Dusty's shoulder and locked her eyes with mine. "Bess, when was the last time you saw your mother?"

I told Officer Lopez about the Somerville Beloved ceremony that had occurred the previous evening and what it had entailed. Lopez listened, but it was the other officer who was writing everything down. "Your mother was beaten this morning, so where do you think she went?" Officer Lopez asked.

"I don't know," I answered. "Todd came to the house, and he was waiting around for her. He was drinking and telling me the ceremony was fantastic. When I asked where my mother was, he mentioned she had gone back to the studio to retrieve something, and she was walking home. He said she was high from success and wanted the time to 'revel in the coolness of the night' or something, but she never came home. Todd drank a lot of beers, so he didn't go out to look for her. I stayed at the house and sent her text messages, but she didn't answer any of them. This morning, Todd was gone, and I took my sister to school."

"If your mother was at the studio and the event went well, can you think of any reason why Mr. Mackey would attack her?" This was the other officer speaking.

I thought about my mother, and the last time I had talked with her directly. It had been at dinner two nights ago when we had the conversation about Annika's angel wings. There had been something then in my mother's demeanor. I remember thinking she was trying to tell me something.

"Bess," Officer Lopez had taken the seat next to me. Her voice was low, but I'm sure everyone else could hear her words. "Your mother's injuries were not the type of injuries we normally see in domestic violence. This wasn't a direct beating. He wanted something. There were other wounds on the body before he went for her face out of fury. What did he want? Why did he take your sister?"

"Leverage," I whispered as the answer dawned on me.

"Yeeees..." Officer Lopez confirmed, stringing out the word. "But leverage for what?"

My gaze drifted up, and I looked at Dusty. "In the hospital room by the chair is my backpack from school. I need to show it to the police." Dusty frowned, but she went into the room. A few seconds later, she came out with my backpack with the green ribbon tied across the straps. Her hands shook as she handed it over to me.

As I spoke to the police, questions scattered around my mind like thoughts that had sprouted wings but had no place to fly, so they were forced to bounce around in my head. I withdrew a hot sauce pack from the front pouch and sucked it back to try and ground my thinking.

"You should go back to Cosmic Hearts and see if there is a backpack that looks exactly like this one but without the ribbon. But I'm pretty sure it's not there."

"What's in the backpack?" asked the male policeman.

"Drugs...or money," I answered. Dusty gasped and slowly sank into the seat on the other side of Officer Lopez. The other officer took a picture of my backpack and went down the hallway, where I could see him making calls.

"Who is he?" I asked Officer Lopez, nodding my head in the direction of the other officer.

"He's the detective who was brought in once it was understood Todd Mackey was the attacker and he had kidnapped your sister. He is responsible for bringing your sister back home safely. Now he is contacting the narcotics division. It looks like everyone at the precinct is going to be caught up in this one."

"Go big or go home," I deadpanned. Officer Lopez looked at me askance, questioning my poor attempt at humor.

"I thought your family didn't like cops," she said.

"We don't," I responded. "Except for when we have to."

"Just like everybody else," she sighed, shaking her head. "So, why don't you tell me what's going on. And just remember whatever you tell me is going to be passed on to other divisions. I only do robbery and property damage. Other officers might need to come back and ask you more questions. Are you going to be able to handle that?"

I nodded. And then I told Officer Lopez everything I knew about Todd and what I had guessed about his drug operation. I was scared, but I was also relieved.

***

At ten o'clock that evening, I was shooed out of my mother's room. Surgery was scheduled for the morning. They didn't want me in there when the team came to retrieve her.

I sat in the waiting room. Ollie came by at two in the morning to try and get me to go home and sleep in my bed. He promised me he would bring me back in the morning, so I would be here when they took her into the operating room. I refused. I didn't want to go home when Echo was not there. It seemed like the only suitable option was to stay in the hospital waiting room. I was waiting for any type of information about anything.

At dawn, before they took my mother to the operating room, a nurse brought an EMT over to me. The man was not in his uniform. He had been one of the ambulance technicians that had delivered my mother to the hospital.

"Are you Bess?" he asked. He was washed and scrubbed and looked like he was going to start his day rather than coming off a long 18-hour shift. I could smell the shampoo he had used to wash his hair. It reminded me it had been a few days since I had showered myself. I'm sure I was ripe; especially given the number of hot sauce packs I had been consuming. Ollie had brought me a large thermos of tea to sip through the night so I would have something else in my system besides pepper sauce.

The EMT handed me a folded-up piece of paper. It was addressed, "To Bess, my little mouse," I slipped the paper into my bookbag, not wanting to open it with people standing around. Besides, there was blood on it.

MERCY

Sunday

Two days went by with no word regarding my sister. I stayed at the hospital. Rueben and Joanie began coming by on Friday and Saturday. They were so caring and sympathetic; it was almost nauseous. They were treating me like a little duckling, newly hatched from its shell. I was that duckling. I was trembling and shaking from the experience and afraid to step away from the nest. I had never seen that level of violence directed on a human being before.

Joanie sat in the hospital waiting room and prayed for me, my sister, and the recovery of our mother. She took a chair next to me and softly mouthed words to Jehovah. I told her to go to the chapel in the hospital, but she refused. Apparently, Jehovah's Witnesses don't use the chapel. Sometimes, when a new person entered the area, I pretended not to know the girl sitting next to me, asking for Jehovah's protection and guidance. But I was glad she was there, even with all the embarrassing praying stuff.

Joanie told me she had led a special vigil at her kingdom hall with her father and the Spanish congregation had joined in as well. Over a hundred Jehovah's Witnesses prayed for my family and our safety. It's strange to learn hundreds of people you don't know are taking the time out of their lives to send hope (in whatever form) for your spiritual benefit. On one level, it feels invasive as I wonder what they know about me and how they judge my family. But on another level, it's touching and sweet. And weird. Let's not forget weird.

On Monday, the third day of my hospital vigil, I received a call from Officer Lopez to come outside to the front of the building. I did. A squad car was there, and I could see Officer Lopez sitting in the back seat, talking to someone beside her. Suddenly, the door swung open, and a little red-haired person charged out of the car and tackled me. The two of us fell back into the flower beds with my arms tightly around her. I smelled the musky scent of her dirty wild hair and felt the fragile perfection of her little body. She was pure innocence and love, and I thought my heart would break.

The police drove us to lunch at a sandwich place a few blocks away. No one wanted Echo to know about our mom just yet. She was told our mother was hurt and was in the hospital to get better. Echo accepted this since she had been in a hospital and gotten better. We ordered a tuna melt with fries for us to split, and Echo dived in like she hadn't eaten in days. The officers just ordered coffee. I wasn't hungry. Still, I selected some fries and deposited them on a separate plate, dousing them with ketchup and hot sauce to claim them.

Officer Lopez, along with the ruggedly handsome detective in khakis, drilled Echo with questions to piece together where she had been for the last 48 hours. I didn't catch the other cop's name, Kling, or something like that. I figured after this, I wouldn't be seeing him again, but I kind of liked the way he smelled like cinnamon.

During the time she was with Todd, Echo was utterly unaware of her possible peril. Todd hadn't told Echo the story about our mother being in the hospital. Instead, he said they were playing hooky and then had to explain what hooky meant. Playing hooky with Todd meant going to a movie in the middle of the day. Todd took her to a movie and bought her a massive tub of popcorn and red vines candy. Echo sat through the film and then a dinner of a burger and a chocolate banana shake, and then played with her toy fairies which were conveniently in her hair.

While they were in the theatre and restaurant, Todd kept popping up, checking on the status of Terry and what was happening at the hospital. Echo was very annoyed he kept leaving the movie and going to the lobby because then she had to explain what was happening in the story when he came back. Of course, Echo didn't know who Todd was calling to get his information, but Officer Kling or something like that said they knew Todd had an inside person at the hospital, which was how he had access to some of his pharmaceuticals.

With no promising news on Terry's recovery, Todd stashed Echo at a friend's house on Friday evening and all day Saturday and Sunday. Echo didn't have much to say about the nice lady except she gave Echo soda and cereal, and she had a cat. Echo talked endlessly about the soda (a treat our mother denies us) and how naughty Smithers the cat was. Apparently, Smithers kept running off with one of Echo's plastic fairies and hiding it in his food dish. Echo spent the entire time of her kidnapping watching television, drinking soda, eating cereal, and playing with Smithers. She slept on the couch with a smelly quilt, but she used it anyway because it was cold. (The police were amused by this detail, and Officer Lopez praised my sister for being practical and then had to define "practical.")

The police surmised when Todd heard Terry's injuries were severe, and consciousness was not happening soon, having Echo as a hostage became more of a liability than an asset. It wasn't going to deliver what he wanted, so he needed to let Echo go. Todd dropped my sister off at Luther's auto shop. I thought it looked like a desperate attempt to make it appear as if Luther was involved. If the police hadn't already vetted Luther and the shop, Todd might have been successful with that sneaky maneuver.

Luther immediately called the police when Echo showed up and when they arrived, my sister confirmed Todd had removed her from school to play hooky. The identity of Todd's female friend, the owner of Smithers, the cat, was not of concern. Echo was back, and she was unharmed. She was only missing a plastic fairy which somehow Smithers had been victorious in claiming.

Pleased to have adult attention, Echo finished her story and polished off her half of the tuna melt and mine as well. She grabbed me continually to give me hugs, wiping her greasy fingers on my clothing. I didn't say anything or push her away. I was glad to have her back.

"How's your mother?" Officer Lopez asked.

I shook my head to indicate things were not going well, making sure Echo was not watching. I fought back the tears threatening to spill out from my eyes. "I need to take her home," I said, gesturing to Echo. My voice cracked with emotion.

"That's just it..." Officer Lopez hesitated and looked over at her partner, Kling or something. "We are not sure where the two of you should go."

"Home is where we should go," I responded.

Detective Kling or something eyed me with a worried expression. "We don't know where Todd Mackey is at the moment, and we don't know where the drugs are located, so we think you two need to be protected."

"We're not going to a foster home," I said emphatically. "That's not happening. You have to keep us together and allow us to continue with our lives. I need to be able to go to the hospital and school. There are responsible adults around us. Don't take us away."

Lopez looked at the detective and spoke in my defense. "I've seen how capable this girl is. They should be fine at the house. At least for a while."

Officer Lopez turned her attention back to me and leaned in. "Listen to me," she said with all seriousness. "These are the ground rules for you and your sister to return to your home. One, you must maintain a regular schedule and stay within Berkeley. If you need to travel outside, you contact Detective Kline or me." (*Kline. His name is Kline*) "Two, this is not a game. Until Todd Mackey or the drugs are located, there will be a unit watching the house."

I frowned at that piece of information, and Lopez frowned back at me. Her frown was uncompromising. "I repeat," she said. "This is not a game."

"What about Cosmic Hearts?' I asked. "Can I go there?"

"Once it has been cleaned up and Ms. Lorazo reopens, then yes, you can go there. Of the adults in your mother's circle, only Ms. Lorazo and the tenant, Olliver DeMatteo, are allowed in the house.

"What about Luther Tucker?"

Lopez looked over at Kline. He shook his head no. Lopez looked back at me and said, "No," even though I distinctly saw Kline's negative answer.

"Why not?" I protested.

"Legal reasons" was Kline's response, so I guess they had found out about the restraining order.

"How about my friends?" I asked. "Can I have my friends over?"

"Can I have MY friends over?" Echo had decided to jump into the conversation. "And a kitten," she added.

Lopez smiled in Echo's direction. "Yes, if your sister says it is okay." Looking back at me, Lopez laid out the parameters. "Friends should be okay, but try to stay at your home, the schools, and the tattoo studio."

"And the library," I threw in. "Finals are coming up."

"Your home, the schools, the tattoo studio, and the library," Lopez responded.

I put out my hand to shake on it in agreement. Lopez shook my hand and then also shook Echo's who had stuck out hers, so she was included as well. "That should be it," Officer Lopez said, standing and stretching her back. Kline went over to the cashier to pay for the meal and their coffees. He reached into his breast pocket and removed a toothpick. It went right into the side of his mouth.

Officer Lopez leaned in and spoke in a confidential tone. "Narcotics believes they will have Mackey in custody soon, but in the meantime, please watch yourself. We're stretching things here, allowing you and your sister to go back to the house, especially with your mother's condition, and ..." she allowed her words to trail off. Echo was becoming attentive to the conversation. Officer Lopez looked straight into my eyes. "Stay in contact. This is not a game."

"Okay, I. GOT. IT." I said. Perhaps, I was too snippy.

Echo and I were taken home. This ended my vigil at the hospital, so I took a shower. Echo kept insisting the police lady said she could have a kitten. Not remembering how she could have reached that conclusion, I dodged the subject by telling her it was mom's decision, and she would have to wait until our mother was home.

Ollie was happy to see us both, and Dusty came by at dinner to celebrate the return of Echo. We didn't call it that, but it was on everyone's mind. I had Ollie take a picture of me hugging Echo on my phone, and I sent it to the last number I had for Luther. A few minutes later, a red heart was messaged back. I was glad my mother wouldn't know Todd had stolen Echo. Things were shaky, but things would only get better. We could move forward and heal.

Dusty was still pale from the shock of recent events. In less than a day, she had learned her business had been used to shelter a drug operation, and she might have lost her best friend. I could see Dusty was trying to pull herself together. There were indications she had gotten some sleep. Her face was scrubbed, and her hair combed. Giant palm trees dangled as earrings under the brim of her cowboy hat.

"The studio is in shambles," she said. "The police scoured the place looking for the backpack."

"It wouldn't be there," I said. "She moved it. That's why he beat her. But I can't figure out where she could have taken it."

"Did she bring it here to the house?"

"No," I replied. "Todd was here."

"The car?" Dusty guessed.

Todd has it."

"Well, I know one place she went that morning," Dusty ventured. "She walked to the bank and made the deposit from Thursday's event."

My head snapped up. "Was it a substantial deposit?" I asked. I had a vision of my mother dumping rolls of cash wadded up in rubber bands at the teller's window and telling them to count it.

"No," Dusty answered. "I told the police and showed them the deposit receipt she placed in the appointment book."

"Why'd she put it there?"

"I don't know, but that's where I found it."

I thought about my mother's movements. Clearly, she had gone back to get the backpack after the Somerville event. The bag may have had drugs in it, but it would have predominately contained cash. She went to the bank in the morning but didn't deposit the money from the backpack there. That would have raised suspicion, and I'm sure the police were checking that. Besides, Todd believed he still had access to the bag. He took Echo because my mother told him she hid it, but she wouldn't tell him where.

If she had driven somewhere far to hide the backpack, we wouldn't know because Todd had her car. I wasn't sure if checking mileage was really a way that the police could determine where people traveled. Many times, in police shows, a parking ticket or a camera at an intersection reveals where a person has been. I seriously doubted if the questions revolving around my mother would be solved by a parking ticket. There just wasn't any way to figure out what she had been thinking or where she had gone.

Before Dusty left, I told her I would come by after school on Tuesday to help with the clean-up. Maybe with the two of us, we would be able to get clients back in the door by Thursday. Dusty expressed her gratitude and gave me an enormous hug. "She'll be okay. Your mom will be okay." She whispered in my ear. I thanked her, but I believe that those words were more to comfort Dusty than myself.

That evening as I lay in my bed, I could hear distant sirens as police cars answered an emergency call. Officer Lopez had said the vehicle positioned at our house would not leave even if there were a burglary or a fire down the street. It was an unmarked vehicle, but evident to anyone who knows what to look for. I've gotten to the point where I know what to look for.

Earlier in the evening, I had tossed Echo into the bath with lots of suds and scrubbed her until she was raw and squeaky. As I conditioned and rinsed her hair, I thought I was possibly eliminating potential clues for the forensic teams if they needed it. However, the police hadn't shown much interest in trying to pinpoint where Echo had been for the last few days. Whoever the woman was, she had probably been fed a string of lies explaining why Todd had my sister.

Smelling like strawberries, Echo lay in bed next to me sound asleep. As I had combed her hair out and braided it to dry, she told me she was going to name her kitten Smithers. I smiled and said, that was a good choice. Last week the name of the kitten was going to be Pepper, and the week before that, the selected name was Georgie. With Todd no longer a member of the household, maybe Echo could finally get her kitten. I rubbed my sister's small blanketed body and allowed my mind to drift and think about orange kittens and where a litter box would go.

My phone buzzed. A text message had come in. I glanced at the screen, hoping the sender was Luther. The number was blocked, but the message was clear. It read, "where's my shit?" A few seconds later, another message appeared.

"Don't make me take your sister again."

II

PURSUE MAXINE

·

IT'S A GAME

I was lying on my bed, gazing out the window and watching a little bird dance around from branch to branch on the tree that shaded my room. My mind was wandering, in the same way, the bird was flitting and chirping. Hop, chirp, bob head down, bob head up, hop, chirp, ruffle feathers. That bird was me – hopping here and there, not knowing where it should perch or where it should rest its head.

My mother never made it to surgery. She was brought out of the induced coma, but then her vitals went wobbly. She had a devastating stroke on Sunday night. They believed she was conscious, but she was locked inside an unresponsive body. This is what I hadn't wanted to share with Officer Lopez when she asked about Terry's condition. Things did not look good.

Echo was home, but I knew there was a threat hanging over her. Todd had made it clear he could get to my sister. I was antsy to take action, but I didn't know what I could possibly do. I shared Todd's text messages to Officer Lopez, who insisted on contacting Detective Kline. The police were searching hard for Todd. Annika had been arrested but released when it was clear she didn't know anything outside of the honest employment she had received from my mother. (Lucky her) Nick Ryder had been questioned while he was in jail. Duane Rodriguez had disappeared along with Todd.

While I spoke with Officer Lopez, we went over the details of my mother's last two days in Cosmic Hearts. Dusty claimed on Wednesday, my mother was there when she arrived. My mother worked steadily and placed calls. Dusty had gotten them salads for lunch. Thursday before the Somerville ceremony, my mother handled a full day's worth of bookings. Chinese food had been ordered. Terry didn't leave the place. Friday, Dusty entered Cosmic Hearts and found my mother beaten on the floor. The studio had been tossed. Chinese food containers with their remaining contents were crushed along with the spilled ink and fallen equipment.

Officer Lopez mentioned the delivery guy from the Chinese kitchen had been roughed up the night before. He was jumped on his way home by two assailants who repeatedly demanded he hand over the bag the tattoo lady had given him. His beating stopped when he fell unconscious. But the attackers took the keys to his residence and searched the place. Luckily his girlfriend hadn't been home, or she would have been beaten as well.

I took a deep breath and exhaled while Officer Lopez told me about the beaten delivery guy. "This is a sign of desperation, Bess," she said. "We all know the bag and its contents were in the studio on Thursday night, so this guy is at his wit's end - grasping for straws. All known associates are being watched. He's going to surface soon, and then we will have him." Once again, Officer Lopez tried to talk me into leaving the house, but I didn't trust the system. I didn't want to be hiding. I needed to be near the hospital and my friends. I needed to be able to see my mother.

"Just catch him, will you," I said.

Ollie blared opera arias throughout the house. Despite the fact the refrigerator was filled with casseroles and food brought by members of Joanie's Witness congregation, he was baking and baking and baking. I don't think he had turned the oven off for the last three days. Ollie was in a frenzy of grief. In a month, there will be twenty more pounds on his frame. And then everyone will be forced to do diet cleanses with him.

Thoughts like this meant I believed we would rally on without Terry Wynters at the helm. But could we? I took Echo to school this morning, aware of the unmarked police car following slowly behind us as we walked. I didn't feel like going to school myself, so I returned home.

I looked at the screen on my phone and went into messages. I scrolled through my multiple attempts to contact my mother on Thursday night after the ceremony, and she didn't come home. I landed on Wednesday, which was the last time we had actually communicated. She had messaged I should come by the studio after school on Thursday. I had responded I couldn't. I was getting Echo and then studying with Rueben. She messaged back I needed to pick something up. I had replied she should bring it home.

As my eyes flitted around the numerous items in my room, random thoughts and memories danced in my head. My brain needed something to do. Finally, my eyes rested on my book bag, propped up near the door. There it sat, waiting for me to grab it on the way out. The lost book bag which started it all. My green ribbon was still threaded through the handles. It was then I remembered there was something inside from my mother that I hadn't looked at.

I quickly opened my bag and snatched out the folded paper. My name was scrawled across the front, but it wasn't my mother's hand. The EMT had probably written it for her. There were brown finger marks on the paper. The EMT's gloves were bloody from working on my mother, and the mess had transferred to the paper as he wrote what my mother said. I unfolded the paper and frowned at what I saw. The words "Pursue Maxine" were written in black ink on the page. They were arranged strangely as "pursue" was written from left to right, but the name Maxine was written vertically. The words intersected and shared the letter "e" at their ends.

Pursue Maxine

Was this a puzzle? The first thing that crossed my mind was this was some type of crossword puzzle. I turned the paper around and looked at my name and childhood nickname on the other side. There were no instructions. Nothing else for me to extract information from.

I stared at the paper. Was my mother leaving me a clue to the whereabouts of the stash of drugs? That had to be it. Had she hidden them somewhere in the shop? Somewhere in the house?

Earlier, I needed to feel like I had something to do - to take action. Now I had something to do. It appeared I had a puzzle to solve. I grabbed my jacket and called out for Ollie. I needed a ride to the hospital.

I figured I could get information from the EMT regarding the message he had written for my mother. But first I had to let him know I wanted to speak to him. Ollie drove me to the hospital in silence. His face grey and hard. The softness had left his cheeks. I realized I was wrong in thinking he would gain weight from consuming all the heavy carbs and baked goods in the refrigerator. He wasn't eating at all. Our family tragedy was his family tragedy.

I reached over and placed my hand on his arm as he gripped the steering wheel. We drove for a few blocks, and then Ollie had to reach down and pull a tissue from the side pocket of the door in the truck's cab. Tears were streaming down his face.

If it weren't for us, he would be pathetic and alone. That's what he said to me, time and time again. He had his sister out in Idaho, but her husband had made it clear Ollie could visit but never stay. My mother's generosity was a saving grace for him, and he was fiercely protective of her. Going behind her back and taking Echo to visit Luther must have been so difficult for him to do. He probably felt like he was betraying her. He was. It must be how the subjects in a kingdom feel when they go against the wishes of their king. Kings are human, and mistakes are made. Are people supposed to ignore the error and pretend it is not a mistake at all? When does the king (or queen as the case may be) get called on their poor judgment? Is it always treason when you challenge the queen's will?

We reached the hospital, and Ollie let me out near the entrance while he pulled around to the parking garage for visitors. I headed for the nurses' station that functioned as a hub for the floor where my mother rested. The woman at the monitor was not the one who had brought over the EMT. I looked at the chart over her head and read the names posted there. None of them stood out, but then I wasn't positive I had caught the woman's name anyway. During the time I spent at the hospital, I had seen dozens of nurses, and I couldn't link any of them to names.

"Yes, may I help you?" the nurse at the desk had bright green eyes, and she had a colorful headband pulling back her spiky dark hair.

"My mother is Theresa Winters in room 304," I said. The woman gave me the sad eyes tinged with pity. I was beginning to see those eyes on everyone's face.

"I recognize you. It's a little early for visiting hours for minors, dear." the nurse smiled. "But if you wish, I am sure it is alright for you to poke your head in for a bit and look in on her. There hasn't been any change I'm afraid."

"Thanks. I think I'll do that. I was hoping to get the name of the nurse working here on Saturday morning. She was a tall woman with long blond hair."

"Could she have had it clipped up high on her head?" the front desk nurse asked, demonstrating a high ponytail with her hands.

"Yes, that's her. Is she here now? I really need to talk to her."

"Her name is Carol. She's probably on break now." The nurse flipped through a few charts and checked something on the monitor. "Yes, she should be back on the floor in fifteen minutes. If you'd like, I can send her to your mother's room."

I thanked the nurse and went to stand at my mother's bedside. There was no change in her condition except every time I went in to see her, she looked just a little bit smaller. It was like she was shrinking into the bed covers. I stood there for a while, just staring at this miniature woman. Her face was a swollen purple bruise. One eye was now covered with gauze (I didn't know why), and the red hair poking out from the bandages was damp with perspiration. Without the vibrant energy that made her roar larger than life, she really was an itty-bitty thing. My concentration was so intense I didn't notice Carol enter the room.

"Hi," she said. "It's Bess, right?"

"That's right."

"I'm sorry her condition hasn't improved."

"Remember the EMT that brought me a letter the other day?" I asked. "Do you think I could speak to him?"

"Roger, yes. I'll find him. I can send a message and ask him to come up to the room when he is done with his shift."

I thanked Carol, and she turned to leave, but then a thought flashed in my mind.

"Have there been any other visitors for my mother?" I asked.

"Outside of the police? No."

"Detective Kline has been here?"

"Yes, they were hoping to get more information from her, but as you can see her..." The nurse smoothed down the linens around my mother's torso. "Her condition hasn't changed. Outside of the police, only family is allowed."

"I'm her only family that can come in. My sister is six, and I don't think she should see our mother looking...not yet, anyway." In addition to her face being swollen, there were black and purple bruises shaped like fingerprints on her neck. I didn't have to have it spelled out to me; I knew what those neck bruises meant. Looking at my mother, I only felt deep sorrow. The simmering rage I was used to tapping into was gone. I looked over at nurse Carol who was gazing down at my mother with what could only be described as love and concern.

"Is there any way of allowing others to see her?" I asked. "I'm sure her business partner and best friend would like to be here, and then there's...." My thoughts drifted because I was about to say Luther or

Ollie, and I wasn't sure how to characterize them to make the nurse understand these men were family. The important thing, however, is that Todd had not been in. It was probably the best news I had heard since the attack. Todd couldn't snake his way into my mother's room.

"I can compile a list of people who have permission to visit," I stated. "I know I'm considered a kid, but there are people who I'd like to be able to sit with her, read to her, play music, stuff like that."

"That sounds lovely," Carol responded. She looked at me and hesitated. I could see she was thinking something and then decided to share what was nagging at her brain. "You know, I hadn't thought anything about it last night, but now that we are talking, there was someone who came into her room last evening while I was here. He was a big fellow, black, and holding a cap in his hands. He entered the room, distressed. And while staring at your mother, his hand flew up to his mouth. He saw me then and backed away. Apologizing that he had the wrong room."

Luther.

Carol continued. "Even though he said he had the wrong room, it seemed like he knew your mother. I understand she is well known in the area."

I decided not to respond.

Carol finished tucking the bedding around my mother and stood up. "Let's go to the floor reception, and I'll send a message to Roger. You can also give me the names of the people who should be allowed in."

"How about the people that should be blocked?"

Carol laughed and patted my shoulder. "Those too." The woman thought I was joking.

As we moved out of the room into the corridor, I saw Ollie had arrived from parking his truck and had folded himself into one of the pale grey chairs in the waiting area. He looked miserable. I tapped Carol and gestured in Ollie's direction.

"That's one of the people I would like to have on the list," I said. Carol smiled. "I've seen him here before. We wondered who he belonged to."

"He'll probably play classical music in my mother's room. I must warn you. He likes opera."

***

Once again, Roger was freshly showered when he visited me in my mother's hospital room. He hovered by the door as if he were afraid to take another step into the sterile space. "I'm glad to see she is still with us," he said, looking at my mother lying on the bed. "She seems like quite a fighter."

I was by the window gazing at the view of the Berkeley hills that my mother couldn't see. "I want to ask you about the letter you gave me," I said. "You wrote the inscription on the outside of the envelope. Did you also write the message inside?"

Roger nodded his head. "It was very peculiar. But she insisted I do it that way. Wouldn't let us do anything for her until I had written the note out. No oxygen. Nothing. Not until I got the note right. I was worried about her, so I did what she said." He winced as he spoke and looked down at my mother lying on the bed. His arms folded across his body as if he was warding off a chill.

"Did she insist you write the words in that fashion – with them intersecting like a crossword puzzle?"

Roger looked back up at me. "Exactly. And those were her words. She wanted me to give it to you directly, but she was worried someone else would see it."

"Did she say who?" I could guess. By this time, the danger had escalated with Todd, but she wouldn't be aware he had taken Echo and disappeared for the weekend.

"No. She kept saying, 'I fixed it. I fixed everything' over and over and that Bess will know what to do. She said if I write the words like that, you would know what she was saying."

But I didn't know what she was saying. It appeared my mother had given me the answers to a crossword puzzle. Crosswords were Terry's thing. They were not mine. Was I supposed to find the questions to these answers? Clearly, I was meant to do something with this, and I would have to figure out what it was. If the police didn't catch Todd, the only way to make him go away was to find the bag. This word puzzle was the answer I just had to figure out what it meant.

WHO IS MAXINE?

"Pursue, Maxine. I fixed it. I fixed everything."
Those were the last words my mother communicated to me. What the hell did she mean? I stared at the cryptic words written down on the blood-stained paper. I read the words repeatedly, willing them to reveal their hidden meaning to me. "I fixed it. I fixed it."

"I fixed it. I fixed everything" seemed to be the message, and Maxine was the woman I had to find, so I would know how she fixed it. But I didn't know anyone named Maxine. And if this woman was a chance acquaintance, how was I going to find her? I checked with Dusty and Ollie, and even Luther. I checked with all the adults who were familiar with my mother's social contacts and clients. No one in the inner circle knew a Maxine or had a clue as to what Terry could be trying to say.

Ollie went through most of the family papers with me, and we didn't see the name Maxine on a relative or a business contact. My maternal grandmother's name was Ellen, and she had a sister named Ramona. My grandfather had a sister named Katrina. I did some further digging on my mother's side of the family, the Wynter's side, but nothing surfaced. No Maxine.

There was, of course, the possibility Maxine could be from my father's side of the family. But the more I thought about it, the more I was convinced it was a dead-end and not worth pursuing. In the past, if I mentioned seeking Charles or his family members, my mother shot down the notion like an expert marksman firing at a clay puck launched into the air. It was a quick smackdown, with particles scattered to the wind. There was no way Terry wanted me to meet Charles. So, to have me pursue someone from his side of the family just felt absurd. That wasn't the path she was guiding me to.

And the reality was this, I believed she hadn't known anything about him. She didn't know anything outside of his first name and the apartment he had lived in sixteen years ago. There was an embarrassment from her lack of knowledge. From what I could tell, she never informed the couple who hosted the dinner party where she met Charles of my existence and had not bothered to learn his last name. But they would know his last name, of course.

I knew the couple. I figured out who they were.

Years ago, my mother slipped and revealed the couple's name in a casual conversation. She was talking to someone about the genesis of a tattoo design. There was an art piece in a friend's hallway that exhibited such a darling, whimsical painting style she had used it for inspiration. The person had asked if she knew the name of the artist of the painting. My mother had laughed and explained Frank and Heather didn't have the foggiest idea who produced the artwork since they had found the canvas at Goodwill. The person interrupted, asking if this was Frank Hudson, and my mother replied no, it was Frank Bloom. You don't know him. The story then veered off as she explained why Frank and Heather had been at Goodwill because that was a whole story in itself. I waited a few minutes and then slipped away to my room, moving quietly and slowly, so as not to draw attention to myself. Once inside my bedroom, I had quickly jotted down the names so I wouldn't ever forget. I wrote the names down and folded up the paper and slid it under my mattress.

Frank and Heather Bloom. Frank and Heather Bloom.

I had heard another story about that infamous tattoo. It was a tattoo frequently requested for a couple of years and was integral in building public interest in my mother's work. The design depicted a charming cat wearing a slightly skewed aviator helmet, a fitted paisley vest with an old-fashioned man's watch swinging from a chain, and galoshes. The cat sported a rakish smile, and it caught the fancy of people who liked steampunk, science fiction, and Lewis Carroll's "Alice in Wonderland" characters. The ink work on the paisley vest, and the cat's ruffled fur was beautifully detailed. It was all about style and charm.

There was a period where she was interviewed about the idea behind her steampunk Cheshire cat. (Later, there would be the mouse, the fox, and the moose. Then she moved into her rockabilly collection). The story she usually shared was that she saw a painting of a tuxedo-wearing cat at a friend's party, and her imagination sparked to the level of a volcanic eruption. Sometimes she added the party had been a monumental event in her life in more ways than one. Most people took that comment as a reference to the line of successful tattoos that factored into her business. Still, I caught her looking at me sometimes when she made that comment, and I began to believe it was at this party she had met my father.

It was strange my mother felt I had to be a secret, a secret from Charles and his family. She always told me she was selfish, and she wanted to keep me all to herself. When I was little, I believed those words. It made me feel special. But as I got older, uncertainty began to creep in. A lot of uncertainty. I began to believe she was ashamed of me -that somehow, I wasn't the daughter I should be, and if Charles ever met me, I would be a huge disappointment. Luckily, my time spent with Luther took those feelings of doubt and shame away. Luther instilled strong feelings of pride, not only in me but in my black heritage. This is something my mother believed I would just absorb by virtue of living in a diverse-multicultural-anything goes city like Berkeley. I have found this type of thinking is misguided. Cultural identity doesn't work in a Kumbaya hand-holding type of way, and it can't be legislated in a city council meeting.

I hope if the day ever comes where I get the opportunity to meet Charles, he will be proud to claim me as his daughter. Now whether the same could be said for me, and I would feel pride in him is another story entirely. We have already seen my mother's choices for bedfellows leave a lot to be desired. It was this notion that always held me back from wanting to find Charles and reveal myself to him. As long as I haven't met him, he can still be the heroic Fireman Charles or the benevolent King Charles of my little girl fantasies. He could be the father I needed him to be, and I could imagine anything. I wasn't sure if meeting the man in the flesh was worth losing the fantasy for.

Ollie did an extensive Internet search for the name Maxine and didn't come up with anything of value. We checked literary references and my mother's old school classmates. Nothing. We scanned her yearbooks and photo albums. Nothing. We linked the name to merchants and businesses in the area. Maxine's Cupcakes and Maxine's Deli were visited and then crossed off the list.

There was a moment, okay two whole hours, where I panicked, believing Maxine was the name of a girl my mother met when she had traveled to Nepal. This was some gypsy-like girl with flowers in her hair, a beaded tunic, and a sunshine smile. She had joined my mother on her spiritual adventure when Terry sought enlightenment and peace, two things she never found.

Dusty talked me down from that idea as she had known my mother when she returned from Nepal, and Dusty was positive if there had been a girl named Maxine back then, she would have heard about it.

Ollie loves cop shows, and he set up a large whiteboard in the dining room. He was copying what he saw detectives do when they are trying to solve a murder case. Ollie created graphs and lists, showing our progress, and writing down the clues we followed as we attempted to unmask Maxine. He wrote up a list of questions to ask when on a phone call so pertinent information was not forgotten. Every crazy idea was tossed onto the board and investigated.

The time spent on the investigation helped with the grief and the vacuum created by the absence of my mother's spirit. As usual, Terry had left us with a challenge, and we were keen on rising to the occasion.

I was wracking my brain. What was my mother trying to say? And why was I even supposed to pursue this Maxine? Had she given the bag of drugs and money to Maxine? If so, why didn't she just tell Maxine to take the backpack to the police?

If there were doubts about the importance of Maxine, the stakes were raised the next day to a dangerous level.

BESS THE BOSS

I don't often drive since I have a bike, and I love the freedom of pedaling on my own and not having to worry about a parking place. I have plenty of responsibilities relating to the household and Cosmic Hearts, and I never wanted to add "errand girl" to the list. One of the great things with bike riding is if it doesn't fit in your backpack, people don't ask you to pick items up. And since my pack is already filled with books and notebooks, I had a ready excuse to decline, and I could always claim extra weight would throw me off balance. Ollie handled the purchases for the home, and Dusty took care of the studio if there were items that weren't brought in by vendors. So, it was a rare thing to see me behind the wheel of a car. But as things go, my bike needed some attention, and I was borrowing Ollie's truck to get the frame straightened and the gears checked.

The family car, or my mother's car, had disappeared with Todd.

A week had passed since my mother had entered the hospital. The police were beginning to believe Todd had fled the area. Either that or he was dead. When Officer Lopez mentioned this piece of information, I was surprised. "He'd be killed?" I asked.

"Oh yeah," she replied emphatically. The police had taken my mother's computer a few days ago (with my permission), and a picture of the book bag filled with drugs was discovered in her email. She had sent it on Wednesday morning. This confirmed she had possession or knew about the drugs. I pointed out to Lopez it also confirmed my mother wasn't a part of the operation. She wouldn't have taken a picture of it and emailed it to herself.

"There was about a hundred thousand dollars' worth of product in that bag," Officer Lopez said. "People definitely get killed for that much. People get killed for less."

Hours after Lopez said that to me, Duane Rodriguez's body was discovered in a warehouse in West Oakland. Officer Lopez called me that evening with the news. The discovery of Rodriguez fueled the theory Todd was dead. Todd's blood was also found at the warehouse. There was no body. Just blood. West Oakland is near the harbor, so there was speculation his body was dumped in the water if, in fact, he was dead.

Despite the belief, Todd was a dangerous man, the police didn't think he had killed Rodriguez. Officer Lopez went mum when I asked her more questions. The only thing she would tell me is Todd had a police record, which is why they were able to match the blood found at the warehouse. (I bet my mother was not aware Todd was a jailbird)

With Todd Mackey in the likely deceased category, the watch on our house was pulled back. Officer Lopez and Detective Kline sternly reminded me the rules allowing Echo and I to stay in our home without an official guardian were still in place.

"HOWEVER," Detective Kline added. (He wasn't as nice as Officer Lopez, and the stupid toothpick in the mouth thing was right out of Hollywood casting.) "Expect a visit from Child Protection Services in the next few weeks. We had to give them your address to check, but since you are involved with an ongoing case, they will wait to come by until we say so."

"And we just might forget to say so," Officer Lopez said softly, giving me a sly smile.

With this freshly planted information in my mind, I allowed my mind to explore what a possible future would look like for my sister and me. I could leave high school and get my GED. Then, I could seek emancipated minor status. Perhaps I would be allowed to legally become Echo's guardian. Those thoughts shifted into the details of what our life would be like. I would stick around and get a job somewhere. I could take classes at Berkeley community college. Echo would remain at her school. We could keep things close to the way they are. Of course, Ollie could stay at the house if he wanted. We would get a kitten, maybe two kittens. Things wouldn't be so bad.

I was waiting at a stop sign, when the passenger side door swung open, and Todd Mackey smoothly slipped into the seat next to me. It was so sudden I jumped a bit in the air, hitting my head on the low cabin of the truck. He had been running because his face was flushed, and his distinctive odor of musk assaulted my nostrils.

"What are you doing?" I demanded. I may have sounded feisty, but I was shocked and alarmed.

"Now, darling, is that any way to greet an old friend?" Todd flashed his movie-star grin. His smile rattled me, and I sucked in some air. Todd smoothed back his hair with both hands, and I could have sworn he checked himself in the mirror.

"Get out of the truck," I ordered. I was trying to maintain my composure, but my body was shaking. I was terrified of what Todd might do. "The police are looking for you, you know." Maybe that would get him to leave. Suddenly, there was a sharp horn blast, and I jumped in my seat. I had forgotten I was still sitting at the stop sign.

"You better get a move on, darling. You don't want to draw attention to yourself."

"Maybe I do," I said. I turned my face to look at Todd head-on. He was smirking. To him, I was just this little girl, an annoying and obstinate little girl.

My direct challenge didn't faze him at all. "I don't think that would be wise for you and that cute little mop of a sister. You both staying in that big house all by your lonesome while your mother is in the hospital."

The car behind me honked again. The driver laid his palm aggressively on the horn for several beats, and the blaring sound filled the cab of the truck in stereophonic sound. I gripped the steering wheel tightly to keep my hands from noticeably shaking and stared straight ahead. I refused to move. Somehow, pulling forward with Todd in the truck seemed like an unwise move. It was like giving him control. The pressure mounted. "We're not by ourselves," I said. "We've got people around us. We're protected."

Todd leaned in and leered. "You mean like now?" He raised his eyebrows in jest and looked around at the emptiness of the cab. "Don't try to kid me, Bess. I've seen how that house is run. And I know the police are not watching it anymore." He laughed. It was a deep, loud bark of a laugh, and I suddenly wanted to cry. "You're the boss. You are the BOSS. Like a video game combatant. You can't get to the next level until you handle the boss. You must take out the boss. And here she is, Bess the Boss." He smiled like he just shared a private joke, and then leaned in even closer to me if that was possible. "Your bossiness is not in question, my little caramel chew. We both know you are not protected."

"We have adults around us." I countered, but my voice cracked and filled with emotion. I focused on the view through the windshield of the truck to keep my emotions in check. The road in front of me beckoned, but I refused to move. The honking behind us continued. The pressure the driver placed on the horn matched the pressure building in my feverish head.

"You can't possibly be talking about homo 1 and homo 2. Those two couldn't build a fire if they had two sticks, a pack of matches, and lighter fluid." Todd chuckled at the thought of Ollie and Dusty, stumbling to work together as a team.

Tears flooded my eyes. These hot tears rolled down my cheeks like steaming liquid embers. My mother had betrayed us. She had told this skulking fiend everything about the household. Without her dynamic and combative nature, we were in a perilous position. Todd would sell us out for his drugs and use the system to dismantle our fragile household.

Suddenly, the driver behind me had enough, and he pulled out with a screech. He drove past, screaming some type of obscenity and took off to the left, burning rubber. I didn't hear the name he called me, but I'm sure it was an attack on my gender. I felt even more vulnerable. I realized I had been secretly hoping the driver of the car would have gotten out and checked to see what the problem was instead of angrily racing off like he did.

Todd grinned wolfishly as he watched the car speed down the street and disappear. "Fancy that. I'm not the only one you piss off." He then swiftly placed his left arm over my shoulder and pulled me into his chest. His voice was husky, and he spoke right into my ear. His hot breath made me shudder. "My little caramel girl, do you think you can lock your bedroom door to keep me away," he whispered.

The tears escaped and rolled down my cheeks. I felt like I was going to burst from fear.

Todd then took his right hand and touched my cheek, turning my face so I had to look at him. It was an intimate and god-awful move. I was scared to flinch or jerk away. I held his gaze as his thumb wiped away the tears, moving down my cheeks. "What a pretty thing you are. You are going to be someone's prize; I can see that. I should have found a way to pick that lock."

"It's dead-bolted," I responded. I continued to hold his gaze. My hatred for this man was rising, forcing out any humiliation or panic. I felt the sheer power of my emotional intensity fire from my eyes like cosmic laser blasts. In my mind, Todd withered away due to the fiery strength of my unrelenting fury.

Todd matched my stare, but there was admiration in his eyes. "So like your mother, you are." He then leaned in and placed a tender lover's kiss on my lips. My stomach churned. I wanted to retch, but I was frozen to the spot in the car seat. I envisioned myself as a column of titanium. I was solid, impenetrable, and an obstacle. I had to go back and be the Boss. I had to be the challenge that couldn't be beaten to advance to the next level. I had to keep Todd from moving forward.

"My mother...what she was...is gone...you...you destroyed...everything..." I didn't get the rest out. The words hitched in my brain. My eyes were unfocused, and his image was blurry, but the words I stuttered out had the necessary effect. Todd pulled back from me and leaned into the passenger side window. He sat silently for a moment. I took the opportunity to turn away and face the front of the vehicle, so I didn't have to look at him. Todd stared straight ahead as if he was waiting for me to pull away. The quiet was becoming unnerving.

"Really?" he finally said. "Well, I didn't expect that. That's too bad. It makes my message here so much more important."

"What message?" I asked. I kept my focus on the street ahead. My hands gripped the steering wheel so tight I felt it was my last link to sanity. My sanity would evaporate if I released the pressure and let go of the wheel. My life's blood would flow right out of me, and I would fall over in a faint. But it mustn't happen. I refused to let it happen. I was Bess the Boss, and I was titanium.

"I want my stuff. Isn't it obvious?"

"We've looked everywhere. No one can find the bag."

"You shouldn't be looking for a bag. You should be looking for a key."

"A key? A key to what?" I asked.

"The safety deposit box" was his response.

The moment Todd said that my brain pinged the way an answer smacks you in the head due to its self-evident nature. Of course. We already knew she had gone to the bank on Friday morning.

But then, as quickly as I saw a resolution, I felt despair. A key is smaller than a book bag. *Fuck.* "I have no idea where the key is," I said.

"Then you have a problem," Todd replied. He slithered out of the truck and shut the door. And despite my attempts at maintaining a titanium composure, the metal fortitude dissolved away, and I began to weep.

What rattled me the most about this encounter with Todd was that I quickly understood why the police found his blood in the warehouse. Several teeth were missing from Todd's mouth, and I don't think they were removed by a dentist.

CHRISTINA CROSS

I finally composed myself enough to drive to the bike shop and get that errand taken care of. I was supposed to meet Dusty at Cosmic Hearts, but I needed to take the time to think about Todd and the apparent threat he presented as a desperate man. There was no denying he was desperate. His missing teeth indicated someone else was placing pressure on him. I remembered when his hand was injured after I tossed the water on Nick. I had been the wrench in Todd's wheel for a long time.

I knew I needed to contact Officer Lopez and let her know Todd was alive. But then, that would bring the police back, and they would whisk Echo and me away.

If this happened, I would never find the key, and I was pretty sure "pursue Maxine" was about finding the key to the safety deposit box." Maxine had the key. My mother's message was left to me. I had to find the key.

It was then that my phone rang. It was Officer Lopez. I hesitated to answer because I wasn't sure I was ready to talk to her yet. I steeled myself and accepted the call.

"We are looking for a key," Officer Lopez said.

"For the safety deposit box," I responded and then immediately cursed myself for blurting that out.

Sure enough, Officer Lopez paused. "How do you know that?"

My mouth moved faster than my brain. "It has to be," I said. "My mother went to the bank on Friday, and she would have had time to hide the bag in the safety deposit box at the bank."

"Did you know she had one?" asked Officer Lopez. "A safety deposit box?" She sounded exasperated with me.

"I forgot," I said. Which was the truth. "But the minute you mentioned a key, I remembered." Which wasn't entirely true.

Officer Lopez than proceeded to tell me how the police figured out my mother had used the safety deposit box. A younger officer, being thorough, was backtracking and talking to people and businesses he had spoken to before. When the officer went to the bank, he talked to the same teller. But this time, instead of just confirming my mother had been there, he asked what my mother had done. The teller answered she made a deposit and visited the safety deposit box. My mother's signature on the deposit box request verified she had entered the vault. The police were trying to get a court order to open the box, but it would take time. "Do you have the key?" Officer Lopez asked.

"No," I replied.

"I was sure hoping you would say yes." She ended the call quickly, and I was back to contemplating the recent affairs in the truck. It was then I realized I had forgotten to mention to Officer Lopez that Todd was still alive.

***

"Give me the appointment book for a second; I have to add someone in." Dusty gestured with her left hand for me to bring it over. She was eating lunch at her station. Carla had brought in food so Dusty didn't have to leave the studio. Sometimes Carla even answered the phone and helped clean the stations and sterilize the tools. I was beginning to like Carla. She didn't talk much, and she still gave off the vibe of a wounded bird, but she clearly adored Dusty.

The recent traumatic events in Dusty's life had allowed Carla to step up and contribute. She was an enormous help with the clean-up of the studio, the insurance filing, and reordering products that had been destroyed or lost. Dusty was able to see clients within two weeks of Todd's attack on my mother. In addition to the appointments, several people were coming in to give their condolences.

Carla had brought in food from Gordos, and Dusty had an enormous burrito balanced in her right hand. I brought the book over, and she tried to transfer the food to her left hand so she could hold the pen to write. The transfer was not happening smoothly, as it truly was an enormous burrito. Her left hand wasn't going to get the proper grip, and her lunch was threatening to burst.

"Here. Can you do it?" She handed me the pen. "Christina Cross wants to come in tomorrow. I need an hour with her. Is there time in the afternoon?"

I checked Dusty's schedule and saw there was a spot to fit Christina in at 2:00. I wrote the name in. "2:00 will work if you move back the 2:45 to 3 or even 3:15. I can make the call."

"Let me see. Hold it up." I displayed the book, so Dusty could see how I was laying out her day. She took a big bite of the burrito and nodded her approval. But then she frowned and pointed to Christina's name on the line. "That's not how you spell Christina."

"What are you talking about? That's how you spell Christina."

"That's not how SHE spells it."

Christina Cross was a regular client of my mother's. I knew her well. She was a funny lady with a big personality who wore a lot of yellow. She loved my mother's cute animal designs and had a menagerie across her backside.

"How does she spell it, then? With a "K"?"

"With an "X." X, and then "tina.""

I erased the name and wrote it correctly into the appointment book.

303

Suddenly, my perception switched. The act of writing the client's name in the book triggered something deep inside. Cavernous deep. A burst of knowledge rose up from within my gut. It powered through my torso, exploding in a shower of light above my head. I was bathed in sudden awareness.

"OH. MY. GOD."

I flipped through the pages of the appointment book going back last week; that Thursday before Todd assaulted Terry. I ran my finger down my mother's schedule for that day. Sure enough, Christina had come in earlier to get some work done. There it was on the page "Xtina" and then a little added note in my mother's writing – *cool cow.*

I looked at the rest of the names listed on the page; Nikko, Michael, Emily, Ariel, and Ian. These were the clients my mother had seen along with Xtina. It couldn't be a coincidence that these names arranged in the proper order, spelled out "Maxine." Here it was. I had found Maxine.

A heady euphoria washed over me, and I smacked my hand down on the counter in triumph. I turned and grinned at Dusty, who was looking at me like I was a few hops away from the loony bin; the burrito was all but forgotten as she stared at me. Her eyes showed concern. It had been a long time since Dusty had seen me smile.

"I figured out who Maxine is," I shared. The stupid grin on my face was not going away.

Dusty still stared with amazement. "Who?" she whispered.

I held up the appointment book to the page on Thursday. "It's Michael, Ariel, Xtina, Ian, Nikko, and Emily," I said the names in order so Dusty would grasp it immediately.

She nodded in understanding. "Holy Shit"

This was not how their appointments were lined up in the book, so with a casual glance, we had missed it. But it was there all along written out on the page. My mother had marked it with the deposit slip from the bank. Michael, Ariel, Xtina, Ian, Nikko, and Emily. Terry really loved her puzzles.

"So, now what?" Dusty asked.

"I need to talk to Xtina about a cool cow."

Xtina Cross was a singer who sang in many clubs and lounges in the Sacramento area. She was the perfect performer for the hotel circuit and the travelers who had to deal with state business at the capitol. At the age of forty-five, the word "adorable" still fit, and as I said earlier, she wore a lot of yellow. Not pale yellow, but bright sunshiny blinding yellow. When she scurried into the shop the next day, you couldn't miss her. The room literally brightened when she came in like clouds had parted, and the sun's rays were beaming through. Xtina Cross does not blend.

"Ohhh, Dusty, it's so wonderful to see you. My heart is broken, just broken, broken, broken. Thank you. Thank you for fitting me in." Xtina threw her arms around Dusty and embraced her with enormous force. I was sitting over by the desk, waiting for Dusty to bring my presence to Xtina's attention.

Dusty extracted herself from Xtina's hug. "Of course, Xtina. You're like family here."

Xtina cupped Dusty's chin in her hands and gave a reassuring smile. "Dusty, I can't believe all this nasty business. I'm devastated, just devastated. Poor, poor Terry. This place will not be the same without her. Are you alright, dear?"

Xtina released Dusty's face, and a thankful Dusty looked down at the floor. Handling genuine emotion was not Dusty's strong suit.

"What can I do for you, Christina? I was surprised to hear you wanted me to do some ink. I wouldn't think you would want the type of animals I specialize in on your backside."

"You're right. I don't. No creepy tarantulas crawling over my behind. I thought you could augment one of the designs Terry did for me. I came in a few weeks ago for her to touch it up, and now I'd like to add something in a commemorative way. You know to make it extra special. For Terry."

Dusty nodded. "I see what you're saying. That's nice. That's sweet, in fact. Do you have any ideas?"

"Something to indicate the loss, but not too morbid, okay. I was thinking maybe flowers like the ones Terry has on her body but held in the animal's hoof. Could you alter the limbs to do that? You have to look at the tattoo. I'll need to lie down somewhere and hoist my dress up, and then you can tell me your thoughts."

It was then Dusty remembered I was there. "Xtina, have you met Bess? This is Terry's oldest daughter."

Xtina's face lit up when she saw me. She flew across the room and gave me the same tackling hug she had delivered to Dusty earlier. "Oh my darling, darling girl. I'm so sorry. You know I loved your mother deeply. She was a treasure, a treasure I tell you. I'm so proud to have her work on my body."

I smiled at Xtina. "Thank you, but you know she's not dead. You don't need to commemorate her."

That brought on an incredibly awkward silence as Xtina's face went red. "Yes, of course," she stammered. "I'm sorry to speak that way. It's just I understood she wouldn't be back. Back to work, I mean."

Hearing Xtina say those words made me realize the truth of the statement. It was unlikely my mother would ever tattoo another body again. I looked over at Dusty with a look begging for assistance because I realized I wasn't sure how to transition to the questions I needed to ask Xtina. I needed to justify my presence as she showed Dusty her behind. Not only that, I would probably have to touch the tattoo to glean the information my mother intended to share. The genuine awkwardness of the situation became glaringly clear.

I took a breath and decided to plow through, hoping Dusty would smooth over any ragged holes I tore open in my brazen request.

"Xtina, I have something I need to ask you. It's a favor, actually."

Xtina took my hand and squeezed it. "Anything. Anything darling. Ask away. What can I do?"

"Can you tell me about the last tattoo my mother did for you? Was it a cow?"

A puzzled expression crept across Christina's face, but I had her full attention. "Yes," she confirmed. "It's a cow – a cow with sunglasses and red lipstick. Your mom put her rockabilly touch on it. I've had it for some time. I think it was the first inkwork your mom did for me."

I was confused. I thought all the Maxine clients were getting new tattoos done. But then I realized that belief didn't make sense. For my mom to compile a list of people, she had to already know what ink they wanted to be done or what ink they already had on their bodies. She contacted them, not the other way around.

Xtina continued talking. "I had wanted to add a bit more to the tattoo later, and then she called me to come in because she had the idea of adding a pink ladies leather jacket. You know, from *Grease*. She did the work for free." She smiled then at the memory either of the leather jacket-wearing cow or the musical or the fact the ink was a freebie.

"Can you tell me more about it?" I asked.

"Like what?"

"Like why a cow." I was thinking of my mother's note next to Xtina's name. She had just written "cool cow." If adding the jacket was my mother's idea, then that would not be a part of Xtina's tattoo story.

"I like cows. Why is this important?" I could sense resistance rising in Xtina. She was wary. The cow was personal to her, and she didn't want to share the meaning. Inwardly I sighed. I needed to know the significance of the cow. I was going to have to touch this lady's butt. I tried a new tactic with Xtina. I looked at Dusty first, signaling (hopefully) she needed to play along.

"Can I see it?" I blurted out.

"The tattoo?"

"Yes. It's important."

"It's on my butt."

"I know. It's just...it's just it would really mean a lot to me. Your cow is one of the last tattoos my mother did before she..." I let my voice trail away, leaving the other person to fill in the blank.

I still wasn't sure how to describe what happened. It wasn't an accident. The "attack" made it sound like it was done by a stranger. "Hurt" didn't cover the depth of the damage, and "beaten" seemed like a punishment. However, Xtina knew what had happened. Whatever image floated to her mind; it was enough for her face to crumble in anguish.

"I need to see it. It will help me a lot." I added for emphasis.

Xtina turned and looked at Dusty with a questioning glance. Dusty managed to muster up a sympathetic nod. It was like they were silently communicating; *help the poor little girl out. Her mom is in the hospital. It doesn't hurt you, and it's no skin off your nose. Just show her your butt.*

Xtina looked back at me and gave a tiny shrug. "Well, who can argue with how people find closure. Where should I do this, Dusty? Or am I hiking up my skirts out here for anyone who waltzes down Telegraph Avenue to see."

We had Xtina lay stomach down on the padded cot and curtained off the area. I locked the front door, flipping over the sign, so it looked like we had stepped out for a bit. The sign said we would be back in twenty minutes.

I hoped Xtina Cross wasn't ticklish.

FAT COW

Christina's story

All her life Christina Cross was known as loud, big, and brassy. She favored bright garden colored clothing in vibrant prints. Sometimes the prints looked better suited for a kindergarten teacher with kitty cats and rocket ships. Christina didn't care. Christina spoke at a volume that ensured she would always be shushed in the library, movie theaters, and just about any public venue. Using your "inside voice" was an alien concept to her.

Are you thinking about climbing out the window while your parents are asleep, to hang out with the gang past curfew? Christina Cross better not be the gal assigned to pick you up. Just driving up the street, she'd have the music blaring, would honk the horn a few times, and then holler your name and tell you to get your ass out here. Let's pretend that racket hasn't gotten your parent's attention. You climb into the car, reminding Christina everything is supposed to be on the hush-hush. Christina will clap her hands over her mouth and squeal louder than a gunshot. "Oh, I forgot you were sneaking out!" There was no chill to Christina.

She was a love her or hate her type of gal. And the people who disliked her always used a derogatory term, highlighting their lack of imagination. They would call her a fat cow.

Back when she was in college, Christina had a run-in with a girl known as Judy Stirling. Judy was the "it" girl on campus. She was a tall skinny thing with breasts that hadn't come naturally to her body. Judy was used to flashing a smile and getting what she wanted. She was shocked, shocked, I tell you when she was not assigned the soprano role in the music department's Sondheim revue. Christina was cast instead. Christina's audition with "Age of Aquarius" from *Hair* and "Memories" from *Cats* was strong and memorable.

Judy voiced her displeasure. She let everyone know she believed the only way Christina had gotten cast over her was that the fat cow must have put out. Judy would moo whenever Christina was nearby. Christina was hurt by the accusations. Still, the injuries cut deeper when she realized people (even fellow cast members) were snickering in response to Judy's claims. People were not challenging Judy and pointing out that maybe, just maybe, Christina was more musically gifted.

That opportunity came for Christina when she overheard Judy griping in the commissary about the Sondheim casting. It had been over two weeks, and Judy still wouldn't let it go. Christina had enough and marched over to where Judy was sitting with her royal court of friends. Feeling like a quivering jellyfish, Christina instead visualized her body as a solid mass and stood over Judy as an intimidating fortress. Judy had leaned away, making a cutting remark about Christina's size and how fat cows give her nightmares. Christina looked down at this skinny creature who needed plastic surgery to gain any level of voluptuousness and said, "I'm your worst nightmare, Judy. I'm a fat cow with talent."

Walking away, praying she wouldn't drop her food tray due to her shaking hands, Christina was rewarded with the sounds of laughter at Judy's table. She smiled inside, knowing the laughter was directed at Judy.

Her rivalry with Judy Stirling didn't end there. Judy continued with her snide remarks around the school, she just wisely took it underground. Christina didn't mind Judy's viciousness as much since her personal status on the campus was growing in leaps and bounds. Christina's bodacious persona was gaining her fans, and it was clear after graduation, she could take her mighty voice on the road.

Years passed, and Christina forgot about Judy. Or at least she told herself she had. She changed the spelling of her name to Xtina and enjoyed popularity in the independent music scene as a lounge singer. Xtina traveled all over the country but liked to keep her tours on the west coast. "Changing time zones is a bitch!" Her public shows were big sellouts.

Social media was a blessing for her. She liked performing in smaller venues as the audience always felt like family. After a show, she was known for staying around for pictures and sharing laughs with her fans. People would bring her the wildest gifts. There were cookies baked to resemble her and strange fan art depicting Xtina in relationships with all sorts of popular male characters in fiction from Doctor Who to Iron Man. Xtina loved it all.

Even with all her fame and money, Xtina admitted to her therapist, who she saw twice a month, that Judy was the mean girl in her dreams. Whenever Xtina doubted herself, a nasty vision of Judy would pop in her head. This vision would call her a fat cow and mock her for believing she could do anything but eat. Many exercises were employed to erase Judy from the equation. The most effective one was writing Judy's name on pieces of paper and placing them in the freezer - "I'm giving her the cold shoulder," Xtina would joke.

"This will work, until you see her in real life, then you truly have to give her the cold shoulder," her therapist responded.

It was bound to happen. Cosmic alliances always fold over and call forth what is bubbling within your mind. It was a small dinner club in Napa, and Xtina was performing for a bunch of happily inebriated wine drinkers. It was one of her favorite moments in her act when she would take requests from the audience. She could sing almost anything, or at least she was good at faking it. The bright light was scanning the audience as they yelled out suggestions from Beyonce to Cher, and then Xtina saw her. Judy Stirling was sitting in the crowd. Xtina could see her leaning over and talking with her friends. Judy was probably saying she went to college with the performer. She was probably saying that girl beat me out for the Sondheim revue. But she was probably NOT saying anything about how she had tortured Christina and humiliated her for years. Xtina watched Judy flick her hair back and lean in, showing off her purchased breasts in a V-cut sweater.

Xtina decided she didn't want to have to look at Judy Stirling one minute longer, and a wicked grin bloomed across her face. "Hi Judy," she said into the microphone, and she waved like they were kids at the playground. "Hey everyone, I went to college with her, and here she is coming to hear me sing. Isn't that wild!?" Xtina smiled the biggest smile she could muster. She was sure the lights were pinging off her shiny white teeth. She had to hold it, or people might see she was shaking from nerves. Xtina spoke into the microphone as clearly as she could. "I'm still your worst nightmare, Judy. But now I'm a talented fat cow with power. And I'm going to have you bounced from this room. Bye-bye." And like that, Judy Stirling was escorted from the premises.

The following week Xtina made an appointment with Terry Wynters at Cosmic Hearts to ink a fat cow on her ass.

FIDO

Later that afternoon, I called an emergency meeting with Joanie and Rueben. I was worried about them coming to my house, so we met in the teen room at the public library Claremont branch. The spot is private, even with the glass walls. With the door shut, nobody can hear you. The closed door creates a glass-walled clubhouse.

I dropped the bombshell about my mother leaving a puzzle for me to solve. At first, my friends had frowned as they tried to suss out what I was telling them, and then they both gave me expressions of wide-eyed astonishment. Ten minutes passed, and Rueben was looking at a sheet of paper where I had created a grid. First, MAXINE was written out as if it were the down answer to a crossword puzzle. I had written the corresponding names from the appointment book across, so it looked like this:

Michael
Ariel
Xtina
Ian
Nikko
Emily

Then after Xtina, I had added a column that said "cow" and then "empowering" and "revenge" as the thematic clues I had gotten from

Xtina's story.

"This is some serious shit," said Rueben. He then passed the sheet to Joanie. She gazed silently at the paper and didn't react to Rueben's lapse in language.

"I have to find all the people on this page and see their ink. The message my mother left me is on those tattoos," I explained. I left out the part I needed to touch the tattoos to really glean the message because that indicates I have some sort of power. And even if I do (have "some sort of power"), I wasn't ready to share that yet. Everything in its own time.

"This is some crazy shit." Rueben looked over at Joanie and added "sorry" under his breath.

Joanie didn't respond. She hadn't lifted her eyes from the page.

"Can't you call them and ask them what their tattoo is and have them describe it?" asked Rueben.

"It's not that easy," I responded. "They might not tell me very much. Sometimes you must see the design. I know my mother's style. Like for instance, I could have asked Xtina what her tattoo was, and she could have just answered it was a cow. I wouldn't have had the extra information that the cow was dressed in rockabilly attire or heard the story behind her wanting a cow to begin with."

Rueben nodded in agreement. "The story is important. This is some crazy shit". His eyes nervously flashed over in Joanie's direction.

"What do you think your mother's message is?" he asked. The question was innocently said, but incredibly stupid, given the situation. Right after he spoke, Rueben immediately murmured, "Nevermind."

I decided to come clean, but just a little bit. "There are missing papers addressing the guardianship for my sister and me."

"Why are they missing?" Rueben persisted.

"They just are," I responded. "You know how my mother was. And if they are not found, Echo and I could be placed in foster care and even separated." I let the last comment sink in.

"Actually, we are looking for a key," I added a beat later.

"A key?"

"Yes, for a safety deposit box. I think if I solve the puzzle, I will find where the key is."

"Why didn't she just tell you where the key is? Why the puzzle game?" I had to hand it to Rueben. He was dotting every "I" and crossing every "T."

"She didn't want Todd to know," was my reply.

There was an uncomfortable silence as my friends absorbed this bit of information. They both knew Todd was responsible for what had happened to my mother, but they didn't know Todd had taken Echo and had threatened to do it again. My friends didn't know about the drugs. Right now, in their minds, my mother and Todd had fought, and things had gotten ugly, really ugly. Given the reason why I had them follow Rodriguez to the tobacco shop weeks ago, they believed the fight was about another woman. With my mother in the hospital and the grim circumstance she was in, they were aware my home situation was fragile.

Joanie finally looked up from the Maxine puzzle she held in her hands. "Will these missing papers place you with Luther?" she asked.

"I hope so," I answered. That was the truth.

"Is this going to be dangerous?"

"No," I said. That was a lie.

"What do you need us to do?" she asked. Her eyes shifted over to Rueben, informing him they were coming on board with whatever I presented to them.

Inwardly, I sighed with relief. On the outside, I gave both my friends a huge smile.

I hadn't worked out all the logistics for seeing the other people that made up MAXINE. I knew Rueben was an excellent wingman in tight situations, and his fluent Spanish could be useful. Joanie had a car.

Having Joanie be the driver kept her out of the action. I thought that would be the best way to protect her and yet keep her as part of the crew. It was funny how important it was to me to honor Joanie's religious beliefs and for her father to trust her in my company. No illegal tasks would be handed to Joanie. Rueben and I could probably cover those things between the two of us. Not that I was thinking we would be doing anything illegal. I mean, how hard is it to track down five people? I had their contact info and a good cover story.

Besides, there was nothing inherently dangerous in finding five people and looking at the ink work done on their bodies. The hazardous component of this insane adventure was what would happen if I DIDN'T decipher Terry's message in time. But I was determined I would. If anyone could unravel the crazy imagination of my mother, it was me.

We headed back to my house for dinner. We were eating through the casseroles left by Joanie's Jehovah's Witness congregation. Ollie had announced it was time to clean out the freezer so he could get back to cooking food and not baking cakes and cookies. Echo was not pleased with this as she had gotten used to having cake for breakfast. (Don't judge; a slice of cake is about the same calories as a bowl of cereal. Besides, she also had a chocolate protein shake with spinach and strawberries in it. Don't tell her about the spinach) Dusty was coming by with her girlfriend, Carla, and bringing a six-pack of beer to share with Ollie.

Echo was trying out her latest schoolyard riddle, and it went something like this:

Echo: knock knock

You: who's there?

Echo: No. Wait. Wait. I did it wrong, ...okay. What's your favorite color?

You: Purple

Echo: Spell it.

You: P...U... R... (and then Echo screeches with laughter and yells "no, no")

Echo: I... T Get it. Get it.

And then you roll your eyes as she gleefully runs off to her next victim. It almost felt like old times.

During dinner, Dusty shared a hysterical story about a couple that came into Cosmic Hearts to get matching tattoos. Apparently, the woman was hesitant and not convinced this is what she wanted to do. The guy was one of those large beefy fellows who believed in the power of his manliness. Dusty said he was drooling over the idea his girlfriend was going to have his name forever scrawled on her arm. Carla kept giggling and snorting out her water while Dusty told the story – clearly, there was a punchline coming.

"It took a full hour for them to agree on an image to go with the names," Dusty said. "He was leaning towards snakes and scorpions, while she was going for the hearts and love knots, and strangely..." Dusty threw out a wicked smile, and Carla snorted, AGAIN. "... a dog."

Dusty paused and then continued. "Finally, they agreed on a snake coiled up as a love knot with their names inked into the snake's scales. It was actually pretty classy."

"Too classy for him," Carla interjected.

Dusty smiled. "Simmer down, babe. I'm getting there. The girl insisted the fella get the design done first. He was all for it. He already had a tattoo, and he was happy to show her the ropes and help squash her fears. He was like, 'I'll hold your hand when you're getting yours. It'll be fine.' He was really playing it up, and she was really acting like he was her knight in shining armor, and she was so happy he was there to show her the way. Interesting, though. She never asked if it was going to hurt."

"Why is that interesting?" Rueben asked.

"Because it's the number one question people ask if they are worried about getting a tattoo," I answered.

Dusty continued. "So, it takes me about an hour to do the guy. He was sweating and grimacing throughout and kept moving, and I wondered how he had gotten his other tattoo done."

"He must have been drunk, Carla added.

"Yeah, probably" was Dusty's response. "So, we're all finished, and I have the girlfriend take a look. The work is good. The snake is tight, and the names "Bryan and Sarah are linked together, but plain as day to see. She stands there, cool as a cucumber now, looking at the tattoo for a long time, a long time. Then, she says, 'The wrong name is there. It should say Hailey, not Sarah' And then she walks out of the shop, I swear to God."

Ollie howled and pounded the table with his hands. Rueben's jaw dropped open. I laughed alongside Carla, who wiggled while she laughed.

But Joanie leaned in. She was intrigued. "Wait. What did he do?" she asked.

"His face was redder than the skin around the new ink," Dusty said. "He didn't say much. After she left, he asked for his money back for the second tattoo, which now wasn't going to happen. I thought that was fair, so I gave it to him." Dusty smiled as she took a swig from her beer.

"I don't understand the dog thing," said Rueben. "Why did she want a dog?"

"Cause he was a dirty cheating dog," Joanie's replied. "That's why."

"Well, if you tie it to the love knot idea, dogs also represent fidelity," said Dusty.

"They do?" asked Ollie.

"That's right," I responded. "Fidelity is trust and faithfulness, and dogs symbolize that."

"Fido is a common dog name, and *fidus* means trust in Latin," Rueben cried out. He then started snapping his fingers, and his eyes widened with understanding. "Omigod, Bess, what if this is how you figure out the puzzle for Maxine. What if the tattoos have double meanings? Like they symbolize something beyond what they are."

I sat quietly, soaking in what Rueben was saying. It made sense. It deepened the layers of the puzzle, and crossword puzzle answers can be deceptively simple and challenging at the same time. Like Terry.

Rueben jumped up and excitedly strutted around the living room. "We are going to get this. We are going to get this," he sang rhythmically as he swayed his hips and rotated his arms like he was the head of a conga line. Echo saw this and joyfully hopped in behind him. "We are going to get this. We are going to get this." The two of them danced around.

I stood there, amused and curious. "Okay," I said, smiling. "Love your enthusiasm. We really need it. But why are you dancing?"

"We are going to get this," said Rueben with absolute certainty. "You know why? Because I got a 1570 on the SAT, and I didn't even study. 1570, baby. Take that and smoke it." And then Rueben and Echo conga danced into the hallway. 1570 out of 1600 and no prep. That is pretty good.

319

WILLINGHAM CATERERS

Michael Willingham was waiting for us in an open doorway on the third floor. He was lanky, with a day's growth of beard on his face, his long hair pulled back and high into a man bun. I used to detest that style on men. However, over time, I preferred its tidy effect over the droopy stringy ponytail men sported. Michael wore an untucked flannel shirt over a white T-shirt, and skinny man jeans tucked into black Doc Martens with untied laces (of course). The whole outfit was supposed to look unpretentious, but I knew those items were all designer, and he was wearing at least six to seven hundred dollars on his body.

Everything about Michael screamed wannabe Renaissance man. However, instead of presenting an aloof demeanor, he seemed delighted to see us. His eyes were alive with excitement, and there was manic energy in his movements as he practically shoved Rueben and me through the door of his apartment.

We had left Joanie waiting in the car out in front of the apartment. I thought it was essential to keep Joanie as distant from the "investigation" as possible. Driving Rueben and me to a person's home wasn't dangerous. It was the deception involved once we were inside, that Joanie (and her father) would have a problem with. I was just looking out for my girl. Besides, as Joanie pointed out, once we pulled up in front of Willingham's building skirting the shoreline of Lake Merritt, it was smart to have a lookout person as part of the crew. It was also smart to have someone who knew where we were and what we were doing, in case - you know, the police asked. Joanie waved us out and then settled into the solitude of the car, reading "The Handmaid's Tale" for English.

I didn't know Willingham at all. He wasn't one of my mother's regulars like Xtina. When I called him following our dinner and Rueben's enthusiastic congo line, he quickly invited me over once I mentioned Terry Wynters. His eagerness prompted me to have Rueben and Joanie along.

I only knew what Dusty had mentioned to me when I casually asked. She said, "he's nice enough, I guess." I practically rolled my eyes at this non-committal, non-judgmental, no-damn-kind-of-description comment. All I had to go on was "he's nice enough," and the knowledge he had asked my mother to tattoo a golden lyre on his bicep. She had called him Wednesday, saying she suddenly had an opening in her schedule and could fit him in.

When I gave Joanie and Rueben this information, they both re-sponded at the same time. Rueben said, "what's a lyre?" and Joanie replied, "he must be a musician." Ignoring Rueben, the 1570 ignoramus, I looked at Joanie and said: "My thoughts, exactly." A lyre is one of those words that must be spelled out for people to grasp your meaning.

However, once I stepped into Willingham's apartment, I quickly realized we were all kinds of wrong about the musician assessment.

"Welcome to my home," Willingham said with a theatrical flair. His spruced-up bathroom with matching hand towels and burning fragrance candles (Ugh. Gag) was to our immediate left. But my nose was picking up some marvelous smells, and I knew it wasn't from those ridiculous candles. To the right was a shotgun hallway that presumably led to the bedroom. There was an ample open space directly in front which held the living room, and we could see a tiny deck with two chairs overlooking the sparkling water of Lake Merritt. But it was what lay to our left that captured our eyes and quickly excited our bellies.

Sitting on the countertop functioning as a divider between the living room and the kitchen was an array of finger foods. The aroma in the apartment teasing my nostrils was an overwhelming fresh smell of chopped farm stand fruit and fragrant pungent spices. It smelled heavenly, like a ripe summer day. I took a deep breath and smiled. Rueben's eyes grew as large as pizza pies as he took in the smorgasbord displayed in front of us.

Michael slapped his hands together and gleefully rubbed them, like the old cliché indicating, "let's get started."

"You two are going to help me out since you're here. I've been playing around with Asian fusion, and I want your opinion on these turkey meatballs." He stepped into his kitchen and gestured for us to move forward as he explained the dishes presented in front of us. His hand gestures were like a magician's, delicate, and quick. I was mesmerized as they danced and spun in the air, pointing at the plates as he talked.

"These meatballs are a combination of tart cherries and ginger. These meatballs are sweet cherries with ginger, and these over here to the far-right have cranberries, mandarin oranges, and a pinch of ginger." He gestured to small yellow index cards, perfectly lined up in front of each platter. "I have little cards in front of each plate, and I want you to rank your preferences. 1, 2, and 3. And then place the cards face down back in front of the appropriate dish. When you've done that, please move onto the fresh salsas."

I wanted to dive into this fabulous opportunity that had presented itself to us, but first things first, Rueben and I were here on a mission, and I didn't want to forget as I savored the food. God, I loved fresh ginger, and it was a spice Ollie detested, so we never had it at home.

Good old Rueben had already speared two meatballs from the tart cherry platter. He almost swallowed them whole and announced: "I thought you were a musician."

Michael's face scrunched up into a tight fist. "Wherever did you get that idea? I've been cooking for years. I went solo with my catering company six years ago."

Rueben looked over at me, confused. I glared back at him because I needed to be leading the questions, and I didn't want Willingham to be on guard, and now he was. There was a long pause. Long enough for everyone in the room to feel weird and awkward. Rueben covered by eating and scooping up some salsa two-fisted. I remained silent, not sure how to save the moment or what to do.

Willingham gave it a try. He arched his eyebrows and smiled. "Well, people have called me a virtuoso in cuisine...". The joke trickled away, and he decided to plunge back into describing the banquet of food.

"This here's a summer salsa with ginger. There are fresh peaches, heirloom tomatoes, ginger, torpedo onions, lemon juice, and a dash of balsamic vinegar! Over here is a spicy avocado and jalapeno dressing. I've dribbled it across salad samples. Cobb salad here and a more Tex Mex salad here. Four samples altogether. One Cobb is with Reed avocados, and the other is Haas. Then I did the same with the Tex Mex salads. Which combo sings to you more? Please take advantage of the index cards for notations. So, while you are doing that, you can tell me why you are here. I love having people over, but you called me."

"What's the Asian fusion with avocados?" I asked. I was stalling, and I knew it. The meatballs were tantalizing, and I popped two into my mouth.

"There isn't any. They just had Reed avocados at the market, and I started getting creative."

I seriously wondered what Michael Willingham served when he

wasn't creative. These ginger meatballs were popping like tiny bombs of orgasmic flavor in my mouth.

Willingham was eying me now, his dark eyes directly focused on me. "What's this all about? You said this had something to do with Terry Wynters. I just got ink done by her. And you two seem really young."

"Yes, I know. It's why I'm here."

"What's wrong? Does this have something to do with the attack?"

So, he did know about that.

"I'm Terry Wynters' daughter."

Michael Willingham drew back, pulling himself to his full and formidable height. He was a rake; thin and tall. "Oh," he said softly. Oh...I'm...dreadfully..." He tightly pushed his lips together and then broke his gaze from my face. "I'm sorry." He looked out the picture window, and it seemed for a second he was watching something on the street. His gaze was distracted. But then he turned back and looked me square in the eye. "I admired your mother quite a bit. I had heard so much about her. I was excited when she called and told me she could fit me in sooner than originally scheduled. Now that I look at you, I see the resemblance. I'm sorry I didn't notice it before."

I shrugged my shoulders. I don't expect people to remark on any resemblance to my mother and me. I'm so over that.

Michael leaned over the counter, focusing on me. "I still don't understand why you are here. I don't usually receive visits from the children of the artists who ink me."

"How much do you know about the circumstances surrounding my mother?" I asked. I decided speaking closer to the truth would be the best tactic. Besides, I wanted to eat the Asian fusion, avocado sampling, or whatever this was displayed in front of me and that Rueben had practically devoured.

"Not very much, to be honest," Michael replied. His eyes softened.

"I only heard she had been attacked. And things didn't look promising." He said the last part very softly.

Good, I thought to myself. He's uncomfortable, so he won't ask too many questions. "I don't know if you are aware of this, but you were one of her last clients."

Michael Willingham visibly shuddered.

"I'm kind of seeking closure, and I am visiting the people who saw my mother at the shop to... (I allowed myself to stammer here) ...well, to see what she worked on the last day..."

"Oh, my dear..." Michael swept me up into his arms, giving me a hug much stronger than it looked like he could possibly deliver. Over his shoulder, I saw Rueben wasn't paying us any mind and had consumed half of the Cobb salad with the Haas avocados (or were they the Reed avocados. I'd need to look at those cards)

"Your mother WAS AN ARTIST. So extraordinary. I sought her specifically to do the lyre on my arm" He pulled back then and looked at me and then over to Rueben. A smile spread across his face. "THAT'S why you thought I was a musician. Of course, it all makes sense now. Why would a man who cooks have an instrument tattoo?"

"I had the same question" were the words floating through my head, but I said, "Can I see it?" The story about the lyre must be good.

"Of course, of course." Michael whipped off the flannel shirt and pulled up the sleeve of his white T to show me the lyre my mother had inked upon his body. The tattoo was fresh and beautifully detailed. Many accents made it recognizable as the work of Terry Wynters. The color of the lyre was, in fact, golden, and sun rays were leaping from the strings as if the music the instrument played was intense and volatile instead of harmonious and melodic. It was the inclusion of the fiery sun rays that made the work compelling and distinct - much more than just a simple harp or lyre.

Michael was looking at my face, trying to read my expression. I'm trying to figure out what it means, and he thinks I am judging the design. "What do you think?" he asked.

"It's my mother's work. I love it. I like the added touch of the sun rays."

"Yes, that was her idea. When she added them to the sketch, I freaked. They were perfect."

Now came the loaded question. "What does the lyre mean to you?"

"When I was a kid, my mother wanted me to pick up an instrument. But I never could find the discipline to practice, and none of the instruments in the orchestra interested me outside of the harp. And that seemed like a useless instrument to learn for a boy. Besides, those suckers are huge and expensive." He sighed and looked out his picture window at the jeweled lake below. "When she passed away, I wanted to get something to remember her by, and an instrument seemed fitting."

"But why a lyre and not a harp?"

"That was your mother's idea, as well. It looks close enough to a harp, and the sun rays are pretty cool."

Something was missing here, but I couldn't put my mental finger on it. Looking at the tattoo and hearing Michael talk wasn't enough. "Can I touch it?" I asked.

"Sure. Go ahead."

I ran my finger over the image, making sure I caught the sun rays that vibrated with intensity. But the story played before my eyes did not connect to what Michael Willingham had said about the lyre. What I saw were multiple images of a little boy drawing pictures of Star Wars looking space capsules and astronauts floating in space tethered to rocket ships. The little boy's room was filled with Buzz Lightyear type of stuff. When he wasn't drawing pictures of space, the little boy was putting together spaceships from Lego sets. Every now and then, I could hear classical music playing on a stereo somewhere in the house, but it was the only musical connection to the story the tattoo showed me.

Hiding my disappointment, I looked at Michael and smiled. "Thank you," I said.

"My pleasure," he answered and gestured to what was left on his countertop. "Now dig in and give me notes. It looks like your friend here has left a few morsels for you."

I helped myself to what I could, and it was delicious. I tried to leave detailed notes on the cards as Michael asked, but how do you differentiate from amazing and fantastic? I made shit up.

Forty minutes had passed since our arrival, and Rueben was telling Michael how he had skipped a level of math in high school, so I believed it was time for us to go.

"I hope we have both been helpful to one another," Michael said as a farewell. "I did admire your mother's work. All the best to you."

I felt grateful, even though the story from his tattoo did not match the story he told me. There were things here that didn't fit. It was like a door that doesn't stay shut. It remained slightly open because there was something keeping it from latching correctly. Later, I would have to visualize the story and images and match it up against Xtina's cow tattoo. These thoughts were whirling around my head as Rueben, and I descended the stairs to the street.

Suddenly, Rueben grabbed my arm and looked at me with a horrified expression. "Omigod! Joanie's still in the car. She is going to be mad when she hears about the food she missed."

I had forgotten about Joanie as well. Ugh. I was a lousy friend. I wanted to kick myself. But I knew of a way to stay in her good graces and not have her ditch us out here in Oakland.

"Why don't you give Joanie those meatballs you stuffed in your jacket pocket," I said.

The shocked look on Rueben's face when he registered my knowledge of the pilfered snacks made me laugh all the way to the car. It felt good. I felt like myself again.

·

ATOMIC ALLURE

"Ariel Sanchez is a pole dancer! Omigod, this is fantastic!" The information excited Rueben, and I quickly explained the differences between a pole dancer and a stripper. (To be honest, I had to look them up myself) Initially, I was terrified about Ariel being a dancer as I had visions of having to sneak into a nightclub with a fake ID and dressing up with makeup and shit.

Rueben's excitement dimmed once the realization of getting to Ariel and her tattoo presented a logistical challenge. I had called the number listed in the client files for Ariel and learned it was a place of business. The voice recording said Atomic Allure. It then talked about the location of the studio, parking issues, and the closest Bart station. Since it was where she worked, I felt weird, leaving a message identifying myself and asking if I could see Ariel's tattoo. I had no idea what Atomic Allure was but searching around online quickly yielded some answers.

For the most part, Atomic Allure was a dance studio, specializing in pole dancing classes. They also did specialty birthday and bridal parties, and the studio could be leased out for events. I found a listing of the classes offered, and realized Ariel Sanchez was an instructor. The website also provided a picture, and I could see the tattoos on her body as she was dressed in what looked like her underwear and high heels. The three other women who were listed as instructors were wearing similar attire.

Ariel Sanchez was a knockout. She had beautiful creamy bronze skin with a luxurious mane of cinnamon-colored hair. Her eyes were the depth of black coffee, and the smile in the picture was inviting - not in a sexual way, but in a way that made you want to take her classes, which I'm sure was the desired effect.

The note my mother had written next to Ariel's name simply said, "phases." I had no idea what that meant. And looking at the picture of Ariel's body on the Atomic Allure website, my mother was not the only ink artist she visited. Ariel had at least fifteen visible tattoos on her body. They weren't connected in a unifying theme but scattered all over her arms, neck, and fingers. Like Xtina Cross, Ariel had been a regular of my mother's, but looking at the photo, I could only guess which ink jobs had been done by my mother's hand.

Joanie and I did a trial run and drove past Atomic Allure to get a feel for the place. It was in a sketchy part of town, and the studio doors were only open when classes started and ended. You couldn't just enter. You signed up for sessions online, and this determined your entry into the studio. There was a bouncer, and I didn't think I could talk my way in.

When we brought the dilemma to Rueben, he suggested I sign up for one of the classes and then be a bad student. I hated this idea because of the truth behind it, (I'm an awful dancer), but it seemed like the only way I could get inside and have an audience with Ariel. While taking the class, I would express an interest in getting a tattoo, which would prompt her to talk about the ones she has. This is where not looking like Terry Wynters becomes an asset. Ariel will not suspect anything. Something inked on her body will have a hint about phases or going through a phase (which is what I suspected). I'll do my accidental touching routine with the tattoo and get the information I needed. Easy Peasy.

Of course, it was not easy. It turns out Ariel doesn't teach any beginner classes. Then I thought I would sign up for her intermediate level and act all embarrassed when I get there and realize it is not a beginner class. That way, I still get to interact with Ariel.

Again, not so easy. The online booking system would not let me sign up for an intermediate class without prior permission from one of the instructors. I couldn't accidentally sign up for the wrong category.

This required some new problem-solving skills. I tore open a hot sauce packet and sucked down the juice. I continued to stare at the computer screen and click around the website. I was trying to figure out how to get myself in front of Ariel without it looking like a girl stalker move. I realized I was probably going to have to tell her I was Terry Wynters' daughter. I had learned with Michael and Xtina that telling them I needed closure had opened the door immediately to them, showing me their ink. People like to believe they are helping you with an emotional hurdle.

I hoped the tattoo I needed to see on Ariel wasn't on her butt. I grimaced, remembering Xtina calling out, "Are you touching it?!" to me when I was touching the cow on her butt. But since it was Xtina, she laughed at my red-faced apology, telling me if I ever needed to stroke her butt again, all I had to do was call. Something said to me that Ariel was not like Xtina. However, my problem with Ariel was physically getting to her. Ariel Sanchez was locked up like Fort Knox.

Then I saw my entry. In two nights, the studio was closed to the public due to a private party. In two nights, I could come up with a plan to crash the private party, but I needed Joanie and Rueben's help. I clicked around some more on the website and stumbled across a visual I thought I could use to my advantage.

My phone buzzed. It was Officer Lopez.

"Any news?" I asked.

"I was hoping you would have something for me," she responded.

This would have been the moment when I should have told Officer Lopez Todd was still alive. I should have said he had contacted me and was aware there was a key to a bank safety deposit box. I should have told Officer Lopez about the message my mother had left for me and that I was attempting to solve it. This would have been the moment a smart person would have come clean with the cops. However, I think we have established I am not a smart person. I am a smart-ass or one of those people who are too clever for their own good.

I mumbled something to Officer Lopez about preparing for finals in two weeks. She asked me how my sister was, and I told her Echo was doing fine. Officer Lopez asked if Child Protection Services had been by yet, and I told her no. She seemed satisfied with that answer. She then spoke about her concerns circling the lack of progress with my mother's recuperation. The current limbo state Echo and I were occupying could get dicey with the county. I decided then to ask Officer Lopez a leading question about restraining orders and custody.

"What would happen if my mother passes away or doesn't get better? Could Luther Tucker petition for custody?"

"Is he your biological father?" she asked. I thought this was an odd question, but then I realized she had seen Luther, and she knew the restraining order came from a domestic dispute.

"No."

"Weeeelll, (she drew the word out like it had three syllables), he could petition, but if anyone sought custody over him, he would probably lose. And it would be expensive, legally, for him. Who are your other relatives?"

"There isn't anyone," I answered.

She was silent. I could hear her breathing on the other end, so I knew the connection had not been lost.

"The court would seek out your biological fathers."

"That could take a lot of time," I responded. And Echo and I would be separated was the underlying thought which I didn't vocalize. "I have a favor to ask."

She sighed, and I almost laughed into the phone. "What?!" I cried. "It's not like I ask for a lot of favors."

"Are you kidding me?" Officer Lopez responded. "Every dialogue with you is a slew of favors. What do you want now?"

"Permission to see Luther Tucker," I said. "For my sister," I added.

Officer Lopez went silent again. "I can't..." she started to say. "WE can't give permission," she amended. "That's a legal issue. We can just look the other way."

"Are you guys, the cops, watching us?" I asked.

"Sometimes," was the reply.

"I thought you were looking for Todd and the drugs."

"We are. But that doesn't mean Mr. Mackey won't circle back to you if he's still alive. And if not him, then whoever he owes money to."

Once again, here was another moment when I should have told Officer Lopez about Todd and the Maxine puzzle. But I didn't trust what her response would be. I couldn't risk Echo and me being yanked from our home and kept apart from each other as the adults tried to figure everything out. Placing us in foster care increased the danger. It put us at the mercy of people we didn't know and in an unfamiliar environment. At the moment, when I was talking to Officer Lopez, I still believed I had some control, and I could figure things out.

I had also just come up with a brilliant way to get into Atomic Allure, and I needed to get Officer Lopez off the phone and call Rueben.

I ended the call with Officer Lopez promising I would keep her posted. Somehow, I believe she knew I was lying.

Rueben was thrilled I was putting him on the next case. After being fed by Michael Willingham, he was sure the pole dancers would be equally exciting.

"Look at the Atomic Allure website and go to their private party page," I told him. I listened while he clicked himself to the spot I needed him to see.

"What am I looking for?"

"See the pictures of previous events? Almost all of the food being catered is Mexican."

"So. They probably have a company they use regularly. My aunt is not going to do the gig."

"You're not looking hard enough," I said. "Look at the tables, not at what people are wearing."

"I AM LOOKING AT THE TABLES," he growled. It was said too forcefully, which meant he was looking at the dancers.

"See the picture with the guy putting down wine glasses. See what's over to the side of his left hand?"

"It's a bowl of hot sauce packets."

"Yes. It's the same hot sauce your aunt uses at her restaurant. The stuff you get for me. Go pick up a box from her before Thursday and meet up at Joanie's house by 6:00. You should wear a white shirt with black pants."

I then explained the plan to Rueben, but once I told him what he needed to wear, he got it immediately.

THE TINY DANCER

E ver since my run-in with Todd, I made it a practice to leave my bike in different spots around the city, so my location was not given away. Some days I would ride the bike to school but then take the bus home. Other days I would lock it someplace around the CAL university campus, enter a building on one side and then exit out the back. I tried to break up my routine as much as possible so there wasn't a routine.

Tonight, I was heading to Joanie's, so I stashed my bike at the North Berkeley Bart station. Her place was about eight blocks away. I didn't want the police to know I was heading to a dance studio, and on the off-chance Todd was watching me, I didn't want him to know either. I locked up my bike, went through the turnstile with my commuter card, and then hopped over the rail on the opposite side when a guard wasn't looking.

My friends were there to meet me. Joanie was the driver to allow her to maintain her distance, and Rueben and I were both wearing white button-up shirts and black slacks. We also both had on black sneakers, but I didn't think our footwear would be noticed. The important thing was to play the role. Rueben brought the box of hot sauce packets from his Aunt's restaurant. I had pegged the caterers employed by Atomic Allure used the same brand. The rest of the plan was simple.

Mr. Whittier waved his goodbyes as we headed out the door. I wondered if Joanie had told him where we were going. With the jackets covering what Rueben and I were wearing; he may not have noticed we were dressed the same.

Since Joanie and I had driven to Atomic Allure earlier, we got there quickly. We knew we could park down the street and wait for the caterers to show up. Since the place was a thriving dance hall, I guessed they wouldn't be setting up for the private event until after the last class for the day.

I guessed right. The catering van arrived about ten minutes before the class was over. We saw the dance students leave, and then the catering company began to move their equipment in. A few minutes later, some servers were dropped off, and they were wearing the uniform of black slacks and white shirts I had seen from the pictures of the website.

"We're going in," I said to my team. "Rueben, grab the box." I patted Joanie on the shoulder. "Once we are inside, leave here and wait somewhere safe for us to call."

Joanie nodded. "There's a Starbucks in Emeryville."

Rueben and I hopped out of the car and ran up the street with the box of hot sauce. We behaved as if someone had forgotten the box. In fact, that is precisely what I told the bouncer dude when he stopped us at the stairs.

"What's this?" he asked.

"We were told to bring it," Rueben answered. He then said his next practiced line. "Someone forgot to put it in the van."

The bouncer looked at us briefly and nodded his head. We were in.

Once we got to the top of the stairs, we zipped up our jackets to hide the fact we were wearing white shirts. We didn't want to actually get pulled into catering work. Two people began to direct us to the kitchen in the back.

"You need to get rid of the box," I hissed to Rueben. He propped the hot sauce box in an out of the way place, hoping he could retrieve it on our way out. He didn't want to have to reimburse his Aunt.

People were milling about everywhere. There were two large studios with mirrored walls, and they each had seven or eight silver poles reaching from the floor to ceiling. Long pads to cushion landings were stacked to the side. I looked around for anyone who could be part of Atomic Allure. But mostly what I spotted were caterers and serving staff setting up tables and pulling out tablecloths and glasses. It looked like there was an office in the far back, so Rueben and I headed that way.

A woman raced out of the office space in a halter dress. It wasn't zipped up so you could see her bra and ample breasts. I'm sure Rueben got an eyeful. She was pinning her hair up while she was moving and almost collided with me.

"What...what are you doing back here?" she demanded.

"I'm looking for Ariel Sanchez," I said.

The woman glanced at Rueben, who was wisely keeping his mouth shut. He diverted his eyes upwards to keep from looking at the mounds of flesh in front of him.

"She's back there. But I'm the contact person for tonight."

I shrugged my shoulders as if to say, *don't ask me.* "I was told to talk to Ariel."

The woman sighed and finished pushing a bobby pin in place on the bun she had been constructing in the back of her head. "Ariel, get out here!" she shouted.

"Why?" cried out a voice from the office.

"I don't know. Some teens want to talk to you." Well, at least she had pegged that right. "I need to find out what happened to the flowers." She charged ahead, entering the bustle of caterers with her dress still undone in the back. Rueben's eyes followed her. I elbowed him to keep him focused.

"I'm dressing for crying out loud!" was the response, but the other woman was long gone. "Dammit. Whoever's out there, hold on for a second."

"No problem," I responded. I wished my voice didn't sound so high and shaky. I wanted to open that box of hot sauce we had brought with us, but I thought it would look weird if we broke open our prop. Ariel Sanchez stepped out from the back room. She was wearing a dressing robe and had her hair in curlers – the ones that twist and give you ringlets. Ariel had makeup on, but she had just begun the process. The foundation was done, but she had only gotten one eye completed with eyeliner and dark shadow. The effect was disarming. I couldn't help but stare at her face.

"Who are you?" she challenged. "I don't know you." Her demeanor was guarded, and I suddenly got worried she was going to call one of the security guys over. Ariel took a few steps towards us. Her picture on the website gave you no clue as to how tiny she was. As she approached Rueben and me, I was reminded of the reality television show about families pushing their little girls into beauty pageants. That's what Ariel Sanchez looked like – a toddler in a tiara, but with mucho attitude.

"What do you want?" Ariel demanded. "We have an event starting in half an hour, and I still have a shitload to do."

"You don't know me," I started. "But you know my mother. She's Teresa Wynters."

Ariel kept her arms crossed over her chest. Her stern bearing did not waver.

"I believe you've gotten some ink done from her..."

"Yeah, so what" was Ariel's response.

"Maybe you've heard, but my mother was attacked about two weeks ago and..."

"I heard she died." Hearing Ariel speak that way directly made me flinch.

"She's not herself," I amended.

"What does that mean?"

"She may not...she won't recover."

Ariel shifted her weight and looked away. "Damn. I'm sorry to hear that". There was genuine remorse in her voice, but then she steeled herself up again. "But what do you want from me?"

"Since my mother has been hospitalized, I've been asking the last clients who visited her if I could see their tattoos."

"What for?" Ariel asked.

I gave her the answer that had worked on Xtina and Michael. "Closure."

"Damn. Really? That's fucked up. Not that you want closure or nothing, but that this could be the end of something."

I nodded. Ariel's words were more valid than she understood.

"I've got a Terry Wynters' tattoo on my shoulder." Ariel began to move the sleeve of her dressing gown up, when she stopped, snapping her finger as if she had a bright and brilliant idea. "You know who else has one of your mom's tattoo? Tina. Tina had a rabbit done, and that's why I went in to get the unicorn. Hey Tina," she hollered over her shoulder. "Get out here for a second."

Tina came shuffling out of the back office. Unlike Ariel and the woman before her, Tina was dressed and had her makeup done. Only her hair was incomplete. One side had already met the curling iron, while the other half was waiting to be introduced. Bedroom slippers adorned her feet as high heeled shoes would be the last thing she put on.

Ariel gestured for Tina to approach. Tina was a very tall girl and standing next to Ariel, they looked like Rocky and Bullwinkle. Ariel pointed at me. "This here is Terry Wynters' kid. Show her your rabbit."

Tina immediately hiked up her dress to reveal my mother's distinctive rockabilly rabbit with the pocket watch. It was possibly the most popular of my mother's designs. Literally, hundreds of people had it or pirated versions of it.

I smiled politely at Tina, who was happy to show off the inked image on her thigh. "It's one of my favorites," I said through a forced smile. Tina beamed.

"This is what I got," Ariel announced as she loosened the ties on her gown. "After Tina showed me her rabbit, I knew I had to get one from your mother." Ariel's hand reached up to the neck of the gown to pull it back. I wondered what the tattoo would be since the only note my mother had written was "phases," and Ariel had just mentioned a unicorn. I inched towards her so that I could quickly move my finger on the skin to demonstrate my fascination.

Unfortunately, I got blocked by Tina, who was still holding her dress up, displaying the rabbit tattoo. Tina started talking, "Let me tell you why I got this." I shot a quick glance at Ariel, and I could tell she had heard this story before, and she was letting her friend take the stage.

"My little brother had this stuffed rabbit toy he called Boo-boo. My brother's seven years younger than me. My moms had him with her second husband, my stepdad. Trey loved his Boo-boo. He'd take it anywhere; to the park, to the grocery store, he'd take it to the movies. My moms wanted to get a second one because she was worried he would lose it, and then he wouldn't be able to sleep. And Boo-boo was getting dirty, you know what I'm saying."

I could see Ariel was getting a bit antsy. She was shifting her weight back and forth, looking at Tina and then over at me. Ariel still had to finish getting ready for the special event. But I didn't want to interrupt Tina, and it looked like Ariel didn't want to interrupt her either.

"So, my step-dad takes Trey to the circus. I don't know if it was really the circus, but it had animals and shit. Trey takes Boo-boo, and my moms warns my stepdad not to let Trey forget his Boo-boo. But of course, that's exactly what happened. My stepdad leaves Boo-boo the rabbit. Trey came home with a balloon but no Boo-boo.

Ariel sighed and looked behind her at the office space where she had been doing her makeup and hair. I needed Tina to speed things up. I couldn't afford for Ariel to get bored and not allow me to see the tattoo I had come all this way to see.

I sensed Tina's story was not going to end well. I was right.

"My moms was furious about my step-dad leaving Boo-boo, and they got into a big fight. Everybody was freaking out. You know what I'm saying..." (I wanted to interject and say, "Yes, I DO know what you're saying) The fight was huge and shit. If Trey couldn't sleep without his Boo-boo, he sure wasn't going to sleep with all the racket our parents were making. And then my stepdad admits he threw Boo-boo away. He says Trey is too old to be carrying around a rabbit, and he storms out of the house. Trey keeps crying and crying, so I decide to go and get a tattoo of a rabbit and let Trey see it, and it would be our secret. I couldn't get a tattoo of Boo-boo, but I liked this one, and I told Trey Boo-boo got an upgrade." Tina smiled when she finished her story. I could see the joy that had powered her decision to help her younger brother.

"So now Boo-boo is always with us," she added.

"Why did you put it on your thigh?" Rueben asked. I had forgotten he was there. My head whipped around to make sure Rueben wasn't leering, but he seemed genuinely interested in Tina and her story.

"I needed to hide it," Tina answered. "I didn't want my moms to see it."

I suddenly had a lot of respect for Tina. I took a hard look at her and tried to imagine what she looked like without all the makeup. I realized she was probably only a few years older than me.

Ariel interjected. "I'm really sorry about Terry and everything, but I need to get ready."

"Yes, please can I look at the tattoo my mother inked. I see you have a lot, but I'd really like to see my mother's work."

"Alright," Ariel sighed. "It's my biggest one. But I don't have time to tell you all about it." She gave Tina an eyeful, but Tina didn't notice. In fact, Tina was off talking to Rueben.

Finally, Ariel loosened the gown enough so that her shoulder was exposed, and I could see the tattoo. It was a large unicorn - about six inches in length. The mythical creature was full-bodied and standing on a skateboard. The unicorn had a sweet face and big eyes, and the mane of the animal was curled in ringlets. The style reminded me of Ariel's hair. A red arrow pierced the heart of the unicorn, and you could see the pointed tip coming out the other side. If the arrow injured the unicorn, you couldn't tell. There was no pain in the features or tears around the face. Quite frankly, the vibe of the design was strange. My mother had not created this. The unicorn on the skateboard was an idea dictated by the client. It obviously meant something to Ariel Sanchez.

"WOW," I said as I leaned forward to touch the ink. Ariel gave me a discomforted look, but she didn't push me away. I swept my finger across the animal's body, running it all the way down to the wheels of the skateboard. I took a deep breath and allowed the story to unfold itself and blanket over me. I got what I needed and looked at Ariel and said, thank you.

"That's okay," she said and pulled the robe back over her body. "Again, I'm sorry about your mom. Maybe I'll have to go to the other lady there if I need more work done."

WHEN you need more work done, I thought to myself. Ariel had dozens of tattoos all over her body. Her arms and fingers were covered. It would only be a matter of time before she moved down to her calves and legs. I knew a tattoo addict when I saw one.

Rueben and I left quickly. Rueben was happy because he had scored

Tina's phone number. The guests for the party were starting to arrive, and Ariel only had half her face done. She shooed me away, and we grabbed the box of hot sauce packets on the way out. I texted Joanie that we were ready, and within five minutes, she pulled up in the station wagon.

Ariel's story had been rich with images and ideas, and I needed to run it past my friends immediately.

THE UNICORN AND THE SKATER BOY

Ariel's Story

The jasmine trees in the neighborhood were in glorious bloom. The pink flowers overflowed in the branches, and the sidewalk was carpeted with the blossoms. The perfumed scent added a level of princess enchantment to the night. Anticipation was in the air. To this day, a whiff of the flower spins Ariel back to that night. Even the moon in its blinding brightness contributed to the portrait of hope and wonder. It was a new moon signifying a new chapter in Ariel's life.

Ariel and her girlfriends, Kathleen and Maya, stepped up towards the house. All the magical components were there: jasmine flowers, a full moon, and being flanked by your best girls, the girls you could trust. Dance music hummed and buzzed from the house. Maya smiled and bounced as she recognized the music of her favorite band. The front porch was decorated with small green and white lanterns. The enchanting moment screamed, "Come in, come in, the party is waiting, and your life is about to begin."

The girls were ecstatic to be at their first high school party. As Kathleen kept reminding them over and over, "This was a BIG deal." They got the invitation from a high school girl they met at the mall. Classes were finished, school was out, and summer was beckoning with its languid open arms. Ariel had been admiring a pair of earrings at the fashion boutique where the older girls shopped at. She and her friends were entering Oakland Tech next year, and they were busy discussing the new styles they would be showcasing in the fall. They planned to do makeovers over the summer and enter high school looking fierce. "Fierce" was Maya's favorite new word. Maya, the science egghead, practiced and experimented with words she overheard from the fashion plates and popular kids. She wanted to make it sound like they were part of her regular vocabulary.

Ariel had tried to tell Maya "fierce" was already retro.

Maya's advice to Ariel was she should go more bohemian in her look. Ariel could braid her hair at night and take them out in the morning to get the ripple effect, and then wear long skirts with cropped tops and these earrings. Maya brandished a pair of wide, brightly colored beaded hoops that were bigger and bolder than anything Ariel had worn before.

"Oooh, those would look fabulous on you," cooed a voice behind Ariel. The word "fabulous" had sounded like it had been sung, and it sent a warm shiver down Ariel's spine. She turned around and saw an olive-skinned beauty with a mass of dark curls piled high upon her head. The girl's green eyes sparkled as she smiled at the younger Ariel. Her gaze swept over Maya and Kathleen, who were standing nearby, going through the skirt rack.

"You guys going to Oakland Tech next year?" she asked. Ariel nodded her head. At least, she thinks she did, she was too caught up in the trance of being spoken to by a high schooler.

"Hey, there's a party tonight at my girlfriend's house - end of school type of thing. Since you guys are going to be at Tech, you should go. Meet a couple of folks." The girl jotted down some information on a piece of paper and handed it to Maya. Before leaving, she turned and looked at Ariel. "You should wear those earrings."

As soon as the girl cleared the store, Ariel took the earrings and marched up to the cashier. "I'll take these please."

Kathleen was stunned at their good fortune of being invited to a high school party, and they weren't even in high school yet. "This is a big deal," she gasped. "It's a sign of things to come. It's like we are already in." They worked out the logistics of attending the party. It turned out Maya lived three blocks away from the house where the party was being held. If they all told their parents they were spending the night at Maya's home, it would be easy to sneak out and walk to the event. Maya's parents were a cinch to handle as they were constantly distracted by the escapades of Maya's older brother, Craig. Craig was already at Oakland Tech and was "a micro inch away from juvey," as Maya liked to say. Maya snickered when she mentioned they were going to a party her brother was probably not invited to. Kathleen nodded her head, exclaiming, "This is a big deal!"

"We know!!" All three of them laughed because they were sharing so much. This was a life event, and they were best friends. No better than that, they were sisters.

Now the girls were standing outside the party, excited they were launching their lives as mega high schoolers. They held the moment and shared beaming smiles. Their eyes glowed. Maya whispered to Ariel, "You look great."

"Thanks," Ariel responded. "You do too," she whispered back and squeezed her friend's hand. And with that, Maya, Kathleen, and Ariel entered the house. But it was Ariel's life that would change forever.

She knew she was in trouble when the boy first approached her. He came up from behind and spoke softly into her ear - through the waves of hair she had painstakingly unbraided and finger-combed. His deep voice resonated and made her tingle.

"And who are you?"

She had never had a boy stand so close to her. "Ariel," she replied.

She held onto the giggle erupting within her as she knew it would make her sound childish.

"Like the mermaid?" Ariel hated when people referenced the Disney princess. Not that she didn't like the movie, but the cartoon Ariel had been so silly. She started to turn around to see this boy and tell him she wasn't a stupid mermaid, but he held her shoulder, keeping her with her back to him.

"No, don't," he said. "Let's talk this way for a while. I love your hair. It's so wild and tempting. Are you wild and tempting, Ariel?"

Ariel was frozen in the moment. She desperately wished to move her head and see if either Kathleen or Maya could see her. Ariel had lost track of them about twenty minutes ago. She had gone to the kitchen to get more punch or whatever the sweet raspberry-colored drink in the large tub of ice was, and they were gone.

Where were her girlfriends? She could hear loud laughter coming from the staircase near the dance floor. Was that them? She wanted to turn her head and seek them out, and she also wanted to urgently turn around and see the face of the intoxicating male voice behind her. The face of the boy, no man, who was making her feel like a sexual being. Yes, that was it. She understood what was happening and the firecracker feeling popping through her body. She was warm and flushed, and it wasn't just the raspberry punch talking. She didn't want to disobey him. Play the game the way he was setting up the rules. His hands were warm and firm on her shoulders. She wondered if she was going to be kissed tonight.

"Are you wild and tempting, little Ariel?" The deep voice quivered in her ear.

"No," she answered. A smile escaped.

"Ahhh, but your hair says you are," the boy whispered.

"How can hair say I'm wild and tempting," she asked. And then the giggle escaped. Darn it. But he was making her feel light and free

347

inside.

"And your eyes say it as well."

"My eyes?"

"Yes, I've been watching you ever since you came through the door with your girlfriends."

"That's kind of creepy."

"What's creepy about watching an enchanted creature? You are beautiful. The most beautiful girl I've seen for I don't know, ages. I have wanted to get you alone, so I could talk to you. But..." He laughed. His laugh was smooth, and the warm breath on her neck comforted her. "You're not a mermaid. You're a unicorn. I've snared a unicorn."

Ariel admits those were the magic words. He called her a unicorn, and she melted, leaning back into his embrace. He held her tight, and after a beat, he said: "let's dance."

And Ariel went onto the dance floor and the boy who thought she was a unicorn followed. They danced to the song in their own personal embrace with her back to his chest. His face buried into her wild and tempting hair. They rocked to the music, and Ariel didn't care if Kathleen or Maya could see her or not. The moment was magic. The moment was hers and hers alone.

When the dance was over, the boy whispered into her hair. "Can I kiss you?"

Kathleen nodded her head. Of course, he could. "But I have to turn around." She slowly pivoted to face her suitor. For a fleeting moment, she was worried he would be ugly. How shallow you are, she scolded herself. But it did cross her mind. It would be her luck the boy who called her a unicorn, the boy who wooed her to the point her nerves sparked electricity and dissolved like jelly at the same time, was a dork-faced troll.

But she didn't need to worry. The face gazing into hers was attractive and kind and framed with hair that could only be described as wild and tempting. Kathleen had never liked long hair on a boy before, but her previous tastes suddenly flew out of her mind and ceased to exist. His hair was spectacular, and her hair was remarkable. A foolish thought flashed into her mind - our children would have fabulous hair.

The boy, whose name was Milo, (she would learn that later). Milo, the skater boy, was a rising junior at Oakland Tech High School. He was a bit of an outsider but admired by his peers for his reckless bravado. Milo cupped Ariel's face with his hands and kissed her on her forehead, where her unicorn horn would be if it existed. For a second, Ariel wondered could he possibly have meant that type of kiss. A chaste kiss on her forehead. Symbolic, yes, sweet and tender, but I thought he was going to really...

Bam. Her thoughts were abruptly cut off by soft, intense lips pressing onto hers. This kiss engulfed her deeply, pulling up levels of wanton desire she didn't know was possible. Her heart flew into the sky, arched into the air, and broke apart like a dazzling firework. Warm lights blazed and crackled, and Ariel felt herself melt into the boy's arms. At that moment, in that time, all she wanted was for him to surround her entirely with his solid body. His hands were moving down her body and the kisses didn't let up. He smelled like peppermint and cedar. She tasted the peppermint in his mouth and knew he had somehow prepared for this encounter by freshening his mouth with a mint. Knowing she was actively being seduced made the desirous kissing and sexual embrace even more enthralling.

The boy pulled back and Ariel's eyes flew open. She saw his beautiful face staring intently at her, soaking her up as if she were a mouthwatering sauce, and he was a slice of bread. She wanted to extend the moment and make time last forever. She loved him in an instant.

"I have to have you", he whispered into her ear. "You are so delicious. You are a delicious unicorn."

All Ariel could do was nod her head. Yes. Yes, of course, he could have her.

It happened so quickly. But in Ariel's mind the moment was pulled tight like a memory swelling and breathing inside her. Later, when she would hear the stories from Maya and Kathleen and other girls about their first times with fumbling neophytes, she was thankful Milo knew what he was doing. Ariel's first time was filled with girlhood giggles and teen passion and no other sexual experience in her life would ever match it.

Once she had nodded her agreement, Milo led her down into the basement of the house. Ariel felt so lightheaded she thought she was being carried. There was a tingling excitement within as she knew what was about to happen – this was it. This was happening, and it was going to be marvelous with this dreamy boy with spectacular hair under a starless night and a moon glowing like embers that will never die.

There were other teens downstairs, coupling quickly on bean bag chairs and in dark corners. Milo navigated Ariel to a vacated loveseat and skillfully took her virginity.

A month later, he would leave her weeping on the front porch of her parent's home.

That's why the tattoo of the skateboard riding unicorn, beautifully inked by Terry Wynters, has an arrow through its heart.

MONTEREY BAY

J oanie had a theory, and I agreed it was a good one. It's a good one, but I had no idea as to where this theory could lead us. Joanie suggested the lyre from Willingham and the arrow with Ariel's unicorn were clues pointing to the Greek Gods. In particular, the twins of Zeus, Apollo, and Artemis. All the Greek gods have multiple symbols associated with them. Apollo has the lyre as the god of music, and Artemis (also known as Diana) was a huntress who used a bow and arrow. This seemed very significant to me. I remember my mother working on a Trojan War-themed crossword puzzle a while ago. I had corrected her spelling of King Priam.

I got very excited until the cow popped up. Xtina's tattoo was a cow. A cow wearing a pink bomber jacket, but a cow just the same. In all the reading I had done on the Trojan War and Greek mythology, I don't remember there being a cow on Mount Olympus.

In fact, the cow paired up with the lyre had produced a lively discussion about Jack and the Beanstalk. For half a day, I was convinced we had it. The clues were directing us to this fairy tale with the boy giant killer. The cow was what Jack sold to get the magic beans. The golden lyre represented the singing harp he steals from the giant. And the arrow was the direction up, as in up the beanstalk.

I felt euphoric for a few hours until I got home from school and took a good look at the other images my mother inked that day to make up

MAXINE. There was the word "Howl," and then the words "Mouse" and "Crab." Now "howl" I could argue (poorly) that Jack howled with glee when he defeated the giant. But try as I might, I couldn't come up with a plausible way to work in a crab or a mouse into the story of Jack and the Beanstalk. I was resigned to the notion I needed to see all the tattoo designs to figure out this puzzle.

My next step in the Maxine investigation involved the crab, and the crab was the design belonging to Ian Kramer. Ian was going to be a challenge. Not logistically like Ariel and her pole dancing, but Ian was a musician, and Ian was always on the move.

I had Ian's contact information and called him under the pretense of follow-up tattoo care. He didn't mention anything about my mother when I called, which told me he hadn't heard about what happened. When I first talked to Ian, it was hard to listen to him because of the noise in the background, so I had to call him back. The second time there was a bad cellular connection because of where the band was traveling. Despite my requests, Ian had said he couldn't come into the studio. Finally, I was able to create enough chit chat between Ian and myself to get the name of the band he was with - Purple Medfly. I would have to go to him.

With the name of the band at my fingertips, I tracked the progress of their tour and checked to see if venues were coming up that were close enough for me to convince Joanie to drive us to. Looking at the website, I was able to discern two things. One, whoever oversaw the Instagram account, and updated their web info was meticulous. There were changes made to the band's info every day. New pictures were posted, the song lists were added, and the webmaster individual also liked to list what the best moment of the day was for the band. Even if the best thing was eating scrambled eggs with bacon and salsa for breakfast. The second thing was this band was clearly a 70's cover band, and Ian was their bass player, which meant he got a lot of action, and I don't mean James Bond action - well, actually I do.

My mother loved music from the seventies. Whenever she talked about these bands, she always mentioned the bass player along with the lead singer. There was something very cool about the guy or gal on the bass. Pink Floyd had Roger Waters. Gene Simmons in KISS, Larry Graham with Sly & The Family Stone, and of course, Bootsy! I think Sting and Flea were bass players as well.

Anyway, I could tell by the pictures posted on the Purple Medfly website that Ian Kramer was the hot one in the group. He had the most photos of scantily clad festival worshipers hanging off him. There were tons of pictures of Ian with bright-eyed girls wearing crop tops, Daisy Duke shorts and floppy felt hats with flowers fastened to the band. Posing with hand gestures as if they were street or something. They stuck their tongues out and pouted duck lips. The only thing that was different from girl to girl was the color and the length of their hair. In all the pictures, Ian flashed a dopey grin with glazed eyes, which made me believe the guy probably drank on stage.

This was information I filed away in the back of my brain as it wasn't anything I wanted to share with Rueben. And having Joanie know was a big no-no. Telling Joanie Ariel's story was about losing her virginity to a boy in high school was stressful enough. Purple Medfly might be playing nearby, but I would never convince Joanie to enter a club with me. And Rueben had a hard time convincing people he was sixteen, forget about twenty-one.

I realized dealing with an inebriated Ian Kramer might be okay. People seemed to be more honest when they have been drinking. Not honest like you're beautiful to someone who clearly isn't, but accurate in a truth serum type of way. If there were secrets to hold back, the brain didn't remember those facts as quickly as when someone was sober.

I kept going back to the tattoo story showing Michael Willingham playing with Lego Star Wars sets. It didn't match up with his claim that since he couldn't play an instrument, he had one tattooed on his arm. For what? Punishment? Michael Willingham and his lies kept toying with me. I wondered if I would have to go back and talk with him again. My mouth also still drooled over those fantastic meatballs.

There was a television show I used to watch all the time with Luther, where there was a doctor who was a jerk. He felt justified in his demeanor because he claimed all patients lie to their doctors. I remember when I first heard the character declare this on the show, I turned to Luther and said, "That's not true. Why would people lie to their doctors?" Luther pulled me in for a hug and answered, "people are embarrassed. They know their bad habits are usually the reason they are in a doctor's office, to begin with, so they lie to the doctor to downplay their bad behavior." I shrugged my shoulders at the time, not really believing what he was saying.

Later in the evening, my mind wandered as I lay in bed, and a thought crossed my mind. I lifted my left foot, so the arch of my sole was illuminated in the moonlight coming through the window. The remnants of the sparrow tattoo, inked on my foot when I was a baby, were barely distinguishable. As I grew, the features of the bird had become blurred and altered, so it was unrecognizable as anything. Someone in the know could possibly suss out the outline of a wing, but for the most part, it looked like a strange birthmark.

However, Echo's sparrow was still discernible. Her growth had not yet blurred the bird's image. Instead, it looked like her foot had expanded out and around the tattoo, distilling the image down. This made the sparrow even more apparent. The thought crossed my mind that one of the reasons Terry had spent hours watching over Echo in the hospital was that she·was terrified of someone·seeing the tattoo. Maybe she could lose her license to work or have it suspended. Or even worse, she could lose custody of Echo and possibly even me.

Tattooing one's children is not a rational thing to do, but in those moments, my mother was not rational. The deep grief growing from her excessive miscarriages created an insane focus on the daughters that survived. We weren't songbirds kept in cages, but pieces of DNA she felt compelled to claim, to stamp with a brand. When I did something noteworthy in school, she would smile and say, "Shoot for the moon, baby. Shoot for the moon". But the way she said it was more for her than for me. It was a mantra spoken to soothe her soul. She was telling a piece of herself to aim high.

Luther would shake his head whenever he heard Terry say the phrase. He was a man who finished what he started, so hearing half a statement drove him nuts. He would add the rest of the words, which were "And land among the stars." It was a phrase spoken often in the house back in the Luther days. Shoot for the moon and land among the stars.

I had been checking the Purple Medfly website daily, looking for opportunities to see Ian Kramer. There were dates set in July and August, but nothing for May or June. This made me believe they were not touring yet. Every now and then, the webmaster would post pictures of the band in rehearsals. I hoped they were hanging out in the East Bay, especially since three of the band members (Ian included) were from the Bay Area.

Finally, after checking for three days, I hit the jackpot. The group was scheduled to show up at the Monterey County fair in a surprise appearance for Memorial Day weekend. This was perfect! Monterey is a beautiful coastal city about two and a half hours away on Big Sur. It is a destination spot. I would need to convince Rueben and Joanie to take the weekend to go out there. Because of the work he must do at the farmer's market and the occasional flea market, Rueben does not enjoy street fairs or carnivals. I guess it feels like chores to him. However, food is a good enticement for Rueben.

I started formulating a plan, figuring out how I could pull this off with Rueben and Joanie's help. The following day I met Joanie at the library to help her cram for her environmental science. I had the chance to present my sales pitch.

"Monterey County is loaded with unique activities. We're finishing off our Junior year. It's been stressful, don't you think? We deserve to get out and grab life by the moments. Monterey is the perfect getaway." I sounded just like the tourist website. In fact, I had written down keywords that would appeal to Joanie and memorized my spiel. However, she was looking at me like I was a talking squirrel trying to sell her a car.

"It will be so much fun," I continued. "Rueben loves clam chowder. YOU...you love clam chowder. We can challenge ourselves to find the best clam chowder on Old Fisherman's Wharf. We can try them all!"

Joanie smiled. She liked the idea, and I literally stole that one right from the Monterey webpage. I was getting to her.

"And after sampling all the clam chowder the wharf has to offer, we could hike to the top of Garrapata State Park. They say it's quite the view!"

Joanie was peering at me with a skeptic's eyes. "I don't get it. Why are you so anxious to leave? Is it even a good idea for you to be gone overnight or for a weekend? What about Echo and stuff with your mom?"

From her point of view, it looked like I was gallivanting to Big Sur less than a month after the attack of my mother. I took a beat before responding. I really needed to have Joanie on my side, but I couldn't tell her about Todd and the drugs or the threats. I couldn't tell her there was a ticking clock involved regarding solving the puzzle. If Joanie knew anything about this, she would go right to her father or, worse, the police. I had to sound reasonable. My requests to get away needed to make sense to her. Rueben, on the other hand, would follow me if I had bacon in my pocket.

"You're right," I said. "It seems sudden. But all this stuff with my mother is getting to me. I'm still kind of in shock. Maybe lost is a better word. I go to visit her and just stand there. I don't know what to do. I don't know what to say. I have so many questions, and she can't answer them. I need to connect and find remnants of her where I can."

"The tattoos of the last day..." said Joanie. She nodded her head as if she understood a whole new side to me.

"Yes, seeing the last tattoos is really bringing it home that there won't be anymore. There is nothing new to add to Terry's gallery pages. There will be no more animal characters. No more ink. The work she has done is finished."

Hearing this, Joanie's eyes teared up, and she threw her arms around me. "Your mother's work isn't finished.", she whispered into my ears. "*You* are your mother's work. You and Echo. It's not about the ink, Bess. It's not just the ink."

I allowed Joanie's words to sink into my heart. I remained still and fought the urge within me to respond. I wanted to say something dismissive and comment about my mother's crazy behavior, but I knew it was the wrong thing to do.

From the way Joanie was holding me, I could sense this wasn't about me. Joanie needed this, as well. Joanie had immediately come to my side when she heard about what happened to Terry. It was 2 am, and she made her father get up and take her to the hospital so she could be there. Joanie wasn't family, and they made her wait down the hall until I came out of the hospital room. She waited for two hours for me. No word. No message was passed. But somehow, I knew when I released my mother's hand and entered the hallway, there would be someone outside for me. I looked up and that someone was Joanie.

Joanie lost her mother when she was eight years old. She understood the shock and the emptiness and the feelings of being adrift. She held me that early morning in the hospital corridor the same way she was holding me now. It was for fortitude and faith, not only for me but for her. Motherless girls must watch each other's back and be the cloak over each other's shoulders.

Joanie talked to her father, and the Monterey plan was in effect. In fact, Mr. Whittier contacted a member of the Jehovah's Witness congregation who lived in Monterey, and she agreed to allow the three of us to spend the weekend in her home. She had an extra bedroom for Joanie and me, and Rueben would be on the couch. I wasn't sure how I was going to pull off the county fair portion of the weekend and getting close to Ian Kramer. I might have to do that on my own while Joanie and Rueben were slurping up chowder.

Or I could come clean and tell my friends that the "I" in Maxine is playing with a band called Purple Medfly. They are performing at the Monterey Fair, which I have every intention of attending. Yeah, I could say that, but lying just seems to be my default.

I really don't know why I didn't tell them.

GET OVER YOURSELF

I am known for being a studious and organized individual and a welcoming presence in a teacher's classroom. But the last few weeks had made it impossible for me to focus on academics. I couldn't think about anything beyond my family, my friends, and my home. Discussions about college exams and personal statements bored me, and I would roll my eyes at the drama displayed in the hallways over grades and test scores. None of that shit was life and death. None of that shit was important.

A few weeks before school let out, Kelly Dallas was having a breakdown in the C building over a B- in French destroying her GPA. "I won't get into Stanford without a 4.3", she wailed. "My life is over! I'm going to die!"

I walked right up to that idiot, zoomed in on her tear-stained face, and said, "Go ahead. There will be more air for those of us who don't give a shit." A nearby vice-principal overheard my comment and goose-stepped me to the office along with the wailing Kelly, who kept crying she was going to press charges. Really? Press charges? Body shaming is an issue. So is slut-shaming. But crybaby shaming? I don't think so. Did she think I had besmirched her character? Or stolen her pride? She had none that I could see. I almost wanted her to get a lawyer and press charges just to prove my case she was an overwrought child who didn't have her priorities straight.

In the eyes of the school administration, having a mother in the hospital after a brutal beating gives one a lot of latitude in their behavior. I was out of the vice-principal's office and sucking my third packet of hot sauce in ten minutes. Kelly Dallas was still texting her parents to pick her up because she was too devastated to walk home. Give me a break. My mother is comatose, and I have a drug dealer breathing down my neck, and I can still function, but this child won't get into Stanford, and now her world is falling apart. Stanford has dodged a bullet, in my opinion.

All in all, Berkeley High School and I needed a break from each other. My counselor, Mrs. Clemson, let me know I was passing two classes and receiving incompletes in four others. I could make up the work over the summer. Mrs. Clemson gave me a bear hug, engulfing my face into her bosom and her cloying flowery perfume. She patted the back of my head, saying, "We're rooting for you, honey. Take all the time you need." I wanted to ask her who was "we"? And what were they rooting for? But I was anxious to get out of there and didn't need to test any more of Mrs. Clemson's patience.

This weekend was the planned Monterey excursion. For a profoundly religious man, I found Mr. Whittier to be quite accommodating. He never made a stink about how much time Joanie spent with Rueben and me. He didn't question our relationship or make incorrect assumptions about Rueben because he was a guy. He made the arrangements with Mrs. Marshall down in Monterey for us to spend the weekend with her, and he gave Joanie gas money. Even though we were staying with a member of a sister congregation, Mr. Whittier expected Joanie to check in every two hours while we were gone. With Mr. Whittier, there was respect and expectations mingled with his parenting.

It was realizations like this that made me feel terrible. I knew I was not matching Mr. Whittier's moral assumptions. I was deceiving his daughter by not telling her the whole truth, and she was such a great friend she was aware of this and not pushing the issue. I knew this would all come back and bite me in the ass. Cause, you know, Karma. Rueben had the biggest hurdle in clearing the weekend as Saturday was a workday in his family at the farmer's market. He needed his older brother to agree to a double shift. I jumped in and offered to work David's shift the following two weekends, so the guy was getting two Saturdays off in the future. David was cool for one of Rueben's older brothers, but he was always smiling at me. By working his shift, it was a win for me as I was ensuring I wouldn't have to deal with David's stupid grin that was always on his face whenever I caught him looking my way.

Of course, in my household, there wasn't anybody I needed to clear my schedule with. Both Ollie and Dusty knew I would be gone for a few days, and Echo would be spending the night with Luther. I knew Ollie disliked the feeling he was responsible for Echo, and her being with Luther was best for everyone around. However, I couldn't help being worried about the law and Child Protective Services. The police acted as if we didn't make a big deal about it, they wouldn't scrutinize the situation. Besides, the neighbors didn't know there was a restraining order against Luther. They were used to seeing him around.

I spent a few hours with Echo playing school, which was her current favorite game. She'd line the dolls and stuffed animals up and then do presentations of whatever was her most recent obsession. Today's topic was peas and how to watch out when a grownup tries to slip these little green balls into your spaghetti or guacamole. Her mention of the guacamole betrayal caused me to smile as Ollie had recently done this to Echo in his attempt to make the green dip lower in fat content. Echo was outraged. The look on her face when she discovered there were peas in the guacamole was priceless. If I were more social media savvy, it would make the perfect kid GIF showing shocked betrayal.

Echo believed it was necessary to train her doll posse on the ways adults were underhanded with peas in one's food. (Please, nobody tell her about the spinach in the chocolate protein shakes) I played along and pretended to be one of the students. I raised my hand, asking obnoxious questions about other vegetables and whether there are good ones or bad ones. Perhaps we can just go by their color, like green is bad and orange is good.

I loved doing stuff like this with Echo as you could really see her thought process in action. She wanted to condemn peas all together as being in the green food group. Still, I knew she liked celery. I was able to get her all worked up and flustered as she tried to explain that celery was the exception in the green vegetable rule. Finally, she dismissed me for talking too much and bothering people in the classroom, and I had to wear the "naughty" hat and sit in the back of the room. Boy was she learning how the world works.

Later Luther picked her up and promised to attend a nighttime nutrition class with the dolls after dinner. Echo ran down the hall to complete her packing and giving Luther time to focus on me. Great. (that was sarcasm)

Luther eyed me for a while. He was standing on the back porch outside the kitchen, so technically, he was not in the house.

"Ollie says that you're spending the weekend in Monterey."

"Yeah," I answered.

"Why?" Luther asked.

"Have you been there? It's pretty nice."

"Yes, it's nice. Why are you going?"

"I just needed a break, and there is a fair going on. Seemed like a good time."

"Ummm, Hmmmm," was Luther's reply.

"What you don't believe me?"

"No."

I opened my mouth in mock dismay. "I'm shocked you think that. Joanie is coming with me. And Rueben," I added.

"Now, I know you're up to something." He wagged his finger. "Joanie is your buffer."

Echo came running back. She had her overnight bag and a handful of her dolls and stuffed animals for the nutrition class on peas. She handed a few to Luther for him to hold, and he cradled them in his arms.

"Don't do anything stupid," Luther said. He turned his back and descended the back stairs.

"Mom says we shouldn't say stupid," Echo admonished.

"I stand corrected," Luther replied. He looked back at me. "I mean it. If anything happens, you give me a call. Running off to Monterey, my ass. You're still playing Nancy Drew."

Okay, so what if I am.

PURPLE MEDFLY

Purple Medfly started the set going right into the guitar riff leading into Van Halen's "Eruption." They followed that with some Cheap Trick and then transitioned into The Rolling Stone's song "Miss You." The lead singer was strutting like a rooster, channeling his best version of Mick Jagger. He wasn't half bad, the mostly middle-aged crowd loved it. However, my eyes kept drifting over to Ian. Earlier assessments of him were correct as the guy was pulling long sips from a container that couldn't possibly be water.

The group played something by Sweet, which I knew my mother had in her music collection and then went into a Ramones medley. Bob Seger's "Old Time Rock and Roll" brought on a huge cheer, and so did Dire Strait's "Sultans of Swing." Purple Medfly was good. They ended their set with a hilarious rendition of "King Tut." The musicians did the whole Egyptian hand gesture thing and had the audience mimic them.

Rueben and Joanie had a good time even though they were listening to 'old folks' music. Rueben was enjoying himself immensely as he was on his fourth corn dog. It had been incredibly easy to get them to attend the Monterey fair. We drove past the perimeter, and I said, "Hey look" while pointing at the Ferris wheel. Joanie responded with, "I love Ferris wheels! Let's go!" And that was that. We bought three tickets and were inside. I wish all my deceptions were this easy.

When the musicians were done, I moved to the front of the stage and stood beyond the metal barriers. A few roadies were positioned as makeshift bodyguards, waiting for the band to meet and take pictures with their groupies. There definitely were folks who followed Purple Medfly regularly. They greeted the musicians by name and took tons of photos, promising to post and promote them on social media. Ian was there grinning for the cameras. He had a loud disruptive laugh, and his movements were uncontrolled and sloppy. Even to my sixteen-year-old, untrained eyes, I could see the guy was both repugnant and drunk.

I began to weave myself through the crowd, moving like a needle in a giant loom. I was focused on the spot I was trying to reach. Still, if someone had been watching me from a bird's eye view, it would appear like there was no rhyme to my reason. I'd take six steps to the left to dodge the low dangling cigarette at the thigh, and then two steps front and a swivel of the hips to escape tripping over a stroller. Then, a quick dash to my right to take advantage of a sudden gap in the crowd as bodies shifted. When I finally managed to foist my way to the front, I was dismayed to find Ian was no longer there. In fact, I hadn't heard his booming cackle of a laugh for a while.

I leaned over the barrier designed to keep the festival goers from entering the designated backstage area. My eyes scanned the moving bodies lifting gear and loading the trucks. I didn't see Ian, and my biggest fear was he had already skipped out. Perhaps he had taken advantage of an offer from a comely music fan and was now out of my reach. I quickly looked to my right and left to see if anyone was observing me. It appeared I was in the clear, so I threw my legs over the barrier and moved across.

Ten seconds after hopping the barrier, I heard my name being hissed. I looked back, and Joanie was staring at me with an expression that was a mixture of annoyance and "what the hell are you doing?".

Rueben was standing next to her consuming a funnel cake. I gestured to the two of them to stay put and moved back behind the stage area, trying to walk as if I had a purpose for being there. Because, well, I did.

It didn't take long for me to locate Ian. I had been correct about the alcohol consumption on stage as the guy was puking his guts out in a bush. He was by himself. The roadies were moving music equipment and packing things up, and no one was paying any mind to the bass player. Perhaps this was a common occurrence.

I took on the role of the concerned Samaritan and dipped down next to Ian. I got low on my knees and placed my hand on the small of his back, mimicking a gesture I had seen many people do with my mother when she was vomiting in the bathroom. I leaned in so he could hear me.

"Ian. Ian, can you hear me."

"Oh, I'm so sick. Shit." He groaned.

He was bracing himself on all fours. The hard retching had stopped, but the body was still heaving. His pile of sick was laying in the dirt in front of him. He clearly had been drinking on an empty stomach as there was hardly any food particles in the mess. It also meant there was very little smell. Thank God.

"Ian, did you need some help?" I just thought I'd say that as it seemed like the right thing to say. My mind was racing as to how I could get my fingers on the tattoo. I was going to have to ask him, and I needed to take advantage of his weakened state of mind.

"That vodka was shit," he cried. "Who got the vodka? They got shitty vodka."

I patted his back and answered. "I'll check into it. Ian, would you like me to get you some water? A cloth to wipe your face?"

He groaned again and then, after a beat, slowly nodded his head.

"I'll be right back. Don't move."

He responded with a high-pitched moan, but it appeared as though I had his trust. I was helping him, and he would accept the kindness. In his condition, he wouldn't remember me later, so I needed to take advantage of the situation quickly.

Now I had the semblance of a plan, and I moved with more purpose. I approached a man with a beard screaming for membership in ZZTop and asked him where I could find a cloth or a rag.

He looked at me suspiciously and asked: "Whatcha need it for?"

I smiled and tried to look sheepish. "Ian is over there. He's sick. I thought I'd help clean him off."

The bearded roadie looked over at Ian in the bushes and rolled his eyes. This was definitely a common occurrence. He reached into his back pocket and pulled out a navy bandana. "Here. Use this. You'll find water bottles over there." He pointed over to where there was a table set up with snacks and beverages for the crew.

I thanked him and dashed over to the table as I could see it was in the process of being broken down and packed away. I grabbed two bottles and hurried over to Ian's side.

"I'm here," I said, and I placed the palm of my hand on his back again. "You want to sit up so I can clean your face off?"

"Not yet. I'm not done." He groaned loudly, but the sound was interrupted by his body heaving. There wasn't anything left, but it would take a while before the reflexive action of eliminating the toxins would cease. Next would come the head spinning, and I was hoping I could get him to talk at that point before the pressure of his pounding head caused him to pass out.

I opened one of the bottles of water and doused the sick on the ground and then piled leaves and sticks on top so no one would accidentally lean or sit in it. That no one being me.

"Who got the shitty vodka?" he gasped out.

"I told you I'd find that out. Right now, I want to help you. Can we get this jacket off, so you don't puke on it?"

He liked this idea and allowed me to slowly peel off his rather nice leather jacket and laid it to the side. I was glad to see he was wearing a tank shirt underneath. Ian was holding the position on his hands and knees, and I could see there was a lot of inked artwork over his body. His shoulder and upper arm on the right side had a design that was difficult to make out at first, but I realized this was the ink my mother had done.

I had to stare at it for a long time before I realized I was seeing a stylized Day of the Dead image of a woman wearing a golden gown like Belle from *Beauty and the Beast*. There was a coquettish nature to the woman's expression, even with the painted skull features on her face. It was not the type of work my mother usually did. Like Ariel's tattoo, this seemed to be a customer request.

Ian was gasping to steady his stomach and the heaving. He took deep breaths and began to slowly push the breath out of his nose. Watching the way he was forcing himself to concentrate on his breathing made me think he had ridden this rodeo before.

I needed to engage him before he started to line up his brain cells and wonder who this good Samaritan was. I figured the Day of the Dead tattoo was the one I needed to focus on and receive my mother's clue. Next to Ian's name, she had written "crab," and there were no crabs on the inked design.

"Here, this should help," I said. I had gotten the bandana wet and began to softly place it on Ian's forehead. The dampness on his brow had a positive effect as I saw the muscles in his face relax.

"How does that feel?"

"Great. That feels great. Keep it up."

"You guys were wonderful tonight. I loved the Ramones songs."

"Yeah," he gasped out. "Those are fun. Say, what's your name? Do I know you?"

That was information I wasn't going to share, so I decided to move closer to my target goal. "I couldn't help noticing the tattoo you have on your back and shoulder. It's beautiful. The woman has a lovely expression on her face, and I heart the dress. It looks like she is dancing. It's really cool."

Ian closed his eyes, and a mournful expression flooded his features. "That's Chloe. That's my Chloe."

"Oh," I responded. "Is she your girlfriend?" I threw the question out there knowing I was striking a match and possibly having it land on gasoline. I had already seen this guy hit on every scantily clad female under the sun. If he had a girlfriend that he was inking on his back, it would just underscore what a cretin he was. But the lost look on his face was beginning to tell me something else.

"She was. She was my girlfriend. She's gone now."

And by "gone," I knew Ian didn't mean she had moved to New Jersey. He meant Chloe had died. The Day of the Dead makeup on her face was confirmation. I was out of my league here. Knowing the story would be unpleasant, I braced myself and touched the tattooed face commemorating Chloe.

"I'm sorry," I said, which seemed like the only thing to say. I added more water to the bandana and continued stroking Ian's brow. My hands shook as the powerful emotions I received from his ink, speared my heart, and then sank and settled within me. Ian didn't notice. I kept my strokes gentle and comforting, operating the way I would if my sister was suffering from a fever. "Do you want to talk about it?"

"Not really," he answered. But then he did. He shared his story with the nameless Samaritan, who already had the tale from the ink on his skin.

ALL FOR CHLOE

Ian's Story

Ian Kramer and Chloe Brandt met at Berkeley High School. In Chemistry, to be exact. Under the owlish glare of Mrs. White, they performed lab assignments as chemistry partners. They laughed at the fact they were both bumblers and unable to execute the exact measurements Mrs. White required. They bonded over spills and toxic fumes.

One day Chloe mentioned she needed a beach vacation. She was coughing due to the plumes of smoke that were either her fault or Ian's. It didn't matter, the entire classroom needed to be vacated so the room could be adequately aired out. There were tears in her eyes, and Ian thought she was crying, but it was really the chemicals. They were both huddled together in the hallway. Chloe was coughing, dabbing her eyes with a tissue while Ian furtively glanced at the other students. The other members of the chemistry class were glaring at them. The toxic duo was going to be reassigned, and nobody wanted to be their lab partners.

"This sucks," Chloe exclaimed. "I need to go and chill at my favorite place."

"Where's that?" Ian asked.

"The beach. I need the white noise of seagulls and waves hitting the rocks. It calms me, and I can breathe."

At that moment, Ian was determined to ask Chloe out and take her to the beach. It would be their first date, and his mom could help him assemble a picnic. Ian was incredibly happy because he had a plan.

As anticipated, Mrs. White scolded the two of them and paired them up with different lab buddies. The new chem partners groaned upon hearing their names linked with the toxic duo, as they could see their grade point averages plummeting. But Ian didn't mind. He didn't hear a word of Mrs. White's lecture or the sulking noises of his new chemistry buddy as the only thing threading through his elated brain was "I have a plan. I'm going to take Chloe to the beach, and she'll love it. It's her favorite place. I can't lose."

Two weeks later, when he was sure the East Bay weather would hold up, Ian asked Chloe out to the beach. He said he would prepare a picnic, but Chloe needed to choose the spot. There were lots of beaches on the coastal line, and Ian wanted to go somewhere Chloe favored. She was delighted, and they went out to Stinson Beach. Ian brought along a wicker picnic basket and checkered tablecloth. They were the kind you saw in the movies. Ian's mother had prepared thick ham sandwiches with mustard and spicy pickles. There was also potato salad, chewy cookies, strawberries, and sparkling water to drink.

The temperature was chilly, so they didn't completely strip down to their bathing suits. But they ran on the beach, laughed and played in the waves and Ian was enchanted. Chloe was too and wanting to make the date perfect and not wishing to hurt Ian's feelings, she didn't tell him she was deathly allergic to strawberries. And Ian failed to notice she didn't touch them at all.

Beach destinations became the focus of their courtship. Before Chloe was in his life, Ian hadn't spent much time at the beach. His mother had always disliked taking her children to the coast. She intensely disliked sand and hated the fact that a good gust of wind could send the grainy particles into what would have been a perfectly put together meal. She also hated the seagulls dive-bombing for your food if you weren't paying attention. Then there was the sand that followed you back home. You just couldn't get rid of it. The sand would hide in your shoes and the cuffs of your jeans. It was maddening. But Ian's mom saw her son was madly in love, so she encouraged the beach trips. Having Chloe in his life had transformed Ian from a snarling seventeen-year-old to a darling lovestruck goofball.

Mrs. Kramer, Ian's mom, wished she could clone Chloe and have her around always. So much got accomplished because, in Ian's eyes, it was all for Chloe. Graduate from high school? Sure, because it was all for Chloe. Go to San Diego State? Yes, because it was all for Chloe. Get an apartment in Oakland? You bet because it was all for Chloe. Chloe loved the music from the seventies, and Ian joined a cover band because it was all for Chloe. They struggled with the struggles young couples do, but their lives were full, and it was all for Chloe.

Their love for beaches expanded beyond the California coast. Once Ian owned a reliable car, they would spend their vacations driving across the country to visit the beaches in the Gulf of Mexico and the east coast. One time while they were at Pickering beach in Delaware, Chloe heard about the horseshoe crabs and their mating season in May and June during the high tides and the full moon. This was something she had to become a part of, so they registered to be volunteers in Delaware Bay for the Memorial Day weekend.

The first night they spent on the beach rescuing the crabs was spooky and exhilarating. The crabs came out of the waves following a primal spawning ritual. Their movements were eerie as they crowded the sands seeking mates. Ian had never seen horseshoe crabs move before, and it was very different than the Maine and Maryland crab sidestep he was used to seeing. The crabs stumbled along. Some found mates, and some kept moving farther and farther away from the water.

A few got flipped on their backs from stones and the uneven terrain.

The head of the rescue team encouraged them to wait until early light to turn the crabs back over. Daylight was necessary to help the ones that got stuck in driftwood and other encumbrances keeping them from being able to return to the water. Even with a bright moon in the night sky, there was the danger of a volunteer not seeing a crab before they heard the crunch under their feet.

Ian and Chloe helped rescue the stranded and upside-down crabs at dawn. Chloe's face was flushed from the excitement, and wild strands of hair flew about her from the brisk morning wind coming off the Atlantic. This simple act of compassion for the sea creatures brought out the best in her. She was making a difference. Ian had never seen her more beautiful.

That afternoon, Ian called his mother and asked her what had been in the picnic basket on the first date he had with Chloe at Stinson Beach. Ian intended to recreate the meal, and he and Chloe would eat while they watched the crabs come onto the beach. Mrs. Kramer recited the items: ham sandwiches with pickles, potato salad, chocolate chip cookies, strawberries, and sparkling water. Ian decided to switch out champagne for the sparkling water. They were celebrating, after all. It was the last conversation where Mrs. Kramer heard any joy in her son's voice.

That evening as they watched the crabs slink out of the waves, Ian told Chloe he had a surprise. He brought out the champagne and poured a glass for the two of them. They sipped and talked about their future. Chloe mentioned maybe they could leave Oakland and live on the east coast. Ian replied he was okay with that. Then, Ian told Chloe to close her eyes for the surprise. He broke off a piece of the ham sandwich with pickles he had the local deli prepare and placed it in her mouth. Chloe chewed and giggled as Ian fed her, but she dutifully kept her eyes closed. Then Ian fed a spoonful of potato salad to Chloe.

She gasped as she recognized this was the picnic from their first date.

Then Ian placed a strawberry on Chloe's lips, and she took a bite. Chloe's eyes flew open. She spat the fruit out, and her face teared up.

"Why'd you give me a strawberry?" she cried.

"It was part of the picnic," Ian answered. He had no idea what was happening.

"No, I'm allergic." Chloe choked. Her throat was swelling, and the tightness in her chest made her wheeze.

They were two miles away from the car, where Chloe had left her bag along with her EpiPen. Ian stood up and looked around for the other scattered rescuers who were on the sidelines of the beach.

"Help!" Ian called. "Help, we need an EpiPen. My girlfriend can't breathe."

A group of the rescuers came to Ian's aid. No one had an EpiPen, so they helped Ian carry Chloe to the car. Three other men hoisted Chloe up so they could run, and others moved ahead using flashlights and lanterns to light up the ground, so the men didn't stumble.

Chloe was in shock and barely coherent. "Don't hurt the crabs, Ian," she gasped. "Don't hurt the crabs."

Ian sobbed and apologized profusely. He promised her everything from the moon and back. "Just hang in there, baby," he said over and over.

By the time they made it to the car and administered the dose, twenty minutes had passed. An ambulance was called, but Chloe had already stopped breathing.

***

Ian's sadness was profound. The guilt he endured because he fed his girlfriend, the morsel that killed her was intense. This story explained so much. The lack of connection, the wandering, the drinking. Ian didn't care anymore.

He had fallen asleep long before he got to the end of his story, but his tattoo of Chloe had told me the rest. Everything Ian said was truthful. His tattoo confirmed he didn't know about Chloe's allergy to strawberries. It was an honest and tragic mistake.

I shifted my body so I could relieve myself of Ian's weight and slowly lower him to the ground. I took a last look at the tattoo and noticed something peculiar about the bottom of the dress the woman was wearing. Initially, when I had glanced at the golden gown, I had thought the detail at the bottom was lace, but now I could see the design was tiny horseshoe crabs. Ian had done the tattoo of Chloe in the memorial makeup and golden gown a long time ago, but these little crabs at the bottom of the dress were recent add-ons. This was the work my mother inked when Ian came to see her on Thursday as the "I" in Maxine. The crabs were the highlight of the story.

I stood up and wiped my hands on the back of my jeans. Folks had drifted away from the staging area as the festival was winding down for the night. My eyes searched the area for my friends. I didn't have to look very far. Rueben was only a few yards away, chowing down on a large bag of kettle corn. Joanie stood next to him, staring in my direction. Her hands were on her hips, and she did not look happy.

PICTURE PUZZLES

A cow, a lyre or instrument, a unicorn, and a crab. I had drawn sketches of these images in my notes. I was not the artist my mother was, so both the cow and the unicorn were a little misshapen. I cursed myself for not taking photos of the tattoos when I had the opportunity. It seemed so obvious now, but at the time, taking a photograph was like it a breach in the personal boundaries the individual was granting me. I was already touching their skin, taking a picture felt uncouth, especially when I realized one of the photos would be of Xtina's behind. My memory would have to serve.

There were circles around the images and added phrases or possible thematic ideas like "Jack in the Beanstalk?" near the cow and "Rock and Roll" because of the leather jacket. The lyre had words like "Greek God" and "Apollo" and "Olympus." All the ideas discussed with Joanie and Rueben were somewhere on the paper.

Joanie was furious with me about Monterey. She said nothing while we were with Mrs. Marshall. But all the way back to Berkeley in the car, she read me the riot act, shouting about drunk men and reckless girls. I told her she laid down more rules than my mother and the cops combined. She ignored my comment and just told me to do what I had to do. She waved her hand like I was an annoying fly. She was angry, and I wasn't sure how I could fix it.

She came over after school to assist with the Maxine puzzle, but her emotions were still simmering with displeasure. Thankfully a eureka moment dispelled the tension when Rueben yelled, "*Fantasia*"! We rushed to the shelves, where I knew we had the movie in our possession. We watched thinking we had the answer as we saw unicorns and Greek Gods on the screen. Then I remembered there was a Mickey Mouse version of Jack and the Beanstalk, and Joanie reminded us about Ariel, the mermaid, and Sebastian, the crab. We were getting ahead of ourselves, but our brains were clicking. Nikko and Emily were the last two people to locate. Their notes had said "howl" and "mouse." We kept thinking howl meant a werewolf, but it could be something else. I hoped howl wasn't werewolf because there isn't a werewolf in any of these movies. That was the problem with these clues, there was always one that didn't fit into place.

"*Hocus Pocus* has a werewolf," Joanie threw out in the discussion.

"No, it doesn't," Rueben responded.

"Are you sure?" Joanie asked. "I'm pretty sure I saw a werewolf."

Rueben turned to me. "Bess, is there a werewolf in *Hocus Pocus?*"

"I don't know. I didn't see the movie."

"You never saw *Hocus Pocus*!?" they both cried out incredulously. I was beginning to wonder how Joanie saw *Hocus Pocus*. There are a lot of contradictions in that girl.

"You guys, please don't tell me the solution to finding the key is Disney," I said.

"Yeah, we don't want to fall down that rabbit hole," Rueben responded. We all groaned.

Joanie and Rueben took off, and I was left to ponder the meaning of the Maxine board I was creating. I drew lines connecting the images in order of MAXINE with question marks around the tattoos I had not yet seen or touched. I was transferring the work from paper and using the board Ollie had mounted when we first were trying to figure out what Maxine was. My Maxine board with sketches and phrases and question marks mapped out did resemble the television show murder boards. I wondered if policemen really did that. Did Officer Lopez have a board up that she was looking at as she tried to solve the crimes surrounding Cosmic Hearts? I doubt she had Jack and the Beanstalk written on hers, though.

Echo came in, holding a picture of a cow. Her drawing showed a smiling cow eating grass under a sunny sky. "Here," she said, handing me the drawing. "Put this one up. Yours is boring."

"Thanks," I said, ignoring her little jibe. Echo had definitely inherited the artistic gene from our mother. Her cow was much better than my cow. I removed my shabby drawing and placed hers in its place. We both stepped back to admire her handiwork and how it beautified my Maxine board.

"What are you doing?" Echo asked. She gestured to the whole board and its contents.

"I'm trying to figure something out," I answered.

"Is it connect the dots?" Echo had a lot of connect-the-dots picture books, and I'm sure my lines linking one image or idea to the next reminded her of that. "It doesn't look like anything," she said.

"I know," was my reply.

"I think you missed a dot somewhere."

"I know," I sighed. This kid was really grinding my gears.

"Maybe the little pictures are part of a big picture." She skipped out of the room and came back with one of her "Where's Waldo" books. She opened her book to a random page. "Look," she said, patting the page showing an immensely detailed drawing of medieval England. "This is the big picture." She swirled her hand around the page. "But then over here is a cat hiding in a barrel. Here's a lady hitting a man with a long piece of bread. Oh look, there's Waldo. And see, right here is a horse eating an apple." She pointed at each image as she spoke.

Small pictures that were part of a big picture. I think Echo was onto something. Perhaps what my mother was doing was building a larger image instead of leading me to a smaller one. I felt on edge, and tingly like something important had just happened.

I got it. My mother was using a crossword puzzle to build a picture puzzle. She liked words, but I was drawn to thematic images. She had crafted this puzzle for me to solve. What was the bigger picture?

"What is that?" asked Echo. She was pointing to my poorly sketched horseshoe crab for Ian Kramer.

"It's a crab," I answered.

"I don't see it," Echo answered. She gave me a pitiful glance and left the room, shaking her head. "I'm going to draw you a better one."

I knew whatever crab Echo designed would look just like Sebastian from *The Little Mermaid*.

It's a rough day when your six-year-old sister gets to put you in your place.

CPS

I approached the house from the east and saw an unfamiliar woman standing on the front stoop. She was dressed in a basic skirt, beige sweater, and a scarf to add some life to the ensemble. Modest brown loafers adorned her feet. In her arms, she held a stack of folders. Everything about her screamed Child Protective Services.

I paused on the sidewalk. My brain racing. What should I do? I could turn and run, give an excuse claiming I didn't see her, and I need to meet with a study group for a class. But then she'd come back another day. And perhaps that day would be frightful and chaotic. Besides, the study group or class excuse might not work. She could be informed about my mutual "time-out" from high school.

I breathed in and out, releasing the air through my nose. No, I surmised it is best for me to confront her now. Perhaps I can make this quick and send her away.

I walked slowly down the street watching her warily. Eventually, she looked over and saw me. A quick glance inside a folder must have confirmed I was Elizabeth Wynters. She waved and gestured for me to come up the steps as if she lived in the residence and not me.

"Elizabeth Wynters?" she asked.

"Bess," I answered. "I go by Bess."

She flipped open her folder and made a notation. Looking up, she flashed a smile, but it wasn't genuine at all. In fact, I was getting weirded out by this woman. She wasn't a predator like Todd. No, this woman reeked of bureaucracy.

"I'm a little early," the woman explained. "I was told you got home around 4:00. And look here you are, 4:00 on the button." She looked around me. "Is there a reason you didn't ride your bicycle?"

My eyes widened. WTF? How does she know I ride a bicycle? Without thinking how it would sound, I asked "Is my bike riding in your file?"

The woman pressed her lips together in response to my flippancy and pushed back the glasses on her face. "Yes," she said. That is in the file. It says you use a bicycle as your mode of transportation. I don't see it, so I was wondering if it was stolen. Those can be very pricey to replace."

I had to keep myself from frowning at this woman. Fear was seeping into my body like a chill in the air. I had always worried our family court file was thick and filled with personal information that shouldn't be public knowledge. The woman's eyes were bearing down on me as she waited to hear the answer regarding the status of my bike.

I didn't want to say where it truly was. I had left in on the CAL campus to shield my movements from Todd. Not that he was following me, but he was following me. My bike had become a liability if I didn't want Todd or whoever to know where I was. I figured the house was safe – even if we didn't have the police on constant surveillance.

Now Child Protective Services was standing on our doorstep to protect the child. That meant this woman was here thinking she might remove my sister.

It was as if the woman was reading my mind. "Where is your sister?" she asked.

"She'll be home soon," I responded.

There was a long pause and the woman looked at me expectantly. It took me a minute to realize she was waiting for me to invite her inside. Talk about the one thing I didn't want to do. It's not that the place was a mess, I knew it wasn't, but inviting her in seemed like she was an invited guest. And nothing was farther from the truth.

Finally, I bit the bullet and said, "Would you like to come in?"

She smiled her condescending smile again. "That would be the idea," she replied.

I opened the door and let her in. I've always believed my mother's anger at people's judgments to be over the top, but here I was witnessing an example of the type of judgment my mother despised. This woman didn't know us - she didn't know us at all and yet she was stepping into our home ready to make a judgment and write a report. Her report would be added to all the other reports in the folder and anybody reading them would believe they knew our family. But there was so much they were missing. For instance, anything about Ollie would only state he was a tenant and not the keeper of the kitchen. Ollie's cuisine and his boisterous sense of humor kept this family content and loved. There would be no mention of Dusty outside the fact she was Terry Wynters' business partner at Cosmic Hearts. Dusty's no nonsense viewpoint kept my mother from falling into too many flights of fancy. Then, of course, there would be no mention of Luther (outside of the restraining order). Luther's attention and support had shown both Echo and me what we were missing by not having a father around. Luther grounded us. He was the solid rock that kept the helium filled balloons from drifting into the sky.

None of those people were in the file. And right now, those were the adults in my family circle.

I watched the woman as she stepped over the threshold and into the foyer of the house. She looked around at the large couch and love seat filled with throw pillows, the worn-down Asian rug, and the multiple art projects in different stages of completion. Some of the art projects were notions of my mother's who wanted to experiment in different mediums. Some of the art projects were Echo's as she mimicked our mother. By the way, if people ever wondered where the nickname "Echo" came from, it was a combination of her physical resemblance to our mother and her proclivity to play in the art world.

I was reminded of this when the woman asked where Eleanora was. I almost said "who," but thankfully caught myself.

"She had a playdate after school," I answered. "She's scheduled to be back at 5:00. Ordinarily, I would be studying during this time period." The comment was said to let this woman know she was interfering.

"Yes, but you're not in school right now," the woman replied.

She did know about that. I realized being placed on a "forced hiatus" in a public school was probably something the authorities would be notified of. Government agencies stick together in theory.

"I might not be attending classes, but I still have work I need to hand in," I said. "We didn't know you were coming. Otherwise I would have had my sister here at the house."

"The purpose of a surprise home visit is to see how you are functioning on a day to day basis and not what you do when company calls."

Company!? Did she just compare herself to company?

The woman walked into the kitchen and looked around. She then pushed open the door to my bedroom and peered inside. It sounds stupid, but I was glad I made my bed this morning.

"This is your bedroom?" the woman asked.

I didn't answer because something flippant was about to fly out of my mouth.

She looked around the back of the bedroom door and noted the locks. She played with the deadbolt, moving the mechanism back and forth. She then made a notation on a piece of paper in the file. I stood there, saying nothing.

The woman then moved towards the staircase that led to Ollie's bedroom and his private bathroom.

"That's where Ollie stays," I said.

"I'll just go have a look," the woman replied. She disappeared up the stairs. Her sensible shoes treading softly as she climbed. I didn't follow her. Instead I listened as she moved about on the upper floor. I didn't hear drawers opening, but she did open Ollie's closet door and move items back on the hangars. After a beat, she came back down.

"That's a lovely space for the tenant," she observed. "Do you happen to know where your mother keeps the rental agreement and his references?" The woman looked about for a desk or office space that would indicate where such important papers would be located.

I knew Ollie's lease was somewhere in his room, but I stated, "you'd have to ask my mother where she keeps it."

The woman looked over at me, with an expression that could have been read in many ways. Did she think I was being a wiseass or just sadly mistaken?

To help her along with the assessment, I replied, "Oh, I'm sorry. You can't ask her right now. Perhaps, later."

The woman ignored me and continued to move through the other side of the house. She glanced into Echo's room and then took her time walking through the master bedroom and bathroom. She moved back into the hallway and stopped. "What's this?" she asked.

She was standing in front of the Maxine board. While she had been upstairs in Ollie's space, I had debated covering the board with a sheet. But I felt that would draw even more attention to it. I was hoping she would see all the other partially completed projects and believe it was like them.

The woman continued to look at the drawings and images taped on the board and the phrases marked alongside them.

"It's a game I'm playing with my sister," I explained.

"How do you play it?" the woman asked.

I opened my mouth and stuff just flew out. "Well, it's hard to explain, but I was teaching her about storytelling and identifying key elements in a story. This is about Jack and the Beanstalk. The cow is there because Jack goes to town to sell the cow which is what launches the story."

The woman nodded. "I see you have Jack and the Beanstalk written here. But what is the crab for?"

"Um, she likes *The Little Mermaid*, and they have a crab in the story."

"And the unicorn?"

"She wanted the land where the giant was to be magical."

The woman appeared puzzled.

"She's six," I responded as if to offer an explanation.

"Teaching a six-year-old the fundamentals of storytelling is ambitious," the woman said. She turned away from the Maxine board and wrote something else in her file.

I kept my mouth shut. I just wanted this woman to leave. "Is there anything else I can help you with?" I offered.

"I need to see and speak to Eleanora," the woman replied.

"She's at a friend's house," I answered.

"That's fine. I'll wait."

The last thing I wanted was to sit with this woman for the next hour. She wasn't particularly interested in speaking to me. That's okay, but I didn't want her to talk to Echo and have my sister blurt out stuff about Luther.

"Would you like me to contact the family and ask them to bring Echo home earlier?" I asked.

"That's not necessary," the woman replied.

"Oh, I insist," I said. "Why hang around here when you could be back in your comfy office? I'll call them now." I rang the Kellys and told them there was a social worker at her home who needed to speak with Echo. They understood and agreed to bring Echo back early. I then asked to speak with my sister, briefly.

"Hey, Echo," I said. "There's a nice lady here at the house who wants to talk to you. Maisie's parents need to bring you home now."

Echo sighed and complained about not finishing her snack. They had just gotten back from the park.

"Echo," I said. I added a firm tone to my voice to get her attention. "There are no orange kitties, got it. No orange kitties."

Echo went silent. Then she said, "Okay," and ended the call.

I was pretty sure she understood what I was saying.

Back when our mother had destroyed Echo's drawing and torn out the section depicting Luther holding an orange kitten, Echo and I used that image to convey happiness. Echo had created the picture to be a depiction of her contentment. Whenever we did things together and I saw her smiling, I would say "Orange kitty?" and she would answer "yes, orange kitty." When we sent her to Luther's while I was in Monterey, I had said "orange kitty," and she cheerfully clapped her hands, knowing she would be staying with Luther. I hoped by saying "no orange kitty", she understood not to talk about seeing Luther.

Fifteen minutes later, the Kellys brought Echo home. The woman went outside and spoke briefly with Mr. and Mrs. Kelly. I could see Maisie in the backseat of the car. The Kellys were the type of people who know how to handle bureaucracy. They had two car seats in the back, indicating my sister had been securely and properly fastened in. I noted the woman peeked and saw the extra car seat as she waved at Maisie.

I had Echo alone for a second. I crouched down and looked her square in the eye. "No orange kitty," I said again.

"No orange kitty," she whispered back. There was sadness in her expression. She got it.

The woman entered the house and closed the front door. I felt a shiver as we were alone with her in the house – even though it was our house. The way she closed the door it was like a sinister individual shutting the door between you and the last possible means of escape. Echo and I took seats on the couch while the woman sat in the chair across from us.

"Well this is delightful," she stated. "I have the two Wynters daughters sitting here together." She spoke with a wide smile as if she was going to interview us for a gossip magazine. "What is your full name and birthdate?" She said to the both of us.

I answered and then began to do Echo, but the woman stopped me. "I'd like to hear her say it" What is your full name, dearie?" she said to my sister.

"Echo Wynters," my sister responded.

"Your full name," the woman said.

I leaned in and whispered to Echo. "The long one," I said.

"Echo Haydn Wynters," my sister responded.

The woman appeared puzzled. "Who is Eleanora?" she asked.

"I don't know," said Echo, and she shrugged her shoulders.

"No one calls her that," I explained.

The woman made a noise with her teeth and moved on.

"And what is your birthdate...Echo is it?" You could tell she didn't think highly of the nickname.

"August 22nd," my sister responded. "I'll be seven."

The woman made a notation which I found odd. She had to have this basic information in the file. Was she writing down the child didn't know her proper name, but knows her birthdate?

"So, what have you been doing since your mother has been in the hospital?" she asked.

"Going to school and playing with Maisie," Echo replied.

"Have you had a chance to see your mother at all?"

Echo looked at me and I jumped in to intervene. "I visit our mother a number of times a week," I offered. "And I bring pictures and drawings completed by my sister, and I describe them to her."

The woman looked at me sternly. "Your sister has not been in to see your mother?"

"Have you seen our mother?" I responded. "Do you know how she looks? Do you know she can't respond or move?"

The woman opened one of her files and began flipping through the pages. "What I have here is she is in a coma, but it says it was an induced coma brought on by her doctors."

I leaned in so Echo would not hear what I was saying. "She's in a coma because she was beaten. The swelling was so bad on her brain the doctors placed her in a coma. Do you know what a person looks like when they have been kicked repeatedly in the skull? We are sparing my sister from that image and I would appreciate it, if you didn't mention the injuries our mother is suffering. All Echo knows is that Terry is sick and in the hospital."

Thankfully, the tension was interrupted by the arrival of Ollie coming in through the back porch. "Who is here?" he shouted.

"We're in the living room," I answered.

Ollie flounced out of the kitchen. "Who is we?" he demanded, but then he saw. There was no mistaking the woman's attire. She was clearly bureaucracy. Ollie straightened his shoulders and tightened his hips as he continued to move.

"Hello," he said, extending his right hand. "I'm Olliver DeMatteo."

The woman gave her name and handed Ollie her business card. "Do you mind if I check this?" Ollie asked. "I'll just call the number on the bottom."

The woman smirked. "I'm not at my office," she said. "No one will answer."

"I'm not calling you," Ollie replied with a laugh. "But someone will answer the line before I am sent to your extension, and I can verify your position. Excuse me for a moment." He gave me a knowing look before heading back into the kitchen.

Damn. Why didn't I think of checking her credentials? That was a smart move on Ollie's part. Not that I didn't believe this woman wasn't from Child Protective Services, but it was smart to show you were checking up.

Ollie came back in the living room and sat in the love seat. "Thanks, Mrs. Woodman," he said. "You never can be too careful. Especially since I return home and find you here alone with the two minors of the household without an adult's permission or knowledge."

"Are you a tenant of the house?" Mrs. Woodman asked.

"Yes, I am the legal tenant," Ollie replied.

"You have a splendid arrangement upstairs."

"Oh, you saw my room."

"I must view the entire premises," she replied.

"Did you view the basement?" he asked.

"I didn't realize there was a basement."

"Mostly storage, but it's still a basement."

"May I ask what your rent is?"

Ollie smiled. "You can ask, but I won't answer. That's between me and Theresa Wynters."

I had never seen this side of Ollie. I liked it.

"Why don't I show you the basement and then you can be on your way," said Ollie.

"I'm not finished talking to the girls," Mrs. Woodman replied.

"Oh, go right ahead," said Ollie, gesturing grandly to my sister and me with his arms.

Mrs. Woodman had lost her intimidating edge. When she tried to ask a question that went beyond our daily activities of school, meals, and sleep, Ollie would lean forward and ask her the purpose of the inquiry. He was really nailing this woman whose nosiness was going far and beyond professional necessity. Ollie made sure Mrs.

Woodman's questions stayed within the parameters. He didn't cross the line and answer for us, but he made it clear to her, who was in charge.

Ten more minutes passed, and then he stood up declaring it was time for her to see the basement. He needed to get dinner started so Echo and I could remain on our schedules. Mrs. Woodman was shown the door leading to the basement. The basement was really a large dirt space under the house, but one side had been leveled and concrete was poured to create a secure storage area for the rainy season. There were stairs heading down to the space from the hallway. Mrs. Woodman peeked down, and then withdrew. I can't blame her. The space smelled like wet musty boots and acrylic paints.

She thanked us for the visit and then headed out the front door which Ollie was holding, wide open.

Ollie shut the door, and then melted to the floor. "Omigod," he exclaimed. "That was exhausting. What a witch."

"Maybe we should have thrown water on her," Echo added.

Ollie and I burst into laughter.

HOWL

Nikko's Story

When Nikko first heard the siren, he panicked. He was doing the driving, and even though he was handling the road okay, there were the four beers he had drunk less than an hour ago. Nikko didn't think he could pass any type of road test. Plus, this was Mike's car, and Mike was in the backseat passed out along with Gates. Blue lights blinded him in the rearview mirror, and Nikko had to remind himself to breathe and see if he was being pulled over. Count to five and see. Every fiber of Nikko's being wanted to yank the steering wheel to the right and make a run for it over the flat terrain. Maybe a wilder person would have followed through with that instinct, but not Nikko. He was the steady, reliable one, even after four beers.

This had been one crazy night. Actually, it had been a crazy weekend. They were on their second day of celebrating, and it took Nikko a full minute to remember what had prompted the partying. Gates' girlfriend had broken up with him, that was it, and both Mike and Nikko had hated that stuck-up female ball of toxic gas. To counter the droopy expression on Gates' face, Mike had whipped out his bong and a new stash of Dragon's Grass or whatever the hell the weed had been called, and the weekend was launched.

Getting high with Mike was always an adventure because he wasn't a guy who liked to stay inside while he was tripping. In less than an hour, the trio entered the Oakland zoo, acting foolishly in front of the animal pens and the families with strollers. That had been fun, Nikko smiled to himself. He rarely got to let loose and do crazy shit with the guys. He was the nerd of the group. Mike was the king, and Gates was the lover boy.

The blue lights were not for him, and after a minute, the patrol car zoomed on. Bigger fish to fry Nikko thought, and Mike must be paid up on his parking tickets.

As if on cue, Nikko could hear the big guy stirring in the backseat.

"That was a cop!" There was a slight moan in Mike's voice as if regaining consciousness was not an easy task.

"He didn't want us," Nikko said, feeling the tension ease away. The cop was only taillights up ahead.

"You okay to drive?" Mike asked.

"Well, I don't have much choice," Nikko responded. "Gates is out, and I had less alcohol than you did."

"True. True." Mike replied, nodding his head at the same time. He winced at the head bopping. "Oh man, I need another beer."

"There's still two left from the six-pack Gates bought this afternoon." Nikko had found himself keeping track of how much everyone was consuming. That's why he felt confident about taking the wheel.

Mike found the beer and pulled the tab. "There's aspirin in the glove compartment. Toss it back, will ya."

Nikko lobbed the bottle and listened as Mike swallowed a handful of pills and drained the can of beer in a single swallow. Never in his lifetime would Nikko ever be able to do that.

"So, where we at, Einstein? What's the plan?"

Nikko was at a loss. He had been heading home or at least in the general direction of home.

"I was heading back to Oakland."

"Where we at now?"

"Stockton. Just passed."

Mike winced and looked out the car window. "How'd we get all the way out here?" he asked.

"We were driving around Lodi looking for those sausages you wanted."

"Oh yeah, that's right. Did we get 'em?"

"Cooler is in the trunk," Nikko responded.

"Those are damn good sausages," Mike muttered. His head fell back, and he closed his eyes again.

They better be Nikko thought. They had spent an entire day trying to find the butcher because Mike couldn't remember the name of the place. "There's a giant cow in front. You can't miss it," he insisted. But then he changed his mind wondering if it was a giant pig and not a giant cow. The munchies were hitting them hard, and hot Cheetos and Takis and beer weren't cutting it. The idea of biting into a juicy sausage slathered with mustard was enough to get Gates and Nikko to agree to the hunt.

Mike insisted the place was legendary, and he was sort of right. After they drove through Stockton and entered Lodi, all they had to say was the meat place with a giant cow or pig out front, and people told them where to go. Gates was having a grand time approaching hot looking girls and asking them where he could find the place with the legendary sausages. One girl told him there would be a line. Gates had some cheeky retort about sausages and being worth the wait, and the girls howled with laughter. Nikko wished he could interact with girls that way. Only Gates could use searching for a meat market to pick up girls, he didn't have to be in one. By the time they reached Lockeford meat and sausage services, Gates had three new numbers in his mobile phone, and the problem of the stuck-up toxic bitch who had dumped him was gone.

However, a new problem quickly surfaced. The guys were starving, and Lockeford sold the sausages uncooked. Mike had forgotten about that detail, but it didn't keep them from buying almost 10 pounds of meat apiece.

"We need a cooler," Mike growled.

The next stop was Walmart, where they purchased a giant cooler, two bags of ice, and more hot Cheetos and Takis.

"I need real food," Gates complained.

They were all in agreement and found a place serving greasy burgers and fries. Gates was texting the girls who had given him their numbers. The guys were high again on Dragon Grass, and Nikko and Mike had assisted with the text responses. But Gates was a master with the way he flipped words and made everything sound like he was talking about sex. Nikko couldn't stop laughing, and Mike was hooting so hard he was on the ground holding his stomach. The seductive wordplay worked, and the guys were invited to a party in Lodi later in the evening.

One of the girls had said they should dress up, so it was back to Walmart.

"What should we dress up as?" Gate asked.

Nikko kept saying he didn't think that is what the girl meant, but Gates was on a roll, and Walmart had a clearance bin of Halloween costumes. That's how a werewolf, a vampire, and the mummy showed up at the house party at ten o'clock. Gates saw the surprised faces taking in their attire and threw out his arms, exclaiming, "You told us to dress up!" Everyone laughed, and they were through the door. Gates could sell anything.

Gates was the mummy, and he wrapped himself with dozens of rolls of gauze tape. He kept insisting on adding fake blood to his ensemble even though Nikko had argued blood was more for the vampire and the werewolf, but Gates didn't care. Nikko had to admit he had gotten the more comfortable costume. As the werewolf, he had fake chest hair spouting out of his jacket, hairy gloves, and a mask. The mask had been removed and was now lying on the passenger seat. Mike was the vampire with a tuxedo T-shirt, a black cape and fangs, which he kept pulling out so he could guzzle beer.

Early Sunday morning and the party was still roaring, but Gates suddenly announced he had to get back home. He was singing in the church choir at eight AM, and his grandmother would kill him if he were late. Mike kept screaming, "You're unbelievable. You're unbelievable." Neither one of them had been in any condition to drive, and home was at least two hours away. Nikko grabbed a coke from the refrigerator and loaded his buddies into the back of Mike's car. The minute their heads hit the upholstery, the two of them were asleep.

Gates started snoring. Mike rolled him a bit to get him to stop. "You know, we should just leave him on his grandmother's doorstep looking like this. Freak her out with all the fake bandages and blood."

Nikko laughed. "Yeah, let's do that."

"Pull over, dude, I gotta take a piss".

Nikko was on a stretch of highway that was dark enough for Mike to do his business and not have anyone see. Besides, there weren't many cars out at three in the morning. The moon was high and full, and it seemed like you could see forever into the distance. The area was so quiet Nikko could hear Mike's piss hitting the tall grass.

Mike finished relieving himself, and Nikko heard him running a distance away, his shoes hitting the gravel of the road. Curious, he looked in the side mirror and saw Mike pull out an abandoned shopping cart. The cart's wheels were wobbly, and Mike struggled to get it behind the car.

Nikko got out of the vehicle and stood beside his friend. "What are you doing?'

"I've got an idea," said Mike. "I really want some of those

sausages." He pointed at the closed trunk. "Open her up. I'm going to cook a few and use this cart as a grill."

Nikko nodded with approval. Besides, he needed something to boost his weariness for the last leg of the trip, and he was sick of Cheetos.

Mike cleared an area a few yards from the car, and they pushed the shopping cart out and placed it on its side. It was easy to get a fire going thanks to Nikko's days as a Boy Scout. They kept the flame low and controllable. It took some time, but eventually, the sausages were sizzling and ready to eat. Using a stick, Mike skewered the jalapeno flavored one and handed it to Nikko.

"Get ready for heaven, buddy."

Nikko bit into the meat and drooled in delight. Without a doubt, this was the best damn sausage he ever had. This was the best damn night of his life, and he was with the best damn friend he could ask for.

Nikko threw back his head and howled in glory at the moon. He was the wolfman, after all.

***

Nikko looked at me in expectation. His tattoo was a werewolf done in my mother's signature animal series of steampunk and elegance. The wolfman bore a resemblance to Nikko, which made me think my mother had heard portions of the story when he chose this creature to be inked on his forearm.

Nikko agreed to meet me at the UC Berkeley campus after talking to me on the phone. We were at a coffee shop near the Doe Library. It seemed like a safe enough spot to meet a stranger. Joanie and Rueben hovered over by the counter where pastries were on display. I could see Rueben buying a couple of treats.

After my stunt in Monterey, Joanie was not letting me meet with men by myself.

"I'm sorry about your mother," Nikko said. "She was a gorgeous lady. I liked her a lot. A friend of mine was thinking about going to her to get some work done."

I wondered if the friend he was referring to was Mike or Gates.

"This ink isn't fresh," I said. "Why did you come to see my mother a few weeks ago?"

"She called me and said she was offering a special for previous clients. She insisted I come in the following day for a consultation."

"She didn't actually do any ink work?" I asked.

"No, we just talked about what I might want. I thought I might get a taco on my ankle." (What is it with men and food?) I hoped my face did not reflect the derision I was feeling inside, and I like tacos.

The word written next to Nikko's name had been "howl." I was pretty sure this was the tattoo I was supposed to focus on, but just to be sure, I asked: "Do you have any other inkwork?"

"This is the only one Terry Wynters did. But here I have two others." He lifted his shirt and showed me a cactus on his stomach and then slid the whole shirt off so I could see the snake inked on his bicep. Out of the corner of my eye, I spotted Rueben tapping Joanie to make sure she noted a man had just disrobed in front of me. Joanie looked over and then looked away as if this was just a daily occurrence in the life of Bess Wynters. After a second passed, Nikko pulled his T-shirt back on. The other two tattoos were unremarkable. The wolfman was clearly the work of art.

I thanked Nikko and took a table in the cafe. Joanie and Rueben joined me. Joanie had purchased a cup of chai tea and laid it down in front of me. Even when she's angry, she is still thoughtful. I told them the story about Nikko and his compadres.

"Maybe we should check out those sausages" was Rueben's predictable response.

Joanie had out the sheet with the notations and the puzzle. She underlined "werewolf" under the howl clue my mother had left. It's funny how we all correctly assumed howl was about a werewolf.

"What does howl mean? Freedom?" she asked. "A release? That's like empowerment or a change of perspective a person has about themselves." Joanie was now convinced Ariel's story about losing her virginity to the skater boy was also about empowerment. Even though her lover had been older, Ariel had decided she would go through with the sexual act.

"Okay," I agreed. "Then let's say the theme is empowerment. Now connect a crab to empowerment. Or a lyre. Willingham's story appeared to be about empowerment denied, not achieved."

"But empowerment is still part of the theme." Rueben jumped in. "It could be like those essays we have to write where the format demands we present the positives, but also mention the negatives, the opposing view."

Willingham's tattoo still bothered me. It was like one of those itches that never goes away when you scratch it. I kept having the notion the lyre was not a lyre. The inked design told me a story about a boy who connected to space stuff, not music, or even baking cupcakes. I was certain Willingham had lied to me about his tattoo. His story was about space. But then how did space connect to empowerment? I also don't see how you make Ian Kramer's story with the crab about empowerment or even anti-empowerment.

Back at the house, I mentioned my "eureka" moment with Echo and that the stories or tattoos were pieces of a bigger puzzle to my friends. That got everybody thinking.

On the board, Joanie added keywords next to each inked image that were, as she put it, the essence of the story. Rueben argued what she meant was "Theme," but Joanie insisted "essence" was a better term, and she didn't care Rueben was taking AP English, and she wasn't. So next to Xtina's cow was the word "vengeance." Willingham had the word "denied" next to his lyre. Ariel's unicorn had the word "desire."

Nikko's wolfman had the word "joy," and Ian's crab had the word "sorrow."

Rueben reached across Joanie and added, "covet" to the lyre, "lust" to the unicorn, and "envy" to the cow.

"What are you doing?" Joanie cried. She slapped Rueben's hand away.

"I was looking to see if this could be the seven deadly sins."

"Get out of here, would you," Joanie said. She was clearly irritated. "This is not about the seven deadly sins. This is not the movie, *Seven.*"

"But, maybe –" Rueben continued to argue.

"Stop." Joanie held up her hand with the palm out. "This is not about sin. I know about sin, and this puzzle is not about sin." She looked at the board for a beat and then added, "I think this puzzle is about love."

I decided to intervene. "Joanie's right. My mother wouldn't leave clues around that had anything to do with sin or judgment."

Rueben was looking at Joanie with a curious expression. "How did you see the movie *Seven*? That movie is rated "R"?

Joanie glared at Rueben. He was riding her last nerve. "You don't have to see the movie to know what goes on it. Especially a movie like that. I know what's in the box. And by the way, I can talk about *Fight Club* too."

"You're not supposed to talk about *Fight Club*," was Rueben's response.

A hint of a smile tugged at Joanie's mouth. When I saw it, I knew they had just buried the hatchet.

Both Joanie and Rueben wanted to solve the puzzle just as much as I did. Rueben because of the intellectual challenge, and Joanie because it meant safety for my family. And me, well, it also meant safety for me but in a much more authentic sense. We got carried off into the topic of movies with cult fandoms attached to them, and I forgot to ask Joanie what she meant when she said the Maxine board was about love.

RUNES

I listened, stunned, as the woman on the other end of the receiver told me her daughter had passed away three weeks ago. The information was not processing. This was impossible. Emily, the E in Maxine, was dead.

"Are you sure?" I asked. "I'm sorry, that came out wrong," I quickly added, as the words were inconsiderate to a grieving mother.

"Where did you say you were calling from?" asked the woman. Aggression had crept into her voice.

"I'm calling from Cosmic Hearts tattoo studio," I explained. "Emily had an appointment scheduled, and I was following up to see if she was happy with the ink work and if there were any questions."

"Well, she didn't make the appointment, did she?" the mother snapped. "How come you don't know that?"

"I'm sorry," I stammered. "I'm not the tattoo artist. I'm just making the follow-up calls. There was nothing here indicating she didn't make the session. My condolences for your loss." I was about to end the call when a thought crossed my mind. "Did she have a tattoo of a mouse?" I asked.

The woman hung up on me.

Not knowing what to do or think, I wandered into the living room and pulled back the curtains to look outside. I stared out onto the street, not really looking at anything in particular. I just needed someplace to direct my eyes. I sipped the remains of my tea as I mulled over the situation. It seemed like everything had just taken a sudden dive into Hellville.

If Emily didn't make the appointment, how could she be the E in Maxine? There had been two other names listed in the schedule, but they didn't contribute to the Maxine puzzle. I believed they were vendors. The other name written in there was Elizabeth. Was that me? I assumed it was me. But why did she write Elizabeth and not Bess? Was it intended to throw Todd off? I believed she hadn't written my full name because that would have drawn attention to this page. Still, looking at the sheet again, the writing of "mouse" was slanted just enough for it to be argued it was me and not Emily.

I thought back to events and conversations occurring several weeks ago. Was I supposed to go into the tattoo shop on Thursday? Yes, I was. But I didn't. Was it essential I didn't do the errand she had asked? No. If it were important for me to show up, my mother would have said so. She would have demanded I come. But she had contacted me so she could write my name in the appointment book. If Emily died three weeks ago, it's possible my mother already knew. Or at least knew Emily couldn't be confirmed. Emily could have been an early entry, and then when my mother couldn't get a hold of her, she had added my given name into the appointment book, so she would have an "E."

Am I the mouse?

I ruminated over what this additional information meant when my phone buzzed. It was Joanie. I answered.

"Go to the Atomic Allure website," she said.

"I'm not home. I'm with Luther."

"Doesn't he have a computer? Go to the Atomic Allure website."

"Just a sec." She was snippy, so I didn't want to argue with her.

I found Luther in the kitchen. He was heating up a couple of frozen pizzas in the oven. He saw me and took my mug so he could refresh my tea. Luther had his music going, and Billie Holiday was singing she would see me in all the familiar places.

"Why do you play that?" I asked.

He looked at me, puzzled. "I like Billie Holiday."

"That's my mother's favorite song, you know."

"Yes, I know. Terry burned this CD for me long time ago. It's got Holiday, Nina Simone, Sade, Aretha Franklin, Etta James..." He pointed to the oven. "You hungry? These pizzas should be ready in about ten minutes."

"Sure," I said. "Hey, I need to look up something on your laptop. Is that okay?"

"It's in the bedroom. I'll bring it out."

I told Joanie to hold on while Luther went to fetch his computer. She didn't dive into chit chat to cover the silence as we waited. Was she still angry at me? Probably. I sipped my tea.

Holiday's fragile voice created a haunting mood in the kitchen as she continued to sing about seeing me. Everybody wants to be seen.

I took a seat at the kitchen table, and Luther placed his open laptop in front of me. I typed Atomic Allure in the search bar and was immediately taken to the studio's website.

"Okay, I'm there," I said to Joanie. "Now what?"

I looked up at Luther standing in the doorway and gestured to the CD player.

"Why do you still listen to it? Doesn't it make you sad?"

He shook his head. "I loved Terry. I still love her. These songs remind me of what we had. Even though it's over, there are good memories, and I intend to hold onto them."

"Listening to it on a CD player is old school, you know."

Luther smiled. "I wouldn't have it any other way."

Holliday continued to sing about finding a loved one in the sun in the morning and the moon at night. The melody lingered.

Joanie was telling me her father still used his CD player as well, and then she instructed me to look at the photo of the pole dance instructors Ariel Sanchez was in.

"Didn't you say Ariel saw your mother a couple of times?" she asked.

"Yes."

"Did it take more than one session to do the unicorn?" Joanie hadn't seen the tattoo, but Rueben and I had described it in detail.

"No, probably not, but it would have been a long one."

"What other tattoos on Ariel's body did your mother do?" Joanie asked.

Looking at the photo, it was hard to tell. Ariel had about twelve that you could see in the picture, and the unicorn had been on her shoulder blade, so it was not visible in the featured photo.

Joanie had another question. "Did you ask Ariel if the unicorn was done on the day before your mother was —" She didn't want to say the rest, but I got her drift.

No. No, I hadn't. I had <u>assumed</u>. It was the largest tattoo on Ariel's body, and it was definitely my mother's work. I rushed the situation because of the pending party, and Tina taking up so much time talking about her ink. I sucked at this detective thing. I admitted my faux pas to Joanie.

"Are we going to have to go back and see her?" I asked. It had been so hard to get to Ariel the first time.

"I don't think so," Joanie responded. "Look at her hand. The one on the pole."

Ariel's right hand was wrapped around the pole as she posed with the other teachers. You could see there were small tattoos on her fingers. They looked like circles. I squinted my eyes and leaned closer to the screen. "What are those?" I asked.

"They're runes," Joanie answered. "Almost all the other tattoos on Ariel's body are versions of runes. If your mother inked her more than once, then some had to be done by your mother."

"How do you know this?"

"When you're a Witness, you learn a lot about other beliefs, especially pagan ones, because of the pioneering work we do in other countries."

"Color me impressed," I said.

Joanie snorted. "I'll get back to you. I'm going to look up what those runes mean."

She hung up, leaving me to wonder if our friendship was still intact. Outside of commenting her father also listened to CDs, Joanie was focused on solving the puzzle, and not talking to me. Maybe that was just so she could close the door on our friendship when things were done. Once we solved Maxine, Joanie could go and find another friend who didn't lie to her at the drop of a hat.

It was selfish thinking on my part, but I had always thought her religious beliefs made her an oddball at school; that she would be alone if Rueben and I hadn't taken her in. The last year had shown me I was viewing it wrong. Joanie was liked and accepted by others. Heck, the cheerleading squad had begged her to join even though she was a klutz and wouldn't wear their super short skirts. The cheerleading squad wasn't banging down my door asking me to try out, that's for sure.

"Wow. You look...you look...bummed." Luther had returned to the kitchen.

I shrugged. I didn't want to tell him I was worried Joanie was dumping me as a friend.

Luther opened the oven and removed the pizzas, placing them on the stove to let them cool before slicing them up. He glanced at the laptop screen open to Atomic Allure and gave me a quizzical look. "Are you and Joanie planning on taking classes?" he asked.

"Hahaha."

"Who's that?" He pointed at Ariel Sanchez.

"She was a client of Terry's."

"Cute."

"Yes?"

"I'm just stating a fact. Don't make too much of it."

I got a text from Joanie. It said, "The rune symbols on her fingers are the phases of the moon. Solved it."

I jumped up. The chair fell back on the floor. "I've gotta go," I said.

"What??" My sudden movement had startled Luther.

"I've gotta go. Call Ollie and have him bring Echo here. Right now."

"Okay?" The concern was all over his face.

"I'll be alright. Just have Ollie come here with Echo. I'll be right back. Everyone should be in one place. I figured out Maxine."

(Actually, Joanie had)

"Who's Maxine?" Luther yelled as I flew out the door.

MOUSETRAP

I ran. Yesterday, Joanie had said the puzzle was about love. I barely registered the comment, believing it was Joanie channeling Rebecca of Sunnybrook Farm.

But she was right; the mystery was about love.

Billie Holiday's emotional and melancholy voice floated through my head. I continued to hear the lyrics to "I'll Be Seeing You," my mother's favorite song.

"Do you want to see something?" she asked.

"Yes," I had responded.

As I ran, the images of the past flooded my memory. They were vivid and sharp. I fixed my eyes ahead on my destination, which was still a mile away. I cursed to myself that in my desire to visit with Luther, I had stashed my bicycle near Alta Bates hospital so the police wouldn't know where I was. It wasn't just the police, of course, but Todd as well.

The memories continued to pour over me like a shower of gold. How had I not seen it? It was so obvious. Stupid. Stupid. Stupid.

"Shhhhh." My mother in the past had placed her finger gently across her lips. A smile spread over her face. This was the beginning of a game.

"What?" I was interested. At that time of my life, everything she did was fascinating to me. I was four. She was my world.

Look at my hiding place. It's perfect for a mouse – like you. I can put teeny tiny things in there. Look, I'm going to draw this big heart on a piece of paper and fold it up and hide it in there. That's my special love for you. And you know what else? This spot is right behind Spiderwand's moon.

The winking moon?

Yes, the winking moon on the other side. Whenever I wink at you, that's code for 'I love you' because my heart is behind the winking moon.

As I raced to the studio, the game all came back to me. My mother had her secrets and her games, and this had been my initiation into her creative expressions. My mother liked to have something mean something else, like her crossword puzzles. When I was a child, a wink said love.

I remembered how quickly I discarded the game when Luther came into our lives. Luther declared his love loudly. He hugged me with arms that bore no tattoos and told me his love was unconditional. There were no secrets or whispers. With Terry, there were always riddles and games.

Had she stopped winking at me? Or had I stopped looking for the winks? Maybe I had believed her love for me had faded as she pursued men and craved more children. All of this seemed so long ago, and the answers were grains of sand, passing through my fingers. Perhaps they were answers that didn't need to be spoken. Despite what I believed; my mother had never stopped loving me. She had never stopped seeing me.

The building was right in front of me. I stopped running and gasped for breath as I stared at the mural, Spiderwand's masterpiece. The depiction of the cosmos merged with humanity. There it all was, right there for me to see - images I had gazed at throughout my childhood. Still, I had blindly (or stubbornly) refused to put together the message my mother was sending me. When had I stopped marveling at Spiderwand's painting? When had I allocated it to merely a colorful background of the past?

Right there in all their painted glory were the images I had been seeking. The pictures I needed to piece it all together. A chubby cow was jumping over the moon with a cat fiddling beneath. There were the constellations and their astrological pairings with Cancer, the crab sitting proudly amongst the stars. There was the wolf on a distant hill howling to the crescent moon. I could now see they were drawn to resemble rune symbols. High at the top, not far from Cancer was a little rocket ship, and I knew it had the number eleven on its side for the Apollo moon program. And there was the child's hand with the beaded butterfly bracelet drawing attention to the winking moon with a little mouse sitting on top. How could I forget about the mouse?! All the images and stories pointed to the moon. The moon was the answer. It had been right there before me.

If I had only looked within.

Suddenly, I sensed movement behind me. Something was moving fast. Before I could turn, I was hit in the back of the head. My knees crumbled, and everything went black as my body smacked onto the pavement.

***

A hard jolt brought me back to consciousness. My head collided with something metal, and I tried to get my arm in a position to buffer the bouncing movement. I was in a car. Or rather the trunk of a car. I could feel the scratchy cheap layer of fabric used to line a trunk's interior. It was dark and cramped, but if I kept my body curled in a fetal position, I could manage the situation. Slowly my eyesight adjusted... BANG. It felt like the car had gone over a speed bump. They were everywhere in the Bay Area. I cursed out loud. My impulse was to scream at the driver and pound on the top of the trunk. But then I realized I probably didn't want them to know I was awake.

I suspected Todd was driving, but I didn't know for sure. This wasn't my mother's car, but he had probably gotten rid of her Volvo a long time ago. The vehicle was reported stolen, so it wouldn't have been smart to keep it around.

I wondered how long I had been out cold and how long I had been in the trunk of the car. A solid form in my back pocket told me I still had my cell phone. I reached around and pulled the phone out. Luther was the number I dialed. He answered immediately.

"Girl, where the hell are you?!" His voice was charged and emotional.

"Luther, I'm in trouble," I responded.

"Where are you?!" he demanded.

"I don't know," I answered.

He began to protest, but I cut him off with "I'm in the trunk of a car."

"WHAT?! What happened? Where are you?"

"The car is moving, so I don't know. First, is Echo with you?"

"Yes," Luther responded. "Ollie just brought her over. He told me about this Maxine business."

"Good because I don't think the house is safe. Or the studio..."

"Bess, Bess...," Luther stopped me. "I'm having Ollie call the police. You keep talking to me. How did you end up in a car trunk? Do you remember that? You rushed out of my place thirty minutes ago."

Good. That meant a lot of time had not gone by. It took me maybe twenty minutes to get to Cosmic Hearts from Luther's apartment

"I was in front of the tattoo studio, and someone hit me from behind."

"Do you know who?"

"I didn't see them, but my guess is Todd." I could hear Luther relay the information to Ollie and then Ollie speaking to the police. When Todd's name came up, Ollie questioned it, claiming Todd was dead. Luther responded I was guessing, and I could hear Ollie tell the police in the background. The car slowed and took a hard right. My body slid with the trajectory motion, and I was crunched into the side of the trunk. Ouch.

"Bess, keep talking to me," Luther said. "How long has the car been driving?"

"I don't know because I was out for a while. But if you say I've been gone for half an hour, then ten minutes. Maybe ten minutes." Luther barked the information to Ollie, who then repeated it to the police.

"Luther, the car is stopping," I cried. The panic I heard in my voice scared me even more.

"Bess, listen to me," Luther said. He spoke precisely and urgently. "Hang up with me right now and dial 911. Do you hear me? Dial 911, hit mute, and then hide the phone in the back of the trunk. Leave it there. We'll find you."

"Luther...," I sobbed. I had barely enough time to do Luther's instructions before the driver of the car came around to the back and opened the trunk.

There was a squealing sound as the trunk opened, like an animal screeching in defiance. Even though it was dark outside, a swatch of light fell across my face, and I had to hold up my hand as I squinted at the glare. The shadow of Todd's familiar form blocked the light, which I realized was a streetlamp. It had been cold in the trunk, and my body was shivering. The shivering could also have been adrenaline and panic.

"Good, you're awake," he observed. "I won't have to carry you. Makes it a lot easier for me." He looked down at me, and a smile crept across his face. His missing teeth made him look even more like a reptile. "I've wanted to do this for a long time," he said, and he pulled out what appeared to be a scarf from his jacket pocket.

For a brief second, I thought he was going to wrap it around my throat. However, his aim was higher, and the scarf was forced into my mouth. He wrapped it around my head twice before securing it tightly behind my neck. The scarf bit into the sides of my mouth. My jaws were forced open in a painful way, and I had to fight to keep from gagging.

"Come here," he snapped and hoisted me out of the trunk. He had a firm grip on my arms and lifted me effortlessly as if I were one of Echo's fairy dolls. A brief image of my sister flashed in my mind. I hoped she wasn't worried about me and that Ollie and Luther were shielding her from what was going on. The phone was tucked into the floorboards of the trunk. They would find me.

Todd had stopped the car in an industrial area of the city. I guessed we were in Oakland. I couldn't smell the ocean, but then again, my nostrils were covered by the woolen scarf covering the lower portion of my face. Todd kicked open the door to what appeared to be a condemned warehouse. Windows were boarded on the outside, and junk was piled up and overflowing on the sidewalk area. He pulled me through the threshold.

The area was dank and deserted. There were signs homeless people had taken up residence at different periods. Bedrolls and blankets were shoved in corners, and empty cans of food were tossed around the ground. I wanted to say something smart like "Hey, is this where you've been staying? Looks like an upgrade." But I was gagged, so the thought went unvoiced. I guess that was the point of the scarf.

Todd was showing no mercy as he pulled me along over the floorboards. The wooden floorboards were loose and lay across the concrete floor. Todd kept a firm grip, holding me tight against his body as he dragged me along. I couldn't use my arms to balance, so I continually tripped over the junk cluttering the floor. One block of wood caused me to stumble, and I fell over. Todd released me as I fell, and I came down hard on my knees. I was thankful I was wearing jeans.

Todd cursed and pulled me up by my elbows. He shook me hard as if it was my fault I couldn't walk straight. I tried to call him a dumbass - but then again, I was gagged.

I know I should have been fearful. I know I should have been scared, but now, I was just angry. Angry and annoyed. Angry that this guy had done so much damage to my family and annoyed at his level of incompetence. What was the purpose of taking me? Even if he could beat me up and have me reveal the location of the drugs, which I knew must be in the safe deposit box at the bank. He couldn't get to them. Could he? I didn't know the rules of having access to a safety deposit box, but I assumed the bank had to have you listed as authorized, and you had to have the key. The police were still waiting to have a judge allow them access. The court's view was it was just drugs, they weren't going anywhere.

Could my mother have added Todd to the list of authorized people? No, impossible. But then...

Who was on the list? Me? Maybe. Unless you had to be over eighteen than I wouldn't be. And my mother would have drawn up this legal stuff back when Cosmic Hearts was being launched. I wouldn't be listed then as I was a toddler. My deceased grandparents, maybe. That was possible. And Dusty. Dusty would have access. Dusty was how Todd was going to get into the safety box. I loved Dusty immensely, but she would roll over the minute Todd threatened to do anything.

My feet hit more debris and glancing down, it looked like crumpled up bags and cartons from fast-food restaurants. We moved through three rooms, and then Todd pulled me up a flight of metal stairs. We climbed about two levels, but it was difficult for me to gauge. We reached a floor with wide-open spaces. The walls were covered with graffiti, and there were large holes in the plaster. I saw plastic sheeting everywhere. I began to panic. Was this the place where the police found Rodriguez's body? And Todd lost his teeth?

"Where's your phone?" he demanded. He growled when he realized I couldn't answer him. (*Hey, dumbass!*) His hands moved around my jeans, patting me down. He looked at me, satisfied that the object was not on my person. I was so glad Luther had told me to leave it in the car.

"Move over here," he demanded. "There's a chair." Todd placed a hand on my shoulder and pushed me down. I felt the edge of the chair as my body fell, and I managed to adjust myself quickly, so my butt hit the seat, and I didn't plummet to the floor.

"There you go," he said. His voice sounded disappointed that I hadn't hit the floor. I took a deep breath and instantly regretted it as I received a healthy snort of Todd funk. The scarf must have been one Todd owned for years and never washed. It's difficult to gag when you are already gagged.

With me in the chair and silenced, Todd then picked up strands of rope lying nearby. He tied my hands and tied each ankle to the front of the chair. He then stood back to admire his work.

In my mind, I was shooting electric laser bolts at him, but I stayed calm as if I had already sucked down three packets of hot sauce. I let my fury simmer.

"Alright, then. I'm going to make this simple," Todd said. "I am going to remove the scarf so you can tell me where the key is to the safe deposit box. I know you know. I've been watching you. You might think your little tricks with the bicycle would throw me off your track, but I didn't need to follow you, my dear. I just needed to wait until you came back to the tattoo studio. And eventually, you did."

I prayed my eyes didn't betray my thoughts. Dammit. Dammit. Dammit. I walked. No, I ran right into the trap.

"Your movements all over the city were amusing. I lost you for a few days. And during that time, I lost two fingers." He held up his right hand and waved it like he was saying hello. That's when I noticed the hand was wrapped in bandages. He smiled, but it was more like a painful wince. He wasn't displaying his crocodile grin.

"I've been patient because I knew you would show up, and I knew you would have the answer I need. I had to convince others of this. It was hard because they don't know you the way I do. Alright, I'm going to remove the scarf. If you scream, I hit you. If you don't give me the answer I need, I hit you. I may have lost some digits, but they didn't take the fingers from my strong hand."

Todd stepped behind me and loosened the knots on the scarf. It slipped enough to allow me to breathe properly, and I spat out the scratchy material from my mouth.

"Where's the key?" Todd asked.

"What are you going to do with me?" was my reply.

"No, no, no," he said, stepping in front of me and wagging a finger. "Tell me where the key is, or I hit you."

I really didn't want to get hit. Images of my mother in the hospital bed was all I needed to spit out what he wanted to hear. "It's in the moon," I replied. I then closed my eyes and lowered my head as if he had defeated me. But I was really hoping he would take my answer and not ask anymore. If I looked at him, he might grasp that my response was not entirely forthcoming.

Todd repositioned the scarf over my mouth and tightened the knots, so it was a gag once more. He came back around and smirked as he spoke. "Now, that wasn't hard. And as a reward, I'm going to share what's going to happen next. I leave you here while I head back to the studio and retrieve the key. Once I have it, I'll be at the bank first thing in the morning with your mom's pal, Dusty. After we're done, I'll tell Dusty where you can be found."

His eyes took me in for a beat longer. I couldn't imagine what he thought as I sat there tied to a chair with his nasty scarf around my mouth. However, many thoughts fluttered through my head. One of them being he would be back because he couldn't possibly locate the key by merely looking in the moon. The tattoo studio was called Cosmic Hearts. There were constellation lights all over the place. He would rip them down and look inside the ones shaped like a crescent moon and come up empty. He would be back, and he would be angry.

But I was gagged so I couldn't say anything.

"Goodbye, Bess. I hope I never see you again, you little bitch."

THIRTEEN THOUGHTS

Contrary to popular belief, being tied up and gagged is not kinky, and it's not fun. Of course, I was not benefiting from lying on a comfy bed with my head propped up with feather pillows. A lavender-scented blindfold was not wrapped around my head, and silk scarves were not attached to my wrist and ankles while a partner lightly touched my thigh with a feather.

Instead, I was strapped to a metal chair in the middle of a room filled with swaths of plastic sheeting and piles of junkie debris. My mouth gagged from the smell of human funk coming from the scarf, and my wrists were scratched raw by the tough fibered rope used to tie them together. I was alone unless you counted the rats. I guessed the scratching sounds I was hearing were vermin moving in and out of the walls. I could hear the roar of traffic, but it sounded distant like white noise. And I really had to pee.

One thing movies never show you is, if a person has been tied up for a long time, how they handle this most basic function. I live in California, and I carry a reusable water bottle in my bag. I drink half my body weight in liquid ounces to stay hydrated. This means I must use the bathroom almost every two hours.

My bladder was bursting.

I thought back to the last time I had used the bathroom. It had been at Luther's house before my ill-fated call to Emily's mother.

I had been drinking tea, but I hadn't finished it, had I? But then I remembered it was my second cup. I tried to calculate how long ago that had been.

I wondered if by keeping a low profile for the last week and hiding my activity from Todd, he believed I had located the key a long time ago. Perhaps he thought I was moving the drugs somewhere else. No, that didn't make sense. He probably had someone watch the bank to make sure I didn't go inside while he watched Cosmic Hearts. It wasn't Duane, so maybe there was someone else sitting in a car with a viewpoint of the bank with tons of fast-food wrappers and styrofoam cups littered in the back seat. Maybe the gross guy at Tobacco Joe's. No, No, No. My mind was going in too many directions.

I took a deep breath, ignored my screaming bladder, and began to itemize what I knew and what Todd knew and to think out my situation. One, I knew where the key to the safety deposit box was. I had solved Maxine. Two, I had semi-lied when I told Todd it was in the moon. I knew Todd would think of the planetary lights draped around the shop. He would go to Cosmic Hearts, tear down the lights and break open the ones fashioned like a moon. Hell, he would break open all the lights. Todd would then realize I had lied to him and come back and torture me. However, this bought me time. Time to do what, I wasn't sure.

Three, I didn't have my phone. Luther's request that I call 911 and leave my phone in Todd's car might work. They would track the vehicle. My hopes shot up with the thought. But then I realized if the police saw my location as Cosmic Hearts (which is where Todd was headed), they might think it's not an emergency. No, they knew it was an emergency, Luther and Ollie had called them.

Four, my phone was with Todd, not me. If Todd were killed in a shootout, nobody would know where I was.

Five, I have to pee.

Six, I was counting on the fact the police allowed Echo to stay with Ollie and Luther, and they didn't move her. If Echo remains with Luther, she'd be fine. However, if Officer Lopez (or anybody else) took my sister to the station and she saw the room for children-in-crisis, Echo would scream for me and create a scene. The children-in-crisis room was where we had been the horrible night when Terry went bonkers over Luther. If there was an emotional scene at the police station, a lot of stuff could go wrong, possibly alerting Todd to Echo's whereabouts. I wanted Todd to be focused on me.

Seven, I hoped having Ollie take Echo to Luther's house was the right move. Todd knew about Luther, he knew where Luther worked, but he didn't know where Luther lived. Luther's home was the safest place for my sister. If anything happened to me, she would already be somewhere she would be protected. Restraining order or not, with everything going down, Luther would fight like a gladiator for Echo. He could have a shot at winning custody.

Seven and a half, I really had to pee, and because my ankles were tied to the chair, I couldn't cross my legs.

Eight, I wish I had peed in the trunk of Todd's car when I had the chance. That way, my DNA and smell would be all over the trunk, and he would be directly tied to my death. I hadn't done it then because the thought of Todd seeing me with a wet crotch was too embarrassing. I don't think I could have handled his nasty comments with no ability to lash back because of the gag. My anguish was mounting as I knew there was no way I could go another five minutes without soiling myself. If I ended up becoming a meal for the rats, they would reach my bladder and find it bone dry.

Eight and a half, I wondered how long I could go before I died. (Once I had the thought, I realized Rueben would probably know the answer to that.)

Nine, how long would I be tied up here? Nobody knew where I was outside of Todd. What if he was killed in a car accident as he headed back to Berkeley and the tattoo shop? What if he got in a shoot out with the cops? What if his boss, the drug kingpin, or whatever he was, finally got tired of Todd's antics and got rid of him? What if the ghost of Wolfie rose up and tore out his throat? I smiled, thinking about the last image. It would be a fitting end for Todd.

Ten, Todd had been lying in wait for me outside Cosmic Hearts. But how did he know I would show up there? Luck, I guess. He couldn't have grabbed me outside of the house as there were too many witnesses. Telegraph Avenue was the right spot to snatch me. Even though there is a lot of traffic, with the homeless, the drug users, and the squatters at various places, people look away more.

Eleven, he didn't know about the meaning of Maxine. He wanted the key to the safety deposit box, and he figured I knew where it was. He was waiting for me, and I had run right up to him. I was too excited with the realization I had solved the puzzle.

Twelve, I had wanted to have the key in my possession before dealing with Todd. I would have the upper hand, and I could clear the box of whatever else was in there outside of the drugs. Now I was worried about what else Todd could get his hands on. Were there papers involving the house and the tattoo studio? Could Todd take everything we owned? Legally, I didn't think it worked that way, but I was still worried.

Thirteen, I wish Rueben was here because he would have the answers to all these questions. Shit, I wish Rueben was here because then he could untie me, and I could escape.

Escape.

Believe it or not, it took that long for the idea to register. I could escape.

MACKEY'S BACK

First things first, I peed my pants. I had to get that out of the way. A person can't plot their escape if their mind is focused on their bladder. I knew it would eventually dry, and the situation demanded it. Still, the act of defiling myself set off a fit of raging anger within me. I hated Todd for so many reasons, and now I had a fresh wet reason contributing to my determination to get out of there.

The space I was in had no light, but my eyes had become accustomed to the darkness long enough to distinguish the different mounds of blankets and fast food containers. I needed to find something; a nail or screw, a plastic knife from the take-out food - something to loosen the rope on my hands and feet. Todd had tied my hands together, but only my feet were fastened to the chair. I made a silent prayer of thanks Todd hadn't tied my hands behind me to the chair. That would have made things more difficult. Then again, my situation was challenging enough.

I braced myself for what I was about to do. I rocked the chair back, tilting it with my feet and creating momentum until it fell backward with a slam. My head hit the hard warehouse floor, but since I had prepared myself for the impact, I was able to lift my head up a little bit, so the thud wasn't that bad. It was still bad, though. Dazed, I lay there on my back, feeling like a turtle or one of the horseshoe crabs from Ian Kramer's tattoo.

I took a couple of deep breaths through my nose in preparation for the next movement. I rocked myself again. This time my hips were doing most of the work. I flipped myself on my side and got my hands situated so I could push myself into a crawling position. Initially, I planned to roll with the chair to the clump of blankets closest to my location. However, with my knees on the ground and the chair on my back, I realized I could move inchworm-like across the floor. This hurt like hell, and I was so glad I was wearing jeans and not shorts. My knees were going to a mass of bloody scrapes and bruises after this was over. IF this was ever over.

I inched my way to the closest pile of blankets. My hands patted around the area, seeking anything sharp enough to cut the ropes. Disturbing the mounds released a foul smell of sour body odor and mildew. There was a ratty jacket rolled up for a pillow. I searched the pockets and found a lighter. This could work, but I didn't want to burn the ropes off. I'd burn my ankles and my fingers and increase the pain I was already experiencing to a whole new level.

Farther to my left was another pile of stuff for me to check. I started to inch my way over. I wasn't sure how much time had passed. I wondered if the police had caught Todd at Cosmic Hearts while he was checking every moon-shaped light or picture we had. There was a lot. If the police were following my phone, then they would be led to Todd. They might have him in custody by now. However, Todd could refuse to tell them where I was. His donkey ass might go for days before he mentioned where I was.

I reached the second pile of trash and discarded belongings. There were torn up paperback books, burned plastic cups and bowls, and a mirror. I saw the telltale signs of white powder on the glass of the mirror and began to frantically check the area for the item I prayed I would find. I did. I found it, and I felt like weeping.

Grasping the razor in my fingers, I steadily sawed away at the bindings at my feet. I thought I'd start there on the off-chance Todd returned. I could run if my legs were free.

The rope fell away from my ankles. I gingerly stood up and away from the chair. OW. I thought I was going to faint from the pain. My legs cramped, and the dried blood on my knees separated from the jean fabric. I hurt and stank, but at least my crotch was dry. I worked the razor on the rope around my hands. I don't know how people do it in the movies without cutting themselves, because I nicked myself many times, but I got my hands free.

Next, the nasty scarf was removed from around my mouth. Every muscle in my body was strained and sore. I leaned against a wall and took deep breaths to fill my lungs and spat out the stench of Todd's scarf. I was free, but I was in bad shape. I didn't think I'd be able to walk. If I threw my body in the direction I wanted to go, maybe I could wobble and stumble out.

That's when I heard it. A car pulled up and halted with a screech. I held my breath and listened. Who was it? Could it be the police searching for me?

I heard a voice scream out, "You fucking bitch!"

It was not the police.

I could hear his screams as he stormed into the warehouse and slammed the door behind him. My heart thumped wildly, and I placed a hand over my chest, willing it to slow down. Breathe, girl. Wait him out. He might not find you.

He charged through the vacant spaces and headed up the stairs to the area where he had left me. His curses were wild and crazed. He sounded like a roaring dragon.

I had no choice but to hide. There weren't a lot of options. The only way out of the building that I was aware of was the door Todd had come through. I couldn't roll myself up in the plastic sheeting of one of the mangy blankets on the floor. In the far corner, a wooden structure like a loft was erected. It looked like the type of scaffolding painters use when reaching high areas. It was about three stories tall. It didn't look sturdy, but someone had taken ropes and tied the wooden base to two window frames at the top of the walls to steady it. There was a makeshift ladder with planks of wood nailed to twin poles, and it leaned against the structure. It was dark at the top. I figured if I climbed up and lay flat, I wouldn't be seen.

That's what I did. I gritted my teeth and climbed. The ladder was flimsy as hell, and I wondered who had constructed this gem of failed carpentry. But here I was using it, so I guess I had to be thankful. The top of the scaffolding was rickety, but there was enough room for me to lie flat. Moldy bedding was lumped in the corner, and some hung over the platform. I hoped if Todd looked up, he wouldn't see anything but darkness and cloth appearing to be an abandoned bed. I also hoped Todd didn't have a flashlight.

He entered the room where he had left me tied to the chair and saw I had escaped my bindings. He cursed loudly. A string of "fucks" leaped from his mouth. He glanced quickly around the room, tossed the old clothing around, and left. I could hear him pulling up plastic sheeting as he charged through the halls, searching for me. I lay still and held my breath.

I thought about knocking the ladder over but knew Todd would hear it falling to the floor and quickly return. In addition to the lumps of bedding, there were long lengths of rope discarded on the platform. I realized whoever used this as a sleeping area, had needed the lines to strap themselves to the scaffolding so they wouldn't roll off.

There was a long silence. I couldn't hear any movement coming from Todd. I waited. My eyes focused on the entryway where the stairs led up to the floor. And then I heard him. Actually, I saw him first. As a glow of light began to ascend the stairs. His steps were soft now as he had to walk carefully to keep the flames going on the torch he had cobbled together. Todd had taken a discarded piece of clothing and wrapped it around a decaying broomstick. The torch burned bright, illuminating the entire area. Shit. I had left the lighter down there, and he had found it.

"I know you are here," Todd spoke. His voice carried across the vast open space. "You didn't leave. You may have untied yourself, but you didn't leave this building. I've searched everywhere, and this is all that is left." He held the torch high and approached the scaffolding. "You must be up there."

I bit down on my lips and held my breath. Maybe if he didn't see anything with the torch, he'd give up and go back down to the ground floor. But then the platform began to sway and lurch, and I knew Todd was climbing up the ladder. His movements were jerky as he held the torch with his left hand and used his bandaged right arm to hook around the wooden planks on the poles and hoist himself up. The platform swung like a hammock, but the ropes securing it to the high windows overhead held – but just barely.

I knew once he reached the top, he would be able to see me, so I pushed myself up and got into a crouched position. I was as far away from Todd and the ladder as possible, right on the edge of the platform. I didn't look down. If I looked down, I would lose my nerve. In my hands, I clutched the rope I had found within the abandoned bedding.

Todd's eyes cleared the platform and looked in my direction. The torch slowly burned. The shadows from the flames flickered across his face. He looked like a demon. "There you are," he said. I could hear the fury smoldering in his voice. "I have no idea why you lied to me. I told you what I would do. I take no pleasure in this."

I didn't say a word. I knew any word out of my mouth could betray what I was thinking.

I watched him pull himself up onto the wooden platform. He

stayed low as the structure swung from his movements and added weight. "You're surprisingly quiet," he commented as he crawled in my direction. With each motion, the scaffolding rocked. "I guess we should be thankful for small mercies."

I held onto the rope, biding my time. I waited until Todd was almost within reach to grab me. His eyes were focused on my face, so he didn't notice the rope I held or that one section was tied to the end of the platform.

I leaped down and swung out on the rope. My hands burned as they slid down the line, and the rough fibers tore up my flesh. When I was about ten feet away, I dropped to the ground. The impact was hard. I landed badly, and one of my ankles snapped. I pitched forward and crumbled onto the floor. Another object smacked to the floor. My sudden leap had caused the platform to violently sway, and the ladder pitched over. Flat on the ground, I flipped myself over and looked up behind me. Todd was startled. He had toppled forward and dropped the torch. His hands grasped the platform as it shook.

I couldn't walk, but I could move myself along the floor. The front of my jeans and knees were scraped raw from my earlier inchworm maneuver. Now, I was going to scrape up my behind. These jeans were going in the trash when I got home.

I stiffly pushed myself backward along the floor with my good foot. The other leg dragged. The pain from my ankle was intense. I cried out every time I moved.

Todd watched me from the swaying scaffolding. "Bess put the ladder back up," he called down to me.

I panted and grunted in pain as I pushed myself away from him. I had managed to get about fifteen feet away. Suddenly, there was a cry of dismay. I looked up and saw there was a fire leaping up behind Todd. He had dropped the torch on top of the discarded bedding. The platform was burning, and his access to the rope I had used was blocked.

Todd screamed and knocked the blazing bundle over the side of the platform. He pounded the orange embers on the structure with his hands and feet. Howling, as his injured and bandaged hand smacked against the wood. "Put the ladder back up!" he shrieked.

"I can't," I gasped. "I can't." There was nothing I could do. I didn't have the strength to push myself over to the ladder and hold it back up. I couldn't stand myself. Also, when Todd knocked the flaming torch and bedding off the scaffolding, it landed on top of the ladder. The ladder was already burning. I tried to yell he should jump - that he'd survive the fall. But the smoke claimed my voice, and I started choking.

The whole area by the scaffolding was being consumed by fire. The plastic sheeting was burning, and chemical smoke filled the space. The smoke blinded me, and my chest heaved as my lungs cried out for air.

I couldn't see Todd, but I could hear him. His anguished cries filled my head as the fumes and smoke from the burning plastic engulfed the room. Todd's screams of terror turned into a high-pitched sound that wasn't human, and then it stopped. All I heard was the snap and crackle of the flames.

I felt confused and sleepy. My head fell back onto the floor, and I knew I was about to close my eyes and give in. There was a crash as the burning scaffolding hit the floor.

My muscles collapsed, and my mind slowly drifted off. I thought I heard a voice shout, "She's in here." My last conscious thought was of cinnamon-scented fingers grabbing hold of my body and lifting me up.

CONFESSION

It was grumpy Detective Kline who pulled me from the fire. The police had found the car outside the warehouse. They were mounting a rescue when the smoke began to roll out of the windows on the third floor. Kline had stormed in and pulled me out before the fire trucks arrived. Thank goodness for that.

I was taken to the hospital and treated for smoke inhalation, and my injured ankle was given a cast. The scrapes and bruises were cleaned and bandaged. I refused to stay overnight and threatened to scream if they didn't release me. One Wynters woman in the hospital was enough. I couldn't stand the notion that both my mother and I were hospitalized. Also, I knew it would upset Echo. Our mother hadn't returned from the hospital yet, and if I were there too, my sister wouldn't be able to handle it. I had to convalesce at home.

I stayed in my room for days and, wisely, people left me alone. I was a storm of emotions, flashing anger, and despair. Sometimes, I would burst into tears for no reason. A person stepping across the threshold could receive a tongue lashing for looking at me. Only Echo was brave enough to enter my room. She'd bring happy drawings of Luther and me and Ollie and orange kittens. Echo would hang them up on the walls with tape to make me feel better. Before she left, she would inquire if I was ready for new riddles. "No, I'm too sick," I would protest.

Rueben came by to see me, but I kept the visit brief. I wasn't up to talking. I just wanted to wallow (SAT vocabulary word) in my gloomy funk. I promised him I would go into detail about the elements of Maxine when I was ready and sent him away.

Joanie sent a text message, "you, okay?". I texted back "Y," and after that, I didn't hear from her. The thought of losing Joanie as a friend added an additional layer to the depression and grief I was carrying. It was my own fault, too, but what could I tell her?

After three days of letting me marinate in my stew of misery and rage, Ollie knocked on the door. He said it was time for me to make an appearance at the police station and give my statement.

During my session with Assistant District Attorney Blount, I told it all. There were hesitations, and the words trickled out slowly. Then they came faster, and the words I needed were presenting themselves and flying off my tongue. I talked about what Todd wanted of me and why and how he had threatened to harm Echo and destroy my family. I spoke of being caught between loyalty and love for Luther and the fear of my mother's wrath. Swallowing, with my face burning and hands knotted in my lap, I talked about the anger at my mother and the resentment surrounding her leaving us vulnerable to Child Protective Services and the folly of drug dealers. I mentioned my search for the key to the safety deposit box and how I had been visiting the last clients of my mother's. I didn't mention the specifics of Maxine or, of course, my strange talent. Still, I made it sound like seeing these people helped guide me towards my mother's emotional state. And to a certain extent, that was true.

And finally, with the feeling of charging over a cliff and plunging into a roaring sea, I talked about locating the key to the bank box, and my dangerous encounter with Todd. How he attacked me outside the tattoo studio, tied me up at the warehouse, and then started a fire that consumed him.

After I was done, my new buddy, ADA Blount, with the superstar tattoo on her wrist, thanked me. She collected her notepad and tape recorder and left the room.

Back when I was in the hospital, I told the police where the key to the safety deposit box could be located, and they had easily found it. Officer Lopez came by the house the following day to share the contents of the box. As hoped, the missing backpack with mounds of cash was stuffed inside. There were also multiple legal documents ranging from my mother's will, the deeds on the house and Cosmic Hearts, and a vital piece of paper. Theresa Wynters had handwritten her request that the restraining order against Luther Tucker be lifted and he be granted guardianship of her two minor daughters. (Yes, she had fixed it.)

Even though ADA Blount had left the room, I remained seated at the metal table. My head was down. My fingers fidgeted. I wasn't done. Detective Kline touched my shoulder. "Bess, is there something else?" he asked.

"Are they still recording?" I asked.

"The ADA took the tape recorder with her," he replied.

"I mean the other recording devices. Aren't they running a video or something?"

Detective Kline laughed. "Believe it or not. This room is not set up for that." He looked at me for a long time. His expression was a mix of concern and curiosity. "Should I bring the ADA back?" he asked.

"NO!" I cried, and a huge sob escaped from my chest. I figured this man should know what type of dark-hearted person he had saved from the fire, and I admitted my terrible secret. If it had been Echo, or Luther, or Ollie or Joanie, or anybody I loved at the top of that burning scaffold, I would have gotten the ladder to them. I knew I would have tried. I would have fought against the enormous pain of the broken ankle and my shaking muscles and made it happen. I would have held the burning ladder with my hands and withstood the burns if it meant someone I loved would get to safety. But it was Todd at the top of the scaffolding, so I didn't. I could still hear his screams, followed by the roar of silence when they ended. I knew that sound would stay with me forever.

I said this through streaming tears, and when I finished, Detective Kline took my hand in his and grasped it with a warm understanding. His other hand reached into the breast pocket of his jacket, and he handed me a crimson-colored handkerchief to dry my face. "He was long gone," he said. "There wasn't anything to be done - anything you could have done. Don't place that burden on yourself."

I nodded in response, but my mind was blank. Every thought, every feeling that had been keeping house inside of me had been released for all to hear. I breathed freely. There was no tightness in my chest. No desire to grab a packet of hot sauce. No desire to burn inside.

I don't know how long I sat in this pleasant state of exhausted mindlessness. But Detective Kline moved at last. He pulled a toothpick out of his pocket and placed it between his lips. He stood and stretched his back, releasing a bit of a groan. Smiling, he took my hand, squeezed it, and led me outside the room where Luther, Echo, Dusty, and Ollie, my family, awaited me.

LOOK UP CHILD

J oanie didn't come by the house until all the excitement had died
down. I was still bandaged from the burns and hobbling on the
cast. When I opened the door, she stood there with her hands
on her hips. An angry scowl darkened her face. "I should be really
angry with you," she said.

"But you're not?" I replied, hopefully.

She crossed over the threshold, forcing me to step back. I wondered
if she was this dominant when she did her pioneering work door to
door. She turned and faced me with her arms crossed over her chest.
"You lied to me," she said.

"Yes, I did."

"WHY? You knew you were in danger. Why didn't you tell us what
was going on? I mean that trip out to Monterey...why didn't you
say something then? Instead, you disappear to chase this drunk guy
around, for what? To see his tattoo?" Joanie theatrically thrust her
arms in the air. Her hands were in fists. "You have to trust me! I'm
your best friend! Why don't you trust me?! I hate this!

It was at that moment I should have told her. I should have said:

Joanie, I have this superpower. I know you don't believe in this kind of
thing, being a Jehovah's Witness and all, but I can touch people's tattoos
and know their innermost secrets. I know the truths of others, so I lie as a
defense mechanism for myself. I know in your book the tattoo touching

sounds like spiritualism, and it makes me a demon in your eyes. So that's why I lied to you, Joanie. I lied to you about the real purpose of the tattoos. I lied about the drugs, and the danger, and the threats. Because I can't tell you the truth without also telling you I'm a tattoo psychic.

That's probably what I should have said. Instead, I said, "I'm sorry."

She looked at me. Tears of frustration were pooling in her eyes. She shook her head as if to ward off the emotion and headed into the kitchen. I thought it was odd she was seeking food, but then I heard the back-kitchen door open and the steps of Joanie venturing onto the closed-in porch. Silently I followed her out there.

The night was dark and clear. Joanie stood on the far side of the porch, looking up at the sky through the mesh screens. She turned as I stepped out, acknowledging my entrance.

"Are you okay?" she asked.

"Not really," I replied. I knew Joanie meant emotionally and not physically. I wrapped my arms around my body, holding myself tightly. It was like I was trying to keep the feelings inside, trying to stay shrouded and protected. I needed to hear Joanie say we were cool. That she forgave me. I waited.

"The stars are really out tonight," she said. "They're gorgeous."

I halfway gazed out at the night sky. There were a lot of stars out, but given recent events, I wasn't in the mood to look at constellations or even the moon.

"You have to understand your mother is everywhere," Joanie said. "She will speak to you in many ways. It took me years to understand that." Joanie turned her head, and I could see tears were running down her face. "You have to be open." She wiped the water from her cheeks and continued to speak. "I know I see my mother every time I watch waves hit the beach. I feel her whenever the wind blows against my face. I smell her when I open a jar of cold cream. You have to find your mother in the world and not be alone."

Joanie turned her attention back to the stars and began to hum a song. Slowly, she moved rhythmically to the music, and then she began to give voice to the tune. I recognized the song at once. It was the melodic "Bridge Over Troubled Waters." It was so beautiful, and Joanie sang it with such clarity and spirit I felt she was conducting church on my cluttered back porch. After a while, Joanie moved up behind me and put her arms around my chest. I was drawn to her and the comfort emanating from her internal channels of strength. It was a direct channel, a connection. She was so positive, so pure. She was the beacon of light, guiding me and illuminating me. She was a bridge. A bridge out of the darkness.

"Look," Joanie's eyes were gazing up into the night, and I saw what she wanted me to see. A beautiful crystallized star hung in the galaxy. It shined incredibly bright and looked like it was suspended there in the night by itself, all alone. "That's you," Joanie whispered in my ear. "That's you. The dazzling fighter. You are the diamond in the sky. You stand alone, but you aren't alone. You're part of an entire galaxy out there. You are not alone."

I focused on the star in the sky and wondered if I should make a wish. A wish for security to steady the future lying ahead. I stood very still and silent. A gentle wind came through the open windows on the porch. I could smell pine in the air. I canted my head, so the evening breeze brushed my face. My body's senses were reaching out. It was like the essence of Bess was reaching out into the night with thin elongated fingers. It seemed like I was seeking a form of communion.

The woman I knew as my mother was gone. Technically, I was an orphan and, on the road to becoming an emancipated minor. It crossed my mind I could search for my biological father, but I wondered would he even want to know about me. I was in no hurry for that hard discovery. Echo was going to be adopted by Luther. Dusty would operate Cosmic Hearts and carry on. In time she would bring in other artists to work alongside her. She told me if I ended up going to UC Berkeley, I could work at Cosmic Hearts and keep the books on track and the store in the black. Our family would always have a financial interest in the store. I also suspected Dusty wanted me to continue using my Sherlock Holmes intuitiveness on her clients.

The danger was over. The future ahead of me looked as vast and promising and frightening as the wide-open black sky over my head. I focused on the crystal star, and tears rolled down my face. Joanie held me tighter and went back to humming the lyrics of the song about faithful perseverance and the grace of the Silver Girl. My chest shook with grief and fear of the unknown. I was still holding it in.

"Let it go. Let it go," whispered Joanie, in between the lyrics. "It's time to shine."

With one giant heave, I felt a release of pain. I cried for the loss of my mother. I cried for the flower garden that radiated all over her skin. I cried for her mischievous smile and the laughter exploding from her body. I cried for her mad crazed dancing. I cried for her inspired creativity. I cried for the secret hugs at night. I cried for sliced bananas and mangos and sugar-cinnamon on my waffles. I cried for the six other sparrows. I cried for what could have been and what had been taken away.

"I want my mother," I managed to say in between my sobs to no one in particular. They were words spoken to the air, the night, to the pain slowly dissipating into the air.

"Of course, you do," Joanie replied. Her body shouldered my grief, carrying the weight with me.

And then we both saw it at the same time. Sailing through the night was a second star. It twinkled and glided across the sky, leaving a short trail of cosmic light. The second star moved and aligned itself with the solitary bright star, and there was a quick flash as they were joined.

Hello Mom.

KORU

"Elizabeth Wynters?"

The woman at the reception desk smiled at me, her bright red lipstick outlined a broad smile and big teeth. She seemed pleasant, but I was scared.

"Is this your first visit?" she asked. I nodded my head. "Then I'll need to see some ID."

She verified my name as someone allowed access and put a check-mark next to it. She pointed with her pen in the direction to my right.

"Go along the corridor to your right here, then down to the nurses' station. It's covered with butterflies. You can't miss it. There is a nurse, Melissa. She will be expecting you. I'm going to call ahead."

I followed the directions, moving slowly. There were flowers and bright insects painted on the walls of the corridor. With each step, I felt both courageous and frightened.

It was Joanie who finally convinced me to come. Actually, she gave me an ultimatum. Either go to The Gardens and visit or attend a Sunday service with Jehovah's Witnesses.

"Won't I have to wear a dress?" I asked. I had been wearing shorts to get around the cast.

"Yes," Joanie answered. Her eyes narrowed, and she folded her arms across her chest. She was challenging me to make the wrong choice.

"I don't have any dresses," I replied.

"I'll lend you one of mine" was the steely response.

I made an expression of disgust, and Joanie smacked my shoulder in mock anger. "C'mon, it's time," she said. "It's time you went. It's been too long. It will be good for you." She placed her hands on her hips and looked down at me. "It's either that or Jesus."

So here I was.

The nurses' station was impossible to miss. Every space of the front counter was adorned with painted butterflies. There was no white showing through at all. A young woman, probably in her twenties, was waiting for me. She smiled and moved out from behind the station. She had the most amazing sparkling blue eyes.

"Elizabeth?" she asked.

"Bess," I responded. "I go by Bess."

"I'll remember that. I'm glad to meet you. It's nice to have you here."

"Thank you."

"If you'll follow me, I'll take you out to the conservatory. It's quiet there today."

I left the crutches at the station and Melissa led the way down a corridor. She opened a door that went into a glass expansion, connecting into a larger room with floor to ceiling windows. It was warm inside as there were all sorts of plants and flowers to be seen. It was like a greenhouse with the pungent smell of dirt mixed with the floral perfume of the multiple blooms.

I inhaled through my nostrils, capturing the multitude of scents. "Wow," I said. "This is fantastic."

Melissa looked around the space, and then she pointed. "She's over by the angel fountain. She likes to listen to the water as it hits the stones."

I looked in the direction of Melissa's outstretched hand at the woman in the wheelchair with her back to us. She was facing the fountain, her head tilted to one side. Melissa took my elbow and guided me as I moved in my jerky fashion with the cast. She stood in front of the woman and leaned down to speak in her ear. As she spoke, she touched the woman's hand, which sat like a claw on the blanket covering her legs. I didn't move.

"Ms. Wynters. Terry. We have a visitor here to see you. She's a lovely young woman."

"I'm her daughter," I added, biting my lip.

"Yes, of course," Melissa said. "I see the resemblance."

The woman in the chair made no movement. She remained still, facing the fountain. The fountain showed an assortment of angels and cherubs rejoicing in the spray of the water. I quickly counted the number of figures displayed. Eight. I thought of the sparrows.

Melissa smiled at her, squeezed the claw-like hand, and tucked the blanket snugly around her thin thighs. "Would you like me to stay while you visit?" she asked.

The first thought in my head was Yes. *Yes, please stay.* The courage I had felt earlier had drizzled away.

"I think I'll be okay," I said, but really, I was trying to convince myself.

Melissa nodded. "Alright. Twenty minutes then. That's about the right amount of time. I'll come back to get you."

"Thank you, Melissa."

Melissa walked away and went back out through the glass walkway. I came closer to my mother and sat down on a bench facing the fountain. It was relaxing to watch the water trickle over the stone cherubs and the rocks and allow the sound to transport you to another place.

I wondered if my mother was doing the same, and this was why it was her favorite spot. How do the nurses know this is her favorite spot? Were they just saying that as a way of putting me at ease? No. I had counted the number of cherubs playing in the water. I knew why this was her favorite spot.

I looked over at the face of the woman in the wheelchair. The woman who was responsible for me. The woman who had made me. The woman who loved and fought fiercely for my sister and me.

"Hello, Mom," I said.

There was no response. The eyes stared at a place in the distance beyond me, beyond the fountain. Whatever she was looking at, it was a place only she could see.

My mother's face was vastly different since I had last seen her. The horrible cuts and bruising around her cheeks, forehead, and neck were gone. But her left eyelid sloped over too much. Thin crease lines pulled at her mouth, and streaks of grey flashed throughout her hair. Gone was the fiery red color. Her hair had a washed-out orange dishrag tinge, and the nurses had brushed it back into a simple ponytail. The vibrancy and allurement had vanished, but her face was relaxed, with no signs of tension. It was a face of calm acceptance.

After being in an induced coma, Terry Wynters had suffered a stroke while coming out of the unconscious state. The stroke had impaired her speech and body movement. She couldn't move, and she couldn't talk. But she could listen, and she could feel.

I took her hands in mine. Her fingers were thin like the bones of a bird. They were cramped on the blanket, but they gave off warmth, indicating the vivid heat of this woman still resided inside. I clasped her hands, which allowed me to look away and talk without staring into her frozen face.

"I'm so sorry, Mom. I'm sorry I haven't been here sooner. For a long time, I wasn't ready. I knew I would just sit here and cry and cry. And me crying would just upset you. So, I waited. I was afraid to see you. Afraid to see you…" "*like this*" *was what I was thinking but didn't say.*

I took a deep breath and continued. "I hope you know I found Maxine, and what you set up for us has happened. You're so clever, Mom. You're amazing, really. You knew I would figure things out even when I didn't think I would. I just had to stop being mad at you and feeling ashamed. I had to believe you loved me."

With my confession out of the way, I was able to look at her. She sat immobile in the wheelchair, still staring out at the place of nowhere. "We're all at the house, and Luther has filed the paperwork to adopt Echo. I mean, Eleanora." I laughed softly. "Luther was surprised when he saw that. He didn't know Echo was named after Billie Holiday." I fell silent and tapped the fingers on my mother's hand. "She misses you. Echo does. I'll check with the nurses as to when would be a good time to bring her here. But I warn you, she has some hotdog riddles she wants you to hear, and they're awful."

I took another deep breath to say the rest. "I've decided not to have Luther adopt me. I'm going to become an emancipated minor, and I want to stay being a Wynters. I hope that's okay." I squeezed her hand when I said that. "I like being Elizabeth Wynters."

Theresa Ann Wynters sat still in her wheelchair. Her hands unmoving in my grasp. Blood flushed her face, and I knew she could hear me. I imagined she was smiling.

AFTERWORD

Thank you for reading INK FOR THE BELOVED, the first book in The Tattoo Teller Series. The next book starring Bess Wynters, INK FOR THE DAMNED, will be out in the fall of 2020. If you enjoyed INK FOR THE BELOVED, please consider leaving a review on your favorite book site. **Reviews help readers find books!**

Sign up to my newsletter for exclusive sneak peeks at my upcoming books, new release alerts, and exclusive bonus content. www.practicinginpublic.com

WELCOME TO THE WORLD OF INK

Author Acknowledgments

This has been such a ride, and the journey continues.

There's a wonderful group of people on "Team RC" and all of them have helped me shape and refine this novel. My writing support group is composed of Joyce McCallister, Colleen West, Marilyn Kentz, and Jannie Dresser. Thanks for your insight and encouragement and forcing me to be accountable. I must thank my "first readers" my daughter, Ripley and dear friends Claire McDowell, Christine Staples, and Sally Payson Hays. I have two special people Katherine Tomlinson and Ehrich Van Lowe who have supported my writing for years and been my private cheerleaders. Thanks, guys.

It seems strange to thank a location, but I must acknowledge the city that fed my adolescence and groomed my political awareness. After leaving Berkeley for college, I understood how unique this city is. I'm grateful for the special genius of Berkeley and its endless inspirations. I will continue to spotlight the treasures of the East Bay and Northern California with this series. I hope you join me on the journey.

About the Author

R.C. Barnes' debut novel *INK FOR THE BELOVED* is a love letter to her adolescent years in the East Bay. The first book in the YA Tattoo Teller series is set in Berkeley and local readers will enjoy following amateur detective, Bess Wynters, and recognizing the areas she travels. For over twenty years, RC (also known as Robin Claire) has worked in the entertainment industry in film and television development. She was a long time development executive at Walt Disney Studios and if you've seen any movies featuring a dog and sled, Robin probably worked on it. Robin has published numerous short stories in sci-fi/mystery and dystopian anthologies.

On a perfect day, she can be found curled up with a book, listening to the rain outside, nibbling chocolate, and sipping tea or wine (depending on the hour). She lives in Berkeley and is the mother of three very nice people.

You can connect with RC online at www.practicinginpublic.com and @rcbarneswriter

author photo by Charles Chessler

Also by R.C. Barnes

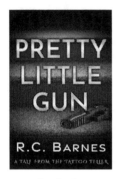

Pretty Little Gun

A tale of Intrigue, suspense, and MURDER

The box wasn't locked. She opened it and a metallic gunpowder smell hit her nostrils. Shelby's eyes widened in astonishment. Lying on top of purple velvet padding was the prettiest gun she had ever seen.

This gun was sweet and small and pink. There was a raspberry hue to the gun's body with shimmery flashes of turquoise. Shelby lifted the weapon from its velvet bed and held it in her hand. Amazement radiated through Shelby. It felt like a warm glow grasping her soul. The gun was a perfect fit as her fingers wrapped the handle. When she turned it around, the iridescent shine flashed like a rainbow.

Learn what Shelby does with the pretty little gun.
Get your copy of this short read introducing teenager Bess Wynters, the tattoo teller, and heroine of the novel INK FOR THE BELOVED.

Go to www.practicinginpublic.com and sign up for my newsletter. You'll receive a free copy of *Pretty Little Gun*.

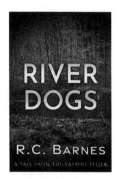

RIVERDOGS

A gripping tale of devastating BE-TRAYAL

Steve Kelly wanted to get high in the woods. He argued it was the best place because you didn't have to worry about the police blinding you with their flashlights or thugs rolling you while you were zoned out. Conrad didn't enjoy going in the woods. He especially didn't like going in the woods by the Maumee River. The place smelled like sewage, and the mosquitoes were ruthless. But there was also something else. "What about the Riverdogs?" he asked Steve.

Were the Riverdogs just an urban legend?

PREDATORS ALWAYS GO AFTER THE WEAKEST ONE.

Get your copy of this short read featuring Bess Wynters, the tattoo teller, and heroine of the novel INK FOR THE BELOVED.